OPENING
Up

OPENING *Up*

LAUREN DANE

FOREVER

NEW YORK   BOSTON

Copyright © 2015 by Lauren Dane
Excerpt from *Falling Under* copyright © 2015 by Lauren Dane

Forever
Hachette Book Group
1290 Avenue of the Americas
New York, NY 10104

www.HachetteBookGroup.com

Printed in the United States of America

RRD-C

First Edition: June 2015
10 9 8 7 6 5 4 3 2 1

Forever is an imprint of Grand Central Publishing.
The Forever name and logo are trademarks of Hachette Book Group, Inc.

The Hachette Speakers Bureau provides a wide range of authors for speaking events. To find out more, go to www.hachettespeakersbureau.com or call (866) 376-6591.

The publisher is not responsible for websites (or their content) that are not owned by the publisher.

Library of Congress Cataloging-in-Publication Data

Dane, Lauren.
    Opening up / Lauren Dane. — First edition.
        pages ; cm. — (Ink & chrome)
    ISBN 978-1-4555-8621-9 (softcover) — ISBN 978-1-4789-0393-2 (audio download) — ISBN 978-1-4555-8623-3 (ebook) 1. Automobile detailing—Fiction. 2. Man-woman relationships—Fiction. I. Title.
    PS3604.A5O64 2015
    813'.6—dc23
                                                                                    2014049906

*This one is for the boy who is the
full moon shining on my Camaro's hood.*

Acknowledgments

Thank-yous go to so many people! 2014 was a year of challenges for me and my family. I'm incredibly grateful to those around me who went out of their way to make things easier for me at what were some of the most stressful times in my life.

Laura Bradford, my agent and friend—thank you so very much.

Leah Hultenschmidt—thank you for working with me so hard to give me as much time and space as you could while I was trying to recover (as well as the work editing me!).

My beta readers—Fatin (who is also my fantastic assistant) and Mary, who always have so much excellent advice and help.

Friends who have pitched in and helped me out—your kindnesses do matter. Thank you all.

Readers—thank you all for your patience and for continuing to read my books!!

OPENING Up

CHAPTER
One

I don't even know who that is, but I'd like to take several large bites." PJ took in the ridiculously badass alpha male across the room from where she and her sister had just been handed drinks at the bar.

"Who?" Julie asked as she paid and they moved to the side. "Point him out. In a non-attention-seeking way!" she added, like PJ was a beast.

PJ blinked a few times before she spoke. "You're a terrible human being."

"I get it from Dad."

PJ tilted her head to indicate the guy whose sheer charisma she felt from across the room. A brunette with a body straight out of a pinup calendar stared up into his face as she stroked a hand up and down his arm.

"She's all right in a totally voluptuous, drop-dead-sex-bomb way. I mean, for those who like that sort of thing." Julie's dry delivery made PJ smile.

"Let's saunter by that fantastic Camaro over there so I can get a closer look." PJ started off.

"At the guy or the car?"

"Two birds. One stone," PJ called lightly over her shoulder.

"Will this end up in some sort of terrible misunderstanding that will embarrass me for years to come? Or, better yet, am I going to have to explain what happened to the police?"

"That only happened once."

Julie's brow rose very slowly. Julie was the elegant one. The one who played the piano perfectly. She'd gone to the schools their parents had told her to. Wore tasteful, perfectly tailored clothes. Now had a corner office at their family's tire company and was set to lead it into the future with their other siblings.

Whereas Penelope Jean Colman had been a "terrible disappointment" because she just never fit anywhere her parents tried to put her. And maybe because she'd gotten her big sister into some trouble once or twice.

"Okay, three times. But I had good reasons for two of them."

"The other was you being innocent?"

"Heck no. Which isn't to say how pleased it makes me that I got away with it."

"He's standing with Duke Bradshaw. The dark-haired one."

Julie did a very nice job of looking natural as she shifted to stand next to PJ, giving her an unobstructed view.

"Duke owns Twisted Steel with someone else. Maybe that's him," Julie said.

There really was no other word for the man but dominant. Easily six foot three, he stood, feet apart, a beer in one hand as he spoke to Duke. This was a man you could dress in a tux and while he'd look fantastic, you'd know he could punch you in the face without losing a cufflink.

She wasn't entirely sure why that made him so hot, it just did. There was a sort of barely restrained . . . *something* about him that made her take notice.

Dark hair, shaved close at the sides, longer on the top. He had it pulled back from his face, exposing masculine features.

"You have that goofy look." Julie poked her in the side.

"Ow! What?" PJ asked without tearing her gaze from *him*.

"You get it at the sight of tacos, too."

PJ nearly choked on her drink. Thank goodness he hadn't noticed her almost dying.

Once she could breathe again, PJ glared at her sister through still-watering eyes. "You're on a roll tonight. Did you take allergy medication before you started drinking?"

Her normally serene sister had a twinkle in her eye. "Someone has to keep me entertained at these things. You seem to like them. I, on the other hand, would rather be home catching up on my *Housewives*."

"What a waste that would be. There are handsome single men here. A bar. Food that's being served from a tray instead of a buffet a hundred people of questionable hygiene have pawed over. Me, of course. All of these things are better than being at home alone watching TV."

"Says you."

"Witty. That expensive Ivy League education was totally worth it."

"I need to dumb it down for state college dropouts to understand." Julie stuck out her tongue.

PJ turned back to look at *him* again. He was too far away for her to see the color of his eyes, but she figured they'd be brown or green maybe. She took note of the septum piercing and the tattoos on both arms visible from the elbows, where he had his shirtsleeves rolled up. It was necessary, for reasons of some sort, that she get a better look.

"Since he's standing with Duke, I say you go on over and introduce yourself. This is an industry party. You're here for Colman Enterprises. It's your job to network. Give him your card." Julie got a little closer, lowering her voice. "And it's good for you to make some connections for your custom work."

It meant a lot that Julie was on her side, excited about the direction PJ's life was headed.

"Come with me."

Julie shook her head. "I see a few people I should at least buy a drink for. Send out a distress call if they're weird and you need me to mace them."

With a wave, Julie headed off in the direction of one of their other clients. Well, all right then.

Ever since PJ met Duke Bradshaw nearly a year before at a race, she'd coveted his work. All the people at Twisted Steel were beyond good at what they did, so the cars and bikes they created and restored were absolutely beautiful. It was art.

Their work had one more thing, the most important thing as far as PJ was concerned. It wasn't just the money or even the art. It was that they loved cars. And motorcycles and racing and engines.

It was that passion that she wanted more of for Colman Enterprises. Her family was great at selling tires. But it wasn't the same as it had been when her grandfather had founded the company. He'd raced, too. He'd understood the heart of his customer in a way no spreadsheet ever could.

For PJ, it was a belief system. It was a love of cars, of speed and chrome and the rumble of engines that was the heart of Colman. That would never change, even if the products and services they offered did.

PJ shook that off as she approached, hearing his voice before she got close enough to say hello.

Mmmmm. Deep and gravelly.

Dark brown eyes—and she bet that when he had his hair down it slanted over them so he'd look hot and mysterious all at once—took her in.

His gaze locked with hers and a smile marked a mouth so carnal she probably would have to light a candle in penance for her very naughty thoughts.

She smiled back and the moment between them heated and slowed. He was *holy shit hot damn and wow* sexy. One of his brows rose. Confident and not a small bit cocky.

He was older. Probably late thirties, early forties. Which was absolutely okay with her. Didn't matter though, because all it took was a close-up view of this male to know he was totally out of her league. He'd rock her world. Maybe set it on fire.

Just having his full attention left her a little shaky. What would sex with him be like? Wrong. Wrong thing to start to wonder right then. Her cheeks heated and she hoped it was dark enough that he missed her blush.

And yet there she continued to stand, finally breaking that moment and turning to Duke. Also ridiculously hot.

"PJ Colman, how are you?" Duke showed perfect white teeth. The dimple to the left of his mouth made PJ bet it tasted sweet.

"I'm doing all right. You?"

"As well as you can be at one of these things."

"Asa Barrons," Manly Man said as he held out a hand.

A *big* hand that engulfed hers as he shook it.

Duke grinned, making him look like a charming wayward boy. No one could stay mad at that face, she bet. "Sorry about that. I figured you already knew PJ. Asa, this is PJ Colman. PJ, this is Asa; he co-owns Twisted Steel with me."

"Colman, as in Colman Enterprises?" Asa let go of her hand slowly and she was proud she didn't gulp audibly.

"Yes." She looked back over her shoulder toward the Camaro and then back to Asa and Duke. "That's one seriously delicious machine."

Asa used that moment to take her in, from the pointed toes of her black heels, up shapely legs, over mouthwatering curves at her hips, to one of the finest racks he'd ever beheld.

The neckline of the dark blue dress she wore—a dress that lovingly caressed her body and yet stayed pretty and feminine—showed off her collarbone and the uppermost curves of her breasts.

And she had good taste. That Camaro was a project they'd finished just a few weeks before. The owner was taking it home to Oregon the following day, so Asa and Duke figured it'd be a good idea to show it off while they could.

PJ stepped to the side to allow a server to pass with a tray of something, and without thinking Asa reached out to take her elbow to steady her. Her skin was warm and soft, and with her so close it wasn't a struggle to breathe her in. Spice and heady flowers.

"Thanks," he said, referring to her compliment about the car. "I'll be a little sad to see it go."

"We argued about the racing stripe." Duke grinned.

"What do *you* think about the racing stripe?" Asa asked her.

He'd liked her smile, but the smirk she gave in response to his question made his cock hard. Christ.

She walked to the car and he followed, barely conscious of anything but the metronome switch of her hips and the long braided rope of her hair hanging to her waist. Purple hair. Light at the top and then darker at the ends.

"I think it's always more about the car." Her voice dropped so that only he could hear. "In general I like racing stripes well enough. My car has them. Though my car is purple, so it's not all stock."

"That so?" He wanted to brush an errant tendril of her hair away from her face, but he resisted.

This was a *work* event. She was the granddaughter of one of the most influential men in racing, and she couldn't have been any more than twenty-five years old. All of that should have been an ice-cold slap of reality.

But his cock didn't give a shit. His cock agreed with his brain that her freckles were fucking hot and wanted to see if she had them all over. And she liked cars. He could tell by the way she looked at his Camaro. Her gaze seemed to caress the curves and lines.

A woman who liked cars on the same level he did was hot. Even if she was totally off the menu.

"Purple?"

"Can I tell you a secret?"

Oh yes, yes she could.

"Go on ahead." He tried to keep the grin off his face.

"I'm kind of a rebel."

He laughed. "That so? I figured, given your hair, that you just liked purple a lot."

"Maybe that too. As for this particular car? The racing stripes are exactly what it needed."

"Duke likes racing stripes on American muscle. The client is a friend of his."

"The paint is fantastic. Perfect work." She walked around, peering closely here and there. "No skimping or cut corners."

"Were you going to judge me harshly if there had been?"

She ran her tongue over her bottom lip before she sank her top teeth into it briefly. He felt it to his toes.

"Absolutely. Paint is a serious thing. Do you need to be reminded of that?"

Christ.

He liked to do the reminding. And he surely would like to remind this woman while she was naked and in his bed. There was something striking about her. An air of confidence that grew as they flirted over machines. Her energy was vibrant. Sensual.

And still, not for him.

He probably should be breaking away to go back over to where Duke stood. Instead he kept talking. "So what do you do at Colman central?"

"I manage accounts. Which is a fancy way of saying I sell tires to people like you and Duke. They send me to industry events like this." She cocked her head and paused before speaking again. "Who does your paint work?"

That was a quick change of topic. "We have paint done on-site. Specialty stuff goes out to contractors. Are you looking for any kind of work in particular? I could give you a better idea if I knew more."

She laughed and...it surprised him. Low and sultry. Not what he expected at all. A brief touch of her hand to his forearm. "*I* do custom paint work. Just wondering who my competition was."

An image of her bent over, breasts heaving against the front of a very tight shirt as she worked on one of his cars, settled in, and he let it.

"This a new service Colman is offering?"

"It's a way to do what I like to do and to expand our reach into new sectors of this business."

Young? Yes. He probably had wrenches older than she was. But she had intelligence to go with the looks. It wasn't as if he thought Colman was the huge success it was without a lot of smart, hard-working people at the helm. But he'd taken one look at that face and body and misjudged her as spoiled, pretty, and rich, and therefore totally useless.

"At some point I'd like to talk with you and Duke about that direction."

"Give the shop a call and set something up." At least he'd get another chance to see that face.

"All right." She looked up, and the upward curve to her lips urged his own to do the same.

Neither of them spoke. It felt as if she waited for him. *That* hit hard. Unexpected to be so moved by this wisp of a woman he'd just met minutes before. It wasn't until she hummed low in her throat, a sound of pleasure, that he realized he'd taken a step closer.

"Excuse me. I'm sorry to interrupt, PJ, but do you have any of Shawn's cards?"

Asa wrestled back his instinct to shove this guy away and have PJ all to himself again.

And was doubly glad when she turned with a smile that was totally different than the one she'd just given Asa. That's when he took in the strong resemblance between her and the guy who'd spoken and figured this had to be one of her brothers.

"Jay, this is Asa Barrons. He's one of the co-owners of Twisted Steel." She looked back to Asa. "This is my brother Jay, CEO at Colman."

Duke dealt better with guys like this one. Asa kept his head in his machines as much as he could. He loved gear with a passion, but people? Not so much.

"Nice to meet you. PJ sings the praises of Twisted Steel frequently." Jay shook Asa's hand.

PJ handed her brother a few cards.

"She was just educating me on her view of racing stripes."

Jay appeared apprehensive, but PJ just laughed and patted her brother's arm. "Don't worry. I'm sure he's not going to stop doing business with us. I didn't tell him I thought they were boring or overdone."

It was Asa's turn to laugh. "Boring?"

Her eyes seemed to light up as her laugh continued to drive him nuts. "Oops, cat's out of the bag now. Please continue to buy our tires."

Jay's eyes widened and Asa wanted to tell the dude to lighten up.

Asa gave her brother a look and made an X over his heart. "I promise we'll continue to buy your tires even though your sister is so irreverent. Maybe *because*." He winked at her and she poked her brother's upper arm.

Jay looked back over his shoulder and then to them once more. "I need to get back to my conversation. It was nice to finally meet you, Asa." He held the cards up. "Thanks."

Before Asa could say anything else, the woman he'd actually been planning on taking home came back through the room looking for him.

"I need to get back to it as well." He held his hand out, shaking PJ's, and then he handed her a business card and took hers.

"Have an excellent evening, Asa Barrons."

The buxom brunette making her way over to him would probably guarantee that. But he couldn't deny the pull as PJ walked away.

He *really* couldn't deny it when she was stopped not even half a room away by Scott Elroy, one of the guys in town who custom-built bikes. And by the looks of it, Asa wasn't the only one who found PJ Colman rather delightful.

CHAPTER

Two

PJ hung up the phone after leaving a message for Asa Barrons. Again. She'd called three times in the month following the party and got his voicemail each time.

She looked across the table at her best friend, Audra. "He's ducking me."

"Or maybe he's just slammed. You said he wasn't hesitant when you brought it up when you met him. They run a busy shop. Making time to deal with another contractor when they already have some and they're backed up or whatever, is going to mean you fall down the list. Even when you're as pretty as you are."

PJ frowned at Audra. "I know you're probably right. What if he doesn't take me seriously? I mean, why should he? He doesn't know me. He doesn't know what I can do. I didn't have my portfolio yet."

She'd been building a portfolio of her painting work so if—no, *when*—Asa met with her, she'd have something concrete to show him.

"Really? So you're going to carry around a portfolio with you at all times? Like he'd have been cool with you just breaking it out at the bar? You know how to do this, PJ. This is like your destiny and whatnot."

PJ snorted. "My destiny?"

"You know what I mean. You were raised to run your family's business."

"And then I turned out to be an artist. The shame of it."

Audra threw her balled-up napkin at PJ's head. "You know my opinion of Howie's parenting."

Howie being Howard Colman Jr., PJ's father.

"Just because you dropped out of college doesn't mean you're not smart. You knew it wasn't right for you. Thing is, you know cars. Your grandfather raised you to love them like he did. And you're artistic and damned good at painting things. I'm sure Asa is just really busy. But even if he doesn't take you seriously now, he will once you're done with him. On a side note, apart from your ability, which we've already established as mighty, he's also going to want to get you into bed. You said you two had that sort of chemistry."

PJ had known Audra since they'd both been kids. It was one of her favorite things in her life that they had such a strong friendship. She knew Audra would say exactly what she needed to hear.

"We did have the tinglies for one another. But he and Duke built Twisted Steel from the ground up. It's not like they could have done it if he'd been following his dick around like it found him water."

"A dowsing dick?" Audra asked.

"I think I saw that in the Jim Rose Circus a few years ago." They both laughed. "He just seems like the kind of man . . ." PJ paused, trying to find the right words. "He's under control. It sort of rolled off him. He's in charge of himself. I'm not saying he doesn't get laid on the regular. I'm just saying he doesn't lead with that head."

"I need to get a closer look at this guy. Which is an excellent segue into me reminding you that you're my best friend, so you need to say you'll do this pinup calendar photo shoot so my boyfriend can keep a job. It pays. There's sure to be hot guys around, and you'll keep your spot as the best friend in the whole world. Which is priceless."

Audra's boyfriend, Tom, had combined forces with some other graphic arts designers and what had been planned as a fun little side project had transformed into a full-blown pinup calendar showcasing the wares of local indie artisans of everything from clothing to jewelry.

And the shoot would undoubtedly take place at a garage of some sort, which gave her another chance to network.

As PJ had told her sister a few weeks before, it was good to attract a whole new kind of business to keep Colman relevant and integral. All those gearheads, the build-and-restore crowd as well as the racing teams, needed paint on their projects. Why not expand Colman Enterprises to fill a market need?

Money was good. Work was good. Doing something nice for a friend was also good.

"Oh, all right."

A commotion followed as a group of their friends came in, including Tom and PJ's ex. Aaron looked around until he saw her and headed her way.

"I gotta go," she muttered, gathering her stuff.

Audra put a hand out. "No. We were here first. This is our place."

"Just not when I know he's going to be here."

It wasn't even that she couldn't get over him or still loved him or any of that. It was more like she was so embarrassed that she'd ever actually fallen for any of his crap that being around him was the equivalent of Sunday dinner at her parents' house.

Tense. Uncomfortable, with the bitter stench of disappointment and passive-aggressive anger in the air. It made her tired and irritated. But he was a good lesson. That's how she'd chosen to think about it.

They were part of the same social circle—which was how she'd found out about the cheating—so they'd see one another frequently. She wasn't going to get rid of her friends, and eventually she'd tolerate his existence again. But she wasn't there yet.

Aaron tried to slide next to PJ but she held a hand out. "No."

His pretty face screwed up a little as he struggled to understand. "Come on, Penny."

PJ curled her lip. "I'm not your fucking Penny. Just go be elsewhere."

Aaron had convinced himself they were somehow meant to be. Maybe because she was the first woman who'd kicked his butt to the curb when she'd caught him stepping out. Maybe it was that he wanted what he couldn't have. Whatever. She didn't care why, really. Although she had been pretty pissed until she got the all-clear back from her doctor, because heaven knew what he could have given her.

"How long are you going to punish me?"

PJ looked at him and then over to Audra, shaking her head. "Is he kidding with this?"

"You know where I am when you realize we're meant to be together, Penny."

"Dude, have some self-respect." Tom, Audra's boyfriend, rolled his eyes and dragged Aaron off. "Come on, let's get more pitchers. It'll give you something to do so my girl won't scoop your eyes out with a spoon."

Tom sent PJ a grin as he swept Aaron away. Audra grabbed PJ's arm and pulled her back to sit. "We already decided you weren't leaving."

Audra raised her glass, patiently waiting for PJ to do the same.

Audra made a prim face and then smirked. "You haven't been out with us for nearly two months. I'm planting my flag right here. This is *our* table and the Ditch is *our* place and we don't give a fuck if Aaron is around. He needs to see you every Friday so he can wallow in the hell he exists in now."

Audra was seriously the best friend anyone could ask for. She always took PJ's side, always had her back, always listened and supported and definitely kicked her butt when PJ needed it.

They all drank.

"I'm going to be sorry I asked," PJ began, "but what you do mean by 'the hell Aaron exists in now'?"

"The one where he doesn't get to see you naked anymore. But he can still remember how awesome it was."

They were still laughing when the guys got back with pitchers and several more of their friends. Audra positioned herself so that Aaron had to sit farther down the table. Enough out of range that PJ could pretend he didn't exist.

She had awesome friends.

"I need you to handle a meeting for me tomorrow," Jay said as he breezed into her office without knocking.

The oldest Colman sibling was the most like their father. Jay had been raised to own every room he entered. To broadcast his will and make it happen. And in his own way, he craved acceptance from Howard Jr. with the same wary yearning PJ did. They were both smart enough to know it was folly and yet they both kept at it.

Still, Jay, though constantly having to war with their uncle for access to their father, was a pretty decent brother. He'd been jammed into his life in ways she couldn't possibly understand. Sure, she was expected to do certain things, but Jay had the weight of their generation on his shoulders. He was the oldest. He'd lead when their father and uncle stepped aside.

It made him a prick sometimes. But she loved him despite his flaws. Even at times like this, when he simply took for granted that people would obey his missives.

PJ finished the last sentence of her e-mail before sending it off and looking up at him. "Can't. I've got a prior engagement tomorrow." She'd be shooting the calendar all day.

"I said I'd play golf with Dad, Uncle Fee, and Shawn. The meeting is just a thing down at the factory. They need some petting. You're good at that."

"So wait. You, Dad, Fee, and Shawn are all going golfing? Is Julie going?"

The look on his face told PJ it hadn't even occurred to him to invite either of his sisters.

"So you boys go off to play and we have to handle the dirty work? I have plans tomorrow, and I can't move them around. Can you find out if they're free to meet today? Though you could stand to hear more voices that aren't Dad's or Fee's."

Her brother was brilliant in so many ways. But sometimes he was so focused he missed things outside his view. He knew money and he knew markets. But he wasn't as good when it came to people.

And he'd say—with some truth—that she didn't spend enough time learning money and markets and too much on people.

"I don't have the time to hold hands, PJ."

"Colman is built on that face-to-face, I'm-just-like-you interaction with not just the people in our industry but our own people too."

"Which is why I'm sending you to pet them."

PJ sighed and then flapped a hand toward her door. "Well? Run along and find out if they can meet me today. But Jay? This is my company too. Julie's company. This is some medieval bullshit and I'm not going to tolerate it."

She and her sister were really sick and tired of the way her brothers, father, and uncle tended to run Colman Enterprises based on decisions they made in places women weren't allowed or invited.

"I'm CEO. Fee is CFO. We don't need to consult you or Julie. But this is just golf."

"That you'd stand there and say 'it's just golf' when that's how men have been making deals—and excluding women, I should add—for decades makes me want to stab you with my pencil right now."

"Jesus, Penelope Jean. Lay off. You grew up rich. You have a job, but this is not your sweatshop. You are not abused."

Ugh. Brothers pushing sisters' buttons; it was an old-ass story, but she *hated* it when he patronized her.

"Oh hey, Jay?" She flipped him off with both hands. "Did you get an A in Smug Bastard 101? I never said a thing about being abused or being in a sweatshop. I said this is my company too. You ought to try listening to me sometimes. I have good ideas."

"You can't even stick with a hair color and you think I'm going to consult you when it comes to decisions for my business?"

His ribbing about his disdain for her feminist ideals was one thing; mainly it was affectionate even if he was a dingus about it. But there was an edge to what he'd just said. An edge that was a slap in her face. *You're not smart enough or good enough to listen to.*

An edge that made the fire in her belly to prove herself to him glow. "My hair color has nothing to do with my ideas."

"Your hair color is an indicator that your ideas are not normal."

"Normal? So I'm abnormal because I have purple hair? Are you kidding me? From the outside you're a perfectly handsome dude in his midthirties, but you're like four hundred and twelve years old inside. Dried up. Yes, I'm *different*, Jay. So? Great-Grandpa ran moonshine. You think that was normal? You think he never took risks? He took risks every time he made a run. Being different is who we are."

"You should have stayed in college and gotten your BA in English. Clearly you know a lot of pretty words that don't mean shit when it comes to payday. Purple hair doesn't sell accounts."

"Did you read up on how to be this patronizing and insulting, or did you just inherit the ability from Dad and Fee?" PJ was proud her voice didn't shake. Sometimes it was hard not to react emotionally to this sort of baiting. She knew some of her family discounted her for being different, and it hurt. Because they didn't take her any more seriously when she did what they expected her to either.

It filled her with futile anger and hurt, but she had gotten pretty good at hiding just how much. "Purple hair sold more than you did last month." She tipped her chin at the navy blue binder on the corner of her desk. "Fee's special numbers say so. Now get out of my office. I'm working and I'm no longer interested in helping you with your problem. Handle your own meeting. I'm busy tomorrow, just like I told you."

He threw his hands up in the air, but he'd been thwarted and she knew he understood that. It was a stupid, petty win, not that it'd stop her from claiming it.

CHAPTER
Three

"Taco Friday is your best idea yet." Asa filled a plate and moved on down the line of ingredients.

Duke shrugged. "I have them from time to time."

"They generally involve food or liquor. You're Shaggy and Scooby rolled into one."

Duke laughed. "Right on. More evidence of how lucky you are to have me around."

Asa snorted. But Duke was right. From pretty much the time they'd met in the army, Duke had been his friend. Had his back, in both the metaphysical sense and the physical one. Duke had saved Asa from getting killed more than once.

The lunchroom at Twisted Steel currently held all eleven employees, so it was loud and raucous. Which might also have something to do with the fact that it was *Beer* and Taco Friday.

It had been a hell of a long last few weeks. They'd pushed one total rebuild out as well as two other smaller jobs. Asa had slept on the couch in his office at least once a week rather than face a drive home after three a.m.

But the work had all been delivered to very happy clients, he was soon to be full of tacos and beer, and all was right with the world.

He and Duke had bought the building the shop sat in five years before, and Asa felt like it was only now truly operating to its full potential. They'd had three employees back then and only used about a quarter of the space. Now they had a showroom, eleven full-time employees, and a host of people they contracted work out to.

There he was, a successful business owner. A homeowner. Asa Barrons, the kid who'd grown up in trailers and shitty public housing apartments in Houston, now had multiple cars, money in the bank, and a life free of chaos and pain.

They had built something together, he and his friend—a business both men could be proud of. It was the ticket out he and Duke had barely known to have dreamed about.

"I'm going to sleep the hell out of a lot of hours," Asa said, taking several long pulls from his beer once he'd collapsed into a chair and set his food down.

Duke settled in across from him. "No lie. I've gotta be back here at ten, though. No way would I miss such a fantastic opportunity."

"What?"

"I told you about this last week. The pinup calendar shoot? They're using the showroom and some of the bays," Duke explained. "Don't worry; I made sure Casey went over everything they have access to. They won't get near any work in progress. Plus I'll be here. Looking at hot women."

"I probably wasn't listening."

"See what happens when you don't?"

Hot women draped over his machines. Now that was indeed a way to spend a Saturday. He'd planned to come in to catch up on paperwork that next afternoon anyway.

Asa tended to keep in his head, especially when he was in the middle of a project. It's all he thought of, the need to put his hands on something, to stamp it with his vision, to watch it yield under his will.

"Thanks for the save. Guess I'll be here at ten instead of noon like I planned."

"I was thinking of heading out to the track on Sunday. You up for it?"

Duke and Asa had recently started a racing team they co-owned with a group of their friends. It brought Asa to the track a lot, and that's when he'd discovered how incredible it was to drive the track himself.

"Hell yes."

Duke tipped his chin. "Fastback?"

On a motorcycle trip down the coast to Los Angeles the summer before, Asa and Duke had found the beat-up shell of a 1968 Fastback and had to have it. They'd spent their spare time since restoring it.

Duke was magic with machines. The best mechanic Asa knew. He'd built the engine they'd wanted as Asa had coaxed all the badass back into the frame.

The result was a growling, hellaciously fast beast.

"Indeed. Depending on the conditions I might take the bike out too."

"Your mom is going to kill me if you eat pavement, you know that, right?"

Fast and hard was his favorite. Nothing else felt quite like driving very, very fast. He didn't have the talent to actually make a living racing. His talents lay elsewhere in the car universe. But he had access to a track and lots of fast machines, and he used that every chance he got.

"My mom uses a cane, you big whiner. You can outrun her. Then again, she doesn't need to catch you. I bet she could throw it and knock you out from ten feet away." Two years before, his mother had to have her foot amputated after complications from diabetes.

"I'm telling her you said that."

"To Pat, that's a love poem." Asa grinned, thinking of how awesome his mom was.

"Speaking of that, the arbor you built over her back patio is really nice."

Asa had gone into the army because it was that or end up in jail. He'd had more anger and potential for violence inside him than he could process. Years spent on the verge of trouble or running from it had left him feeling out of control and exhausted.

So he'd enlisted and then spent several years using the opportunity to make himself into a better man. A better son. To keep himself from landing in trouble in the army, he'd sent home most of his pay. It had been enough to get his mom and two sisters into a safer neighborhood.

He'd kept sending his mom what he could, even once he'd returned to the U.S. and left the military. Eventually, after the surgery, he'd convinced her and his youngest sister to move out to Seattle. It meant everything to him that he could provide for her at long last after she'd fought so hard most of her life just to survive.

"She needed some shade back there. Those big windows made her kitchen and living room way too warm." He didn't like her to be uncomfortable. "Anyway, what were you doing over there? You spoil her worse than I do."

"I had a bunch of green peppers. I know she likes them. No big deal. She bragged on you so long I made her stop because I was getting a complex. Then she made me a grilled cheese sandwich and tomato soup to cheer me up. Your mom is rad."

Asa snorted a laugh. "Just don't tell her about the motorcycles at the track. She'd make my life hell if she found out I was racing."

Twisted Steel was magnificent.

PJ turned in a slow circle as she stood in the middle of their showroom. Just to her left, a 1970 Chevelle. Candy-apple red.

Big windows fronted the space, but they managed to still give it a sort of intentionally gritty feel inside with black leather couches placed in a way to look at the cars and bikes on display like art.

She loved it so very much. Bold and clever. It took itself very seriously when it came to the product but also had a little bit of tongue-in-cheek self-deprecation. Delicious design choices all over the place, including a custom Harley Softail in black matte that gave her a little shiver.

She'd thought it impossible for Asa to be any hotter, until she saw this place.

"If you're done getting all wet over cars can we get your makeup done?" Audra called out.

"Do you see this?" PJ pointed at the Softail's back tire. "It's so fat and delicious. I might actually be maybe a little wet, yes. But I'm just telling you that because we're so close."

PJ plopped down in front of a makeshift makeup station mirror.

"Go look at your outfits with Stella so she can get you styled for each." Audra had taken on the task of organizing the shoot. She pointed at a rolling rack of clothes that had PJ's name on it.

"I see a theme here." Stella, who was acting as their makeup person for the day, took in each outfit.

Tom bounded into their space, amped up on coffee. "What? She's like a ridiculously sexed-up girl next door. Guys love that. We all know it. So work it and sell my decks!"

"You can't be here now. I have it handled." Audra shoved him out and closed the door to the small conference room where they'd set up.

"He's like a hamster on crack," PJ muttered.

"The cutest hamster ever, though. Here." Audra shoved an outfit PJ's way.

The first dress turned out to be a pale blue-and-white gingham. She wore it with red glitter pumps, and Stella teased PJ's hair up in the back and curled her bangs before dividing at the nape of her neck into two braids.

Thick liner, red lips, and a beauty mark and she found herself shoved back out.

"PJ, come over and meet Frank, he's the photographer." Tom introduced them. "We're set up in the shop so come on with me."

She tried not to trip and fall as she kept stopping to gape at things. Where the showroom had been all about the art of the completed project—a perfect experience for a potential client— the shop, with its bays and workstations, was clearly the heart of the operation.

High windows sent shafts of light down onto the shop floor and to the offices that ringed it. It was orderly and tidy without being compulsively so.

She skidded to a halt when she saw the car she'd be posing with.

"Sweet mother of Bob Dylan," she breathed out at the sight of the deep blue 1950 Cadillac roadster convertible before her.

"I take it that means you approve?" Frank asked her.

"I might need some alone time with this car later."

"I know the owner. He might allow it."

She turned to catch sight of Asa walking over. *Walking*! Ha. *Prowling* was a far better word. The air seemed to hum around him, and she found it a little harder to breathe. Especially when he came to a halt just inches from where she stood.

"This is yours?" She might have an orgasm just looking at the car. And now she knew it was his.

He nodded, the corner of his mouth hitching up slightly. "Morning, PJ."

"Morning, Asa. I'm going to have a moment with your car, but I won't do anything she doesn't want."

He stepped closer. "What if she does? What if she wants it all?"

Man, was she in over her head. Just flirting with him was

taking all her effort. What would he be like in bed? What would he kiss like?

"I'd want to take it slow. Just the tip. At first. If she didn't like it we'd stop."

The smile on his mouth made her tingly.

"I might try that one. *Just the tip* has mixed results."

Oh, well. That one made her a little dizzy. And by the look he wore, he knew the effect he was having.

"I doubt that."

"What?"

"Mixed results. You strike me as an overachiever." PJ lowered her lashes a little as she took in the heft of all that steel. Of course he had a Caddy. Big, strong, bold. Totally in charge. Just like him.

"So if I'd given *you* the 'just the tip' line?"

She smiled then. "I don't know. Why don't you try it now?"

PJ rather felt as if she was having an out-of-body experience. There was no other explanation for the words she'd just spoken. Out loud.

Asa opened his mouth and everything inside her seemed to still, just waiting to hear what he'd say.

And then Tom called out to get to work and they reluctantly parted.

Asa tried to pretend it was his choice to watch the shoot when really there was nothing else to be done. She sat in his car. Her skin up against his seats. He bet it would smell of her for the rest of the day. That soft, spicy sex she seemed to throw off like pixie dust or something.

He'd put off returning her call and then had gotten so busy with work he'd legitimately forgotten about it for days at a time. But then she'd come back to his imagination so intensely he'd not called her back on purpose. This sort of raw greed she evoked in him had him nervous.

She'd taken him by surprise. Yes, she was beautiful. Gorgeous face. Fantastic body. Big blue eyes fringed by long lashes. Lush lips. She'd changed her hair from purple to a blond he was pretty sure was her natural color.

Pretty women weren't that rare, though. Certainly not in his world.

She appealed to him in ways he wasn't entirely comfortable with or even able to really put into words. It was her freckles he thought about more than her amazing tits. The sound of her voice. The way her eyes had lit when she talked about cars.

Across from where Asa leaned, the photographer directed her to put her forearm against the steering wheel, where Asa'd just had his hands half an hour before.

In his car. Touching his things. Satisfaction settled into his bones even as something else stirred to life. A hunger for her that only worsened when she leaned forward, one leg out of the car. Her skirt rose, exposing the tops of her stockings. Big blue eyes lined to emphasize the depth of color, the wide, nearly guile-less nature of them. Her tits heaved up at the neckline of that dress.

The whole picture was a slick, hot fist around his cock.

Sweet and hot. Innocence and pure, raw carnal pleasure prom-ised in the curve of her lips.

"No one else in her family looks anything like her." Duke handed over a cup of coffee.

Asa tipped his chin in thanks. "I'm pretty sure *I've* never seen anything like her. Ever. If she's like this now, at what? Twenty-two?"

Duke winced. "Dude, I would *not* be having these thoughts about her if she was twenty-two. Close, though. She's twenty-five. The youngest."

"If she's like this at twenty-five, what will she be like at thirty? She'll be unstoppable."

Duke jabbed him in the side. "You're defiling her in your head right now, aren't you?"

Hell yes. An image of her bent over his desk—her hair messy, backs of her thighs hot with welts he'd left from his favorite crop, her pussy wrapped around his cock as he fucked her—took root in his brain and would not let go.

"Man'd have to be dead not to notice that body." He turned to Duke. "And that age. I'm too old to keep up."

"I'm old enough to admit it might be a hell of a good time to find out if I could or not."

Once they finished with Asa's Caddy the crew moved it outside. Asa grabbed another cup of coffee and a bagel before sauntering out to discover PJ had changed into shorts and a work shirt open to the waist, where it was tied in a knot.

Her hair was artfully messy and wrapped in a bright red bandana, the same color as the bra showcased. She wore her glasses this time, and they perched on her nose, the hoop of her eyebrow ring visible when she arched her brow.

All that skin drove him wild. He wanted to touch. To kiss and lick. Especially that sweet triangle where her breasts and body met at the center of her cleavage. And yet, it could still look nearly sweet on her.

Nearly.

One of the assistants handed her a bottle of handcrafted soda, a root beer Asa really liked. He liked it even more when they leaned her against the front of the Chevelle in the showroom and she wrapped glossy red lips around a straw they'd put into the bottle.

An audible rush of air escaped his lips. The need to see that color at the base of his cock after she'd left it there seemed to take hold like a fever. He made himself turn to tear his attention away. He knew he should leave for a while, but he couldn't quite force himself to leave the shop while PJ was there.

He moved over to Duke and some of the other guys, hoping for a distraction. They hung out, working a bit, talking a lot, watching the shoot as it moved between models, settings, and products, but toward the end of the day, the photographer approached.

"Hey, Asa, I have a question."

"Shoot."

"Tell me you love me," Audra said quietly as she took the outfit PJ was about to change into out of her hands.

"I love you. Why did I tell you that, true as it is?"

Audra looked through the clothes on hangers and pulled out a body-hugging black sleeveless cocktail dress, then glanced back over her shoulder to PJ. "Keep the corset and the stockings and garters."

She thrust the dress PJ's way. "This."

PJ gave it a skeptical look. "I'm going to regret that dough-nut I ate earlier." She stepped in and Audra managed to get it zipped.

"Shut up. You look fantastic. As to why you love me? You love me because this last shoot is with Asa."

Audra said this as Stella started dealing with PJ's hair again, this time smoothing and pinning victory rolls.

"It is? Why? I'm not complaining or anything."

"They wanted someone hotter and darker than the other male model."

It wasn't like PJ hadn't noticed Asa watching. He'd wander away once she was done, but every time it was her turn, Asa found his way back to where she was, sliding his gaze over her like a caress.

Normally she was pretty easygoing when it came to flirting and being around men she was attracted to. But Asa was different. More intense. More everything. Having him watch her was fore-play. It made her breathless and nervous.

And she liked it.

PJ slid into towering heels, and with a backward glance at the mirror to be sure everything was in place, she headed out to where Asa stood in black pants, black motorcycle boots, and a snug T-shirt that stretched over the muscled wall of his chest.

Hoo. Boy.

His gaze found hers as she walked closer. Asa fastened a watch but never took his attention from her.

"PJ, you know Daniel, right? He has a line with watches and wrist cuffs for men," Tom explained. "We thought since you looked so great in Asa's Caddy, maybe the two of you could do this shoot. What do you say?"

She looked up at Asa and his expression nearly sent her to her knees. All smolder and overwhelming sexuality. PJ licked her lips, trying not to appear nervous and giddy.

"I want natural light for part of this. Come on outside. We're set up." The photographer dashed off.

Asa held out an elbow. "Those heels look pretty high, and the shop floor can be slippery sometimes."

Smiling, she took his arm and walked out with him. His skin was warm and taut against her palm.

Outside they had her stand with her back to Frank, facing Asa.

He encircled her waist with his forearm, splaying his palm right above her ass. He was hot and firm and had a hard-on. All her favorite things.

"Asa, with your right hand, grab PJ's upper arm."

All the air left her when he wrapped his fingers around her biceps. His cock pressed against her and with her heels, they were cock to pussy. She wanted him to push her back against something, anything, so she could get at what he had in his jeans.

The tension in his muscles brought a head-to-toe shiver. There was so much strength humming from him, it made her wonder just how much he held back. And *what* he held back.

His pupils seemed to swallow his irises. He bent his head when Frank told him to, his lips against the side of her neck.

Her nipples beaded so hard against the front of her corset and dress, she was sure he could feel it against the wall of his chest.

"Fantastic. I want to try one more thing. Asa, get in the car. I want PJ to lay across the seat, her head in your lap."

She didn't blush, but a burst of heat settled between her thighs. He took a reluctant step back, letting go of her arm.

Stella took her, fixing PJ's hair. "Girl, you've got me all hot and bothered just watching you two," she murmured.

"Not just you." Even knowing everything had been staged by the photographer, PJ was still aflutter after all that up-close contact with him.

Audra, who'd changed back into street clothes, waggled her brows.

Asa held his arm out as they removed the watch he'd had on and replaced it with a leather cuff.

He got in the car and she went to the passenger side.

"Don't make her struggle," Asa barked to the photographer's assistant. "Help her."

How could she just sit there and pretend it wasn't hotter than the sun that he'd just ordered someone to be careful with her? Jeez.

She sat and then Frank positioned them both as he moved around. "Turn around here and rest the back of your head on his thigh."

His really muscly thigh.

Asa looked down at her, wishing this were real. Wishing it were just the two of them. His cock was so hard it seemed to throb with each beat of his heart.

"You okay?"

She smiled up at him. "I can think of worse ways to spend a weekend."

He smiled back.

"Asa, put your hand on her chest, rest it there."

He did, pretending he wasn't itching to slide the top of her dress down to bare her breasts. He wondered if she was pierced anywhere other than her eyebrow. Wondered what sort of ink marked all that pretty skin.

This close he could see the freckles dancing across her collarbone and the curve of each shoulder. He bet that under her makeup she had even more of them.

"Cup her throat. Gentle, like a caress."

Both of them sucked in a breath, but he bet for different reasons.

Except when he wrapped his hand around her throat, she exhaled hard, her pupils widening. She must have been able to feel just how into this he was, poking her in the back of the head. He was so hard it was beginning to hurt.

The photographer spoke in the background. "Perfect. Jesus, PJ, you're so pretty like this. Fantastic. You can get up. Asa, swing your legs out, I want her on your lap and your hand on her thigh. Get that last watch on him."

Asa barely noticed them change out the jewelry because then they had her straddle his lap, artfully arranging the hem of her dress to give a glimpse of a stocking and the strap of her garter belt.

Her pussy was right over his cock, and he had to exercise iron control not to rock himself against her.

"Sorry about this. I'll try not to smoosh you."

She was teasing, but he heard the thready tones in some of her words. Took in the jump of her pulse just below her ear. But goddamn, the heat of her was scalding.

The photographer took Asa's hand and placed it where he wanted at PJ's hip. But then he said, "Stella, get her hair around his fist."

But before Stella could move, Asa had done it. Like he was meant to.

He locked gazes with her as Frank took pictures. Asa hadn't wanted to kiss someone this badly since he'd gotten out of high school.

"Perfect. That's it. Thanks to both of you."

It took another few seconds to make his hand loosen and let go of her hair. And before anyone else could step in, Asa helped PJ off his lap and stood as well. There was no hiding how hot he was for her, so he just kept it casual as he kissed her cheek.

"You were a pro through all that," PJ told him.

"That so?"

"Definitely. I have something for you," she said. "Will you give me ten minutes? I need to change. It's not going to require anything from you, so get that look off your face."

"I'll be here. My office is that door up there." Asa pointed and she nodded and left.

Duke snorted. "You doing okay? Need some pain reliever?"

"Hey, fuck off. You try not getting hard when that is on your lap. Or when her hair is wrapped around your fist."

He'd be remembering that for a while to come. Probably with his eyes closed and that same fist around his cock.

CHAPTER
Four

When she tapped on his door a few minutes later, she'd changed into jeans and a long-sleeved shirt, the lines of her face exposed by her high ponytail.

This PJ was dressed far more appropriately for a shop floor, and even without the party clothes she was beautiful.

"Hi there." She waved, smiling.

Asa returned her smile as he stood and indicated a chair. "Come in and sit."

Some people came into the shop and held themselves still, trying not to get anything on their clothes or set anything on fire. PJ was comfortable, easily dropping into the chair, a folder on her lap.

"I apologize for taking so long to return your calls. It's been crazy here and we've had some major deadlines to meet, so everything else fell by the wayside." He held up a soda. "Thirsty?" When she nodded, he popped the cap and handed it her way.

"Thanks. And I understand that it gets busy sometimes." PJ placed the soda on the table to her left and then slid the folder his way. "That's my work."

He looked from that face down to the photos, sifting through them. He held one up. "Tell me about this."

Her smile raised his respect for her. She was proud of doing good work. An excellent sign in someone you're considering doing business with.

"That's the new Colman Enterprises logo for our racing team. I hand-paint them on all the cars."

Clever work. She had a good eye. A real understanding of the overall placement of all the elements. She'd gone with a clean design, drawing the eye on what would likely be a car covered in a whole lot of busy graphics.

Which was how Asa had noticed the logo when he and Duke had been out at the track. "I was just telling Duke we needed something like this for our team. He and I saw one of the Colman cars at a drag race in California. Really nice work."

"Thank you." She didn't downplay it like some people would. She was proud of her skill.

"But we send out our custom work already. We have people who handle our accounts."

"I know you do. But I'm better. Okay, not better than Richie Carlyle. But no one is. Give me twenty years."

"You have a gig with Colman, don't you? The next generation, right? Why this?"

If she'd quit or had been fired, he'd toss her some work to help her until she got something else.

"I do have a job with Colman." She paused, clearly trying to decide something. "My family's business is great. But it needs to move into other sectors of our industry. Yes, we sell tires. And we're good at it. But the world is changing, and we have to change with it. I think Colman can do more than sell tires and sponsor racing teams. Innovation is how we started. I like to think it's how we'll continue to be relevant into the next generation."

"And custom paint does that? Not shock absorbers? Or air filters?"

"We tried shocks for a while. It didn't work for us." One of her brows rose. *See, I know more than you assumed I did.* "We have so much to offer a significant portion of our market we've previously taken for granted. Neglect loses you customers."

She had the kind of confidence people have when they're on solid ground. She knew what she was talking about. He liked that.

"What market portion do you mean?"

"All the hot rods, custom and restoration build operations. You buy our tires already. And that's great, thanks for your business. But we can offer you more. So I'm starting with some smaller jobs and building contacts."

Asa bet her ease at presenting herself came from being put to work as a kid. She sat there in one of his chairs, eyebrow pierced, ink on her back—a lotus, he thought, but he couldn't get a full view—as well as in a few other places he'd glimpsed.

She wasn't as buttoned-up and straitlaced as her brother. But she took herself seriously and he dug that. Not as a quality in a woman but as a quality in anyone he did business with.

"Like I said, your work is impressive. I'll talk to Duke and get back to you."

There was a pause. He normally would have filled it with an invitation to drinks or something, but he wasn't ready for that. Being alone with her outside a work situation might send messages he didn't intend to send.

She stood and he followed suit, his body so close he could feel her warmth. He made no attempt to step back.

Her smile was slightly teasing. "Thanks for your time. I hope to hear from you soon. You have my number."

"I'll walk you out." He held the door for her, then escorted her through the shop and out the showroom. She bent to grab a duffel bag, and he smoothly snatched it first. "Is this yours?"

"Yes. I designed that logo too."

He looked down at the bag, approving. "Did you get a degree in marketing or something?"

She laughed. "No. I dropped out of college, much to my family's terrible disappointment." She pointed at her car. "That's me."

He looked up and skidded to a halt. "That's yours? *Yours?*"

A 1969 Camaro Z28 with deep purple metallic paint and white stripes sat a few feet away.

"It belonged to my grandfather. When I was little and he was still able to drive, he'd take me out in it. We'd go to Dick's and have burgers and shakes. After his last stroke when he couldn't drive anymore, they moved it to a warehouse where it sat under a tarp until he passed away. He left it to me."

She unlocked the trunk and he dropped the duffel in. He noted the general level of care that'd been put into the car.

"This is Howie Colman's Camaro."

She grinned. "Yes. Though Jay had a fit when they read the will and Gramps left it to me. He tried to get me to auction it a time or two. He had kittens when I painted it purple. Hates it when I drive it too."

"Your brother seems rather irritated by everything about you. What's his problem anyway?"

"Thank you. I think I'm the one with the problem, judging by everyone else in my family." Her laugh wasn't bitter. "He loves the company." She shrugged and then ran her palm over the roof. "I love cars. My grandfather loved cars. It's what Colman could be again."

He nodded. Respecting that a great deal.

He opened the door for her and she slid inside. "Don't forget to talk to Duke and call me to offer me some jobs, Asa Barrons."

She started the engine and it roared to life. He stepped back and she waved before driving off, leaving him in his parking lot trying to piece through what had been a most unexpected Saturday.

Full of tingles and feeling like she'd done a lot of great work for the day, PJ headed over to her sister's place. Julie lived in a very tidy, elegant condo in Bellevue with a great view of the water. And a lot of distance to Colman central up in Edmonds.

Julie loved numbers. She fit just fine in their brother Shawn's office handling money, and she and Shawn had a great rhythm. PJ had long ago stopped wishing she had that same sort of click with her siblings, or anyone in her family, really.

Her sister opened with a hug and handed over a cocktail as PJ entered. "Just finished this batch. Come on, I need to check on dinner."

As usual, Julie's hair was done perfectly. It framed her face just so, hung just right. A split end wouldn't have dared to exist on Julie Colman's head. It simply wasn't done.

PJ took a sip of what turned out to be an excellent dirty martini. "Nice. Thanks."

"I spent three hours down at the factory today. Jay said you cut out on it?"

"He said what? That pissant! He came to me yesterday and asked if I'd cover it. Which I was open to doing last night because I had the shoot today. Then he insulted me about a dozen times and I told him to fuck off." PJ grabbed a pita chip from the bowl on the counter and pointed for emphasis. "I'm sending my legion after him."

"I don't know why you let him get under your skin. You only let him win when you do that."

"Because he's a smug asshole who wanted me to cover a meeting where real employees had to be talked to so he could play golf with all the Colmans who have a penis. How can I let that go?"

Her sister grimaced. "Yes, he's all that. We should have shown up for that golf game. Just to see Jay's and Fee's faces."

Fee was their father's far younger brother. One of those *Hey oops I'm pregnant at forty!* moments for their grandmother. He and Jay were a lot alike, which made Colman Enterprises doubly annoying at big meetings.

Though to be fair, she also knew part of it was that Jay understood Fee was the doorway to their father. For whatever reason,
their father looked to Fee for his opinions more than he did anyone else. Jay was smarter than Fee, but not craftier. Julie would
have been way better at Fee's job, but he'd hold that seat on
the board until he was ready to scamper off and chase women
full-time.

"I don't like to play golf. They should try making decisions at
business meetings set up just for that. Ugh. What's for dinner?"

"Citrus-infused chicken. Farro salad with feta and tomatoes as
a side."

"Yum."

Julie's expression said she knew exactly how yum that was. The
Colman women might have opinions the men in the family didn't
care about. But that didn't mean the women weren't confident,
hard-as-nails people in their own way.

"How did the shoot go?"

After refilling both their glasses, PJ sat up at the kitchen island
and gave her sister a general overview of her interactions with Asa
that day.

"I think my car impressed him more than my body, my face, or
my painting."

"Considering how much you love cars, I think that's a compliment. You're beautiful, even when you pierce your face." Julie
shuddered. "And other parts. But pretty isn't rare. Anyway, that's
nice. You two having shared passions is a good thing."

"He's got this...ugh, I can't even describe it right. He's so
much. He doesn't just look at me, it's like he looks right into me.
He makes me fluttery and blushy. I've never met anyone like him.
He's like turned to twenty-five on the one-to-ten dial. Know what
I mean?"

"Yeah. I do. What's your next move then?"

"Well, I gave him the photos of my work. He said he was going to talk to his partner about it. I'll give him until Friday before I check in. I'd be happy if he called first, but I get the feeling it's going to take some more poking to get him to move on anything. I'm assuming he's stubborn. He's definitely got that *I do what I want* vibe going on."

"You should be used to that by now, so you already have a leg up. Get some plates and stuff out and I'll handle the food." Julie pointed to the table and PJ moved to obey.

She and her sister talked about the fight PJ had with Jay, Julie frowning the whole time.

"I can't believe he said all that. He doesn't mean it. He just said it because he knows it pushes your buttons."

"But he said it. And it's not the first time. I'm trying to contribute! I'm trying to bring my ideas to the table so I can be an active participant in Colman's future."

"You hate hearing this, I know, but you have to prove yourself."

"For how long? I dropped out of college *three years* ago. I've been trying to show everyone how serious I am ever since."

"You're twenty-five. No one takes twenty-five-year-old women seriously. No one takes pretty women seriously. No one takes women with hoops in their eyebrows seriously. No one takes women with boobs like yours seriously. You dropped out of college, you pierced your face, and you're telling one of the most uptight guys on the planet that you have ideas. Jay and Fee and Dad already think women are best at adding shit up and looking pretty."

"So the only way to get anyone to take me seriously is to be an old man?"

Julie thought this was hilarious. "Well, since that's probably not going to happen, I'm telling you to remember your struggle. You're different. They can't even deal with the vagina part. You add blue or purple hair and face piercings and they just lose their shit. But don't let that stop you. Penelope Jean, you are a badass. That comes with a price tag. You know it. You've chosen this path.

Understand its strengths and limitations. You have to be twice as good as any man your age. Whether that's fair or not, that's reality."

"Can I tell Jay you said he was uptight?"

Julie's mouth fought a battle with a smile.

"Go on. You know you want to."

Julie waved a hand, laughing. "You're a bad influence."

"I know. It's a gift. But you're a good one. So there's hope for one of us."

"Just keep being PJ. This is a male-dominated business. Our company is male dominated too. I have faith in your ability to never let anyone ignore you for very long. Jay is testy because he knows you have a point but he's scared of new things." Julie shrugged.

"You always know what to say."

Her sister smiled. "All my facial piercings are on the inside, but I've got your back on this. You have good ideas. Colman *should* be listening to you. Keep talking, baby sister, keep talking. You're good at that too."

"Har. Enough about me. How was your date?"

Julie exhaled long and slow. "It was okay. He's nice. Maybe too nice? I don't know."

"Did he kiss you?"

"At the door. Which he walked me to like a total gentleman."

"And?"

"Meh. It was proficient."

"Proficient?" PJ curled her lip. "I wouldn't even want a car that was 'proficient,' much less a kisser."

"It wasn't bad. He had some technique. We just didn't have any energy as a couple. If he calls again I'm going to say no."

"Or you can say yes, fuck him, and see if he can top proficient. And if not, then you say no. Because if you fuck him on the second date he'll definitely call again."

"You should write a dating advice column in the *Stranger*." Julie raised a brow. "I don't fuck on the second date."

"Two words for you, Julie. Gavin Suarez."

Her sister blushed madly at the mention of her ex. "Well, that's different." Julie had been engaged when she'd met Gavin, who was sitting next to her on an airplane headed from Seattle to Washington DC.

A week later she came back home, broke her engagement, and banged Gavin like a gong until he left six months later to spend three years working for an international aid organization based in Belgium.

"The guy was worth you breaking an engagement over. You let him into your underpants while he was still a relative stranger. I don't know why you don't see these things are the hugely import-ant exclamation points on you needing to run this dude to the ground and claim him before someone else does."

"It's been two years. Someone else probably has."

"None of them are you. You said he told you he wasn't seeing anyone and that he was coming back here to the Northwest when he finished things up. For you."

"I guess I need to see what happens next year then, huh?"

"Honestly, you're so smart and awesome at stuff I'm just shocked at the depth of *I don't want to* over this issue. This guy means something to you. Why are you running from him?"

"Nothing can happen between us right now. He's half a world away. I could visit him and then what? Love him but from here? Where I can't even touch him?"

Frowning, PJ took her sister's hand and gave it a squeeze. "You love him."

Julie nodded. "But it does me no good. Because he's there and I'm here. He told me I should see other people. I guess that means he wants to."

PJ shook her head. "Or maybe he thinks you want to and he's

trying to be nice because he loves you too. In any case, scrap plans to bang proficient kisser and save your ladygarden for Gavin."

"Ladygarden?" At least the sadness had eased around Julie's eyes at the joke.

"You got really mad the last time I said 'pussy.' I could say 'vagina,' but that's boring. 'Flesh pocket'? Do you like that better?"

Horrified, Julie recoiled, her eyes widening to the point that all PJ could do was laugh.

"What? I'd rather have a flesh pocket than a Hot Pocket. At least my stomach won't cramp with the former."

"Stop!" Her sister managed to get the word out through a gale of laughter.

Her work cheering Julie back up was done, so PJ sat back with a smile and narrowly avoided the cherry tomato Julie tossed at her head.

CHAPTER
Five

Hey, Asa. Someone here to see you."

He looked up from the screen to their office manager, Lottie.

"Thank god, something else to do." He stood. "Who is it?"

"Hi there, Asa. I was in the neighborhood, and since I hadn't heard back from you and a few weeks have passed, I thought I'd drop in." PJ Colman stood there, a bright smile on her face.

Lottie hid a smile as she left, but that didn't dampen his pleasure at the sight PJ made in his doorway.

"Want something to drink?" He looked her up and down. She was more businesslike than the times he'd seen her before. Navy blue high-waisted trousers and a long-sleeved white blouse. Her hair was pulled back from her face, which he liked just fine indeed because her face was really easy to look at.

And yet there was something about her . . . something that always cried out for his attention. A pop of color at her arm where her sleeve was rolled up and her ink was exposed. The earrings, which at first glance looked like cameos but were really skeletons instead of women's faces. Just little things that made up a unique package.

"I like that you're not only giving in right away but offering me refreshments. I'd love something to drink."

He moved to her, wanting to brush a kiss against her cheek. But she was there on business, so he reined it in, telling himself it was better anyway. Flirting, sure. No kissing. Kissing those lips would be disastrous. He knew he wouldn't be able to stop until he'd bared every part of her to his touch.

Which would also be disastrous.

That didn't mean he didn't want to be around her for the next while. He liked her. "You're persistent. I know that already. So I might as well give in, take a break, and agree to give you a job so we can see how you work."

He and Duke had talked about it a week before. Her work had been really good, and they did need to expand to new contractors from time to time. Duke also rightly pointed out it didn't hurt them at all to have a better relationship with Colman Enterprises either. If PJ was the next generation and she wanted them to be part of the customer base from then on, it was smart to support that.

"Well, of course you should."

He laughed as he led her toward the break room.

"We've got soda and water and I think those flavored water things with vitamins. Duke thinks they're health food."

"Damn, I want to work here." She took in the break room.

"You don't have a break room at Colman HQ?"

"We have a room with a fridge, a sink, and a microwave. My mother has a deep and abiding love of Costco, so she goes all the time and there are waters and sodas in the fridge. But *you* have ice cream bars. In a special ice cream bar cooler. How is that even a thing I never knew break rooms had? Now I'm questioning everything, Asa. My entire foundation is sort of shaken. If you say you have doughnut delivery I'm probably going to cry."

"I won't tell you, then. There's a Top Pot up the street. I can take you there if you like."

She smirked. "Are you mocking me, Mr. Barrons?"

Oh.

Yes.

He liked that bit of formality from her very much. Especially as it was a tease.

"If you get a hankering for ice cream in the middle of your day, feel free to come over and help yourself."

She slid the top of the cooler open and pulled out one of the chocolate–chocolate chip bars and didn't pay him any mind until she'd unwrapped it and found a seat. "What? Did you think my manners were good enough to turn down an offer of ice cream? I'm only human."

He grabbed one of the same bars and joined her.

"So a job, huh?" she prodded, and then took a bite.

"Duke and I think you do good work. We like having plenty of people to call when we need good work done on our machines. Understand we'll start small and simple to see what you can do. But given the stuff of yours we've seen, we're not worried."

She smiled. "Awesome. When?"

He watched her eat that ice cream and nearly broke down.

She wasn't even really trying that hard to be sexy! He was a grown man with excellent self-control, and this woman made him crazy.

He should have called her back the week before to tell her they'd agreed to toss her some work. Could have had Duke call her.

He should have done a lot of things, but he didn't want to. He wanted what was right there in front of him.

"Finish your ice cream and I'll show you."

"Excellent." She sat back with a smile. "Today is a pretty good day. How are you? Other than super lucky to be here with me eating ice cream, which clearly is a yay."

He laughed. He'd been stupid to resist this. She was fun to be with. "Any afternoon a man can take a break and eat ice cream with a beautiful woman is a yay."

The watching-her-eat-it part was pretty fantastic too, though he'd refrain from saying that.

They finished their ice cream and he led her out toward the shop.

He cast a quick look at her clothes and shoes. She wore heels but not stilettos. "Watch your step." Without thinking he put a hand at her elbow to steady her.

They stood in the back stairwell, just five steps up from the shop floor, but at this part of the stairwell it was just the two of them.

She looked down at where he held her, his hand against the fabric of her blouse, and then back up, her eyes going wide and then half-lidded.

The need was back, gripping him as the heat between him and PJ continued to build.

It grew. And grew until he leaned down and brushed his mouth over hers. His brain screamed at him to stop. Until his cock took over and shoved the brain far away.

Her lips opened on a sigh and he groaned as her taste flooded him, his tongue sliding over her bottom lip. She made a sound so sweet and demanding he'd have given her anything she asked for at that moment.

This was good. She caught his attention, to the point that nothing else registered.

Her bag was between them, which was good because he was so hard he'd have scared her if they were body to body. But she was so fucking sweet he ached for more. Even as she put a hand on his chest and he broke the kiss and stepped back.

He started to apologize, but the look on her face told him that would be a mistake. And he wasn't sorry. He wanted more and he couldn't have it, so he'd have to let that kiss be enough.

PJ supposed she was probably going to hell for not telling Asa she didn't need his elbow because the soles of her shoes were treaded like work boots. She wore them all the time when she was in their different shop spaces at Colman.

But his hand was so big. And warm. And she liked it when he touched her. Then he'd kissed her. It surprised her, but she caught up quickly enough, opening to his mouth, to his tongue, which was quite talented.

He kissed her so well she forgot everything but where he touched her.

Sounds came from around the corner and she didn't care. She should have cared, but she didn't. She'd waited how long for him to do this? Wondered if she'd been imagining real heat between them even as she knew that hard-on he'd been sporting was real.

And it was better than she'd imagined it would be. The kiss and that hard-on.

She put her hand on his chest, and he groaned low in his throat and stepped back. She saw it in his features. He hadn't meant to lose control. He was as surprised by that kiss as she was.

And he'd loved it as much as she had. But he felt guilty. She saw that too. If Asa apologized, she was going to kick him.

He thought better of it—maybe he noted the violence in her eyes—and waved a hand, indicating she should proceed.

Smiling, she moved along as he led her through the shop, bringing her to stand in front of a 1971 El Camino.

"You're kidding me. Really?"

She was usually much more confident, but she wanted this so bad! Working on this truck would be such a fantastic job. As good a time as the kiss. Though she wouldn't say that out loud.

"This is a pretty simple job. The client wants initials woven into a design on each door, below the handle. Give me three choices and I'll pick one."

"Nope." She thrust her bag into his arms and began to walk around the truck.

"Nope?"

She laughed without looking up at him, her gaze roaming greedily over the El Camino. "Bet you don't hear that often. I'm not giving you three designs. That's a waste of my time. I don't need to anyway. Who is your client? Male? Female? Young? Older? Letters in the name?"

Struck silent for long moments, Asa simply watched her. She clearly had something going on because she bent and took a picture of the area with her phone and then stood with a smile.

"I work freehand. If you don't like my design I'll remove it and refund your money. Can I work here or do you need me to take it off-site?" She waited for his reply, and then when it didn't come immediately she moved to him. "Here's the thing, I'm sure you're thinking, *What the hell, she should be grateful and do it the way I said.* Maybe you're right. But while I *am* grateful for the chance, this is creative for me. I have my own process and it doesn't include you or anyone else but the owner of the car. I'm worth it."

"That's a bold claim."

"I'm more than happy to show you."

Oh danger, danger, danger.

Asa liked the way she flirted. Straightforward. She wasn't overly coy.

He reminded himself she was too young. Even if she kissed like she was made for him.

And he had to admit, her refusal to provide three samples was reasonable. He liked her spark.

"You can do it here. We have painting bays. Client is male, thirty-eight. He's a cop. Saved up for years for this job, so I want it to be fan-fucking-tastic, dig?"

One of her brows went up, the one with the ring. His cock hardened at the haughty expression it lent her features.

"Just so we're clear, *all* my work is fan-fucking-tastic. *You* dig? I don't do it if I don't do it all the way. Why else would I be here?"

They stood there not speaking, letting that chemistry between them build. Again. It ebbed and flowed like that every time they were near each other. Playing with fire. He knew it. Suspected she did too.

Which made it even hotter.

Even harder to pull back each time from taking a step into something intimate between them. Which, of course, he'd complicated by kissing her. Still, he couldn't find it in him to feel bad.

"We're waiting on some custom pieces for the dash, so I'll have one of my guys take the doors off and you can work on them while we wait."

"What's this guy like? Is he an Ed Hardy–wearing cop? Earnest cop next door? Hot cop you dated in secret back when you were a senior in high school?"

Fuck.

He scrubbed a hand over his face. He totally had to let that one go. There was no way he could go down that road.

"There's a story?" he heard himself ask like he stood in another room.

"He was hot. Bad. Bad and hot. One of my best friends' older brothers. He's still hot, actually, but engaged. The stuff he taught me." She drew in a slow breath, pleasured at the memory. Her lip caught a moment between her teeth and she looked up at him through her lashes. "I like older men, I suppose."

He pressed the tip of one of his keys into his thigh to keep from taking her hint.

"He's an inked cop who is super active in his community. Works with youth. He's a very cool guy."

She pulled a notebook from her bag—the one he still held—and scribbled things down here and there as they went back and forth for a while.

"If I get this right in one," she muttered as she began to sketch, "when I'm done with this job you can give me the next one right after I deliver."

Cocky.

He wished he'd had her kind of confidence at twenty-five. It had taken eight years in the army for him to learn how to get his emotions under control, and once he'd done that, he'd gotten his shit together and begun focusing on what he'd do in his life after he left the military.

But he shouldn't be encouraging it.

"All right. And if you lose?"

Her gaze left the paper and locked with his. "Do you have some terrible punishment for me?"

And he planned to send Duke a case of beer for walking in right before Asa answered that question honestly.

Moment broken, she smirked and handed him the pad. "No need to discuss what happens if I lose. Because, duh."

He looked down and then handed the pad over to Duke.

"This is for Mort?" Duke asked.

Asa nodded.

"Damn. You're good, beautiful. And you have perfect timing because those parts just came in." Duke looked over to her. "Can you do this now? This guy is one of our good friends. He's waited for this a long time. If you can do it now we can get it to him a little earlier."

"I need to run home and get my stuff. I can be back in an hour. I'm happy to do this for Mort."

"I'll have the doors moved into a paint bay for you." Asa paused. "And when you're done, your next job will be ready."

She flashed them both a smile, grabbed her bag from Asa, and headed out, waving over her shoulder and saying she'd be back.

"Sweet fucking shit, she's hot. Just like a really bad girl wrapped up in a sweet girl-next-door costume," Duke said as they watched her drive off.

"She's just a kid." Asa flagged one of his guys down and told him to get the doors off and moved.

"That person who was just here, trading so much sexual whatever you two have that I could feel it five feet way? That's a woman, Asa."

They continued on to Asa's office. Once they were out of earshot of everyone else, he resumed the conversation. "What I'm looking for is on the more *experienced* end of the spectrum. That woman who was just here is hotter than fire, absolutely. But what I want from a woman isn't in her wheelhouse."

Duke scoffed. "Why? You're kinky, not gay. So obviously she has what you need in her wheelhouse just fine."

"Shut the fuck up. You know what I mean."

Asa liked percussive toys. Crops and paddles, mostly. He loved the sound of the crop splitting the air right before it landed on skin. Loved the crack of that contact. Loved the sound a woman made when she *really* liked it.

He couldn't imagine PJ's reaction if he ordered her over his knees, hands flat on the ground as he paddled her, each strike placed right so that the force traveled straight to her clit.

Of course, now that he'd thought it, the image of her, skin pinked from a leather slapper, whimpering until he walked his fingertips from her thighs up through her pussy had cemented itself in his imagination.

She'd be wet. So wet and hot her body would melt around his fingers when he teased inside.

"Yeah, so if you could stop thinking about whatever it is you want to do with her, that'd be great. You're making me uncomfortable now."

Asa gave Duke a look. "Can I help you with anything else? In case it missed your notice, we're at work and there are things to do that aren't about fucking with me for amusement."

"None of them are as much fun, though. I need to call to check in on a special order I thought was coming today instead of your stuff. When I'm done I'll come out and help."

"For a dick you're pretty cool sometimes. Thanks." Asa grabbed one of the hair band things Lottie kept bringing him—so he'd stop using her rubber bands—got his hair up and out of his face, and headed down to get back to work. And to pretend his office didn't smell like that spicy perfume she wore.

CHAPTER
Six

Julie gave her an encouraging smile from her place at the other end of the table. It was the second Wednesday of the month, so all the top management had gathered in the conference room for the staff meeting.

Unfortunately, their father was still in California. PJ had really hoped to impress him with her presentation.

Shawn looked down at the agenda and then over to PJ. "You're up."

"As you know, I've been looking at ways to further integrate Colman Enterprises branding into other sectors of the industry, with an emphasis on the hot-rod and custom-build people. Over the last three months I've done custom paint work for several shops in the area, including Twisted Steel."

Her uncle frowned. "We don't sell paint, Penelope, we sell tires."

"I'm aware of that, which is why I'm working on this presentation. It doesn't all have to be tires. We already offer other custom services as the need arises with some of our bigger clients. I have the skill, and I'm continuing to build on that. I just attended a class a few weeks ago and plan to keep on with that sort of education and training. Over time my connections will continue to grow as my reputation does."

"It's a waste of time." Fee was grumpy and had been divorced five times. She wasn't sure if he got divorced a lot *because* he was grumpy or if getting divorced a lot *made* him grumpy. Whatever the case, he thought women were stupid and helpless and that she and Julie should shut up, play nice, and let the men run Colman. He liked to point out his daughters as examples of this.

One of these days PJ was going to tell him he shouldn't confuse his estrangement and half abandonment of his daughters with being well behaved. They avoided him because he was a terrible, toxic person.

"It's *not* a waste of time, actually."

"How much Colman money did you fritter away playing with paintbrushes?"

"If you let her finish a sentence she might be able to give us specifics on the financials of this, Fee." Shawn said this to their uncle without looking at him. Her brother winked at her and also gave her a definite push.

Talk money.

"Right now as vice president, I have accounts. Some of them are pretty important, though most large accounts are with Jay and Dad, which makes sense. I most certainly earn my keep. In fact, in ten of the last eighteen months I've been in the top two sales slots. But if you split my clients between Shawn and Jay, I could handle the custom paint work on my own. We have bays here and the accounts with the paint suppliers I need. I don't use brushes usually, but I already have the equipment."

"And we pay you to play while we take a loss?"

She reminded herself not to rise to the bait her uncle tossed her way. Instead, she took a deep breath and continued as if he weren't being a disrespectful asshole. "No. Actually, I believe I can make as much money, if not more, with custom jobs. I recently spent several months learning how to mix and create custom colors. Not a lot of people take the time and get certified, which means my work is not only truly custom, but at the upper end of the spectrum especially, I'm rare. Which means as time goes on, I'll continue to make money for Colman. I'll be doing something I love to do, something to serve car people, which is why we're here, isn't it? Bottom line? It's profitable. You don't need me to sell tires. You have plenty of people who can do that just fine."

"We don't sell custom paint. That's not what we do."

"We didn't sell tires at one point either," Julie said. "Shawn, Jay, me, and PJ, we're the future of Colman. If we're allowed to shape it as we go, to fit who we are as a family moving into the future, it's going to remain vibrant. PJ is smart. She's talented, and those grease monkey shops love her. They love her, they love Colman. I just can't see this as a losing situation. Especially when she'll be bringing a profit in."

"She claims."

PJ hit a button on her keyboard and an image popped up on the big screen at the end of the table. "Those are my receipts for the last three months. Broken down per job and by profit after expenses."

There was savage satisfaction when her uncle's face changed as he added it all up.

"Obviously we need to establish things like hourly rates and that sort of detail, but this is not only viable it's smart. This is adding to what we do in a way that is relevant to me as a Colman but also relevant to car people, which is part of our mission statement."

He frowned again. "Just because we *can* do something, young lady, doesn't mean we *should*."

"Why shouldn't we? I'm not indispensable as a sales rep. I'm using my skills in ways that benefit this company and expanding our client base." Then she turned to Jay. She'd tossed him a sweet deal with the offer to split her accounts between him and Shawn.

Jay loved money and he loved power. Those accounts would give him more of both. And he loved Colman. He might think her vagina clouded her thinking on most things, but that offer of those accounts was what she planned to use to crowbar her brother onto her side.

Shawn had recommended she come up with a few different ways to be compensated in her new position, so she'd gathered the financial information, and as she did it, she'd realized what a huge thing he'd done for her. She probably wouldn't have included it at first, thinking to make her point verbally in her presentation. But Fee never would have taken her word for it, and without the data, others wouldn't be so eager to come down on her side and risk her uncle's grumpy wrath.

"I've e-mailed everyone copies of three different approaches to compensation for this new position and I'm happy to talk about each one. I've included pros and cons of each as well."

"Don't get ahead of yourself," Fee bitched. "Your father isn't here, so we can't vote on anything anyway."

He wasn't. Yet another disappointment in years' worth of them. She'd reminded him of this meeting several times and not once had he said he'd be gone.

"I'm not asking you to vote today. Naturally I expect you all want time to read the material and make a decision. I'm available if you want to speak about this more."

Fee grabbed his things and rushed from the room without saying good-bye. Jay stood. "I'll look at everything. I'm not convinced adding more things won't actually hurt Colman."

"That's fair. We'll talk when you're ready."

He nodded and then spoke again. "This is excellent work." Jay then left, along with everyone else but Shawn and Julie.

Shawn gave her a hug and kissed her cheek. "You did good, Penny-Lope."

She rolled her eyes at his use of her nickname. So many people mispronounced her name when she was a kid, her mother finally gave up and allowed the use of PJ instead of Penelope. But Penny-Lope had stuck with Shawn.

"You saved my butt with the suggestion about the compensation comparison."

He winked. "Nice work tossing half your accounts to Jay. He's greedy enough that it'll be a factor for him. Not that I'm complaining about my half of those clients. I need a new car. My transmission is making noises again."

"Colman has three full-time mechanics. All in a garage about two miles from here. Why are you driving a car with a dodgy transmission?" Julie shook her head at their brother.

"Okay, so to be more accurate, I want a new car."

Laughing, the siblings headed out to their own offices and jobs.

Audra leaned across the table. "What is the story with tall, dark, and pierced?"

"Asa?" As if anyone else was on her mind these days.

"Yes."

"Months now he's looked at my tits and he's looked at my ass. In that way, you know how they do. I know what it looks like when someone is imagining me naked. He does it all the time. Flirts with me like crazy, but he holds back. I thought it was that he had a girlfriend, but now I'm not sure. I don't think he'd go as far as he does with his flirting if he was seeing someone. Maybe he just doesn't dig me that way and I'm too stupid to see it."

"Please. Have you looked at yourself lately? You're adorable. And gorgeous and sexy. Maybe it's the business thing? Like you two work together at times, so maybe it's that. If it is, just change his mind. Flash your boobs. Makes them forget what they were going to say." Audra raised a glass.

"Well, here's the thing. Twisted Steel calls me regularly now. I'm their go-to person. That's great and it makes me happy to know this thing is working out. But I want him. Oh man, do I want him. At the same time, it's hard enough to be taken seriously. If I go hooking up with Asa, how's that going to look? What if people think I banged my way into a job instead of earning it?"

"A round of shots first and then we'll continue to discuss this." Audra tried to get their server's attention, but it was crazy busy so in the end, PJ headed to the bar to get them herself.

Of course as she stood there, several of her friends already at the bar passed her back a shot, and then another, so by the time she made it back to the table they'd been joined by half a dozen more people.

"I might have already gotten started." PJ grinned at Audra.

"I'll say you got started." Audra took two quick shots. "That's better. No wonder you look relaxed."

"Whatever. Stress is bad for you."

"We need music." Audra stood, rooting through her bag for change.

"We do. I need your change," PJ told everyone at the table.

The jukebox was one of her favorite things about the place. The selection was fantastic, with every type of music imaginable.

She was happy. It was a *good* day, even without the shots and music that made her dance as she and Audra sang along.

That's when she realized the prickle on the back of her neck was someone watching her. She turned and halted as she caught sight of none other than Asa.

Well.

"So that happened," she said to Audra without taking her gaze from Asa.

"Go break off a piece of that. My god. And then you have to tell me every last really dirty detail at brunch on Sunday."

PJ faced her friend. "Such confidence! You don't think you'll be seeing me until Sunday?"

"He's currently looking at you like he wants to eat you up with a spoon. You're pretty and relentless when you want something. He wants what you have in your pants."

"He looks like he does. Yes. But he's wily."

They both continued to watch him and he watched PJ right back. Walt, the server, walked by and PJ stopped him, arranging to have shots sent to Asa's table. She waved at Asa and then turned to go back to her table with her friends.

"Why are you headed over here instead of jumping on his peen?" Audra asked.

Asa'd had his chance to catch all the softballs she'd pitched his way over the last five months. She wanted him, yes she did. But that hadn't worked.

Maybe he liked to do the coming over.

Or not, but she wasn't going over there. He knew she was into him, but she had some pride, for goodness sake.

"He knows I want to jump on his peen. He needs to work for it. But nothing says I can't be as alluring as I possibly can to help that along."

Audra nodded. "All right then! By the way, you look seriously hot. He can't miss that part."

She didn't sit. The booth was full anyway, so she stood with Audra near the windows, just next to the table. Trixie Whitley's "Undress Your Name" came on and PJ swayed a little.

"This song is sex on a stick."

Asa couldn't take his attention from PJ. When she'd seen him first a few minutes before, he figured she'd come over and say hello. He could flirt with her and jerk off when he got home, thinking about what he should have done instead of saying good night.

But she waved and went back to her friends. And then she'd sent over drinks, which were currently warming his system and eroding his decision-making skills. He'd be making bad choices in no time.

Thing was, she wasn't looking over. Or paying any attention their way. Her group seemed lively enough. More men than women, and certainly he wasn't the only man in the bar looking at PJ right then.

None of them mattered though. She seemed to throw off some sort of pheromone that pushed his every damned button.

She'd changed her hair. Again.

It was still blond, but this time it had streaks of blue shot through it. He bet she twisted it up into one of those bun things she liked. So you'd see mainly blond but a flash of color. Unique, like her.

Who was that guy leaning so close to her? Asa couldn't see his face as the other guy bent to speak to PJ.

"Who is that guy on PJ?"

Duke, who appeared annoyed to pull himself away from the voluptuous brunette halfway in his lap, peered across the room. "Isn't that Craig Salazar? He does transmissions, I think. Yeah, up in Lake City. He appears to be pretty enchanted by Penelope's breasts. Can't blame him."

There it was. If he continued to sit there with his friends, she'd leave with Craig and he'd have survived another day not giving in and fucking her.

Question was, could he? For months he'd been circling her. Knowing he should leave it alone but always finding himself unable to do it. Could he sit there after he'd tasted her? Neither of them had mentioned that kiss at Twisted Steel, but he certainly hadn't forgotten it. Could he really let another man take her from that bar? To have what Asa could if he just made a move?

With PJ, though, it wouldn't be just a move. He knew that right to his toes. What he felt about her, he knew it would be more.

Which brought him right back to the question. Was it enough to let her leave with another man?

Asa shot Duke a look and got up. "I'll see you later."

"Finally." Duke tipped his chin in good luck before Asa headed over to where she stood.

She leaned against one of the scarred and carved-up wooden posts lining the long room. Smiling.

A great smile. Full of pretty, perfect white teeth. A dimple peeked to the right of her mouth. Her mouth. Christ. The memory of that kiss slammed into him.

But those big blue eyes widened and then went half-mast when she finally noted him approaching. And that smile she'd been wearing with her friends changed into something else entirely just for him.

And then she shifted to brush her hair back over her shoulder and he was gone.

She waited. And he liked that too.

The problem was that the place was jam-packed and it took him longer than he wanted to get to her.

Once there he didn't bother scowling or paying any mind at all to the other dudes around her trying to catch her eye. He had her focus and that was all he needed.

The weight of his attention stole her breath. She knew Craig was talking, but her brain didn't care one bit about anything but the way Asa prowled toward her. He towered above most of the patrons in the bar as he actually sort of rippled at the shoulders and across his chest as he moved.

People scampered out of the way as he passed through, his features showing irritation each time a knot in the crowd slowed him up.

His hair was down that night. Close shaved at the sides, the bulk of it would fall down over his eyes and then he'd shove a hand through it. A simple thing really, but when he did it, it was sexy times a million.

So utterly badass and male.

She'd seen him on his knees the week before when she'd stopped in to Twisted Steel for a job. PJ had come around the corner and nearly run into him.

He'd looked up at her and it hadn't mattered that she was standing. Even on his knees Asa was in charge.

There'd been a flash of hunger in his expression. Just for a breath or two as she'd stood, stunned into stillness. Staring at him.

He'd let it go then, the same way he had over and over for five months, and she'd wanted to punch him in the throat but managed to raise her brow at him and keep on her way.

They'd had that damned kiss the month before and then nothing!

Only now he wasn't hiding the hunger in his gaze. And he wasn't walking away. The difference in his approach told her that.

A delicious thrill raced through her as he came to a halt just inches from touching her. Close enough the heat of him was a caress. PJ was pretty sure she gulped, but it couldn't be helped.

"Penelope Jean, you're looking lovely this evening."

A shiver at the low tones in his greeting.

"Thank you very much, Asa. You're looking ridiculously gorgeous, as usual. Really, you're sort of a menace."

The predatory smile he gave her was full of stuff that was going to make her sweaty. She hoped. Hell, she was sweaty already!

"Thanks for the drinks."

"Of course." If he walked away again she might actually tackle him and demand he tell her why he tortured her so much.

Instead he took one more step, bending to speak into her ear. "Have you had dinner?"

She shook her head. "You going to remedy that?"

He held out a hand and she took it.

CHAPTER
Seven

Asa paused once they'd reached the sidewalk. "I don't know the neighborhood very well. This place is between Duke's house and Twisted Steel, and I've only come in a few times. Any ideas?"

"The Italian joint across the street is really good. Family run and owned. Thai two blocks that way, also really good, and if you're vegetarian or vegan they've got a lot of options." She went ahead and took a risk. "They both deliver. My house is just a few blocks away."

"I like that option."

"I should probably let you hold off making that decision for certain until we get to the end of the block just up here." PJ pointed.

He snorted when they did and faced a rather daunting uphill walk. She'd gotten used to it, but sometimes she had to admit she thought twice about the last few drinks at the end of a night at the Ditch because facing this walk while really tipsy wasn't any fun.

"This just means I can have a little extra helping of whatever we decide on for dinner. I guess you're less likely to get mugged if criminals have to make this walk." He started up the hill and she took up at his side.

"Another benefit. I love this neighborhood. Just a short walk and there are bars and restaurants. Most of the time Audra and I walk together. Usually with her boyfriend. They live across the street from me."

When they got halfway she spoke again. "One more up and then two over."

"No wonder your ass looks as good as it does. This is a great workout."

Flattered, she smiled. "Thanks."

Asa wasn't sure what he had expected, but the duplex she led him to wasn't it. "I'm on the top floor." They climbed more stairs—and he watched her ass some more—until she unlocked her front door at last.

He might have needed a Sherpa to get there, but her apartment was big and would be bright during the daylight hours. Because of the slope being so steep and the apartment being on the top floor, the windows and the slider to her deck all faced Shilshole Bay and Bainbridge Island.

"Menus are in that little holder next to the fridge. I'll be right back."

He pulled out an Italian menu and one for an Indian place and then went to look around. Not extravagant. The furniture was nice, but nothing someone making a good wage couldn't afford. The neighborhood was good, yes, but not trendy, so he bet her rent was decent. What he didn't know was why she hadn't just bought a place. She came from money, so he'd assumed she had a nice house somewhere.

Like he'd assumed that after the first job or two she did for them she'd wander away bored.

But not only had she continued to do great work, it was timely and handled professionally. He knew she'd hooked up with other shops and was freelancing for them as well.

His assumptions had been pretty unfair, and he had to admit

he wanted to get to know her better—and not just what parts of her body she liked to have licked.

She came back in, this time shoeless. "Sorry, those boots need to be resoled. I shouldn't have worn them today. Did you decide?"

He handed her the menus. "Choose."

She drew in a breath and then looked down. "They make the naan fresh. And the samosas are excellent. I have beer that'll go with it. Shall I order then? Do you have any preferences?"

If she had been just five years older, he'd feel so much better about the way his cock seemed to want to bust through his zipper when she'd simply obeyed. Ordering women around was fine—and sometimes it was scorching hot.

But there was something deeper between him and PJ. Normally, though he expected exclusivity when he was sleeping with someone, he didn't get bound up when things ended. But he had a deeper attachment to her already. One he was still wary of.

Too late for second-guessing. He was there in her apartment and they both knew why.

"Surprise me. I'm not vegetarian."

She called in the order and opened her fridge. "Want a beer out on the deck? It's a nice view and it's pretty warm for late May."

He nodded and followed her out, where she settled on an outdoor couch of sorts. He took the beer she handed his way when he sat beside her.

"Thanks."

They drank in silence for a while as late evening settled in around them.

"How long have you lived here?"

"Three years now. I came over to hang out with Audra and saw the 'For Rent' sign, and that was that. I've lived in a giant house, and in a tiny studio, shared apartments, but this is the first place that's felt like home."

"Home is good. Important. I feel that way about Seattle in general. I didn't grow up here."

"The accent sort of gives it away."

He laughed. "You can take the boy out of Texas, but the accent seems to live on. I grew up in Houston. And then in the army I lived in Iraq, and as fucked up as my old neighborhood was, believe me, living in a place where every day people tried to kill me was worse. And after I got out I landed here with an uncle. I hadn't planned to stay, just work awhile, get an idea of what I was going to do, but it was like I just relaxed. I loved the rain and the gray and the green."

He hadn't meant to share all that.

PJ nodded. "I get to travel a lot. It's one of my favorite things. But every time the plane approaches SeaTac I'm so happy."

Neither spoke for a while. Her perfume rose and he leaned close to breathe her in where shoulder met neck. She tipped her head back, giving him access.

He was damned the moment his lips touched her throat. This was exactly where they'd been headed since the first time he'd laid eyes on her at that party months earlier.

Her fingers sifted through his hair and then she yanked, demanding. Groaning, he managed to get his beer on the table before taking her mouth.

PJ swung a leg up and straddled his lap to face him and he hissed at the heat of her as she undulated, rolling her hips.

He nipped her bottom lip, holding her close as he sucked her tongue and then backed off, licking slow until she'd melted against him. Then he nipped her lip again and kissed his way down to her chin and up her jaw to her left ear.

She made a sound.

A low moan. Needy.

"Shhh. Trust me to get you there. Now that I know you like this . . ." He licked the hollow beneath her ear again to underline his point. "Well, now that I know it makes you give me *that* sound? I'll be sure to do it again and again."

She wrapped her arms around his neck. "Promise?"

He laughed. "Oh yes."

"All right then. Get to it. But not too hard because the delivery guy will be here soon."

Well, that sucked.

Since he was already violating his rules, he might as well enjoy it. He needed to remember he had a lot more experience than this silly flailing indicated.

"All right. Let's see just what we can get up to before anyone knocks on your door." He cupped one of her breasts through her blouse and she arched into his touch.

Just right. Everything was just right. The right size. The way she reacted was right. The weight of her on his lap, the way she smelled, her taste, everything.

Not willing to let go of her breast, he used his free hand at her waist to hold her in place. "I'm wondering how long it takes to make you come, PJ."

"You're already past the surface streets and on the freeway," she said in his ear before she sucked the lobe into her mouth.

He shivered. "Good to know."

She did that thing again, undulating so she ground herself against him, and the power between them shifted as she began to own her allure. She was confident and certainly not hesitant about demanding what she wanted, but this was new.

He dug it.

Warm flesh greeted his caress when the hand he'd had at her waist slid beneath her shirt and across her back.

"Do you have ink back here?" he asked, stroking fingertips over her skin.

"I'll show you if you like."

He certainly did like.

*   *   *

The doorbell rang twice and he groaned, standing and holding her like she weighed nothing.

"Food's here."

Hormones made her slightly woozy for a moment as she worked to get herself back in order.

"I'll handle it." He put her down carefully, and they both headed back into the apartment.

He walked like he was in pain, which she supposed if she had a penis she'd understand. "Why don't you relax a little? Drink your beer," PJ said.

He gave her a look that approached an eye roll as he continued toward the door. But she let it pass because he was hotter than the sun and she'd finally gotten him nearly to her bed. Also, she realized Asa was a handful. Like the other alpha males she knew, he'd have to be managed without realizing he was being managed.

He opened the door with a smile so intense the woman on the other side carrying a tote of takeout seemed to black out for a moment as she tried to process over six feet of hot, clearly sex-disheveled man standing in front of her.

PJ let him take the bags and then inserted herself so she could sign the credit card receipt.

"How much do we owe you?" Asa asked.

"I've got it, Asa. Can you please take that to the kitchen?"

The delivery driver looked back and forth between them and shoved the receipt into the space. PJ grabbed it before Asa could. "I already paid when I called it in."

He made a sound she knew meant he'd be giving her his opinion on this turn of events when they were alone. Whatever.

She signed the receipt after adding the tip and closed the door, locking up when she finished.

"I asked you to dinner. I should pay."

"Huh." It wasn't a question. She needed him to understand she wasn't some silly woman who needed taking care of. "Next time you can pay."

He frowned and she got all hot for him again.

"I'm wondering if I should tell you how hot you are when you glower at me. Will it make your ego worse?" She put the bags down and moved to him. He excited her. Made her feel bold and strong. And yet, also precious.

He fought a smile but she saw it and he knew that too, so he encircled her waist and pulled her in close.

"I don't glower."

She rubbed her cheek along his beard. "Oh, you totally glower. *Grrr. I'm glowering. Fear my testosterone.*"

He snorted a laugh. "But you don't. Do you?"

She shook her head. "I don't fear it. I like it. It's sexy. But." She paused to tiptoe up to kiss him quickly. "I do push back if necessary."

He took two handfuls of her ass and pulled her totally snug against him. "I'm wondering if I should tell you how hot you are when you set me straight," he echoed back at her, teasing.

"You definitely should." Not that she thought he'd back off in any case. This was a man who did what he wanted.

She wasn't hungry at all. Not for the food on the counter.

A low hum of pleasure seemed to vibrate along her spine as he drew his fingertips along it.

He took up so much space in the room. So confident in his skin, the way he moved, like a man who was 100 percent cool with what he had going on. That confidence of his was so totally sexy.

"It's very hot. One of the most appealing things about you, as it happens."

He kissed her and she sank into it, let herself fall into the feel of his beard tickling her face, of the firmness of his lips, the sharp nip of teeth, and his tongue—oh god his tongue—sensuous, licking, tasting her.

His cock, hard against her belly, drove her crazy as she restlessly moved from side to side, brushing herself against him.

Asa groaned into her mouth. "Cold takeout. After."

She took his hand and led him back to her bedroom, totally glad she'd changed her sheets just the day before and the place wasn't a total mess.

"You keep surprising me." He stood in her doorway, looking around.

"That doesn't sound like you know if it's a compliment or not."

PJ loved her bedroom. In shades of cool blues, deep purple, and a tiny bit of saffron, she'd made a place that was her sanctuary. Fluffy bedding, comfortable enough to read in all day on a Sunday. Heavy curtains covered the windows because she liked to sleep in total darkness, but when she pulled those back, sunlight streamed in. A chair she'd reupholstered during a community college class she'd taken with Audra the year before sat in a corner with a small side table and lamp.

It was a calming place she sank into every night.

"It's beautiful. Feminine." He walked in and looked around. She liked having him in her intimate space. Made her want to rub on him, mark him like a cat. "You're most certainly those things."

"My layers surprise you? Did you expect cinder-block shelves and a mattress on the floor? Ah, because I'm young."

He didn't deny it, though he sort of tried to be really hot and make her forget.

"I didn't say that. I figured you'd have style. Clearly you have good taste in cars and men."

She snorted and then popped open two buttons on her blouse.

"But my being younger bothers you?" Her fingertip hovered at the next button, the one that would totally expose her bra.

"It's not that."

She slid the third button free, delighting in the look on his face. Greed.

PJ could work with that.

"It isn't?" She unbuttoned the blouse all the way, sliding it off. The dark brown of his eyes seemed to go nearly black as he took her in. So much intensity and focus that the power subtly shifted between them again.

"Take them all off. I want to look at you." There was no way to interpret that as anything but an order.

Licking her lips, she unzipped her pants and stepped from them, his gaze on her like a physical thing. Her underpants followed, then finally her bra.

He sucked in a breath as he moved to her. "Jesus, you're fucking beautiful."

It wasn't like she hadn't had a man look at her like she was pretty before. Or that Asa was the first guy to get hot over her body. But this was different. Naked before him while he still wore his clothes rendered her more than physically bare.

He was so big and sexy there as he circled her, looking at her body. It left her breathless and a little nervous, which was sort of hot too. She was too into whatever was happening to obsess on whether that was weird or not.

"This is fantastic work." He traced over the petals of the lotus that sat across the middle of her back in blues and pale purples.

"Thank you." She'd gotten the tattoo when she'd decided to drop out of college and follow her own damned path.

"Are you Buddhist?"

"No. Did you know the lotus is actually a part of the mytho-religious structure of multiple cultures and religions? A beautiful flower that grows from muddy water. Rising above, reborn as something more than those muddy roots."

He kissed her neck as he slid his hands from her shoulders

down to her fingertips. He turned her wrist up, moving it close so he could examine the ink there. A little outline of a stick drawing of a cat's face.

"My grandfather was an awesome guy. He used to call me Kit-Cat. Not like the chocolate bar, but like a feline. Anyway. He used to send me postcards when he traveled for Colman, and he'd sign them with this little cat face."

"I saw him race once when I was a kid. The local boys' club gave out free tickets and my mom took us all. He was already in his sixties then but still badass."

Asa came around to face her after thinking he needed to give himself a moment before he focused on her tits. But the ink on her back, the curve of her spine, and the sweet swell of her ass had wrapped around his cock like a fist. Freckles dusted over her shoulders and that only made her more beautiful.

He had a thing. For curvy brunettes with red lipstick and great tits. In their thirties and forties.

And here this blond, sweet-as-fuck package wrapped around what was turning out to be a dirty core was all he could think about. Those big blue eyes of hers, the way her bottom lip had the tiniest bow in it. Sweet, yes. But not innocent or naïve. He'd never met anyone like her.

And the story about her grandfather, fuck. Together with the way she essentially told him yes he was bossy and that was okay with her but when he went over the line she'd slap him back, only made him want her more. Strong, powerful women were hot as fuck, and this one got to him in ways that he'd be nervous about. Later.

She looked up at him, her lips curved into a smile. Not trying to hide herself or be coy. Also really fucking hot.

"Howie Colman was an absolute badass. He taught me how to drive."

"Yeah?"

She nodded.

Scrolling tendrils of green wound their way from hip to hip. He danced his fingers over the super-sensitive skin. "Pretty."

"It's a work in progress. I added this frog here." She pointed at her side, where a little green-and-brown frog had been added. "I'll add little things when something happens that I want to mark."

He liked that.

Not as much as he liked the barbell in each nipple. He tugged a little, twisting the bar, and she arched toward him with a moan.

"Tell me what you like about this."

She caught her breath. "It feels good."

He leaned in to nip her neck. "That's not an answer to my question. Do you like the pain?"

He licked across her nipple, leaving it slick, and then tugged on it with his teeth before he did the same with the barbell.

She sank her fingers into his hair, holding him. "I like that better." She went quiet for a bit, but he could tell she was trying to put it into words. "I don't like pain. Not without pleasure."

"Me either, darlin'. The pain is a way to get your body ready for the pleasure. Like a wave pulls back, gathers force, and crashes over the shore again. The balance is that place between them."

"The first time it burned a little longer before it melted into pleasure. I think I must be very selfish because I want the pleasure faster."

He cocked his head and thought about that. "That's my favorite too. The shock of the pain and then the rush of chemicals to flood you with pleasure."

"I want to see your body." She tugged his hair to bring his face to hers.

He kissed her. "Impatient."

"Damn right. I've been imagining you naked for five months now."

Laughing, he stepped from his boots and then teased her slowly as he peeled off his T-shirt.

"I'm having a moment. I may need to sit down. But if I sit down I can't touch you, so that's out." She got close enough to do just that. "Hmm. I suppose now we'll have to test just how you like your nipples and those piercings played with."

She bent her head to lick across first one and then the other nipple. He tried not to pant as she tugged a little harder than he had. And when she sucked it into her mouth hard and fast he couldn't stop the way his hips jutted forward, seeking contact with her body.

He soaked it in as she ran her hands all over his chest and arms. She sucked in a breath as she traced the tentacles twisting around his shoulders and biceps.

"Wow," she whispered as she circled him to take in the rest of the tattoo.

In teals and muted grayscale, the massive octopus took up Asa's back. The artist had used the space on his skin perfectly. It nearly looked graceful, even over all the powerful muscles on Asa's back and forearms.

And in one of the tentacles curled on his side was an ace of spades. "What's this?"

"Just something left over from the army. Ace was my nickname. Not overly imaginative from Asa, but I had that ace of spades done first and then the octopus came after and my tattoo guy worked it into the new design."

"It's incredible." She gave in and pressed her cheek to his back. So hard. Yum. "Do you have a thing about octopus? Octopi? Octopuses?"

He spun quickly, his hands at his button and zipper, and she sort of forgot what she'd been saying.

"They're smart. They're capable of changing their shape and size to adapt to any situation."

Asa Barrons was a survivor. A guy who was proud of how hard he'd worked and what he'd built, and from what she could tell, he had every right to be.

"Show me what else you've got going on."

He unzipped his jeans torturously slow—the look on his face told her he enjoyed the tease—and stepped from them, along with his shorts and socks. Looking at him totally bare, she nearly fell over.

Not only was he powerful with muscled thighs and hard calves, one bearing an intricate biomechanical-style tattoo, but his cock. Hoo, boy.

"You're pierced."

He handled himself firmly, and she tucked that away.

"I am."

He had a barbell frenulum piercing, right below the head of his cock. A shiver ran over her skin. She'd never actually been with anyone with a pierced cock. But she *wanted* it. She licked her lips and the sound he made was nearly a snarl.

"Go on then."

She dropped to her knees, brushing her lips up his left calf, behind his knee, up the inside of his thigh to lick up the line of his cock, pausing at the barbell. She studied it, tongued it gently, tugged on it with her teeth, and then she looked up into his face and swallowed the head of his cock, down past the piercing, tonguing it.

"Goddamn, yes."

He stared down at her, gaze fiercely lit. The hand that slid from the top of her head and down to her jawline was gentle until he shifted, wrapping her hair around his fist and holding her from taking the head back into her mouth.

Suddenly she wanted it so much it surprised her. Straining to get closer, she licked across the head, shuddering at the groan he gave in response.

"Starving for it."

She hummed her assent.

Magic.

PJ on her knees, those pink glossy lips wrapped around his cock, her cheeks rosy after struggling against his hold to get her mouth on him, was utterly breathtaking.

He rolled his hips, slowly fucking her mouth. She was tentative with the piercing. At first. Then she pushed a little, tugged a little harder, flicked her tongue faster.

He rode up to the thinnest of moments before climaxing and then pulled back. Her brow furrowed and she frowned.

Hauling her to her feet, he backed her to the bed and rolled on with her, tucking her body beneath his.

He had to take the reins and slow things down. Need beat at him with closed fists but he'd waited for this, fought it, and now that it was happening he needed to pay attention.

He shifted to keep the majority of his weight off her, his body between those luscious thighs. Her pussy was slick and he groaned when he brushed through it with the line of his cock as he settled.

When he reached her mouth, he took his time, kissing her long and slow until the heat between them was warm honey. He licked down her throat to the hollow there, circling it with the tip of his tongue.

She sighed softly, and the nails she'd had digging into his shoulders relaxed as he licked again and then nibbled across her collarbone.

"I love these freckles," he murmured over a spot he'd licked and then blew over.

"Good thing, since I've got so many."

He licked a trail down her chest, around the outer swell of her right breast, circling up to the nipple.

It drew tight and darkened as he twisted the barbell a few times. He loved the way women's nipples looked when they were pierced. All that pretty, puffy glory of the nipple, feminine and soft, with a ring or a bar through it. The soft made even more alluring by the hard.

She gasped and shivered as he grazed the nipple with his teeth and then kissed his way over to her other breast to do the same there.

When she writhed, he lost a lot of his control as the scalding hot seam of her pussy slid against his cock.

He backed up a little, going to his knees between her thighs. This way she was wide open to him and he could get a look or a touch or a kiss of his favorite parts of her body.

She gazed up at him, her breath coming a little faster, lips glossy and swollen from sucking his cock and all those kisses.

He grabbed his cock at the root and slid the beads in his piercing and the head of his cock over her clit.

She sucked in a breath.

He did it again and then gave her clit a parting tap with his piercing. Her gaze blurred a moment and she got hotter and wetter against his cock.

"You like that?"

"Yes."

"Next time I want you to tell me, understand? I try something new and it revs you up, I want to know." He tapped harder, and then once more. "I'll be able to tell, of course. You're so wet right now, just waiting for me to put my cock inside." He dipped the head, brushing it against her entrance and having to shiver himself at how fucking good it felt. At how much control he had to use to keep from plunging inside.

"I'll know, but I want you to tell me."

Her gaze sharpened and that light came into it. A challenge. Damn it, she pushed his buttons. All the good ones.

Grinning, he shimmied down, ignoring her attempts to get him back to where he'd been. He spread her labia wide and took a lick and then another because she tasted so good. He played his tongue along the underside of her clit until she got very close and moved to her thigh, kissing and nibbling, and then over to the other side.

"You hate me!"

Laughing, he bent his head and as he held her open wide, sealed his mouth around her clit and sucked it slow. Over and over, in and out until she slammed a hand to the bed.

"I really like this part," she said right as she came.

Christ, she made him laugh.

He got up and settled on his back on the bed and she joined him, snuggling on her side facing him, licking up his neck.

"Liked what part? Coming or pussy eating?"

She paused, thinking. "Well, I certainly like to come as a result of some excellent pussy eating. Pussy eating is certainly more pleasurable when there's a climax involved. But I like coming from all sorts of sex-related type activities, just for future reference."

"I'll keep that in mind. Climb aboard."

"I'm hot for you, I can't lie. Well, I mean, your face was just buried in my pussy, so I suppose that was a clue. Anyway, like I said, I'm totally down with this, but I don't fuck without condoms. Just a rule."

"Good. Neither do I. But I'm not going to fuck you. Just yet."

He dug that she respected herself enough to demand protection. He most certainly did. It went hand in hand with the challenge in her eyes and the way she seemed so gloriously at home in her sensual skin.

She rolled up to her knees, throwing one over his waist to settle herself against him.

She bent to kiss him, nibbling his earlobes and getting off on the way his breath caught. The power of affecting a man like this one roared through her as she backed up and slid herself over his cock. "Do you know how ridiculous you are?"

"In a good way or a bad one? Oh fuck yes, grind that pussy on me."

"Well." She paused to do it again, sliding her pussy up and down the line of his cock, closing her eyes as the bloom of pleasure spread from her clit outward each time the beads on his piercing and the crown of his cock stroked over her. This was a million and a half times better than masturbating any other way. She wished she could just go into Babeland and buy an Asa for herself to keep around the next time she got horny.

"I'll need to add dirty talk to the ridiculous list," PJ said. "A good one, obviously, because if it was bad I wouldn't be getting you all wet right now."

"I'm glad you have standards to go with all your other positive attributes."

He could be all dark and broody one moment and then make her laugh the next. There was something so exciting about being with him.

She began to ride him for real, undulating her hips as she moved her body up and back on her calves, her hands braced at his hips.

"You're ridiculous because you're so sexy and hot. An alpha male who rides motorcycles and drives a cool car. You're covered in ink and muscles; you've got tall, dark, and dangerous down pat. I never gave much thought to size. Probably because no one came to the table with what you do. However, I plan to look into the whole idea of being a size queen. Because yeah, I like what you're packing."

She bent to kiss him quickly but he caught her lip between his teeth and tugged. "Make yourself come once more and then I'll fuck you."

There were literally zero flaws with that plan.

Two years before, with a long-term boyfriend, PJ had gotten herself off in front of him and he'd sort of . . . *judged* her for it. Like hello, she'd had his cock in her how many times and he was judgy about the fact that she knew how to make herself come?

She pushed the memory from her head because she knew for sure that *this* man thought it was hot. So there.

Levering so that her hands rested behind her, on his thighs, she rubbed herself along the line of his cock over and over. He felt so good, his gaze roaming all over her body, his cock hard and delicious against her clit each time. She knew it wouldn't be long.

"That's it, fuck. So gorgeous. Take what you need, PJ. Yeah."

After she'd come a few more times and slept, she'd be able to contemplate all the ways Asa was sexy, including his mouth. Right then, though, he put his hands on her and she forgot everything else.

He rolled and tugged her nipples as she ground herself against him, his gaze moving from her face to her tits, down to where her body slid over his cock again and again.

She made a sound she hadn't even known she could make, a low moan that seemed to drag from her gut slow and hard right as she came all over his cock.

Asa shook it off. Cast off the feeling that this woman wasn't the same as anyone else in ways he maybe hadn't really considered. He knew it, and he knew this was inadvisable, but he had no plans to stop now. The problem might be how to stop later. But for right now, he planned to gorge himself on her.

He waited until the last wave of her climax hit, then shifted to grab the condom he'd tucked under her pillow when he'd taken off his jeans.

When he turned, she watched through half-lidded eyes. Asa liked this part, when a woman was boneless with pleasure and he was about to make her feel even better.

"Hands and knees."

She stirred lazily but got into place with his hand at her hip.

"Wait. I want to see you put the condom on over the piercing. I should know this. For future reference."

He pushed her to her back and she smiled so beautifully up at him he had to pause just a moment to take her in.

"I really just wanted to look at your cock with that piercing again. But I'll happily watch you hold it while you put the condom on."

He barked a laugh, leaning down to kiss her because there was nothing else to do but taste that sweetness.

"You put it on then."

"Okay." She lost that laziness as she got to her knees and took the condom, ripping it open. Bending, she peered close as she slid it around the barbell and then down into place. "I told you already how hot that is, right? Probably a lot. But yeah. Wow."

He traced the pad of his thumb over her lips and she sucked it into her mouth. His balls tightened against his body.

"Head down. Ass up."

She nibbled on his thumb before letting go and doing as he'd said.

He paused to look his fill at all that beauty before him. Acres of beautiful skin, all her ink, the curve and sway of her body.

And the furls of her pussy bared to his gaze and attention. He moved close enough to grasp the base of his cock and tease through those wet folds until she made a demanding little sigh and thrust herself back at him.

This heart of a woman was it, as far as Asa was concerned. But nothing prepared him for the way it felt as he slowly pushed into her body and the heat and snugness of her pussy brought sweat beading across his forehead.

He groaned as her inner walls gripped him, and that was before she groaned like she'd never felt better in her life.

"Don't make me do all the work."

She didn't say anything, but clearly she'd heard him because she pushed herself back against him, meeting his thrust.

Each time he slid all the way inside, she made a sound. A deliciously-on-the-verge-of-orgasm, *oh-god-fuck-me-harder* sound that shredded the very last bit of his control.

He pushed a little harder and the sound she made was deeper and she fluttered all around his cock.

"Tell me."

"Fuck me harder."

He sucked in a breath and began to fuck her harder, digging deep each time she pushed back that extra bit. He bent a little, bracing his weight on one hand as he reached around her body to find her clit with the other.

No protests that she couldn't. Instead her inner muscles contracted around his cock the moment he made contact with his fingertips.

She added a little swivel each time she pushed back to meet him, so Asa let that be the strokes against her clit. She set the pace for that while he continued to fuck her, each stroke a little harder, a little deeper.

A breath separated him from orgasm, and when she cried out and gripped him tight, there was nothing but falling into climax right along with her as he stayed deep.

After what felt like a never-ending orgasm, he pulled out carefully, kissing her hip as he got out of bed to deal with the condom.

She'd gotten back into a T-shirt and her panties when he came back. "Now I'm really hungry. I have pie. I just remembered that. My mom made it." She paused to kiss him as she walked back out into the main area of the apartment.

Okay then. He pulled his jeans on and headed out after her.

CHAPTER

Eight

"Come again?" PJ asked her father.

"We've decided you need to return to your position as vice president of sales. Colman has no need to expand our services with painting. It's not what we do. We can't mass-produce it. We make tires and we make a very healthy profit selling them. That's what we do."

He hadn't asked her to explain any of her ideas. Hadn't commented on anything, and this was the first he'd spoken of it since she'd brought it up two months before.

She hardened herself. Letting any of them know how upset she was wouldn't help. Chances were it would do the opposite. Plus, she had enough pride not to let it show, damn it.

"Dad, we don't have to mass-produce it. It's not what we do now, no. That's the point. It doesn't have to be. It makes us a profit and it's about cars. That's our mission, that's the heart of Colman. Why not let me have this as something I bring to the table? I have a client base. You've seen the numbers. I've spent the last two years learning and honing my technique. I have a portfolio, if you'd like to see." Why couldn't he let her have this one thing? This thing she'd thought of and made into a success? This thing that would make him finally realize she was as worthy as her other siblings and not just some silly flake.

"*I said no*, Penelope Jean, and I don't want to hear anything else about it. And I don't want you wasting company time to go to these classes of yours."

It would have been dramatic to say it felt as if her heart was breaking. In truth, he'd done that a long time ago, and she hated to hear herself begging for just a scrap of his attention.

"I've never *wasted* Colman money. I've paid for these classes and tutorials myself. I take them on vacation days or at night and the weekends. This doesn't steal from Colman. This makes us stronger and better."

Julie spoke up. "She's right. This is a very profitable thing for Colman to do. By splitting her existing clients between Shawn and Jay, we keep the profit she made. Which means what she brings in is all *new* profit. All new revenue stream. And more clients who turn to Colman when they need services."

Shawn rapped the table. "I agree."

"You don't have a vote, Shawn." Their uncle shrugged.

"This is my company too. This is something I can do to make Colman mine. Put a stamp on it." She appealed directly to her father. Jay would land wherever the power was, and she knew where Fee stood.

Fee interrupted before her father could speak. "You don't need to do it. You have a job here. Do that one."

PJ sighed. She'd spent the last few days really thinking about what she'd do when and if this happened. She'd spent the night before with her sister drinking Cuba Libres in the bar at John Howie Steak as Julie had listened, offered advice, and steered PJ around the more disastrous options.

"And that's your final answer on this issue, then?" She looked back and forth between her father, uncle, and oldest brother.

Jay's gaze held a warning. He knew her better than their father and uncle. Knew what she was going to do.

"You *are* putting your mark on Colman Enterprises, Penelope

Jean. Your mother and I worried about you when you dropped out of college, but since then you've really buckled down and made something of yourself. You don't need to paint things. You already do all our logos. That's enough."

All her life she'd taken the scraps he'd tossed her way and pretended they were enough. But this time, this time they weren't.

"No. It isn't enough." PJ stood up. "I quit."

She didn't stop walking, even when Jay yelled her name.

Shawn caught up with her as she dropped her keycard and keys in the inbox on her desk.

Though no one had noticed, she'd been taking home little bits and pieces of her stuff over the last two weeks because she'd really begun to feel like it was going to come to this. So she didn't have much but a small box of her things under her arm.

"Let me walk you out. Julie says she'll talk to you tonight; she's yelling at Jay right now." Shawn took the box and put his free arm around her shoulder. "Big move you just made in there."

"She's really yelling at Jay? Can I watch?"

"No. She can get to him in ways none of us can. Anyway, you made your point, babe. I don't think I've ever seen Fee stunned speechless. I owe you a really good bottle of wine for that moment." Shawn kissed the top of her head and waved off people who wanted to approach her and talk about what had happened.

Outside, he opened her trunk and put the box inside before getting her door. "You can do this, you know. I'd rather you do it here. And I think that's still going to happen. You know where I am. If you need money—"

PJ hugged her brother. "I'm totally good. Being the Colman black sheep means I save lots of money not buying ball gowns or estates on the water." She grinned. "Really. I have money in the bank, and though I've billed these jobs through Colman, I have a full schedule for the next few months. I'm building this business. I wanted it to be with Colman, but whichever way, it's me."

"Okay then, do it hard-core, Penny-Lope." He winked. "I believe in you. I also believe the monthly dinner is going to be super fun now. Let's you, me, and Julie meet for drinks before we go over there."

She smiled at Shawn. "You're so sweet. I'll talk to you soon."

When she drove away, though she was sad about how her father had reacted, she was proud she'd stood up and refused to be pushed aside.

Now she had to prove herself on her own.

Asa had been bent over his workbench when her legs caught his attention. Penelope Jean Colman in the flesh. She walked his way, her hair up in a high ponytail swaying in time with the switch in her hips.

Damn, she looked good. And thanks to that night two weeks before, he knew what she looked like naked, bent over things while he took her from behind, and what she looked like on her knees.

She dropped her sunglasses into a case and replaced them with her prescription glasses and gave him one of those smiles of hers. "Afternoon, Asa Barrons. I came to collect an ice cream and to drop off an invoice."

Like apple pie and coffee with a dollop of bourbon. Yes, that was PJ.

He needed to deal with the invitation in her eyes, and needed to do it right, because he liked her and he liked the work she did for them. And because he wasn't a dick.

"Drop off your invoice with Lottie. I'll grab us some ice cream. Meet me in my office."

He watched her walk away and then gave himself a stern lecture.

Still, though he was sure their conversation was going to be unpleasant, he found himself hurrying along to see her.

Then stood in his doorway looking for a moment.

She glanced up from her phone, sliding it back into her bag, giving him her total attention. He had to admit he loved that. Most people talked to you with a phone they half watched while they spoke. Asa found that disrespectful, though Duke just told him he was old-fashioned and to deal with it.

"What did you bring me?"

He held out two ice cream bars, not surprised at all when she took the dark chocolate dipped in dark chocolate. She had a decadent side. Sexy as hell.

Wrong direction! He needed to gut up and get this said, and he might never get to that point if he kept up those sorts of thoughts.

She took a bite and closed her eyes with a pleased hum. "This is the best thing about today. Thanks."

He leaned against the corner of his desk, his legs stretched out. They also blocked her exit, which was not what he should have been doing, but whatever, he was tall. He had to stretch his legs sometimes, didn't he?

"Did you see the stuff for the next few jobs? I told Lottie to set up a box for you in her space."

PJ watched him carefully. "Yes. Thanks. You're being weird."

"I am not being weird." Of course, his denial was far too vehement—another danger sign where she was concerned. She was a test to his control.

He had earned that control with blood and a hell of a lot of hard labor. No matter how hot she was, he needed to keep it. That control made him a man he could be proud of.

She slowly raised the brow with the piercing and then pushed her glasses up her nose. Imperious. He nearly groaned and one corner of her mouth tipped up slightly. She knew that got to him.

He changed the subject. "Have you ever thought about surgery? For your eyes, I mean." And ended up being weird again.

She paused and then ate some more of her ice cream. "I like

glasses. Plus, I can't even put drops in my eyes. I am the worst with that stuff. The few times in my life I have to have drops, my brother Shawn sits on me while Julie keeps my eyes pried open."

Asa guffawed. "Sorry. I just..." He tried to stop snickering.

She flapped a hand his way. "So, as I've made clear, I'm not a good candidate for letting lasers near my eyes. I also take eye-bright and other supplements for eye health because I like to avoid being a woman in her twenties calling her brother and sister over every time she needs eye drops." Then she grinned.

The ground at his feet was shaky. He *liked* her. When he was around her, he was pleased. Satisfied that she was in his shop.

The only other people he felt that way about were his mom and sisters.

She watched him. "So, you gonna tell me what's going on with you, or am I going to keep pretending you're not being sketchy?"

"Sketchy? I'm not sketchy!"

"Oh, so you're mad that you're acting weird and I'm calling you out on it? That's sketchy. Go on and deny it, buster, but you know what I'm talking about and I'm not playing that game. Not with anyone."

PJ mad was blistering hot. He had to breathe out in one slow exhale to pull the tattered shreds of his control around him.

Sometimes when he was seeing someone he would divert them when he didn't want to deal with whatever they wanted to talk about. Which was, actually, shady.

"Drug dealers are sketchy. That clerk at the deli across the street is sketchy. Don't go over there in the afternoons unless you're with me or Duke." He paused and swallowed hard. His dad was sketchy. Asa would never, ever be that. "I'm not sketchy."

Her anger softened and she cocked her head. "I'm truly sorry that I hurt your feelings. It was a poor choice of words. I'm just saying that it's important to me that I never let myself be lied to.

It's not cool. So you can say you don't want to talk about something and I'll respect that. But I'm not going to pretend there's not something we're not talking about. Do you get that distinction?"

"I accept your apology. Thank you. I apologize for overreacting." He sighed, reaching out to close his door. The way he'd acted only underlined why this had to stop. He couldn't be doing this at work.

"What happened two weeks ago, it can't happen again. I mean, it was fantastic, don't get me wrong." He didn't want her thinking he hadn't enjoyed himself, because *fuck yeah* they had mad heat in bed.

The look on her face told him she wasn't going along with this the way he'd hoped she would. "So if it was fantastic, you want to stop why?"

He had to tread very carefully. She might be young, but she was smart and the gleam in her eye told him she was dangerous when pissed off.

Which made him hard, and then he frowned at his lap.

"We have heat, I can't lie. That night was . . . well, it was unreal. But I have a rule and I broke it with you."

"If you tell me you're married or with someone and you fucked me, I'm going to punch you in the balls."

He winced. "No. I'm not with anyone or I wouldn't have slept with you. My rule is that I don't enter any relationships with people I work with. It creates complications." And damn it, he *felt* it when he was with her. Which led him to other reasons, but ones he wasn't going to get into right now.

It was easy to sleep with a woman for a while and then move on when they both got tired. But this was more. He could feel the outline of something far bigger than he'd really wanted to deal with.

He'd already done things he'd never done before. Lost his control. It mattered what she thought and how he made her feel.

Casual sex that would end after a time would ruin this thing they were building. He and Duke loved the work she did. It was best to nip this in the bud.

PJ dropped her half-eaten ice cream into the trash can. "Complications?"

"Yes, complications. Like this one we're having right now."

"I came in to drop off an invoice and have an ice cream bar. I didn't leap on you or wear an *I Love Asa Barrons* button. You started this whatever-it-is you're doing right now."

This was not going the way he'd hoped.

"No, that's not what I'm saying."

PJ drew a breath and fought her temper. She'd had such a weird day and decided to drop by Twisted Steel. No big, just a few minutes of fun, maybe tell Asa about how she'd just quit her job and then go about her business.

Instead he was talking about *complications* as if she didn't want to keep this thing between them mellow in public, especially in a work setting.

And then, like a man, he doubled down. "You're too young for me. I'm too old and jaded for you. We're not right for one another for a host of reasons. But I like you. I like the work you do. I certainly like flirting with you and having you as a friend."

She blinked, incredulous. This guy teased her for months. Flirted. Looked at her like he wanted to take a lick every time she was around. Ate her pussy in her bed before he fucked her. *Three times.*

"This is the hill you want to die on? Really? A we-can-be-just-friends speech?"

"No. I'm sorry. I'm not handling this right. It's why I have the damned rule in the first place, to avoid this business. We were already friends, I like to think. It's a this-is-why-we-can't-fuck-anymore speech."

This was so fucking dumb. If he wasn't as hot and didn't take up as much of her thoughts as he did, she would have stormed out.

He was being dumb.

"Okay, so I think it's totally fair that you have this rule. It would have been better to have known before, but whatever. I do now. But why this assumption that I wouldn't also want to keep the fact that we're sleeping together private? It's hard to be taken seriously when you're female. When you're young it's worse. I have to constantly overcome an assumption that I'm a spoiled, dumb, pretty but useless burden. Sort of like how you're acting right now. I haven't given you a single reason to think I'm going to boil a bunny or start sleeping on your porch and telling people we're married."

He scrubbed his hands over his face, and she didn't feel bad for agitating him. He was being a dingus.

"I like riding crops. I like to use them on the backs of a woman's thighs and her ass. I like to flog her nipples and her pussy."

She shivered, but not from horror. *My.*

"All right." She held a finger up. "So can we admit I've disabused you of the other reasons you've tossed at me?"

He frowned, his dark brows pointing in a sharp V. His hair had started to come out of the tie holding it back from his face because he kept shoving his hand through it.

"I admit no such thing."

She rolled her eyes and his brows flew up. "Oooh, are you mad at my impudence? You can say whatever you want, but I won those other arguments."

She held a hand up and kept speaking. "You made that announcement about crops because you've concluded I wouldn't like that? Or that I'd be shocked and run the other way?"

"Do you?"

"Like crops? I don't know. I've never been cropped. Cropped? Is that what it's called?"

"You're killing me."

"I'm killing all these dumb excuses. You're calling a halt to this based on what, that I *might* not like it? I mean, look, if you don't dig me that way, fine. But now you're just throwing stuff at me and flailing around."

"It's not dumb. You're too young. I'm thirty-seven years old. More than that, those were a really rough thirty-seven years. You're not that."

She stood. "So your cock is going to send me to dirty hell? Do I get a say in any of this, or have you already decided that a decade and some change makes such a difference I'd run screaming if you slapped my ass with a crop?"

"Your being younger is a reason. You don't know what you like yet. Us working together is a reason. If it ended badly it would ruin our working relationship and our friendship."

PJ grabbed her purse. "You know how you feel about the word 'sketchy'? That's how I feel about men explaining to me how I feel and what I believe. You're full of excuses and they're all bullshit. I've already made it clear I don't play like that. Have a nice day, Asa."

"Don't leave it like this." Asa blocked her way to the door. "One hundred percent truth. I do like you, PJ. I want us to continue being friends. I want you to continue doing work for us too."

She grabbed the doorknob and pulled. "I'll continue to do work for you." She kept pulling because it gave her something to do other than cry or get even angrier.

"The rest?"

"I don't know. But I do know if you don't let me out of this room it won't happen at all."

He opened the door and she moved out to the hall. She'd planned a parting shot over her shoulder, but really she just wanted to go home. So she kept walking and hoped he appreciated looking at her ass, because he was a dumbshit who blew a chance to look his fill any time he liked.

*   *   *

PJ showed up at her sister's door two hours later, once she knew Julie had gotten home. When Julie opened up, PJ shoved a six-pack and a bag full of burgers and rings at her sister.

"This appears to be more than just quitting your job. Come in and tell me."

"Only if you tell me about what happened after I left."

"Deal. Come on and let's get these beers open and plates for our burgers."

"I told you I slept with Asa Barrons."

Her sister raised her beer. "You did indeed. Just from watching the two of you together that first night you met it was pretty clear you had the hot hot tingles for each other."

"See, what I love about you is that no one would ever guess you'd say this stuff just by looking at you. Anyway. After I left Colman I went home, dropped stuff off, changed clothes, and then thought, *Hey, I'm going over to Twisted Steel to have ice cream and flirt with Asa.*"

"Don't even say he blew you off or I'm going to run him over with a tow truck."

"I love you." PJ hugged her sister tight and then gave her the story. "I was pretty much like, dude, we'll keep it chill in public, but we can still have sex. I'd bat away one thing and he'd bring something else up."

"Ew. Well, whatever. Better to know now than after a few more times with him when you've really started to like him. You can have sex with hot guys, PJ. Plenty of them around. You're gorgeous, so that part is covered. If this guy wants to be a dick, who cares? His loss."

PJ dunked an onion ring in some ranch dressing. "I'm just over it. People thinking that because I'm young I don't know what I want. Or that because I'm female I don't understand things. What even is that? Jay totally eats that shit up."

Julie sighed, knowing PJ was still dealing with quitting her job too. "I don't get it. To be honest, even if you weren't my baby sister I'd have supported your plan. It's economically clever. Nimble. Fee? Well, he's just foolish and so desperately freaked out that he's not very smart. He blocks you because you're smarter as well as totally full of girl cooties. He manipulates Jay because he's got Dad's ear and Jay has the biggest daddy issues of us all. Jay is going to do whatever he thinks Dad will give him a Scooby snack for."

"I'd like a freaking Scooby snack sometimes, you know? Why does it feel like I'm never going to get any of Dad's time and respect?"

"I don't know what his problem is."

"I know it took me a while to find a direction. I understand it takes time to prove myself. But it just...it's never felt like he liked me very much. Oh sure, he loves me because I'm his kid and he's not a Sith Lord. But I'm beginning to wonder if there's anything I can do to satisfy him. It's not like he ever said anything about my sales record either."

Julie sighed heavily. "He has the most trouble connecting with you. Which isn't because of you."

"Ha! Of course it is. Part of it is that I'm female. I don't know where Dad and Fee got that. Grandma was awesome and Grandpa always treated us with respect. But another part is that he and I just don't fit. I've tried doing exactly what they said they wanted and even then it's not enough."

"He's a jerk, but he doesn't like anyone. I feel like even though I'm technically higher up at Colman they listen to Shawn way more than me. They don't listen to Mom at all."

PJ had left Julie alone when she'd quit her job earlier that day. "And here I am whining about my problems and I've made one for you. I'm sorry I didn't see it."

Julie flipped her off. "No apologies. You have to leave to come

back. Do you know what I mean?" Her sister shrugged one shoulder. "You have to do it this way. They're not going to hear you if
you stay. And if you'd stayed after that crap from earlier? Being
told, *Hey, be quiet and sell tires, we don't need your newfangled ideas?*
Oh man, if you'd stayed, they'd do it to you again. Because you
took it. Your leaving actually supports me more than your staying
and taking that."

"I can do this. But I'm freaked. Just between you and me."

"Freaked about what? You're good at this. You have clients
already. You have a shop space. They underestimated you, PJ.
Don't do the same. Fuck them and fuck Asa. You got this."

"I'm so glad I came over here instead of revenge-making-out
with an ex. That would have ended so badly."

Julie laughed. "If I hear you're getting your lips anywhere near
Aaron, unless you're hitting him with a bar of soap in a sock, I'm
going to kick your ass."

"You're vicious. And also, um no. No Aaron of any type. I have
other options for the sort of instant feel-good drunken make-out,
and then there'd be regret the next day. Maybe." PJ grinned. "Don't
you have that guy friend? You've never actually had intercourse but
you've made out half a dozen times. He's hot. You're hot. It's fun
but you're really not ever going to be with him and he doesn't want
that anyway."

Julie's eyes widened. "There is not such a thing."

"Oh my god. Julie, there is totally such a thing. You won't nec-
essarily be kissing that friend, but one of your friends is that guy.
What about Noah? I'd totally make out with Noah if he was that
friend."

Her sister shook her head. "You think you know someone.
Okay, who? In your group, I mean. Who is your make-out friend?
No, wait, let me guess." Julie thought as she ate. "Well, so I'd *like*
it to be Chris."

"Chris is on-fire hot, but I'm not his type. He's never even looked at me twice. It's Craig. He just broke up with someone two weeks ago. Prime rebound time."

Problem was, she didn't want to make out with Craig and masturbate alone before she fell asleep.

"You have a look."

"I'm going to focus on getting PJ's Custom Work set up. I got asked to do some more modeling, which is great because it's like five or six hours' effort and a nice check. I don't actually need it; I have money in the bank, so get that look off your face. But it keeps me busy and making connections too."

"And he'll hear about it. Asa."

"Maybe. Of course he needs to suffer, be shown just exactly what he's missing. He digs me, Julie. I know it. I can see it every time he looks my way. We have major chemistry. Like when we're in the same room it's sort of intoxicating. And yet I can't moon or pine. I have too much to do. Also, hello. No. I'm not going to be doing that."

"So essentially your plan is to be you and to do it so well he can't resist. Which is a good plan, I think."

They clinked beers and went back to gossip. "Jay," PJ demanded.

"He's a spineless jerk. He knows he was wrong and as much as he's capable, he's sorry for not backing you up. But he's desperate for Dad to pet him and tell him he's pretty. And he's smart. He's a good person to take over when Dad steps down. But he needs to stop being a tightass."

They snickered a while. "I sort of feel bad for him," PJ said.

Their oldest brother had never really had the childhood the rest of them did. He traveled with their dad from a very early age, and their father never lost his reserve. Not with Jay, who wanted their father's approval and affection so badly he'd alienate his siblings, and not with his other kids or his wife, for that matter.

Julie said, "Yes, sure. It sucks. But we all have our shit to shovel. He has to figure it out and stand up on his own two feet.

We all know Fee would be a disaster at running the company. Jay's going to have to take him on at some point."

PJ tipped her chin at her sister. "Why don't you do it?"

"No thanks. I don't want to run the company. But I'll gladly shove Fee out an airlock and take his spot when I can. Can you believe he told me I was too pretty to be wasting my time at a job where I wasn't meeting rich men regularly?"

PJ reared back in horror. "What the ever-loving fuck?"

"Ridiculous. Anyway, do you have plans tomorrow?"

"I have a job first thing in the morning, but it'll be a quick one. I'll be free by one or so. You want to grab lunch and a movie?"

"Yeah. Let's. I have a date. Seattle Opera and swanky French food down at the Market. I need something showstopping for it."

"Right on. I feel the need for some new lingerie and shoes."

One more clink of the beer and they'd polished off the first round. By the time PJ fell asleep in the guest room at Julie's, there'd been at least four more. But it was good. Being there with her sister was good, and Julie was right. PJ'd had to leave in order to ever come back on her own terms.

CHAPTER
Nine

P J had just finished some detail work for one of Duke's motorcycle jobs. He stroked a hand down his beard and grinned as he took a closer look. "Thank you kindly, Penelope Jean. This is excellent work."

Duke was a mellow guy. Usually. He was full of empty sweet talk. Duke's main setting seemed to be charming flirt. But when he complimented her on her paint work, it was genuine.

"I've got a client here in ten minutes. Can you come by the showroom in fifteen? He's after a really unique color, so I thought you might want to talk with him about some options."

"Yes, that's great. I'll be there. Thanks, Duke."

A few steps from the door he turned back to face her. "He's not a bad guy."

Seemed Asa's paranoia about complications might have some basis in fact. "I don't think he is. I think he's a nice guy, as it happens."

Duke grinned again. "He's a loyal guy, yes. Brave. He saved my life. He carried me for three miles after I'd been shot."

"I believe that. I'm glad he was there. I imagine you probably did your share of saving a time or two."

His grin slid off his face for a moment before it was solid again.

"You do what you need to. I don't know how to do this, and normally I'd rather not get into his business this way. But don't give up on him."

Duke stepped back and spun, heading out. "See you soon," he called as he went.

PJ was still thinking about that little exchange when she walked into the showroom just a few minutes later. Duke stood at the front desk with Asa and the guy who was most likely Duke's client.

It hadn't even occurred to her that Asa would be there, but it was too late to avoid him. It wasn't like she didn't see him when she was at Twisted Steel, but she tried to stay out of his way when she could.

Still, she wasn't above being glad she'd fixed her hair and cleaned up before coming in to meet a customer.

Asa was in what was pretty much her favorite stance. Feet apart, arms crossed over his chest so his muscles bulged and his ink showed. He was so imposing and delicious, though she noted he needed to shave the sides of his head again.

She raised a hand, wanting to touch it, but waving and shoving her hand in a pocket before she grabbed hold and did something disastrous.

"Hey there." PJ kept it friendly.

"PJ, perfect timing," Duke said. "Alan Steadman, this is PJ Colman. She's great with color, so I thought she could give us some input for your truck."

Asa tipped his chin again. "Good to see you, Alan. Looking forward to this project, man."

He moved to one of the desks a few feet away and started working at the computer. PJ chose to believe that even though he could've easily done the work in his office, he wanted to be around her. Which may or may not have been true, but that's what she decided to go with.

* * *

Asa had spotted her walking across the lot from the painting bay toward the showroom. Her hair was glossy in the sunlight. The blue had faded and he wondered just what color she'd choose next.

When she came in he noted the sequined sneakers and held back a smile. She'd been surprised to see him but smiled anyway. He tipped his chin.

He missed her looking at him the way she did at Duke. Easy, no tension. Open.

He didn't miss the way Alan looked at her, that much was certain. He should have gone back to his office to update their calendar to accommodate the '58 Chevy Alan had just agreed to pay them quite a bit of money to customize. But he stayed close enough to hear instead.

PJ showed Alan several different shades of green and a few of purple and orange. They all went out, presumably to look at the vintage Schwinn bicycle she'd recently finished. It was tangerine orange with an orange metallic banana seat and acres of chrome. A birthday present for the teenage daughter of a local tattoo artist. PJ had outdone herself with the color. The paint had been expensive, but it was the coolest bike Asa had ever seen.

It was right as they came back inside that Alan made his move and Asa saw red.

Alan listened to PJ, but at the same time, Asa noticed the guy checking her out, and he knew PJ would notice that too. Alan got closer and she stepped back. Before Asa could get up and punch Alan for not giving her space, Duke returned to them and thanked PJ and then called Alan's attention back to where they'd been working on putting together the plan for the job.

She looked at Asa and waved.

He could have gotten up and gone to her. Should have. The thought of her going out with a fucknut like Alan burned in his belly. But he stayed and she turned, leaving.

But not before she shot him a look that said she knew he'd seen that business with Alan. The pierced brow slid up and he couldn't help but smile at her. She shrugged and left, and he didn't stop watching the sway of her ass until she'd gone back inside the painting bay.

"He's here." Audra cruised over and handed PJ a drink.

PJ knew Asa would be at this event. Lots of hot women. Cars. Tattoos. Bikes. Plus Twisted Steel was one of the sponsors, so there was that too.

She was so glad she'd opted for something soft. Her dress was a figure-hugging navy blue summery number that hit her mid-thigh. Audra had given her a braid crown, but her hair hung loose in the back.

"You're like fresh-faced catnip. It's disgusting and awesome all at the same time."

PJ snorted. "Come on then. I see someone I need to talk to."

Audra shrugged. "Okay then. He's totally watching you, by the way."

"Good. Dumbass."

She schmoozed and drank and flirted for another hour or so before she allowed herself to think about Asa. And once that happened, she couldn't do anything but look for him.

That connection zinged between them when he glanced up from his drink and locked gazes with her.

"Here he comes," Audra murmured.

It was like her skin knew he approached, like a caress that got more definite the closer he got as he stalked across the room to her.

He was so intense, his focus totally on her. How could he pretend this thing between them didn't exist?

He stopped well inside her personal space. She looked up at his face, captivated by the sight. Asa was arrestingly attractive. Not pretty. Not even handsome. But absolutely a person who drew your eye. He carried himself with a confident masculinity she found sexy and charming all at once. He might have a New World face, but he had an Old World manner.

It made her feel...safe. Like she could say anything to him. And then he'd gone and been dumb.

"Hi," PJ said.

He could have kissed her if he hadn't been an ass. Instead he gave her a look that singed, realized it, tried to school himself, and annoyed her in the process. Why would he hide how hot he was for her?

Clearly there was backstory she didn't know. The problem was that she wasn't sure he'd let her close enough to share.

"Hey. Can I buy you a drink?" he asked.

"Sure."

He tried to do one of those hand-at-the-small-of-your-back things to escort her to the bar, but she stepped out of his reach. He could have touched any part of her he wanted, but he'd blown her off, so he got to *not* touch her.

Asa wasn't the only gorgeous man on earth. He wasn't even the only one at this party. So if he wanted her to move on, he should understand what her moving on looked like.

She knew he'd noticed it when she was at Twisted Steel the week prior and one of their clients had hit on her. She knew he thought about her because he'd shown up at the photo shoot she was in over the weekend and pretended he wasn't looking at her.

She ordered a rum and Coke and he got a beer, and they headed off to a quiet corner.

"That day." He paused. "You came to Twisted Steel and had just had this important thing happen in your life, and I added to what was probably pretty heavy already. I'm sorry. That's not what friends do."

While he avoided looking her in the eyes for longer than a few seconds, he tried very hard not to look at her boobs. And failed. *Ha.*

"It's fine. It's over and done. I got the message." Because he deserved to suffer, she flipped her hair back behind her shoulder and straightened enough to stress the material at the front of her dress.

"I may have sent a message I didn't mean to. If I'd known about you leaving Colman I would have acted differently."

"Like how? Hm? You'd have fucked me in your break room and then told me a week later that I was too young and didn't know what I wanted?"

If only. She'd have totally liked the first part of that plan. It was the rest that sucked.

"That's not what I said." He looked so miserable she felt sorry for him for a few moments before she hardened her resolve.

"Isn't it? Unless you're here to tell me you were wrong and you think we can make things work, just stop." She paused, but when he said nothing she shrugged and continued on. "All right then. Apology accepted. You didn't know. I need to go back over to Audra, we're headed out in a few. It was good to see you."

He'd been naked in her bed. Hell, he'd been in *her*. He'd licked her in places she'd never been licked before—PJ tried not to smile as she remembered the way he'd licked over her asshole and she'd squeaked and jumped off the mattress.

He'd opened to her and been intimate with her and then told her what she felt and was capable of understanding. He needed to understand why that was so dumb. He needed to accept that he was a total douchenozzle and do some groveling.

And she needed to continue to run into him from time to time so he always had her in his thoughts.

One day they'd laugh at this story. He'd be all, *Oh yeah, I was a dick but thank goodness I finally wised up.* And she'd smile and nod.

Right then, though, she leaned in close to him when she had an excuse so he got a whiff of her and her hair slid against his skin. PJ kissed his cheek and barely resisted rubbing her face across his beard.

Instead she slowly eased back. "See you around."

She knew he watched her walk away. Probably because his gaze seemed to burn into her skin. Also because several other men in the room watched too. Good. He needed to see that as well.

"Hand me that bowl there, the one with the potatoes." Pat Barrons pointed at the bowl her son then moved within her reach.

"If you're not going to tell me what's making you so grumpy, at least stir the beans."

He did, his sister wisely avoiding his eye. They'd bust out laughing and their mother wouldn't be pleased.

"I'm not any more grumpy than usual, you know."

"Don't stand in my kitchen and lie to me, boy."

"It's nothing."

"It's a woman. Dice those onions. I need two." She'd set herself up at the counter he and Duke had lowered for her a few years prior. His mom would gather all her supplies and then cook from one central place near the stove.

Not coincidentally, it gave her the perfect perch to keep an eye on—and lord over—everyone in the living room and dining room.

She made him dice onions because he wasn't just telling her. He'd break eventually; he always did. His baby sister, Courtney, smirked but kept her attention on pouring the cornbread batter into the cast-iron skillet and popping it into the oven to bake.

Pat Barrons had gotten pregnant with Asa when she was just fifteen. His dad had been a few years older but already a seasoned criminal and piece of shit by the time Pat finally called the police on him after he'd hit her.

His paternal grandparents had then swooped in and taken Asa. Pat had spent the next years fighting with Asa's grandparents and his father—when he was out of prison anyway. She'd been able to win visitation but had to stay on top of them to get it. Sometimes they'd control her behavior with the promise of access to Asa. Finally, when he was seven years old, she'd won full custody. After that, they'd picked up and moved from Dallas to Houston.

Asa hated his father's family for humiliating Pat that way. She'd been powerless and they'd abused that because they could. They pretended it was charity when it was the worst sort of vanity.

She'd worked at least two jobs the whole time Asa grew up. It was the price for keeping her independence, and he got that. Understood how important it was that she not be beholden to anyone again.

They didn't have much. It didn't get any better when she had his younger sister, Lettie, and then Courtney a few years after that. There'd been a man for a few years, Lettie and Courtney's dad, but he'd up and gone soon enough.

Right around that time Asa sort of went off the rails. His life was a dead end. He'd wind up in jail just like his dad. He wasn't going to head off to college. He had no future and he acted like it for long enough that his mother had begged him to join the army to do something with his life.

Asa's mother had never asked him for anything. So when she'd cried, saying she was worried he'd end up dead or an addict, when she'd actually begged him, he'd gone down and enlisted.

His mother didn't have a lot of education herself, but she was determined her children would grow up into adults worth knowing.

Needless to say, Pat Barrons could be relentless when she wanted to know something and no one was talking.

"You were going to tell us about the woman," she prodded.

"There's no woman."

His mother just stared at him for long moments before turning the chicken she was cooking.

"Okay, so there was. Is. Whatever. It's not a thing. I can't even say it's over because it never got started. Happy?"

"I'm never happy when you think you can give me that attitude." She gave him a prim look and Courtney snickered.

"I'm sorry." And he was.

"I know, baby. So tell me about this woman. Did she dump you?"

"No one dumped me. I told you, it's nothing. A woman who does our custom paint work. I like her, but she's too young, and we work together. It's a recipe for disaster. So we'll be friends."

Courtney turned and gave him a long, measuring look. "Did *you* tell *her* this or did *she* tell *you* this?"

"I told her." And then at the party last week she'd asked if he was willing to try being together. He hadn't answered because he couldn't find the strength to lie and say he didn't want that. Taking his silence as answer enough, she'd sashayed away, the sway of her ass burned into his memory.

"It's a good thing he's so handsome," his sister said to their mother.

"And so smart with metal, even if he did ruin his face with that ring in his nose. Tell me what you did to this woman."

"Why do you assume I did something to her?"

"Well then, what did she do to you?"

"No one did anything. It's fine. She's too young for me. That's it. She and I had some flirting and stuff, and then before it went any further I let her down easy. I want to be her friend still. She's fun. But too young. Hell, Courtney would love her. PJ's not too much older."

"It's not like I'm your daughter. I'm your sister. If she's older than I am she's legal. Does she giggle? Is she dumb? Sometimes the women I see you with, well..." Courtney's brow rose as their mother chuckled.

If only PJ were dumb. "She's not dumb. The opposite. She's articulate. She knows how to run a business. She might giggle sometimes. But not excessively or inappropriately. Why are we talking about this?"

"Because you're grumpy and Mom called you out and you were explaining to us what this woman had done or hadn't done to you."

"See if I bring you those chocolate croissants next time," he muttered.

"I take it she didn't respond well to being told she was too young?" Courtney asked.

"No." But he needed to remind himself that she was moving on and that was what he wanted.

He and his sister ferried things to the table. She poked him. "Don't think I'd let you out of here alive if you took those chocolate croissants. Just so we're clear."

"You're a Barrons all right."

His mother looked at him before she slid the chicken from the pan and onto a platter. He grabbed that and took it over to the table, knowing she wasn't done with the PJ thing. She was simply biding her time, gathering all her information and planning how to hem him in exactly how she wanted.

"All right. So to recap," his mother said as she came over to the table and sat at the head with her children to either side, "you and this woman had 'flirting and stuff.' " She sent him a look and he tried not to grin. "She wasn't happy about it, which probably means she wanted to be with you and you backed off. She's headstrong then, which is good because you're too bossy for your own good. You'd run right over a woman who didn't push back at you. But this mood of yours..."

She kept plotting as they filled their plates and began to eat.

"Are you really going to make Mom say it?" Courtney asked. "You know she's going to be right, no matter what it is she says. I'm guessing you sent this woman packing and she found someone else who liked her luggage just fine."

Pat thought that was hilarious, but Asa wasn't such a fan.

When he'd found out he'd given her the let's-be-friends talk right after she quit her job, he'd felt like a total shithead.

And last week, when he'd seen her at the party and apologized, she'd looked so pretty, like one of those spun-sugar eggs they used to have at Easter. Everyone else had been vampy, glossy red lipstick, and she'd been pink lips and a blue dress. He'd been unable to think about anything else since.

Their mother sent a raised brow to his sister. They were already ganging up on him and he was just trying to do the right thing.

"Of course other men want her. She's beautiful and ambitious. I'm happy for her to find someone her own age."

"Asa! You put a five in the vice jar right this instant." His mother pointed to the jar on the counter she made them put money in if they cursed or lied. Of course she turned around and bought them things with it, so it wasn't a real punishment by that point, but still.

"Why? What'd I do?"

"You're a liar liar pants on fire, that's what you did!" Courtney pointed her fork his way.

"She needs to find someone closer to her own age. It's best for her. More stable."

Courtney curled her lip at his excuses before she waved her fork at him again. "You're decently handsome. You own your business. You're respected and talented and you have a house. You're even nice to your mom. You're a catch, even if you're still a total liar. Ew. You don't really want her to find someone else, so why are you being such a quitter right now? You want Duke or someone like him to go out with her instead? Honestly?"

The idea of Duke seeing PJ the way he had? No way. "Offsides, Court!"

"Whatever. Asa, you're nearing forty. You just going to 'date' forever? Like you're twenty-seven instead of thirty-seven?"

"I resent the air quotes around 'date.' I date for real. I'm not a jerk."

Their mother patted his hand. "Stop poking at your brother," she said to Courtney before speaking to Asa. "No, you're not a jerk. So, she's pretty and she's smart and educated. Other than her age, which is . . . ?"

"Twenty-five." He cringed.

But his mother waved it away. "Thank god. I thought you were going to say she was nineteen or something. Twenty-five, Asa. That's not too young for you. You said yourself she wasn't silly or giggly or immature. So? Did she just not, you know, do it for you in the bedroom?"

He clapped his hands over his ears. "We're not having this conversation."

"Well, they have doctors for that now. You can take pills. If you're having trouble," his mother teased.

"Now you're just giving me a complex for your own amusement." His mom's eyes danced, and he couldn't help but smile at her. A smartass woman was his weakness. "I hope you're happy."

"Generally I am, because my son takes care of me and my house. My daughters do the same. I'm sassy, which is an important quality in a woman with only one foot, you know. I don't think you have issues with your zip zip." She made a sound effect that he planned to never ever hear again. "So your issue is with this PJ. Is she snotty? I mean, should you break things off because she's awful?"

"So, how has the steering been on your car, Court?"

His sister snorted. "Fine. Duke asked me the same thing two weeks ago. Why don't you want to take a chance on this woman?"

Because she meant something and he was not going to be like his father and break a woman whose heart was as beautiful as PJ's was. "Because I don't. We're friends. That's all we're going to be. Now, I'm done talking about PJ. I mean it."

CHAPTER
Ten

Laughing, PJ and her friends spilled into the Ditch just before eleven. Of course, it was packed by that point, so the sound of music and the low hum of talking swallowed them up as they headed to the bar.

"*Shit*" was all she heard before Audra yanked her back into the alcove where the bathrooms were, shoving her inside the ladies' room.

"What the hell?" PJ slapped her hands back.

"Asa is here."

PJ narrowed her gaze. "Let me guess. He's not alone."

Audra waved a hand. "He's got a gaggle. Way easier to defeat that than if it was just one woman. But let's get you fancied up so you can go out there and gather a gaggle of your own."

Bags opened as makeup was touched up. Audra stopped PJ with a glare when PJ moved to rebutton a few buttons on her blouse.

"You have fantastic tits. Use them, for god's sake!"

He could get super-sexed-up women with few clothes and lots of motivation to fuck him. Any day of the week. Which was actually really annoying.

But none of them was PJ. Despite his little tale about just

being friends, she knew he wanted her. Knew that for whatever reason, he was drawn to her in a way he wasn't to other women. She needed to remind him of that.

"Bear with me here," PJ said. "I've been doing a lot of thinking about this. He's possessive. He has to be there to watch when his cars are used in photo shoots. He has a thing about his chair and his tools and that stuff."

Those chicks shoving their tits his way were a fun distraction. But what if a man like Asa decided a woman was his? Boobs weren't the key here.

"That makes sense. So we need him to aim all that possessiveness your way." Audra lifted a shoulder before stepping back from where she'd done something to PJ's hair.

"Exactly. This is why you're my best friend. Because you know things." PJ winked.

By the time she headed back out, her eyes had been lined darker to emphasize the blue, her lips now a glossy pink.

They strolled through the place and PJ pretended it wasn't even a thing that Asa was off at a far end of the room surrounded by women.

She turned her thousand-watt Colman smile on the bartender like she planned to sell him tires. Except his gaze slid down her throat to her cleavage. PJ knew she'd been right not to flaunt but to hint at it, because there were mounds of mammaries as far as the eye could see in that place.

"Can we get a round of shots with a beer back, please?"

"Darlin', you can have anything you like." The bartender winked.

She laughed. "I'll keep that in mind."

They did the shots, but before they'd taken the first sip from their beers they'd already been joined by two male friends. Who, thank goodness, were ridiculously gorgeous. Craig was there again, drowning his sorrows in liquor and harmless flirting with women he'd never do more than kiss because he was still crushing on his ex so hard.

She dropped her change into the jukebox and made some choices. Audra added hers, and they turned and headed back into the room.

"He sees you," Audra said as she waved at some other friends who'd arrived.

"Good."

This silly age stuff was done with tonight.

She hoped.

Asa needed to come to his senses or be punished by watching her look hot and other men appreciate it. And if he didn't, maybe it was time to actually consider moving on for real.

"He came here. He wanted to see *you*. This is your bar." Audra handed her another drink.

"He best step on it, or I might just decide the attention all these boys are giving me is just as good as anything he could provide."

A flash of pink across the bar caught Asa's attention. PJ stood with her girlfriends, necks of beer bottles between their fingers, smiles on their faces as they got chatted up by... *fuck*, by Asa's friends. Including Craig, who'd been sniffing around her before.

It was for the best. She wasn't for Asa. She'd probably be better off with one of those other guys standing around ogling her. He knew he was no doubt better off with one of the women surrounding him right then.

Women who entertained him, but he didn't think about it much more than that. Women who liked it hard and rough. Who were old enough to know what it was they wanted.

Though PJ had made a fair enough point about him telling her what she felt and wanted. It had been sort of dickish. He probably should have talked it over with her more before breaking things off entirely. It wasn't as if they'd remained friends like they had been before that conversation in his office. She'd kept her distance and he'd felt it.

One of the men with PJ put a hand at her waist and Asa was three steps in her direction before he even realized it. He paused then, watching through a haze of annoyance that she'd even consider letting a dumbass like Craig Salazar touch her in the first place.

Much less give him the smile she just gave him.

That smile said they had some history. Some intimacy. Had they slept together? Had Craig seen her naked with that look she got right before she came? Had she licked down Craig's spine? Nibbled the backs of his knees? Which, by the way, had been an unexpected pleasure.

Asa frowned.

She had a fantastic smile. A fantastic mouth.

He flashed back to the first time they'd been together, that mouth of hers wrapped around the head of his cock. Her tongue dancing over his piercing.

It had been so fucking good he'd reeled for days. And now she was...with someone else. And he realized suddenly that wasn't okay after all.

Craig leaned down from where he stood behind her, sliding an arm around her waist. He spoke in her ear and Asa could see her blush from where he stood.

"Excuse me," he said to the group of people he'd been standing with as he moved away from them and toward PJ.

He could hear her laugh as he approached, like a hook; he was caught until she looked up from what she'd been doing and noted him standing there.

Mine.

Those big blue eyes peered up at him. He held a hand out and she took it without any hesitation. He pulled her to him and danced her away from her admirers. Stealing her away all to himself.

"I surrender," he said in her ear.

She turned so they were nearly nose to nose. "Yeah? What does that mean?"

"It means I want you. It means you want me and I've been dumb to think I could cruise on by and let you go. I don't want to."

He kept her close and she didn't make any attempt to move away from him. Damn, he liked the weight of her against his body. Couldn't wait to get her back to his place so they could continue in private.

However, he got the sense it was going to take more than a squeeze and saying he wanted her to get past the wariness in her eyes.

"Can we talk?" he asked.

"Aren't we talking now?"

"You're going to make me work for it, aren't you?" He couldn't stop his smile of appreciation. She was so much stronger than he'd given her credit for.

"Everything worth having is worth working for, don't you think?"

He kissed her. In front of everyone in the club. In front of all her friends and every man who even entertained a fantasy that he could have her the way Asa did. He *claimed* her.

Oh yeah, this was much better than the last discussion she'd had with Asa, that was for certain. He'd hauled her close and hadn't let go, and then the kiss...

He tasted her for a few moments. It was sweet, gentle. She sighed into his mouth and he gripped her a little tighter as everything sweet and gentle fled. His kiss heated to scorching, carnal hot as his tongue slid into her mouth and owned it.

This wasn't just a kiss of reunion. This kiss told everyone in that room that she was with him. Seemed like her plan to awaken his possessiveness had been pretty effective.

It sent shivers all over her as his taste settled back in to her system. She wasn't prone to making out in public, but wow, this was pretty fantastic. She might have to reevaluate her prior stance on it.

He nipped at her bottom lip and she stared up at him. "I'll make it worth your while if you agree to come to my house so we can talk. We could go to your apartment, but I don't want to walk up the hill. And all my gear is at my place. I have champagne and beer and food and a lot of condoms."

"I'll agree to the former. We'll see if you get to use the latter after I hear you out."

His grin told her his thoughts on the matter, and truth be told, she wanted him. This was what she'd hoped for. Now he needed to grovel a bit and they could get on with the fun part of the evening.

"I need to tell my friends I'm leaving."

"Okay." He spun her neatly, his arm around her shoulders, holding her close as they headed through the crowd.

Craig's eyes widened as they approached and Asa stiffened, so he'd clearly seen that they'd been flirting. Hell, Craig had suggested they go back to her place and finally actually fuck to see if they had something.

It had been halfhearted, but a nice thing to hear anyway.

"Hey, Asa," Craig said.

Asa tipped his chin as a hello. PJ turned to him. "I'll be right with you. Just need to tell Audra I'm going."

He kissed her again and she avoided rolling her eyes. If he wanted to mark his territory she'd let him. Temporarily, until she got a better read on whether he was in this all the way or just to get his dick wet.

"Well, that worked." Audra handed over PJ's stuff before hugging her.

"Maybe. We'll see."

"I got you on that. Don't go through with it if he's an ass. I know it's a great ass, but you can get great ass without letting him walk all over you."

PJ snorted. "Thanks, Mom."

She waved at everyone else and headed back over to where Asa and Craig remained chatting.

"Ready. See you later, Craig." She shifted to hug him and at first Asa held on, but then he let go.

Craig hugged her quickly and stepped back. She'd have to get the story later on what Asa had said.

"I'm glad you're not wearing a skirt because I'm on my bike. You can have my helmet," he said once they reached the sidewalk.

He'd come to her bar. Clearly he'd hoped to see her. She'd have been more impressed if he had two helmets, but then again she might have thought he brought it for another woman and that would have sucked.

"Can we stop by my apartment so I can grab a jacket? I also have a helmet, so then you wouldn't be doing something danger-ous to keep me safe."

He indicated his bike and she paused, mouth wide open for a moment. A custom Softail. Matte black. Simple and super badass. Masculine. Yum.

"It makes me hard to see you look at a machine like that," he murmured into her ear before he licked it and made her wet.

"Did you build this?" She ran covetous fingers over the seat.

He handed her the helmet and she got on after he did.

"I did. It was one of my first projects. Come on, let's get your stuff."

The ride wasn't nearly long enough, less than a minute to get from where he'd parked his bike to her driveway. PJ promised herself she'd get a heaping amount of hanging on, plastered to his back, when they left for his house.

Sure, she didn't actually need to hold on at all. But she would, because hello.

When he keyed the bike off, she slid free and handed his helmet over. "I'll be right back."

"I'm sure you will be." He swung his leg over and stood, taking her hand. "Let's go."

Okay then.

"It's a mess, I'll warn you now." She unlocked the door and they went inside.

He looked around and rolled his eyes. "This is messy?"

"My laundry is on the couch unfolded. I have work stuff all over my table. My shoes are everywhere. I was rushing around this week."

He pulled her to him. "Do you have to work tomorrow?"

"Yes. In the afternoon, most likely. You should know, I'm using a painting bay at Twisted Steel."

"Stay the night with me then. I'll take you to breakfast before I drop you either at the shop or here."

"Your tune changed." She put a hand at her hip.

He sighed. "Pack a bag. We'll go to my house and talk. Okay?"

She hoped like hell he was going to take responsibility for this and that she wasn't making some fruitless trip to his place only to have to call a cab and leave.

He looked really good and she wanted him so much, but she couldn't let her hormones make her choices right then.

She shrugged after giving him a close look and then headed to her room. And he followed her and tossed himself onto her bed as she grabbed a change of clothes for the next day and tossed them into a backpack. One quick trip to the bathroom and she was ready to go.

He looked her helmet over once they'd gotten back to his bike. "I don't like this one. Why do you have it?"

"Um. Wow, you're pushy as hell."

He pulled her close. "I'm testy because I want you so much. Also, this is a shitty helmet. It's not safe."

"You could have had me at least a dozen times over the last six weeks, mister. So don't get testy with me. And the helmet was some sort of freebie I got at work."

"You can't use it. Nope. You can have mine. I have extras. We'll get you a better one soon. There are plenty of great days left to take a bike trip."

He handed her his helmet again and tossed hers in a nearby trash can. She had no idea why it was so bad. She rarely used it, but the two or three times she had it had seemed fine.

"You okay wearing the backpack?"

She tiptoed up to kiss him quickly. "I'm fine. God. Get on and let's go."

He raised a brow. "There's something really wrong with me, but I missed your attitude."

"You got some of it over the last month."

He grinned, kissing her one last time before he got on the bike. She put the helmet on and climbed up behind him. "I don't like it that you're not wearing a helmet. I can use that other one until we get to your house."

He keyed the bike on. "It's a ten-minute drive. We'll be fine. If I get a ticket you can say you told me so. Or smile really pretty at the cop and get me out of the ticket to start with."

CHAPTER
 *Eleven*

He wasn't sure why, but as they pulled up his driveway and into the garage he was self-conscious. Hoped she liked his place. Hoped she liked what he had to say too.

He took the helmet she handed over and hung it on the grip like he usually did. "Come on."

He led her up and into the house and she paused after he took the backpack. "Wow, this is a gorgeous view."

"I bought this house and then spent several years gutting it and rebuilding it. The view though, I didn't need to do anything to that."

When he'd first bought the house it had been in terrible shape. The prior owners had trashed an already outdated house. But he loved the neighborhood in Cedar Heights with its views of Lake Washington, sort of a mirror of her view, only to the east instead of the west.

"Want a tour?"

She nodded and he took her hand. "Living room. Kitchen through there." They walked through and she peeked in here and there until they reached his bedroom, which took up the entire third floor of the house.

He put her backpack on a chair and opened the French doors to the deck. The scent of very late night wafted in.

She faced him and he tipped her chin up with a finger. "Want to talk outside or in here?"

"If I talk to you in here, I'm going to be distracted. Your bed is there." She pointed. "And you're naked there. Also distracting."

"Go on out and sit. I'll get us something to drink."

"I've had plenty to drink." A claim and also a way to set him straight. She expected him to be up-front and open and not play around.

He followed her out, lighting the candles on his deck and choosing to sit next to her on the smaller chaise. Now that he'd made his move, he wanted to touch her. Plus, she was prickly, which to his horror only seemed to make him hotter.

"I was wrong about you," he said.

She continued to watch him. She wore her glasses that night, so the blue was extra vivid, outlined by the black in the frames. Her body language was open but a little guarded. She smelled really damned good and was all curvy and sexy and he wanted to dirty her up at least three times.

If she was open to what he liked, he had plans for the crop that'd just arrived in the mail the day before. He breathed deep to relax, but all he got was a huge whiff of her and his cock ached.

It would happen. They both knew it. That knowledge became a physical thing as the space between them got smaller and smaller.

But she wasn't going to make it easy on him.

"I should have given you, this, us—whatever—a chance instead of blowing it off."

"Because I was too young to know what I wanted."

Okay then, he just had to own it. "Yes. I misjudged you because of your age. And I don't know why, because from the beginning you've known what you wanted just fine. I have a sister who is a little younger than you, okay? I just don't want to be that old guy banging young chicks."

She frowned a moment and then burst out laughing. "You're not old. I'm totally young, but it's okay for you to think that's hot. I want you to think I'm hot. That's sort of what I'm aiming at."

"I totally underestimated you. I'm sorry."

"And the whole co-workers thing?"

"Yeah, I kinda blew that when I kissed you several times in the middle of the bar back there. Maybe I don't like it when clients hit on you."

"So you think they won't if you kiss me in public places?"

"Since I'm groveling and all, I should probably tell you something."

"Which is?"

"I like it that people know you're with me. I like it more than I'm totally comfortable with. Before, I said you didn't know what you wanted and that was unfair. But it's too late now. The truth is, you may not be ready for what I am once I decide something belongs to me."

"Are you trying to scare me?"

"No. Just trying to be honest. I like you. I didn't lie about that before. I've missed our friendship, and the other stuff." The naked stuff as well as hanging out and eating ice cream. "I can't promise I'll be easy all the time."

She kept smiling, cocking her head as she looked at him. "I never would have guessed."

He grinned. She really had no idea what she'd just agreed to. If she thought he was protective about his machines...

"I accept your apology, and we're cool. But I need you to know I'm dealing with my family, who don't take me or my ideas seriously. Now that we're doing this, whatever it is, I won't take that from you. But let's be clear, I'm not afraid to let you whip me, tie me up, hit me with a crop." One of her brows rose and he growled, hauling her into his lap.

"You're playing with fire, so get to your point if you have any more to say." He ground his cock up into her pussy, the seam of her jeans pressing against her clit hard enough to feel *really* good but not hard enough to get off.

Her eyelids slid halfway down and those luscious lips opened on a gasp.

"I forgot my point." She licked her lips and he groaned. "Oh yes, so I'm down, let's do it. But I won't be with anyone who doesn't take me seriously."

He stilled, reaching up to cup her cheek. "PJ, I take you seriously, or you wouldn't be here. I'm sorry your relatives are being assholes, but you know I'd hire you any day of the week. Hell, I do it now."

She watched him for long moments, and he'd begun to mentally compose his next volley when she took her glasses off and set them to the side.

He'd done a good grovel. It had been heartfelt. He'd listened to her. Now she really wanted to move on to the naked part of the evening. "So, tell me what you're going to do to me. Are we going to get all wild and kinky tonight?"

He stood, keeping her in his arms. He dipped to grab her glasses, then took her back into his bedroom and put her down near the bed.

"You carry me around a lot."

He paused and nodded. "I like the way you feel in my arms."

Okay then. It wasn't like she minded. It was sort of awesome that he was that strong. And hot.

"So." He circled her, leaning in to pull the headband from her hair. He dug his fingers in, massaging her scalp until she groaned.

Those fingers tightened and he yanked her head to the side, exposing her neck.

Her breath caught, but not from fear. Desire raced through her, sharp and dark.

He bit and then licked her ear. "Your nipples just got hard."

She shook her head.

"No?" His free hand skimmed up her belly and over her left nipple. "Liar."

"They've *been* hard. I liked what you did with the hair. You came to the Ditch tonight to see me." She had to hear it from him.

"Yes." He bit her neck.

"To wallow in all those women to taunt me?"

He spun her and she threw her arms around his neck. His mouth crushed hers, his tongue demanding entrance as she gave over right away. He left her dizzy and breathless.

He was like a really fantastic roller coaster. She wanted more and more.

The kiss ended when he wrenched away. "To see you. I came to see you. The women were there already."

She bit his lip hard enough to make him yelp.

One hand on her hip, PJ glared his way and used the other finger to point. She stepped close enough to touch, poking him in the chest over and over. "Don't you be flip. You came to my bar and then let women rub all over you and you wanted me to see you and get jealous. And what? To chase you? I've *been* chasing you, Asa. From day one."

He took her hand in his and kissed her fingertip. "You've got a temper. I can respect a woman with a temper. Also, you make it look really good."

Oh, this man. She was in so much trouble. But she wasn't ready to give in just yet. "I've had enough. Just in general. I like you. I think we have great chemistry and you are fantastic in bed. I'm young, but I'm not dumb. Got me?"

He nodded. "I came to your bar and then let women rub all over me to get your attention. But then you were there and I saw other guys around you and it sucked and my crafty plan went to hell because it was me who was jealous."

"Come here." She beckoned with a crooked finger.

He stepped to her again. "Am I safe?"

She tiptoed up, shaking her head. "Not at all."

"Good."

She licked over his bottom lip before pulling her shirt free from her pants.

He took over, unbuttoning, bending to kiss the skin he exposed and then undoing another button and driving her crazy once again.

His beard tickled against the curve of her breast where the edge of her bra met her flesh. "Back at the Ditch you saw me way before I came over, didn't you?" he asked.

Her breath caught as he dragged the edge of his teeth over the nipple he'd exposed as he pulled her bra down.

"Yes."

He hummed, sliding his lips across to her other breast as he also managed to get the rest of the shirt unbuttoned and off.

"It made me crazy." He dropped to his knees, hugging her around her waist before he rid her of her bra and then kissed down her ribs. "I don't much like to share."

She yanked his hair to tip his face to hers. "Keep that in mind the next time you're in a bar surrounded by women who aren't me."

He kissed his way over her belly as he pushed her pants down and off, along with her socks and panties.

"Yes indeed. Makes a man proud to be alive." He looked her up and down as he stood.

"What does? Also, you're still wearing clothes."

"Your fucking spectacular body. And yes, I'm wearing clothes because I want it that way."

Oh. God, that was sort of hot. Okay, really hot. Was it bad that she found it hot? Who the hell knew? She found it hot and went with that.

He took her hand, tugging her across the beautiful hardwood floor. "Did you do this yourself? The flooring?" she asked.

"When I ripped out the carpet that had been here, this was beneath it."

"It's beautiful." The room was very much Asa. Gray and chocolate bedding on a big platform bed. The art on his walls was distinctively modern. She skidded to a halt and then turned to look at the painting on the far wall.

"This is fantastic. Who is this artist?"

Asa joined her. "Nathan Altman. This is a reproduction; the original is in a museum, where it belongs. This one is *Self-Portrait*. I also have *The Watchmaker* downstairs."

She loved the way he talked about art. Loved the passion and awe in his tone.

"I like waking up to see it every morning."

"I can't believe I've never seen this painting before. I'm totally ignorant about art, apparently."

He turned her, leading her to a giant set of dressers. He opened a top drawer and pulled something out.

This was better than Christmas morning. She couldn't wait to see what he had in there.

He turned. "This came in the mail yesterday." He gripped the handle of a black-and-wine-colored crop so hard it creaked, and then looked up at her.

All the spit in her mouth dried up when he stepped back, drawing the flared end of the crop over her nipples as he did.

A flick of his wrist and the snap of the leather sounded over her nipple. Shock urged her to move back but she held on, and the pleasure of it seemed to drown her.

He cursed under his breath and moved to the other nipple. This time she leaned into it. Heat at first as she hissed. And then it wisped away, replaced by a surge of pleasure.

She moaned and he kissed her over and over. Long, drugging kisses until she wondered if she was going to turn to goo right then and there.

"Bend and brace your hands on the footboard." He stepped back and she swallowed, moving on still-gooey legs.

The *whick* as he snapped his wrist and the crop split the air seemed to scatter sensation over her skin. The breath gusted from her lips as she gripped the footboard.

"You're going to kill me." He drew the crop over the skin at the backs of her upper thighs and up over each ass cheek.

"H-How so?"

And then bright, sharp pain as the crop made contact with her thigh just below her right butt cheek.

"Because you're so fucking beautiful." He placed a hand at the middle of her back, pushing her down, thrusting her ass out farther. "Trust me now."

"I like all you're doing. You know, in case you were curious. And I do trust you."

He kissed her back, and the next time he made contact it seemed to send the energy forward from where he struck the backs of her thighs straight to her pussy.

Again.

And again.

And again, though he bent to blow across her skin, heated by the crop's strikes.

"Stay right here," he whispered against her flesh before he moved away, back across the room, and then approached again.

With her eyes closed she could take the sounds of his clothing and picture him undressing right behind her. Looking at her all offered up like a dessert.

* * *

Asa had to pause to take his clothes off and get his control solidly back in place. He was so hard his cock tapped his damned belly. Precome beaded at the slit. He hadn't been this hot for a woman...well, since the first time they were together.

But this was different.

The backs of her thighs and the cheeks of her ass were red and she hadn't just gone along with it because he wanted it.

He tossed himself onto the bed and held a hand out to her. "Come up here and sit on my face. I want to bury myself in you."

Her gaze, which had been lazy, sharpened as she scrambled up to the bed with him.

She kissed his ankle first. And then up to his knees. Up his thighs and to his balls.

He hissed as she licked down the center and then up the line of his cock to the piercing.

"This is a new one." She tugged one end of the heavier-gauge barbell he'd put in before leaving for the Ditch.

"I think you'll like how beads feel when I fuck you."

She looked up his body, still licking over his cock. "You knew this was going to happen when you came to my bar."

"I sure fucking hoped so."

"I love that you dressed your penis up for me."

He shook his head, smiling. "Come on up here." He was close enough as it was, but with her mouth on him he'd never last long enough to fuck her. And he most certainly planned to do just that.

She got to her knees, straddling his body as he shifted down the bed a bit.

"Why did you pierce your nipples?" He tugged and rolled them a little until she writhed.

"I think it looks sexy."

"You're correct."

"Why did you?"

"I like a little pain. I think it looks badass. My nipples are extra sensitive now too, so it worked out well."

Enough talk.

He urged her up with fingers at the backs of her thighs and she shifted until he looked straight up at the glossy folds of her pussy, all within licking and touching distance.

"Get down here," he nearly growled when she hovered just out of reach. He grabbed her hips and pulled her to his mouth, and she gasped.

He loved eating pussy like this. Serving himself of her body, feeling the tremble in her thigh muscles as he fucked her with his tongue and then danced it over her clit.

The skin against his fingertips at the backs of her thighs was on fire. But she squirmed, grinding herself against his mouth as he caressed her.

He'd expected her to give over to him, and she had. The way she felt. The way she tasted on his tongue made him angry that he'd held this off for weeks when they could have been doing it the whole time.

There was a moment when he considered tearing his mouth away to tell her to play with her nipples. But she tasted so good he decided against it and drove her hard and fast into climax.

He tipped her to the side and she landed on her back next to him in bed as she tried to catch her breath.

But she should have known he wouldn't allow that. He rolled, pinning her with his body, and kissed her so hard he stole the bit of breath she'd managed to get back.

She held on because that was all she could do. So much was happening she simply let it, let it wash over her and trusted him to keep her from floating away.

PJ wrapped her legs around him, wanting him to stay put because he felt so good.

But Asa did what *he* wanted, so he kissed down her neck and over all the freckles on her shoulders, licking down her chest to her nipples.

"I've been dreaming of these." He sucked a nipple into his mouth, tugging on the ring she'd worn that day. "I'm not the only one with new jewelry."

"Since you were a jerk, I bought new jewelry, new underpants, and changed my hair. Boys have liked these changes, which was nice since I wasn't sure you'd ever see them."

He bit harder than he had to and she yelped.

"No more of that," he said seriously. "Wait, so other people have seen this?" He circled her nipple with the tip of his tongue.

"It would serve you right if they had."

He grinned at the answer. "It would. But luckily we don't have to worry about it."

"You're very sure of yourself."

"I'm totally sure of myself." He got to his knees between her thighs. "Sometimes it takes me a while to get where I need to be. But once I'm there, I'm very sure about it."

He gripped his cock at the base and teased along her pussy with the head and the beads on the barbell.

"Am I still supposed to say when I like something?"

"I think the squeak in your voice does a good job, but a man can't complain when a beautiful woman tells him she likes what he's doing to her."

"I don't squeak!"

Of course he then reached out and squeezed her clit between his slippery thumb and forefinger and made her do just that.

"Liar."

"Well, you pinched my clit! Who doesn't squeak then?"

"I wouldn't know. Yours is the only clit I'm squeezing these days."

She wanted to laugh, but then she just sort of sighed when he pushed inside a bit and then pulled back.

"First, I'm going to fuck the hell out of you. Then we'll relax a while and start round two."

He rolled the condom on while she watched like a deviant, but it was so hot to see how carefully he pulled the latex around the piercing. Or maybe it was just the way he handled himself in general.

Either way, she liked to watch.

"Feet on the floor," he ordered as he got out of bed.

Oh. Well, yes.

He stood behind her, caressing down her back and sides until she relaxed, and then he pushed into her in one long, hard thrust until they both grunted when he got all the way inside.

"Now then. Fuck me."

PJ lazily turned her head enough to see him.

He gripped her hips and pulled her back so she got what he meant.

PJ braced her elbows and began to push herself back, fucking herself onto his cock. And then she pulled forward and pushed back again until she got a rhythm going and the pleasure of it made her warm inside, even as heat raced through her and the friction inside her body began to build.

Asa looked down at her as she got to her tiptoes and thrust herself back at him harder and harder. Her tattoo seemed to glimmer against the sheen of sweat on her skin. Her hair slid over her shoulders and neck like a river of gold. With streams of pink, but that was all right too. More than all right. It was sexy.

Her freckles stood out on her shoulders so he bent to lick over them. Her sigh was one of pleasure, and he smiled against her flesh at the sound.

"So beautiful."

PJ hummed.

Asa held off as long as he could. He didn't want to leave her body, didn't want to come and have it be over. But his dick didn't give a shit about what his brain wanted. His dick knew it would come again.

"You're even more beautiful when you come." He reached around to her clit and squeezed it, this time with the intent of making her climax. "Ah, you don't squeak when you want to come, do you?"

She made a frustrated little sound in the back of her throat, and he was glad she didn't see the amused smile he wore. She had a temper—which he found irresistible—and she'd kick his butt if she thought he was making fun.

Instead though, he reveled in her. In how alive and vibrant she was. How unafraid she seemed of the thing happening between them. Hell, *he* was scared of it!

Her inner walls gripped him so tight he saw stars for a moment. "Mmm, your pussy just rippled all around my cock. So close, aren't you?"

She gasped and buried her face in the mattress as she groaned with her orgasm. He didn't have any time to tell her he wanted every sound she made when he was responsible for her pleasure. His own climax hit him so hard he had to lock his knees to keep from sagging to the floor.

He snarled and leaned down to take a bite just beneath her shoulder blade as he came so hard it felt like his entire life shot from his cock.

"Get in bed. I'll be right back." He got rid of the condom quickly, and when he came back into the bedroom she was look-ing at his books. He approached her and pulled her close, her back to his front.

"Now see? You could have been having this multiple times a week, every week," she murmured.

He kissed her temple. "I know. But really, it was a terrible punishment not having you in my bed."

"I do hope you've learned, young man."

Grinning, he hugged her tight. "Come on. I'll grab you a T-shirt and then we can crack open the champagne."

CHAPTER
Twelve

You're awfully chipper today." Duke looked him up and down.

Asa poured himself another cup of coffee and brought it over to where he'd put his doughnut.

"I'm not chipper."

"It's a Saturday morning and you're not glowering, hungover, or totally stoic. I mean, you warm up by one or so, but it's ten. You're here at ten on a weekend and you're grinning at me like an idiot."

Asa ate his doughnut before he answered. "It's just a good day, that's all."

"Is that good day connected at all to the pretty blonde in one of our painting bays?"

Asa shrugged. "She and I worked things out. We're good."

"Oh, you mean after you dived into her mouth in the middle of a bar last night?"

Duke had been there the night before, so of course he'd seen the whole thing.

"She needed kissing." And she had. Sweet Penelope Jean had needed a whole lot of kissing and caressing and loving up all over, and he'd been happy to deliver it.

Duke snorted. "You staked a claim."

"That too." He'd stopped fighting his attraction to her. And after the way they'd been not only last night, but that morning before he'd driven them both in to Twisted Steel, he'd been right to finally make a move.

"Okay then. So this is a thing."

Asa paused a moment and then decided that yes, it was a thing of some sort. "It's a thing."

Asa tended to date around and be friends with the women he had sex with. Kissing PJ in the middle of the bar last night the way he had was more than just a *Hey, we're seeing each other* move. He'd been saying, *Mine*. He'd known that the night before. PJ knew it too.

That was an entirely different type of thing for him. But PJ was an entirely different type of woman, so he supposed that was only fitting.

"All right then. Good."

Asa grabbed a cinnamon roll. "We going out to the track Wednesday?"

"The way you're stuffing your face this morning I better eat that last cinnamon roll or you will." Duke grabbed the last one and put it on a plate. "So, Wednesday. Yes."

That upcoming Wednesday was the monthly grudge match out at the track with all their friends. It was mainly a lot of shit talk, great cars, and fast driving, which made it something Asa never wanted to miss.

"Just got off the phone with Mick a few minutes ago. He's coming out on Wednesday too, says he'll meet us there."

Mick had been in the army with Asa and Duke. Asa had gotten out first, then Duke. They'd both ended up in Seattle, and that's where they'd created Twisted Steel. In those early days Mick had lived with Asa and Duke for about eighteen months before he'd given over to moody, restless behavior.

And then out of the blue Mick reenlisted. Asa couldn't imagine what demons he could've been facing at home to send him back to a place that just might have killed him.

"He okay?" Duke met Asa's eyes.

They all had shadows. Even Asa sometimes didn't feel fully home. And he caught a darkness in Duke's eyes from time to time too. But Mick did everything harder than anyone else Asa had ever known, and he knew some pretty hard-core people. It led to self-destructive bullshit sometimes, like returning to a war zone after you'd done your duty and were lucky enough to finally get out.

"He just got in at eleven last night, he said. His brother picked him up, so Mick's there until he decides what he wants to do." Duke shrugged.

"He just wants to fit in somewhere," Asa said.

Asa knew that hunger in ways Duke never could. Duke was the kind of guy everyone liked. He had an easygoing manner that made people talk to him. He was the cool dude people wanted at their table.

Asa had come up harder. He'd had to scrap for a place in the hierarchy of that shitty four-block area he grew up in. Had to dig himself in and keep anyone from thinking they could prey on him.

Mick had had his own scrapping to do. Though he came from a large family, they told him they loved him but hated his sin. Which meant they steadfastly judged him for being bisexual and he never felt like he belonged anywhere.

That's why Asa wanted Mick in Seattle. Because he and Duke were the family who'd give him a place to land and call home.

"You're probably right. God knows most of his family doesn't seem to want to give him that."

They finished up their coffee and headed back down to the shop floor. Asa normally worked six or seven days a week.

Twisted Steel was his. He'd built it with his sweat and his

brain. He and Duke had made something special, and through that, Asa had found a place he fit. Had finally found a way to be comfortable in his skin.

"I'm going to finish that door on the Camaro." Asa headed over in that direction as Duke turned to the left.

Things were mighty fine in his life indeed.

PJ capped her lipstick and dropped the tube back into her bag. She pretended she wasn't nervous and did a terrible job at it.

"Stop. You're making me jittery." Julie patted her hand.

"My paint is right there, Julie. Right. There. People are looking at it and talking to one another. What if they're saying what a horrible job I did?"

"Did you do a horrible job?"

"Hell no! That's triple metallic. That is totally badass."

"Obviously. Now that we've got that cleared up, stop panicking."

"This is like the first public thing Asa and I have been at since he sort of claimed me all *Officer and a Gentleman*–style at the Ditch. I've gotten two dirty looks already."

"Where is he, by the way? I'm so annoyed that everyone else has met him and I haven't. For god's sake, *Jay* knows your boyfriend and I don't?"

"You could have come with me that first night to meet him. And Jay doesn't know my boyfriend. Jay knows who owns Twisted Steel. Different thing." PJ scanned the crowd to see if she could find him.

Just over the last few minutes the number of people who'd showed up had surged as the time for the first heats got closer.

"I should just look for the women and he'll be there," PJ said, tone dry.

"Really? Is that weird? I don't know if I'd like that."

PJ caught sight of that dark hair and he turned like she'd called his name. He started her way.

"It is weird. I don't like it. But we've just started seeing each other. I have to deal with it because women seem to be drawn to him like bugs to a porch light. You'll see. Here he comes."

He stalked over to her and she watched every step. He had on a form-fitting T-shirt and his hair was pulled back from his face. He wore sunglasses and dark boots.

"I said, *goddamn*," Julie whispered.

PJ grinned so hard her cheeks hurt. "I know. He's even *more* like that when he's in bed. All prowly and grrr and stuff. It's so hot."

"How do you even let him out of bed to start with?"

PJ laughed, leaning in very close to give her sister a one-armed hug and whisper, "His cock is pierced."

"You get the fuck out of town!" Julie turned to her, eyes wide.

"I should have told you before. I thought you might be weirded out, but I misjudged you."

"You certainly did if you thought I wouldn't want to hear all about this later when it's just the two of us. I'm not sure if I should worry about you or give you a high five."

They were still laughing as Asa finally got over to them.

He kept coming until they were body to body, nose to nose, and he kissed her. Not a full-on carnal mouthfuck like he could also deliver, but a very nice hello all the same.

"I've been looking all over for you." He turned to Julie and smiled. "You're clearly related to PJ." He held out a hand. "Asa Barrons."

"We just got here about ten minutes ago. We were looking at my car and then trying to find you. Asa, this is my sister, Julie. Julie, Asa."

"It's good to meet you."

Julie smiled up at Asa, already a little besotted, like every other woman seemed to be. "Nice to put a face to the person PJ talks about."

Asa relaxed when Julie responded so warmly. Tenderness

curled in PJ's belly at the sweetness of that vulnerability. And because her sister was being so lovely and thought Asa was hot and charming.

And that was before he gave her the smile. A smile just for PJ. Sexy and sweet and super dirty. He schooled his features back to charming rogue and turned his attention to Julie. "Can I get you two a drink?"

"I can't stay, actually." Julie shrugged. "I have a meeting back at Colman with Fee."

"That's our uncle," PJ explained to Asa.

"The one who treated you so badly." He got all surly when he said it, and PJ wanted to sigh wistfully and twirl her hair around her finger.

"Yes, that's the one." Julie answered him first.

"Julie is the heart of the financial end of Colman. Our uncle is a figurehead, but it's really Julie and to some extent our brother Shawn who are the guiding force there. Julie should be in charge, but she has no penis, which is apparently a prerequisite for that job as far as Fee and our father are concerned."

Asa choked back a laugh and then said his good-byes to Julie, who gave PJ a discreet thumbs-up before she got into her car to leave.

Asa took her hand and led her over to the Twisted Steel tent area. "Have a drink. Are you hungry? We've got burgers and chips."

But before she could answer, he dipped his head and kissed her, and this time there was definitely some mouthfucking going on.

Heat licked at his belly as he finally gave in and sank into her taste like he'd wanted to since he'd caught sight of her across the field.

She slid her arms around his neck and held on, giving over, opening up to him. He hummed his pleasure at that and the curves against him.

When he finally broke away she smiled up at him. "It's a good thing I wore that kiss-proof lipstick."

He laughed. "Still looks juicy." He stole another kiss before turning her toward the bar area.

"Listen, Asa." She put her hand on his forearm to stay him. "Thank you."

"For what? Kissing like a rock star?"

She rolled her eyes before getting serious again. "For the car." She jerked her chin at the Oldsmobile she'd done the triple metallic job on.

"It was my pick. Regardless of who I'm with, the work you did is top-notch. It's good for Twisted Steel too." Each month the different members of their group brought work to show off, and Asa had chosen the Olds not only because her work was fantastic, but because the kind of high-end custom client they wanted to attract would love it too.

"Thank you for that."

He realized then that she'd been concerned. Her work was so good, it had never occurred to him she'd ever doubt herself. But of course she would, just like he did his own work at times.

"You're welcome. Let's keep making money together."

"You got it."

Her attention shifted and the intimate bedroom smile she'd had on tightened to something entirely different and totally platonic. He liked that.

Which was why when he turned to see Craig standing there with a hot redhead he didn't punch the guy.

"Hey, Craig. Carmella, how are you?" PJ hugged the redhead and Asa let his mind wander just a bit until his pants got a little tight.

PJ turned. "Asa, this is Carmella Rossi. She's Craig's cousin."

He nodded at Craig and then looked at the redhead. "Oh hey! I know you." Asa turned back to PJ. "She's Duke's neighbor." And back to Carmella. "You have that awesome little dog right? Like a miniature Doberman?"

Carmella nodded, smiling. "Yes. Also, my uncle is Craig's dad. I do the books at his shop so I talk to Lottie in your office at least once a month."

They made a little small talk for a while longer. Asa'd been hoping Carmella was Craig's date but clearly not. Asa put his arm around PJ's shoulders and she turned her head to look at him.

"First heat starts in ten. I need to head back over to the track. Want to come with me so we can get you a good place to watch?"

"Yes, please!"

He kept her to himself for a few minutes more as he took her behind the tents lining the track. It was marginally quieter and far less crowded.

"We're right up here." He pointed. Duke stood with Mick and another one of the guys from their team.

Asa didn't miss the once-over Mick gave PJ. Or the downturn of his mouth when he finished.

"Hey, PJ." Duke, grinning, danced her away from Asa, hugging her.

PJ laughed and turned back to Asa where he was standing with Mick. She gave him one of her prettiest smiles. Warm, totally genuine.

Mick eyed her carefully.

"PJ Colman, this is Mick Roberts. Mick, this is PJ."

She held a hand out and Mick gave it a halfhearted shake. By that point Asa was pissed.

He stepped between Mick and PJ, trying to be nonchalant, as he spoke to Duke about the first heat.

They'd decided the day before that Asa would drive the muscle car heats and Duke would do the stock. Asa was up first in the Fastback, adrenaline already coursing through his system.

Asa grabbed a pair of noise-dampening headsets for PJ, but

she held up her own pair with a smile before she put them on. Sometimes it was easy to forget how steeped she truly was in car culture. He needed to remember that.

Still, when she wasn't paying attention, he looked closely to be sure her protective gear was appropriate, given that wreck of a helmet she'd had before.

He guided her off to a space they'd cleared for a few people to stand and watch away from the action, and she gave him a thumbs-up. He kissed her hard and she gave him two thumbs up.

Asa tossed a glare Mick's way as the men headed toward the car.

"We'll talk about how you acted later. But for now, you stay the fuck away from her if you have a problem. You got me? Any problem here is between you and me. PJ isn't part of it. I won't allow it."

Mick shook his head. "Just looking out for you."

"Again, let me underline for you that this is an Asa-Mick issue. This has nothing to do with PJ. Am I clear?" He'd beat the shit out of a friend for being a dick any day of the week. They'd hash it out one way or the other, but that had nothing to do with PJ, and Asa wasn't going to let anyone make her feel uncomfortable.

Duke slapped the back of Mick's head. "He understands."

Duke liked PJ, so Asa knew his friend would keep an eye on her.

PJ watched, heart in her throat, as Asa busted his ass in that Fastback. He was so damned good. Intense. His concentration was fantastic, but it was his reflexes that made him so very masterful.

Fearless, he dominated the track like he dominated her in the bedroom.

She paused, smiling at that silly bit of internal narration, but it was true. Asa was totally in charge, and it was the sexiest thing she'd ever seen.

He came in second in the first heat and first in the second.

They brought the Fastback in, switching out with Duke and his stock car.

Asa worked the team for Duke, like Duke had for him, but every once in a while he looked back over his shoulder at her, and it sent all sorts of pulses of goodness through her.

Not that it kept her from noting how much his army friend Mick didn't like her. He was not having any PJ in his life. Not one bit.

Which was too bad, because she was there. Period. But she hated it when people didn't like her for secret reasons! She hadn't done anything to him at all, so what was up his butt?

She'd just have to give it time and space. Maybe he was jealous at how much time Asa spent with her or some other stupid guy thing. Maybe he didn't like blondes. Or he thought she was too young or too whatever. Maybe she'd find out just what his deal was.

For the time being, though, there were fast cars racing, which was sort of like her birthday or something. The smell of fuel and burning rubber, the chitchat, the overwhelming noise levels as machines hummed, roared, idled, and everything in between all around.

A lot of her time as a child had been spent on a track, off to the side watching or in the bleachers if it was a big track. It was like homecoming to be there.

CHAPTER
Thirteen

Twisted Steel was second overall, with Asa ranked highest by one and a half points.

Grinning, he strolled over and kissed her after he'd come off the track.

"Congratulations."

He kissed her again. "Thank you. I'm just going to wash up and change my shirt. I'll meet you in the main tents with the food."

She'd seen Audra head that way just a few minutes before. "All right. I'll see you in a bit."

She put a little extra sway in her walk as she headed out.

The crowd in the main tent was energetic. Lots of gearheads. Mechanical geniuses. These men and women loved car culture. They loved racing and celebrating the old things as well as the new.

Some of them had come to accept her in the months she'd been doing custom work around the Sound. Some she knew second- or thirdhand from Colman as well. Others were like Mick. Suspicious of her. Most of them would be all right once they got to know her better. The rest? It didn't matter. She was with Asa.

Still, it was nice to see all sorts of friendly faces, so when she went in, PJ let go of that discomfort with Mick. It was time to relax and have a drink with her friends.

Audra held up a beer. "Just grabbed this for you. You have great timing. Tom and the guys are getting us food."

PJ took the beer and her stomach growled. "I was on my way to get a burger hours ago and then I got waylaid." Or rather Asa had kissed her and she'd forgotten about everything else.

Tom returned with a tray of burgers and fries. "I just got us a bunch of everything. I figured Asa would be hungry too."

"He didn't eat before the race. I know that much."

Tom grinned, waggling his brows. "You do, don't you?"

Audra punched his arm and he pretended it hurt.

"Who's the hot man-meat with Asa?" Audra asked.

PJ turned and stifled a groan. "That's Mick. I don't know much more than that he was in the army with Duke and Asa. They're all close friends."

"Now why don't you tell me the real story and what he did to make you not like him?" Audra didn't miss much, PJ had to give her that.

"I have no idea what you mean." PJ attempted a prim tone.

"You went all disapproving and your eyes narrowed just a teeny bit. I've known you since before you had boobs. I know when you're repressing something."

Ugh. How much did she *not* want to do this? "I'm going to grab us another round. I'll be right back."

"No way." Audra shoved Tom. "Tom can go. And then we can talk."

Tom groaned but headed off, and the two them bent their heads together so PJ could speak quietly and be heard, relating the story about how Mick had acted.

"He doesn't like me. I don't know why. Maybe Asa dated his sister back in school or maybe Mick hates women in general. Maybe I did something I wasn't even aware of to offend him. Whatever it is, he's not a PJ fan."

"How can anyone not be a PJ fan?" Audra asked.

They laughed, straightening up, and were changing the discussion to non-Mick-related topics when someone bumped into her. Ray something or other. She knew he worked at a body shop over in Lake City.

"Sorry about that." He put his hand on her shoulder, and when he didn't remove it quickly she stepped back.

He appeared to have gotten the message, but was still friendly. "It's PJ, right? You did the paint on that Olds?"

"Yes, that's me."

"Amazing. Did you leave Colman?"

She nodded. "I did. I started my own custom design shop."

"Really? Wow, congratulations. Things are going well, then?"

Asa approached, talking with Mick and Duke. He scanned the crowd until he found her. She waved, smiling, and they headed over.

"We just brought some food over less than five minutes ago if you want some of this. Tom went to get beers, so he'll be back."

Asa kissed her, wrapping an arm around her waist. "I have a special request order coming up. The cook is a friend of my mom's, so she takes care of me." He stole some chips off her plate. "I'll happily take a few of these, though."

"Who's your friend?" Mick asked, tipping his head at Ray. His tone implied *friend* meant PJ banged him on the side or something.

And PJ knew she wasn't alone in that perception because Audra's eyebrows practically hit her hairline. PJ reached out to squeeze her friend's hand to keep her from jumping on Mick's face and pulling his hair out.

"Mick, this is Ray. He does bodywork for Andy Benton up in Lake City." Duke winked at PJ. Duke was awesome and she would have kissed him in gratitude, but Mick would probably see it as her blowing him.

They did that chin-tipping thing men did to say hello. Tom approached with beer and a bunch more food arrived at the table.

Her phone kept buzzing and she finally checked to see her mother had left a message and two texts.

She touched Asa's arm. "I need to call my mom. I'll be back."

"Is everything all right?" He brushed the hair back from her shoulder.

"I think so. It's been a week since I've checked in and she's a little testy." Her mother wasn't one for being put off when she wanted to be heard. It was the one area in which Lenore Colman was actually aggressive.

His concern faded into amusement. "I get that too. Moms are good at it."

She ducked out but didn't go too far. In fact, from where he stood at the table eating and hanging out with their friends, he could see her leaning against a fencepost with the phone to her ear.

After a glare at Mick, Audra said her good-byes to Duke and Asa and headed to another tent along with Tom and several others, leaving him alone with Duke and Mick.

He would normally have asked PJ's friends to stay and called Mick out, but he wanted to do this in private. Once it was handled, he'd talk to Audra because this situation had lost him some hard-fought ground with PJ's circle.

"Now that we're alone, I've dialed Jesus, so he and I want to have a talk with you. Mind telling me why you're being such a dick to my girlfriend?" Asa polished off his burger and paused to drink some of his beer.

Duke had shifted so that he stood between Asa and Mick. The two had gone at it more than once over the years; that was how they worked through a lot of shit. But what had just happened needed words too.

"You're embarrassing yourself, Asa. Ask Jesus why you're dating a goddamn Girl Guide or whatever she is."

Duke sighed. "What's it to you anyway? You lay low for years and suddenly you're back here ready to pass judgment on something you know pretty much nothing about."

Asa had to admit Duke said it better, and less angrily, than he would have.

"What? Being gone means I can't say what needs to be said? I had my own shit to handle." Mick shrugged.

Asa let Duke do most of the talking. He was better with people. "Yeah? How'd that work out for you? I mean that truly, because we've been asking you for a week straight and you don't seem to want to answer. You in some kind of trouble and that's why you're starting shit? Keep our attention on that? What are you running from? Or hiding from? Let us in. We get that you're hurting, but you can't take it out on PJ. She doesn't deserve it. She's good people, and in case you haven't noticed, she makes Asa happy."

Ignoring that opportunity to tell Duke and Asa what was up, Mick rolled his eyes. "Asa, what can you be thinking? I mean other than how taut those tits are. You're her 'what do I do the year after college' fuck."

Asa was lifting Mick off the ground before he thought about it. Duke yelled at them both to stop it. Asa shoved Mick back as he set him down and he stumbled a few steps.

"Chill the fuck out," Duke said genially. But he kept his body between Asa and Mick. "This isn't the place and your girlfriend is just across the way. I think she's had enough bullshit for one day."

Asa glanced over but she was still on her phone, so he looked back to Mick and pointed. "You're out of line." Asa was surprised he'd managed to get the words out at all, given how hard he was clenching his jaw. "*No one* talks about her that way. You got me?"

"No, Asa. I *don't* get you. Who are you? This is...I don't even know. Did you find her after the homecoming game?"

A red haze slid over his vision and he stepped forward, his fist already in the process of cocking back for a solid right to the face.

Duke shook his head. "Asa!"

"What the hell's going on?"

Asa looked over his shoulder to find PJ standing there, holding her phone, red-faced because it was clear she'd heard at least some of the worst parts of that exchange.

"Nothing at all. Just a misunderstanding I was clearing up."

The look on her face told him exactly what she thought of that line. "Okay then. Well, I'm going home now."

"What? Why?" Asa stalked over, taking her hands.

Her gaze narrowed in a way that had him shifting his body, keeping his thigh in knee-deflection range. She pulled her hands from his hold and he frowned. But she wasn't going to be swayed or charmed. Not right then.

"There's a *crowd* watching us. Your friend obviously has some sort of problem with me, and I'm way too tired to figure out what it is tonight. No, actually, I don't care what his problem is since all this played out in public in front of our friends and the people I want to hire me in the future. And when I ask what's going on, you tell me *nothing*. Not a fan of *any* of those reasons."

She looked around Asa to Mick, who flinched when he caught her expression. "And you? Eat a bag of dicks. Asshole. The fuck you think you are?" PJ gave him the finger and turned just as Audra approached wearing the look women get when a dude has seriously messed up.

They headed to the parking lot.

"Go on," Duke urged. "Watch it, though. She has dick-kicking in her eyes."

"She needs to kick Mick, not me," he muttered as he caught up to the women, who'd neared PJ's car.

"I've got it from here," Audra said through her teeth to Asa when he stepped in their path. She was really, truly pissed and ready to defend her friend.

Asa ignored Audra and spoke to PJ. "This is stupid. You don't have to go. It's a misunderstanding. He'll change his mind about you once he gets to know you."

"Oh, okay then. I'll just wait around for your asshole friend with no manners to judge me. Because that's going to happen. Oh, wait, no it isn't. He has no right, and you have no right to ask me to do so. I'm going home and I'm going to bed. Call me tomorrow." PJ waved a hand over her shoulder as they got to her car just a few steps away.

"Are you all right to drive?" He moved around Audra and then, exasperated, threw his hands up. "Audra, back off for a second."

"You can fuck right off, Barrons. I know you did not just talk to me in that tone." Audra looked him over slowly and PJ rolled her eyes.

"Audra. It's cool. You go on back. I'll call you tomorrow. It's not a thing. I'm just done."

Audra hugged PJ and then stalked off after giving Asa a dirty look.

He took a risk and stepped close once they were alone. "I don't want you to go." Which was odd. In any other circumstance he couldn't imagine not having just said, *Okay then, see you later, drive safe.* But he didn't want her to leave. He wanted her to sleep over like she had the weekend before. And he didn't want her to feel bad because of Mick's attitude.

Her expression was more amused and less annoyed, which he appreciated, as he was risking his balls standing so close.

"I watched you race, which was very sexy. I hung out with my friends and had burgers and half a beer. So yes, I'm cool to drive.

I'm going home, where I plan to get into my pajamas and catch up on my DVR. Call me when you can."

He was pretty sure that were their situations reversed, he'd be far less understanding. He kissed her quickly. "This isn't like Mick. He's usually ridiculously protective and mannerly. I don't know what's going on with him, but I'm going to talk to him right now."

She raised her brow but didn't say anything.

He opened her door. "I admire your restraint right now. I also need to tell you how hot it was when you flipped Mick off and told him to eat a bag of dicks. You're a little bit crazy, aren't you?"

"Young and crazy. Asa, you're going to have such a good time with me."

He snorted a laugh and hugged her to him, kissing her forehead. "I already *do* have a good time with you." He remembered why she'd stepped away to start with. "Oh hey, is your mom okay?"

"Yes, she wanted to make lunch plans. Thank you for asking."

"I'm going to kiss you. I'm giving you warning so you won't maim me when I get that close."

"Take your chances, Asa."

He slid a palm around the back of her neck and held her close as he kissed her. She sighed into him, relaxing.

"You're lucky you're so good with your mouth." She kissed him once more and then got into the car.

He closed the door and tapped on her roof before stepping back and watching her drive away, well aware of just how lucky he was.

And then he headed back to where Mick was.

"Just what the fuck is your problem?" Asa asked Mick as he approached where Mick stood with Duke, away from the main tent. Things had died down and people were back to drinking, so at least that much happened.

"How old is that girl?" Mick asked.

"I believe the term for females over eighteen is 'woman.' She's twenty-five."

"You're how old? Forty-five?"

Asa flipped him off. "Thirty-seven."

Mick rolled his eyes. "She's too young for you. She's your mid-life crisis and you're her sugar daddy."

"Sugar daddy?" Asa barked a surprised laugh. "Is that what this is about? She's got more money than I do. She's a *Colman*. As in Colman Enterprises? She has her own business, which is successful. She's not too young for me, and I'm not having a midlife crisis."

"Anything younger than a decade is officially too young. I have socks older than her."

"No, you don't. You're so full of shit." Duke shook his head. "She doesn't need a sugar daddy. She's got talent. Real talent, and all the connections she needs on her own. Her family is more steeped in car culture than we ever will be."

Asa shoved Mick toward where the Oldsmobile was. "See that paint job? That's her. All her. Triple metallic. Perfect. She doesn't need me for this. She's got it on her own."

Mick prowled around the car, peering closely at it until he came to a stop at Asa's side again.

"I'm impressed by anyone with that sort of skill. But she's so young, Asa. Innocent. I bet she has freckles and polishes apples she takes to the teacher."

"And so what if she does? She's a big girl. She knows how to say no, and that's all it would take." Not even that. He was in tune with her. Listened to her responses so he could avoid a situation where she'd have to say no in the first place.

"Take my word for it, Penelope Jean isn't doing anything she doesn't want to do. I've come to know her over the last months. You owe her an apology and some chocolate." Duke shrugged. "Also, she didn't polish an apple for you. I seem to recall you got the finger and an admonition to eat a bag of dicks. She brings me cinnamon candy popcorn because it's my favorite."

Asa laughed. "PJ is capable of handling herself, but in this case, you're my friend and she shouldn't have to. I won't let you hurt her, Mick. She's important to me."

Mick leaned against a light post.

"Is this chick even your type? I've never seen you with a woman like her."

Duke spoke this time. "Interestingly enough, she seemed to be *your* type. Don't think you looking at her ass was a secret. Something you want to tell us?"

Mick blushed hard enough that Asa could see it even in the dim light.

"I've never hid that I like women too. She just reminded me of someone for a moment. That's all. She's pretty, no lie. Great body. She's just not your usual. Young. I jumped to conclusions and got protective and weird."

Mick slid a palm over his head. That sound, the scratch of skin on the stubble of the scalp their friend shaved regularly, was so normal, something Asa had heard during every situation imaginable.

This was Asa, Duke, and Mick. Like it had been for years.

"Jesus. I bet she's going to make me pay. She seems the type," Mick said.

Young and crazy, she'd teased him. Asa'd had his share of crazy women, and she really wasn't in that category. Which was a very good thing. But she had enough of that energy, enough sass and sense of self that she embodied the things he dug about those sorts of intense people without the restraining-order parts.

"She's not a pushover. And you were an asshole. Also, I should have told you this up front, but she's got a temper, which you've seen a bit of. That middle finger was just the tip of that iceberg. Wear a cup."

CHAPTER
Fourteen

She'd just settled into bed and had started to drift off when the knock came at her door.

Asa had texted her earlier to see if she was still up, but she'd just wanted to go to sleep, so she'd ignored it. Also, she was annoyed at him and his friend and she didn't want to deal with any more foolery from them that night.

She pulled on a robe and headed out, looking through the peephole to be sure it was him. And it was.

Seeing him sent all her annoyance skittering away. He looked so good out there on her porch. He'd smell good too. And make her come at least once. But since he'd be feeling guilty she could probably count on a minimum of two orgasms.

She opened up.

He gave her a smile but stayed outside. He held up a couple of shopping bags. "I come bearing gifts. Chocolates. Caramels. Some wine. Me."

PJ put a hand at her hip. "You're trouble." Which was why she would let him in, of course.

"I know. But I'm usually worth it in the end. Can I come in?"

She stepped to the side, locking up once he'd come in.

"Mick is going to be calling you this week to apologize. I feel like I should tell you a little about him. Not to make excuses for what he's done, but maybe to help you understand some."

"Come in. I was in bed. Bring the chocolates, caramel, and you."

He snorted, getting rid of his boots and then following her to her room.

She slid the robe over the top of her door and got back in bed.

"Am I safe getting in there with you?"

She grinned. "You're an adrenaline junkie, Asa. Take your chances."

Laughing, he pulled off every last stitch of clothing and jumped in bed with her.

"Mick was in the army with me and Duke, as you know. We met early on. He and Duke were in the same company, and I came along after one of their buddies got killed."

He shook his head, his gaze going far away for a moment, and she realized how little he spoke about this stuff.

"He's the youngest of seven kids. They're very religious and he's bi. They didn't kick him out or send him to therapy, but they have quietly and gravely judged him for being gay since he came out.

"He's my brother, like Duke is my brother. He's protective and he saw you as a threat because you're young and pretty. He thought you were out to use me. But we hashed it out. Duke and I both talked with him about you. He's a hothead, but he's also got honor. He's not used to fitting anywhere. But he does with us, and you came into that space and he freaked. I hope you'll give him a chance once he apologizes, but if you don't I get that too."

Well, how could she not give the guy a chance after that story? "I'm not a heartless brute." She snuggled down under the covers and he spooned her from behind.

"I have an idea. Something to help you sleep," he said, nuzzling the back of her neck.

"Stop talking, that works best," she muttered and he laughed.

"I'm sorry." He said it quietly, his lips against her pulse on her neck.

"For what?" She turned to face him.

"I invited you somewhere and then you got treated poorly by my best friend. That's a shitty thing to have to deal with. It shouldn't have happened. I'm sorry you had to."

She sighed. "It's all right. I mean, it's not cool that he was such an insulting dickbag. But if he's sorry, truly, and he apologizes, and it was because he wanted to protect you, I can get past it. Shit happens. Wait till you meet my family. It'll be so much fun."

He guffawed. "I've met your oldest brother and your sister."

She rested her chin on his chest, closing her eyes a moment when he played his fingers through her hair.

"I'm still sorry."

He wanted to protect her. It hit her hard, so she turned her face to kiss his chest over his heart as she tried to get her head around what it was that Asa had just shown her such a private side of himself.

He'd made himself vulnerable, and she wasn't sure he'd even realized to what extent he'd done it.

She breathed him in, kissing his skin once more before raising her face to his. "It wasn't the first time there's been some sort of drunken shoving thing at a race. Or a party. Or any gathering of our friends. I've seen you in a few of them. At the time I didn't know it was you."

One of his brows rose. "Really?"

"Once up at Mukilteo I saw this brawl. Fifteen, twenty dudes. Fists flying. *People* flying." It had been epic, even for the knock-down, drag-out guys there. And then they'd all sat down—or lain down, in some cases—and drunk beers together as they bled. It was so weird and yet oddly endearing.

He groaned, putting a hand over his eyes. "Yeah, that was me."

She laughed. "I know. Your hair was different. But I remember the swinging fists. Tonight when you tossed Mick back after picking him up I realized it was you."

Asa was a man who had a great deal of creative talent. He was a smart businessperson as well. But he wasn't above a fistfight when he thought it necessary.

She'd never dated anyone like him before, but that he was so rough and hard but never touched her with anything less than great care only made him hotter. That he wanted to protect her and shield her from hurt was a powerful thing. It made her feel so beautiful.

"You're not kicking me out the door?"

She sat, confused. "Why? Do you think I expected you to punch Mick or something?"

Asa snorted. "He's got the hardest fucking head I've ever punched. It really would have hurt, so I'm glad he saw reason."

"You've already punched him? In the past? Was it about me?"

Asa sat and she exhaled hard at the sight of his abdominal muscles bunching as he did. And of course the cock. And the bar.

He stole a hard, fast kiss. "When you look at me like that I want to fuck you and cuddle you all at once. It's confusing. Anyway. It wasn't about you. Some guys need to be punched in the face from time to time. He's one of them. I'm probably one of them too. But I wasn't asking if you wanted me to leave because I didn't punch Mick. You just admitted you know I've brawled around. You're not the going-out-with-a-brawler type. Aren't you turned off by that?"

"You're not the first person to say I'm confusing. It's a flaw." She laughed when he stole another kiss. "I know who you are to me. And that's what counts. If you used all that to threaten or harm me it'd be different. But you don't. You like to punch people who appear to be okay with punching and being punched, and while I admit to being totally confused by it, it's who you are. I like the Asa I've come to know over the last seven months."

He paused, thinking. "So you wouldn't freak if I told you about the bare-knuckles fight league Duke and I are in? I guess Mick now too. Which needs to happen because he's better than all of us."

"God, I think you just got the same look you do when you see my boobs. I'm going to get a complex. Maybe I need to start punching people. Do you need a moment alone to think about your team's extra-special new knuckles?"

He wasn't sure what he'd expected from her when she'd opened the door earlier. Generally, unanswered texts said, *Leave me the fuck alone, I'll let you know when I'm ready to talk to you*. Or she could have been asleep and that's why she hadn't texted him back. But the truth was, he'd figured it was the former instead of the latter.

He'd come anyway because he'd let himself want sleeping next to her and it had been yanked away from him. And because her temper was so fucking hot he couldn't help but poke at her a little.

She'd listened to what he'd said about Mick and had been kind. Asa knew Mick well enough to be sure his friend would be one of PJ's biggest fans inside a month. Oh sure, she'd make him pay a little, especially if Mick didn't give it enough grovel. But that would only make him like PJ more.

And then she'd let him come into her bedroom and hadn't even flinched when she'd brought up that brawl he'd been in. Duke had broken his ring finger on his left hand and Asa'd had bruised ribs and a black eye for a few days.

"Did you think I'd run off screaming and crying? Do you really believe I'm so fragile that I didn't understand what sort of man you were before I let you in between my thighs? Or did you think I just was so hot for your cock I didn't care? I *was* hot for your cock, by the way. Still am. But it doesn't surprise me you'd willingly let someone punch you in the face. Please tell me you at least take your piercing out of your nose first."

He caught her hand, bringing it to his mouth to kiss her palm. "I don't know what I expect from you sometimes. You're something entirely new to me."

Her smile softened. "I may not have done everything you have, but I'm not fragile. If everyone in your fight group is there willingly and you all get something from it, I don't care. It's not like you're rampaging through Seattle beating up passersby."

Ah. "I don't think you're fragile. At first, yes, because you're so pretty and blond and young—and I already apologized for that, so don't frown—but anyone who's been around you for longer than ten minutes wouldn't think you were fragile."

She waved a lazy hand. "I've spent a lot of my life trying to be the person my father would finally see. Finally listen to. I dressed like I was expected to. Did what I was expected to. And then I just...I dropped out of college." She snorted a laugh. "I dropped out of college and you'd have thought I burned someone's house down. Anyway. I wanted to prove myself on the job. I didn't want to go to college. I wanted to learn things differently and so I tried to be the best I could at Colman.

"I've been working so hard to prove myself their way. But they never considered me capable. I can sell lots of tires. I was top-notch at it, and they'll miss that, probably. But I can guarantee my uncle and my father haven't even considered how shitty and paternalistic it was to tell me I was only allowed to make my mark at Colman in a way *they* defined for me up front. *They* think I'm fragile and useless and silly. And I've spent years trying to change that. So. Yes, I have a button about it, and that's why."

He pushed up to sit in the middle of the bed. "Panties off and get in my lap.

She complied quickly and Asa sighed happily as she wrapped her legs around his waist and settled on his lap as he started the story.

"In high school I had a job at a florist. I worked in the mornings when they got their flower shipment. Up at five, and then I could work a few hours before my first class. I learned then that a lot of roses we used in arrangements were pretty and all, but they barely had a smell. But there was this climbing rosebush near the bus stop. In an empty lot, so it was something that drew your eye. The blooms were bright pink and they didn't just open up, they seemed to explode outward with scent. They weren't perfect like those faintly scented ones we sold for sixty bucks a dozen on Valentine's Day. They were wild and heady and a thousand times better."

She watched him. Vulnerable. He brushed his thumb over her bottom lip.

"*You're* that wild rose, PJ. So pretty at first glance, but the longer I look, the more beautiful you are. Unique. You're vibrant and sensual. There are a lot of words I'd use to describe you, but fragile isn't one of them."

"I was going to make a joke. And then I thought how rude it would be of me to do that instead of thanking you for such a beautiful compliment. So thank you."

He kissed her chin.

She tipped her head back, arching her spine, her pussy hot and wet as it grazed his cock.

He yanked her shirt off, caressing all over her upper body, taking extra time with her nipples and the rings in them.

"I missed you on me." Her whispered words a plea.

She shredded him.

Without even knowing it, she took him apart. He shifted forward a little to kiss her chest, between her breasts.

She held his head, bringing him to her body as they both just soaked each other in.

"I missed being on you too. I had plans for you at my house. You need to come over tomorrow."

Thursdays were the one day he tended not to go in to work. He

wanted to spend the day in his bedroom with her, and he wanted
to punch Mick all over again for ruining that.

"Maybe."

He heard the laughter in her response and he nipped her skin
and then over to her ribs. She shifted, laughing until he'd rolled
on top of her again.

"Yield." He'd meant it to sound teasing but ended up feeling
and sounding far more serious about it.

Yes, that's what he wanted right then.

She looked up at him with those big, beautiful blue eyes. Waiting.

She stole his senses. He found himself opening up with her in
ways he hadn't planned. But she listened. It wasn't like he'd been
lonely before PJ. It wasn't as if he didn't know women looked at
him. But PJ didn't just check out the outside and appreciate it. PJ
focused on all of him. Gave him her full attention, and it made
him feel ten feet tall.

And he knew she'd think it was a small thing, but it was
everything.

She rolled him over and scrambled atop his body. She kissed
him, tasting with sweet kisses, followed by slow sips. It seemed
impossible to be turned on and totally relaxed all at once, but
there it was.

She kissed down his neck, over to each ear, and then paused at
his nipples.

"I love that you're so sensitive here. It makes me so hot to lick
over the bars." She did just that and they both moaned.

The flare of her hips as she shimmied down his body called to
him, made his mouth water.

"More," he growled, and she drew a deep breath as she got into
place on her knees between his thighs. She scored her nails up the
sensitive skin of his thighs and over his balls.

She held his gaze, but he couldn't stop himself from moving
from her eyes down to her hands on him, to her tits.

Dipping her head, she gave hot, openmouthed kisses to his hip bone and to his cock at long last.

She played with the piercing over and over until he was so hard he throbbed. And then she swallowed the head of his cock. One. Two. Three times and then all the way to the root and back up.

He cursed as that last move dragged him to the edge, since he had no plans to come just yet. He liked watching her suck him off. Liked the way it felt even more.

Asa had plans for PJ, and they included fucking her hard and fast while he held her hair in his fist.

He shivered. Yes, that needed to happen, and so he needed not to come just yet.

But that didn't mean he was ready to end this. He watched down the line of his body as she took him into her mouth over and over. Her ass moved from side to side, her tattoo so pretty and sexy in the dim light of the room.

She pressed two fingertips against the space just behind his balls and he grunted, thrusting up into her mouth.

"Yes. Fuck yes."

She hummed, her tongue on the bar so it vibrated through him, and he let himself get so very close he had to actually grab her by the shoulders and haul her off.

"Hey!"

"You're only hotter when you pout. You know that, right? Your lips are swollen from my cock. You're pouting because you want more. Jesus."

He rolled off the bed and rustled in his pants to grab the condoms he'd brought.

"Feet on the floor, top part of your body on the bed. You know how I like it."

She managed to get off the bed and then gave him a look over her shoulder that had him hurrying back her way.

He put the condoms just out of her reach, but in her view. So she'd know what he was planning. When he was ready.

But for right then, he had other things to do. He stepped to her, kissing his way across her back and down her spine, dropping to his knees.

She thrust her ass out and he nipped her cheek, right where it met her thigh.

"Hungry for it?"

"Yes!"

He licked his way up the inside of her thigh, spreading her stance wider with palms at her ankles. "I need you all wide open for me. I want all of you right here."

She made an inarticulate sound into the mattress. Her muscles jumped as he nuzzled her open.

"Nervous?" He licked against her clit a few times.

"Less so now," she said.

He smiled and went back to it. There was something about going down on a woman from this angle. Totally open and vulnerable, all that slick, sweet pussy where he could touch and taste. That she offered herself that way only made him want her more.

The burn of her blush was even hotter against the cool of her comforter where she'd buried her face.

It wasn't like no one had ever gone down on her before. Hell, Asa had gone down on her before! But this...She'd never actually had it like this. Totally exposed to him.

He'd told her to trust him and she'd said she did. So she let go and enjoyed it. Let go and fell into how good it was, how he made her feel with those work-rough palms holding her thighs wide open.

He took what he wanted and she gave it to him. Loved it that he wanted her so much, and when she came she'd been so into it that she didn't realize he'd stopped and was thrusting his cock into her until he reached the hilt.

"More. Please. Please."

He gathered her hair and yanked, pulling her back as he leaned close. "I'm here." He flexed his hips, getting so impossibly deep she made a sound she didn't recognize.

"So hot. I can feel you through the latex."

He snarled things in her ear. Dirty things. Sweet things. He fucked her with his words as easily and skillfully as he did with the cock inside her body.

He surrounded her, molding his body to hers; the sheer size of him held her, stole her breath.

She hadn't really even stopped coming, and this time a rolling aftershock orgasm hit her.

He cursed. "Jesus. What's going on, beautiful? Hm? I want to do it again because you feel so good."

But she was caught in the feedback loop of it. Snagged in the sticky-sweet pleasure of that state, post–multiple orgasms, where everything he did felt amazing.

He sped, fucking her so deep and so hard that each time he slammed home she saw stars against the closed lids of her eyes.

He held her hair tight enough to sting. Everything in her wanted him to come. Wanted to make him feel so good he couldn't do anything else but climax. Wanted to shake his control.

She squeezed her inner muscles and he slapped her ass hard enough to send that crack through the room and a flash of heat through her.

He growled and she pushed back at him. He sped again, harder and harder, her nipples abrading the comforter beneath her. She dug into the bedding for purchase but found none as he pinned her to the bed and came on a strangled whisper of her name.

"I yield," she wheezed, and after a few seconds he remembered his order right before things went naked and sweaty, and laughed.

*   *   *

"Do you have a few minutes?" Asa came into the living room the following day. She'd tucked up on his couch, near the windows, to steal some time to read and enjoy the quiet.

"Dude, my vagina is not magic. If you want some, you have to pick a different place."

He burst out laughing and then someone else walked into the room. Mick. Jesus.

"Thanks for letting me know someone was here." She shot a look at Asa.

He put his hands out defensively. "I didn't know you were going to say that!"

Annoyed, she rolled her eyes and latched her gaze on to Mick. "Why would I give you, or *him*, a few minutes?"

Asa made a sound. He tried not to, she'd give him that. But he made it anyway. Pissy that she'd be mad he essentially dumped his friend on her with no warning and now she'd said all that in his presence and he could use it to hurt her, again.

Mick took a breath. "I owe you an apology. You don't owe me anything at all. I'd very much appreciate it if you'd give me a few minutes of your time."

"Hmph." She put her book aside and tipped her chin at a chair she was sure he'd sat in dozens of times.

"I was really rude to you. It wasn't just inexcusable because I have better manners than that, but also because you're with my brother. I don't normally act like that to women."

"What's your problem then?"

Asa shrugged at Mick. "See? I told you."

Ugh, all this secret brotherhood stuff might be more maddening than she'd originally considered. Had Asa debriefed Mick on her?

"Did you, Asa? Did you give him a primer on how to handle me?"

Mick tried to stifle a smile. PJ shouldn't be that annoyed. Asa'd fucked her into a nice, calm space. She'd stolen some leisure time to read and relax. He'd even made her breakfast to coax her to his house since he'd slept at her apartment. It had been a particularly lovely morning so far.

But she was annoyed nonetheless.

"I did not." Asa frowned. "I told him you had a temper and to watch out. From an *admiration* standpoint, I should add."

"Listen, you." She gave them both a look. "*Both* of you. I don't normally have a temper if people don't go out of their way to agitate me. You both get a motherfucking A plus. God."

Mick burst out laughing. "Please say you forgive me so we can be best friends."

"I have a best friend already. She saw you both in action, so if you think *I'm* hard to deal with, wait till you see *her* again."

"My problem was that I'd been gone a long time and I came back and saw you in a place I didn't know you deserved. But instead of listening to Asa and Duke, who told me you did, I was petty and defensive. You didn't need that. I do want to get to know you, and I hope you'll give me a chance to do that. I'm not an asshole. Not most of the time."

"If you are, you'll get a lot more of me than you did last night. You get me?"

He took her hand and kissed it. "Damn, it really is too bad Asa found you first."

"Hands off." Asa frowned some more. He had a line between his eyes, clearly from all the alpha-male scowling he did. Good thing for him it only made him more handsome.

"Shall I leave the two of you alone to work this out?" She lifted a brow at Asa.

He simply moved to her, picked her up, sat, and put her in his lap. Which she allowed because it was hot.

"Stop." He kissed her.

She would have told him to make her, but he might have, and

it would have been embarrassing to do in front of Mick because her vagina did not care at all that Asa was a bossy dude who'd made her very sore from all his attentions over the last twelve hours or so.

She narrowed her gaze at him and he hugged her tight. "I think we should go to lunch. Mick will pay, since he's been an asshole." Asa said all this smugly, like he'd neatly packaged all this silliness up and was ready to move on.

"I have a job." PJ peered at the clock on the wall. "In three hours."

"Perfect. We'll go to lunch and I'll drop you off and be back to get you later. Don't forget we're going out for a ride tonight."

"We'll go to lunch, but I'll drive."

He looked like he was going to argue, so she put a finger over his lips. "No. I said what I was going to do. You're gorgeous and I adore you, but you need to hear that answer and not argue."

He frowned at her extra hard and she kissed him quickly, getting up. "I'll be back out in a few minutes."

CHAPTER
Fifteen

PJ parked her work truck and headed into the building. This was a newish contact for her. The client had actually looked her up and asked if she'd be willing to meet with him at the restoration shop where his Chevy was being worked on.

Working with new people was a hugely important thing. Sure, she had a lot of clients up in the Seattle area, but down in southwest Washington she didn't know too many people outside the tire world.

This shop was newer, and though she'd called to ask Julie to look them up, they didn't do any business with Colman, which could be a huge gift or a terrible problem. Either way, there was no knowing until she went inside.

The place wasn't as magnificent as Twisted Steel, but really, she'd been in a lot of garages and shops and very few of them were. It was a good-sized operation, though, which was encouraging.

"Hi there. I'm PJ Colman. I'm supposed to meet with one of your rebuild clients today," she said to one of the guys inside, giving him the client's name. They didn't seem to have a receptionist or an office manager, at least not there right then.

"The owner is right in that office there." He pointed and she headed in that direction after thanking him.

She tapped on the door and the guy inside motioned for her to come in.

"Can I help you, sweetie?" he asked, and she shoved down her impulse to curl her lip. *Sweetie?* She sensed this flavor was misogynist with that tone. She bet he didn't like icky girls in his sandbox.

But this was a job and she was a business owner now. Maybe he called everyone pet names. Maybe he'd grow on her. Maybe he was a total tool. She might as well try to make the best of this. It wasn't the first time she'd been patronized, and it wouldn't be the last.

Her smile went cooler as she stood taller. "I'm PJ Colman. I do custom paint. Joe asked me to come down to talk with you two about some options for his Chevy."

He looked her up and down without speaking until she crossed her arms and glared.

"Is he here?"

He raked his gaze over her body again, lingering on her boobs. "He just called. He's running a little late. You're not what I expected. Or maybe exactly what I expected."

She was still trying to remain professional and aloof, but the longer he acted this way the harder that got.

"I'll wait until he arrives then."

He stood, following her out into the open shop area. "Don't you want to know what I expected?"

Sighing, PJ turned and looked him up and down slowly like he had done to her. Only she was dismissive. "Did you have something to say?" She peered at his work shirt. "Gary. I assume that's your name, but these days, one never knows if it's a work shirt or a fashion statement." She gave him one last opportunity to prove he was actually a good guy, or at the very least that he wasn't going to be a nightmare to deal with.

"Just that I expected you to be some big-titted blonde who

couldn't tie her own shoes. You appear to be basically competent and not overly whorish."

"That's a relief. I decided to wear my overly whorish shirt tomorrow."

"You got this job because you're riding Asa Barrons's dick. Look at you." Distaste ruled his features.

He looked upset. *Him*. Like he hadn't just called her a whore. Yep, woman hater. She was done here. There was no way to deal with guys like him. You couldn't explain anything to them or even expect that they'd remain civil and professional. He'd be a problem the whole time.

"I got this job because a customer paying *you* a great deal of money to restore his car saw some of my work and called to hire me. However, I won't be working through this shop, so I'll let him know that."

She turned to leave and he got in front of her, his face very close. "You think you can threaten me? I don't care who you are, little girl, you don't have the stones to threaten me."

That's when the guy who had pointed her to Gary's office when she first arrived rushed over and got between them. "Dude. Chill out."

Gary snarled around the guy's body, "Fucking bitch."

"That's Ms. Fucking Bitch to you." PJ was surprised she didn't stutter the words because she wanted to shake.

The mechanic who'd gotten between them opened the door for her. "I'm sorry about that. Are you all right? Let me walk you to your truck."

She wasn't. She needed to be away from there when it came so she could pull over out of their view.

"Please, just leave me alone. I need you to back up and let me do this."

She didn't even look his way as she found her keys and hit the alarm to unlock her truck.

"I'd say he didn't mean it, but he's an asshole. I'm sorry that happened to you." He said it from a distance, giving her the space she'd asked for.

She opened her door and finally looked at him. "Thanks for getting in between us."

"Listen. If you decide to press charges, my name is Pete. The cops can talk to me. I saw most of it." He ducked his head and went back inside, and she managed to get three freeway off-ramps away before she had to pull into a strip mall parking lot and let the shaking take over.

Duke crouched next to the spot Asa measured the gap where the doorframe on the old Ford had been bent. "Got a second?"

Asa frowned but nodded. They headed to grab some coffee. "What's going on?"

"You know how that guy called here asking for information about PJ?"

It happened from time to time. They got calls asking who did the upholstery, paint, whatever. Usually they shared the details. Their world ran on word of mouth, so if you referred someone one time, the next year someone referred your business.

"No. I mean, I know it happens, but not all the particulars. Is this about the place she was supposed to go this morning? She got up at five to be down there in time." He wasn't panicked. Yet. If it had been urgent Duke would have spit it out already.

"That same guy, the client. He called and told me what happened when she was there."

Asa's mind went very still. He knew he wasn't going to like what Duke was about to say.

"She called him about three hours ago and told him she wasn't going to be able to work with that shop anymore, but if he wanted her to do the paint work outside of that, or through another shop, to let him know. He said she was very calm but it was weird.

Then he got to the shop and one of the mechanics told him what happened."

Duke relayed what he'd heard Gary Weston, the owner of the shop, had said and done to PJ. In full view of his employees and customers. And that the mechanic had to get between Asa's woman and a guy Asa remembered as nearly as big as he was. Someone was going to be very, very sorry.

"*The fuck?* For what?"

"I don't know, man. Joe, the client, he felt awful. Said he tried to call her cell after he found out what happened, but she has it on voicemail. She was so nice he wanted to be sure she was all right."

Asa saw red as he paced, pulling his phone from his pocket. Her number went straight to voicemail, so he texted her, but she didn't reply.

"Why didn't she tell me?"

Duke just looked at him for long moments before deciding to take pity on Asa. "Because she likes to do things herself. Because she's upset and she knows if she comes to you like that you'll be even more keen to kick Weston's ass."

"I warned her she wasn't ready for what I was. Guess she'll have to deal with it." She was his. *His* in an old-school way. To protect and cherish and take care of.

"I'm going to give you some advice. I know you haven't asked for it, but you need it anyway." Duke leaned back, settling in for what Asa thought of as a dude lecture.

But he always had something thoughtful to say, so Asa tried to rein in his impatience at not hearing from PJ yet and focus on Duke. "What?"

"It's a good thing you've saved my ass a dozen times, or I'd kick yours for being such a shithead. You two have something major and it's good for you. It's like she puts you in a more Zen place or what have you. She's serious about cars and this is important to her. If she sees your response as interference, you're going to do some damage."

"Are you telling me I can't punch that asshole Gary?"

Duke laughed, but it wasn't his good-natured dude laugh. This one was darker. This one was the laugh of the guy who brawled and raced just as hard as Asa. Once he got riled, Duke was wicked dangerous.

"Hell no, I'm not saying that. You should absolutely punch him in his face. But separate it from PJ's Custom Designs and Twisted Steel versus his shop. Make it about Asa and Gary."

Asa paused, pushing a breath out and then dragging one in. His control went back into place, but when it came to PJ there seemed to be a whole new set of rules. Entirely new ways to seriously dig on this woman who was quickly taking up a very integral part of his life.

PJ sat in her truck for a bit before she went inside Twisted Steel. What happened back at the shop down south was upsetting and all, but she had to keep moving or she would dwell. She knew herself well enough to understand that. Luckily she had work to do to keep busy.

Asa had texted her several times and had left a few voicemails. She'd needed the drive back up to Seattle and then a milkshake before she'd sent him a text saying she was on her way back to the shop and that she was fine.

And she was better once she'd opened the side door and taken in the smell, the sound of Van Halen's "Runnin' with the Devil" blaring as Duke worked on a motorcycle off to her right, the way the place soared in every direction, full of hot dudes fixing stuff.

This had become a place she loved to be. A place that felt more like home to her than Colman ever had. Some of the guys had held her at a distance at first. She was young. Strike one. She was pretty. Strike two. She was from a well-known family, which also made her suspect. And then she went and started dating Asa.

If she'd been thinking with her business sense instead of her pussy, she probably would have held him off for at least another year so she could establish herself first.

Slowly but surely, though, she'd earned their respect. It wasn't perfect. She knew she had a lot of work to do before they'd accept her totally. And when they did, it would be as PJ and not that young hottie the boss was banging.

Lottie saw PJ approaching and waved. "Hey. You have some receipts in your basket. I deposited some money. We got paid from a few customers this week."

"Excellent."

"Asa's been looking for you. He just went into his office to make a call."

As much as PJ just wanted to go out and finish the rear fender she'd started yesterday, she knew if she did, it would only make things worse.

"Okay. I'll go grab some coffee and by the time I'm ready he'll maybe be off the phone."

"There's pizza in the fridge in the break room. We had it for lunch. There's a lot left if you want some."

She could have said no, but why would she turn that down? "Cool. I'll be back shortly."

He stalked into the room as she was sliding the pizza box back into the fridge. He didn't stop at the doorway, or even just a few feet away. He didn't stop until he'd pulled her to him gently.

"I was worried about you." He kissed her forehead. "You've had your phone off for hours. You can't just not call me back when something happens like that."

"I didn't even think you'd know. I didn't think *anyone* would know. It happened, I left. After I called my client I turned off my phone and came back up here. How did you find out?"

"Not from you."

She blinked at him, trying to remember he was worried and hadn't been able to connect with her. "This is not my favorite thing."

She stepped back and he frowned, glowering at her for a moment.

"Are you really going to be mad at me? *At me?*"

He shook his head, the glower softening. "I'm sorry. I was worried and you didn't call me back. You were out there and I wanted to talk. I'm selfish, I know." He pulled a chair out at the table. "Sit. Please. Eat your pizza. I'm getting coffee, you want something?"

She sat, keeping an eye on him. "What are you up to?"

He brought his coffee over, topping up hers as well. "I'm not up to anything. I just want to know what happened."

Instead of moving across from her, he chose the place next to her and proceeded to take up all the oxygen.

Leaning against him for long moments, she moved to her coffee again before finishing her pizza. And then she told him what happened.

She knew he was pissed. It radiated from him. "Are you mad?"

"I don't think 'mad' is a word that applies here, PJ. But first, are you all right? Do you need to see a doctor or file a police report? What do you need?"

He was trying really hard to get all that alpha male under control, and it was actually exactly what she needed.

"He didn't hit me or anything. He just got in my face and he was so vicious. I don't get it. I've never met the guy. I was polite. The customer called me, not the other way around."

"Can't imagine it was very pleasant to have a man a foot taller than you scream in your face that you're a whore. *I'm* upset and it didn't even happen to me."

"I need to get over it. This shit happens."

He craned his neck so he could see into her face. "This has happened before?"

"I can honestly say no one has gotten in my face in the middle of a business and screamed I was a whore who got a job because I was riding someone's dick."

His eyes went hard and she regretted saying that out loud. On one hand, it was nice to feel defended and that what had happened was outrageous and awful. On the other, she didn't want to stir this situation up. This was a place her personal and professional lives bled into one another.

"But do I get judged because of my gender or my age? Yes. Every day. And not just by strangers. My dad does it."

Another frown; this time PJ knew it was partially in relation to the mention of her father. "I'm not buying that *you* need to get over someone else's bullshit. I don't know what his problem is. I've spent about fifteen minutes in person with the guy. Until today I didn't have any beef with him."

"Apparently he's been thinking a lot about your dick and who rides it."

He put his arm around her shoulders. "I'm sorry you went through that. And I'm sorry you didn't feel like you could call me."

"I didn't call anyone but the client to say I wasn't going to be at the meeting and that I was available if he went elsewhere or wanted me to do the work at a different shop."

"I know people have failed you in your life. I'm not that guy."

His tone was so vehement she knew there was a story there. It wasn't the time or place to dig any deeper, but it underlined how much she wanted to know him, even if he was overwhelming and bossy.

"What are your plans tonight?" He finished his coffee.

"I'm having dinner with my mom and sister. I should be done by nine or so."

"Come to my house after? Spend the night."

She stood, balling up her napkin and washing out her cup and putting it in the small dishwasher. "If you're sure. Text me if you want me to bring anything special with me."

They parted at the bottom of the steps, she heading out to the paint bay and he back to work on the front end of the Dodge they were supposed to deliver in three weeks.

CHAPTER
Sixteen

B is on Main in Bellevue was a place her mom and sister went to a lot. PJ enjoyed it and certainly loved the food, so she was all too happy to accept the invite, which was more like a pointed order.

PJ hugged her mother and gave her a kiss on the cheek after sliding her bag under the table.

Lenore Colman had been raised to be someone's wife. And she did a great job. She'd aged gracefully. She'd had little things done here and there, PJ knew that much, but it was deft and her mother pretended it never happened. As PJ and Julie felt it was their mother's business, they said nothing.

Her home was beautiful. Tasteful. If you stayed in her guest room you'd find a basket with pretty soaps, maybe a sleep mask and some snacks she remembered you liked from the last time she saw you.

Her parties were perfection. She knew how to have you over to eat, no matter the reason or situation. Sometimes she made PJ feel like an utter failure because no matter how hard she tried, she'd never measure up.

"Champagne cocktail?" Julie asked.

"Yes, please." The server left to go handle that as PJ looked back from her menu to her mom and sister. "You both look great. How are things?"

Her mother smiled. "Tell me about *you*. Or should I say, tell me about Asa. Honestly, why you think I wouldn't have heard about this boy, I don't know. But I saw a picture of the two of you. He's quite fierce looking, but Julie says he's very sweet."

"How did you see a picture of us?" When had that happened? *How* had that happened?

"You put it on your whatsits? On the Internet. You post pictures of your work too. I like to look at what you do. It's very impressive. You had on a lovely red dress and he had on a black shirt that buttoned up. Does he really have a ring in his nose like a bull?"

PJ burst out laughing. "He does have a piercing there, yes. Not a ring, a horseshoe of sorts." She brought her phone out of her bag, showing her mother some pictures of them.

"It's actually a little handsome on him." Their mother's nervous laugh and blush made Julie grin across the table at PJ.

Julie looked to their mother. "It's all a front. He's scary on the outside, but quite sweet and charming. A dry sense of humor. A sign of intelligence."

PJ nodded. "He's quiet and very intense. He listens more than he talks. Definitely smart."

Her mom nodded, clearly approving. "Your father says your young man owns a custom-build shop."

"He and his friend Duke co-own it, yes. Twisted Steel. He does the bodywork and some machining. He's thirty-seven. I just wanted to tell you that myself. It seems to scandalize some people. It hasn't really mattered between him and me, though it took me months to get him to ask me out because he thought I was too young for him."

"I think in some circumstances you might be too young for

someone. But you're a Colman and you went after what you wanted until you got it. Well done, darling."

Her mom gave really good compliments sometimes.

Happy and feeling very loved, PJ raised her glass to her mother. "Thank you, Mom."

"You should invite him to dinner."

Even Lenore Colman might not be able to pull off *that* dinner.

"How about we all meet somewhere instead? That way you can visit with him and someone else can do the cooking. You and Dad like Salty's, so let's go there." PJ had no plans to bring Asa into that house. Not the first time he met her parents. A restaurant was a public place. Her father would behave, and if it was awful it would be easier to escape.

"All right. I'll set it up and give you a call about it." Lenore sat back, satisfied, and it occurred to PJ all too late that her mother had set that trap rather expertly.

Well played.

That handled, her mother moved to the next issue on her list. "Are you going to speak to your father any time soon, Penelope?"

"I've seen him once since I left. Which was two months ago at this point. I've left him messages. I've sent him e-mails. I don't know what else I'm supposed to do except to hear him telling me he doesn't want to talk."

"You're saying you've left more than one message for him?"

"Yes. I've left messages for him at work and on his cell phone. I've e-mailed him three times." She shrugged and tried to ignore the hurt that he'd simply pretended like that part of the situation did not exist.

They'd all had brunch together when Jay's birthday had rolled around. Her father had been mildly disapproving and had avoided everything but brief interactions. Certainly nothing about why she'd left Colman or how she was doing out on her own.

Her mother's mouth hardened briefly. PJ and Julie shared a look.

Their mother hadn't been told that detail, though why her father thought he could hide it from her was beyond PJ's understanding.

"I left because what I wanted to do wasn't going to be possible at Colman. I tried to make it happen there, but Dad and Fee won't listen and Jay is going to do whatever Fee says because he has Dad's ear. I know you don't want to hear it, but it's true."

"You'll understand better when you're older. Your father needs you to take over. You and your siblings. You have to make sacrifices for family."

"Sacrifices? Mom, what have you been told?" They'd carefully stepped around the situation because PJ hadn't wanted to put her mom in the middle. But the more they spoke, the clearer it became that their mother hadn't been told everything.

"Why don't you tell me? Start from the beginning."

So PJ did. She started with the first jobs painting the Colman logos on the cars they sponsored, and went right up through the meeting where she'd presented her plan and had it shot down.

"I'm looking at three different places right now to open my shop. I'm paying my bills. I have new clients lining up. All this attention and a lot of this money could be going to Colman. But it isn't, because I'm supposed to just sell tires as my place in the company because that's what Fee says."

"Your uncle is a damned fool. Your dad and I are going to speak about this. I must have missed it when he explained it all to me. But it's not all right with me to have my children estranged from their family and from the business they'll carry into the next generation." Her mother's expression was enough to make PJ *almost* feel bad for her father.

Her mom patted her hand. "Leave this to me. Your uncle is a pain, but he can be gotten around."

"Just ask all his ex-wives," Julie muttered.

Their mom gasped and then she laughed, blushing. "You two."

PJ left an hour later feeling a lot better than she had when she'd shown up.

She knocked on Asa's door just before nine and he opened up.

"Come in." He took her overnight bag as she passed. "Would you like a beer? I was just out on my deck drinking one."

"Yes, that sounds fantastic. I'll grab two since you have my bag."

Longnecks dangling between her fingers, she followed him up to his room.

"How was dinner with your mom and sister?"

"It was all right, actually. My dad had lied to my mom about the way I left and the reasons for it."

"How did she react when she found out?" Asa asked.

"She was surprised and upset. I'm always making waves, so I guess I figured her silence on the matter wasn't that unusual. But she didn't know."

These fucking people made him want to punch things. "Yeah, so I think for this discussion you need to be naked and in the bedroom."

"What?"

Asa smiled down at her, pausing a moment before he buried his fist in her hair and positioned that sweet, sweet mouth of hers just how he wanted it. After he'd kissed the tension out of her spine, he let go.

"That's better. Now, naked and in bed."

She got undressed and he took his time admiring her body. The curves of her, the lotus on her back, tonight a pink streak at her temple that matched the nail polish she wore.

So beautiful.

He got in bed and she snuggled up next to him. He clinked his beer to hers. "Now. Tell me about your family."

"Will you tell me about yours?"

Asa brushed the pad of his thumb over the swell of her bottom lip and she sucked it into her mouth, biting him and then licking as she let go.

"Stop changing the subject."

"I'm not." She grinned. "Okay, so I was a little. But I want to know more about you."

"That's fair." He kissed her quickly before settling back. "So you're close enough with your mom to have dinner with her and Julie. But she hadn't actually spoken *to* you about how and why you left Colman? You've talked to her since then, right? It's been two months."

He had to have heard wrong.

"There's a lot of not talking about it in my family. It makes them uncomfortable when I confront them."

"I don't get it. Their youngest daughter actually walked out on the family business because she was told to be quiet and do what she was told, and neither of them has spoken to you about this? Or you to them?"

"I tried!"

Asa heard the unshed tears in her voice.

Putting his beer aside, he pulled her into his lap. "I'm sorry. I don't want to upset you."

"It is what it is. I need to accept that my dad's never going to connect with me. Not on any level. I've known it since I was about fourteen, but I kept lying to myself. Hoping something would change. Trying to be exactly what he wanted, and when that didn't work, I struck out on my own and I proved myself. I don't expect him to make me CEO or anything like that. I don't have the experience or education to do it. I just wanted to do custom paint, and I proved I could make a profit. My grandpa would have been proud. Why can't he?"

"You were close to Howie then?"

She smiled as she tucked herself into his body.

"Yes. He was my best friend when I was little. He'd show up at our house and take us out for a drive. Or he'd steal us all away for a week at their house. Shawn and I were closest with him and my grandmother."

"Was he close with your dad and your uncle?"

"No. I was a kid, so I don't think I got all the nuances in their relationship. But my grandpa was a firecracker. He loved to laugh. He loved to have fun. He wanted to wring the absolute most out of life, and my father is not like that at all."

"Kids rebel. Maybe being straitlaced is your dad's way of giving the finger to his parents."

"Maybe. My uncle is a jerk and that's his rebellion?"

He held her a little tighter. "Some people are just jerks. He might be one."

"Now you."

"You'll meet my mom soon enough. She knows about you and she'll want me to bring you over. She's . . . most people love her. I told you my youngest sister lives up here too."

"You have another sister?"

"Yes, she's a professor at a small private college. First person in our family to go to college and she just kept going and going." He grinned and PJ tipped her head back to look at him.

Part of the reason he was so displeased with her family was how hard his mother had struggled just to get her child back, all while Howard Jr. worked to make his daughter feel it was rocking the boat just to talk about things.

"You grew up in Texas, so how did you end up in Seattle?"

"I have some family up here." His father's brother, one who'd helped Pat try to get Asa back. "When I got out of the army, my uncle told me I could crash in his guest room if I needed a place to land. Then Duke joined me out here and the rest you know."

She gave him a look. "I don't think so. That story was pretty scant on details. You didn't tell me anything about your dad. But I'll let you tell me the rest when you're ready. Today was really shitty, so you should help me forget it."

Clever that she'd let him have the space around the story of his father while also reminding him she wanted to know. She just seemed to intuit how best to coax him closer to her, make him yearn to share stuff he rarely talked about.

They both needed the sweat of sex to get rid of the day. They'd deal with everything else tomorrow. He also wanted to connect with her, to regain that intimacy they'd lost when he'd handled that business about her morning with her at Twisted Steel.

"How about this? Why don't I help you remember it instead? Just as the day I gave you the best orgasms you've ever had."

She gave him a coy look from under her lashes. "If you're sure. I mean. For science and all I guess we should."

Yes, he was a taciturn man. He liked to listen more than he spoke. But he loved to laugh. With her it was more than that. She didn't just make him laugh; she teased him. She made him happy in ways he hadn't realized were possible.

"It's handy that you're always game."

"For science, Asa. How could I turn my back on that?"

"Very brave of you. Face me. I want you to know who brings you pleasure."

She did as he'd told her to. "I don't need to be looking at your face to remember you make me feel good."

"I like that." He kissed her, tasting her in little nips. "But I still want you to do what I told you."

Her breath caught and he smiled.

"Today I made it about me instead of you when you came into Twisted Steel. Don't misunderstand me, I'm pissed off. But not at you. And you deserved to be put before how I felt or what I wanted to do."

When Asa was twenty-two, he'd had to take his medical files

and a bunch of things his mother had tucked away in an attic. His old report cards had been inside. Even from the time he'd lived with his grandparents. And a report from some counselor he'd seen in junior high.

Due to Asa's unusual circumstances as a young child— being taken from his mother and forced to live with a family that saw him as a physical manifestation of sin and the concomitant physical and emotional abuse he experienced until reunited with his mother at seven years of age— he has manifested difficulty in forming deep attachments and this may hinder his ability to lead a successful life as an adult.

He'd confronted his mother about it, asked her why she hadn't ever told him. And she'd said, "It doesn't matter what that counselor said. You do have trouble getting close to people. But once you do, you'd die for those people. And there's not a goddamn thing wrong with that, Asa."

He hadn't expected PJ. She'd floated into his life and nothing had been the same since. But when he'd heard that story from Duke and then watched her face as she talked about it, he knew for certain PJ was one of those people he'd die for.

Which meant he had to take better care of her.

She cupped his cheeks and kissed him. "We're good."

"Okay then." He slid his palm up her belly, up the valley between her breasts. Up to cup her throat as he pulled her in to take her lips. He kissed and kissed her until she was squirming against him, wanting more.

Asa groaned into her mouth, "You're so wet, so hot. It's so good." Her skin pebbled and he nipped her bottom lip. "On your back."

Slowly, as if she were just a little tipsy, she moved off his lap and settled, her back against the pillows.

"Normally I'd order you to make yourself come. But right at this moment *I* want to make you come."

Her smile was patient as she waited. That would change, though. She'd get less patient the longer he paused. It was one of his favorite things about her. He licked around her knee, watching her nipples draw tighter and get darker.

"Hands over your head." He loved the way that position accentuated the arch of her back, the beauty of her curves. The cant of her hips that opened her up perfectly to his mouth as he slid his lips over her pussy and then parted her with this thumbs, exposing her clit to his tongue.

The sound she made seemed to slice through him, letting all that yearning he felt for her spill out.

The span of his hands as they lay on her thighs, holding them wide for his mouth, made her nearly as breathless as whatever he was doing with his tongue.

He was so fucking big. In every way. It rendered her a little giddy each time he touched her. Even when he was rough or ordered her around, he never used his size against her.

Even today, when she knew he was really angry, she never felt unsafe with him. It made her feel . . . cherished. Adored.

One of his hands slid up her belly to her nipple. She blew out a breath when he pinched just shy of pain and then backed off.

She hummed at the heat sliding all through her. He was just *so good* at eating pussy, she didn't know what to do with herself other than let him do whatever.

He nuzzled her clit until she was right on the very edge of climax and then paused, making her growl her dismay.

"Ah-ah-ah. I'll let you come when I'm ready. I like to tease you until you get really demanding."

She craned her neck to look at him better, without moving her hands, of course. He'd totally stopped fucking her the first time she moved when he'd told her not to. That had sucked. But only for about five minutes, because he wanted to come too.

His smile told her he knew she'd stopped herself from moving because she remembered that.

He got back to it, sliding his tongue deep and then swirling it up to her clit, circling over and over until she came so hard she was a mass of twitching muscles and warm, pleasured female.

He rolled her over to her belly, kissing her shoulder as he did. "I liked that," she mumbled.

He rustled in the nightstand and she smiled, coming out of her stupor a little as she heard the cap of the lube click open after the crinkle of a condom wrapper.

"Mmm." It seemed like that sound was better than any word she could have said. And since he'd left her sort of dopey postclimax, she'd happily leave it at that.

Then the lube, cool and slick, spread over her asshole and she made a markedly *less* enthusiastic sound. She'd withhold judgment to see what he planned to do with all that lube. Fingers, maybe. Cock? Nope.

He moved closer, pulling her hips up, also a very good sign. Until he circled the head of his cock around her asshole. This time her sound was a full-on *no thank you* grunt.

Asa, being Asa, must have taken that as a challenge, because he pressed in and as she'd remembered, it *hurt*, and not in a good way.

She made another sound, *damn the man*, and scrambled up the bed to her knees, facing him. "I'm on the train to nopetown with that."

"I take it you object?" He smirked. *Smirked.* And it worked on him. He was delightfully mussed up. His hair was down and it managed to tumble over one of his eyes and make him look ridiculously hot.

Still, she needed him to know she didn't answer knocks at her back door. "Asa, when it comes to butt sex, my philosophy is this." She indicated her body, and his attention followed, his gaze blurring. " 'All these worlds are yours except Europa.' " She pointed to her ass. " 'Attempt no landing there.' "

He'd never in his life had a romantic partner quote *any* book to him while fucking, much less use a science-fiction novel quote to tell him no thanks to ass fucking.

It was just such a PJ thing that all he could do was burst out laughing, pulling her close. "There's nothing else I'd rather be doing right this moment."

It was her turn to laugh. "Nothing? Me saying no to anal is so amusing?"

He nodded, kissing her. "Everything you do is something I'm interested in. That you quote Arthur C. Clarke underlines my very good taste."

He wasn't so hot to fuck her ass that he was actually disappointed. He liked what he liked, and he had to allow her to feel the same.

"Joke time is over. Hands and knees. I'm all suited up, let's not waste a condom."

With a lazy smile, she complied, thrusting her ass out the way she knew he liked. He petted down her sides and over the curves of her hips, brushed kisses down the long line of her spine as he pushed into her balls-deep with a groan.

This was what he was meant to do. Exactly who he was meant to be with.

He let the pleasure build nice and slow. Or rather he did for several minutes, until he couldn't stop going deeper and harder. She battered his control on every single level.

His fingertips dug into flesh and muscle at her hips as he held her, thrusting to the hilt over and over. The need to roll around in her, to rut and fuck, to bite and lick and mark forever crawled over his skin as he reached up with his right hand to grab a fistful of her hair, hauling her back as he pushed forward.

"Going to be soon. Make yourself come."

There was no doubt she'd obey him, so he knew that first clasp of her inner walls was coming. He cursed as it did, that rippling squeeze that told him she was stroking her clit like he told her to.

Yes. *His.*

He lost himself in her. In the labyrinth of her beauty and sensuality, of the way she felt around him, and when she came in a hot rush, her body squeezing his cock, she pulled him in with her. He came so hard his teeth tingled, the sweat on his thighs sliding against the sweat on hers.

He pulled out and she stretched, watching him walk into the bathroom, then grinned as he returned her way.

PJ handed him a beer. "Let's finish these so we can move toward round two."

She truly was perfect.

CHAPTER
Seventeen

Come out to dinner with me and my friends tonight."

PJ looked up from the stencils she'd just laid down for the first layer of flames on the hood of the '58 Ford Fairlane she'd been working on for the last day or so.

Even after eight months of knowing him, each time she caught sight of Asa it made PJ's breath hitch. It didn't seem to matter that they spent at least five days a week together since that night at the Ditch a little over a month before.

He still managed to get her worked up just by looking at her. Or really, if she was being honest, he still managed to get her worked up just by looking at *PJ*.

Even when they were both busy they'd find the time for a meal or a cup of coffee. It gave him the opportunity to glower at her if he thought she wasn't taking care of herself. She found the kinds of juice she liked in the fridge at Twisted Steel, and there was never a shortage of chocolate-dipped-in-dark-chocolate ice cream bars in the cooler.

He didn't make a big deal out of it, but he did the same thing at his house. Little touches here and there that made it clear he'd been thinking of her comfort or pleasure when he was grocery shopping or whatever.

The best, most intense thing was the way he gave her all his attention, even when they were just doing something simple.

Asa didn't pay attention to too many things. It took a great deal to get him to stop thinking about fenders and engines. Most people and topics didn't get that full Asa-Barrons-is-listening-to-you-with-all-his-being look. It made her feel special.

And slowly but surely she'd become part of his circle. They'd watched her carefully at first, these guys who looked like hard cases but had squooshy insides and big hearts. They didn't know what to make of her, or of the way Asa had sort of claimed her and that was that.

By that point though, most of the guys at the shop talked with her or waved at her or included her in invitations for Asa. Part of it had been cars. Their shared language, she supposed. Duke had been great, and even Mick had loosened up.

PJ stood tall, stretching her arms above her head to loosen the knots from being bent over the tape-and-stencil application. Plus it made her boobs stick out and she never planned to miss a perfect opportunity to remind Asa what she brought to the table.

His eyes glazed over a moment and he smiled. "Naughty."

"Will you discipline me?" She caught her bottom lip between her teeth.

He moved very close but didn't touch her. "Funny you should mention that. I have some new toys. You should stay over after dinner tonight."

Her breath caught and he groaned.

"You just full-on flushed. Your pupils got big. That makes you wet, doesn't it? Trying something new?"

She nodded, trying to ignore the fact that just behind him, just outside the bay she worked in, there was a whole crew of guys doing their jobs too.

"Are you wondering what it could be?"

She nodded again.

"Good. I'll pick you up and we'll head over together. Sushi okay?"

"I'll meet you at your place. I'm going over to Audra's tomorrow, remember?" Her friend was having her wisdom teeth pulled in the afternoon and so PJ planned to spend the night there to keep her company.

He frowned, clearly unable to understand. It always seemed to confuse him when he couldn't get his way. As if the idea of anyone not just giving him exactly what he wanted was incomprehensible.

Amused by how adorable he was and how annoyed he'd be if he knew she was thinking about his adorableness, PJ gave him a mock pout. "We're at work or I'd pet your beard to soothe that frown away. Sushi is great. You get to drive from your house to the restaurant. That's good, right?"

"You do realize I know you're managing me, right?"

She laughed. "I should hope so. You'd be very stupid if you didn't. I have better taste than to date a stupid man. What time should I be at your place?"

"I'll leave here at six or so. We're supposed to meet up at seven thirty."

"All right. I'll see you later."

He gave her the super-hot Asa sex face. Every dirty thing he'd done to her and imagined doing in the future seemed to broadcast over his features, and it never failed to make her hot.

His smile told her he knew it too. "Come to my place with me now. I'll make you a sandwich. After."

She shook her head and took a step back. "Stop it, you. I have to get the orange down so it can dry. This is work. You can molest me later."

"I plan on it." He turned to go and she watched his very fine ass until he'd turned the corner.

*   *   *

PJ had been looking down, zipping her bag after she'd dropped her keys in it. She'd knocked on Asa's door, but when she finally straightened it wasn't Asa there, but a woman. A really pretty young woman.

"Uh..." PJ paused and the other woman smiled.

"Sorry! I'm Asa's sister, Courtney. Come in. He said to tell you he'd be back shortly."

PJ went inside and dropped her things on the bench in his front hall. "I'm PJ Colman. Is everything okay?"

"Our mom. She's been having trouble with one of her faucets. She doesn't need it right now, but it makes her happy to know he'd come over, and he likes to be needed."

Well, that was pretty freaking sweet.

"I'm glad everything is okay. He sent you over here? He could have just texted me."

"I was here when my mom called. I borrowed his tent and was returning it, so I said I'd stay and wait to tell you in person. Anyway, it gives me a chance to meet you."

"Oh. Well, hi. I'm glad to meet you too."

They settled in his kitchen.

"Can you believe this was actually a wall with a tiny window when Asa first bought the house?" His sister waved a hand at the wall of windows leading out to a deck spanning the entire length of the second floor.

"Why would someone do that?" The view was spectacular. Lake Washington glittered in the distance with the Cascades' white-tipped mountains farther beyond that.

"Right?" Courtney shook her head. "It was dark and it seemed way smaller too. Asa has a way of seeing right to the heart of things. He has a great instinct like that."

PJ grinned. "That was an awesome way to compliment and warn me at the same time. Bravo."

Courtney tipped her head back, laughing. "He said you were smart and funny as well as pretty. Come on then and let me keep poking into your life. I need to report back on you to my mom and sister. We're all dying for details."

"He must love that."

Courtney nodded. "Yes, of course. He's so serious all the time. Always was. He worked extra jobs so he could help my mom get us into a better place to live. Even when he enlisted, he sent nearly all his money home to us. But we're grown, my sister and me, and our mom is fine. He needs to lighten up in ways that don't include driving too fast."

"Ha. Don't hold your breath." Asa liked to live on the edge. Fast was like breathing to him.

"At least he has a thick skull. When he was a kid he was legendary for how crazy he was. We didn't have a lot, but our mom found the money and the parts and stuff so each one of us had a bike. Asa rode his off the top of the roof of the church. He rode it *off* things. *Into* things. There was a public pool we'd go to all summer long. He and his friends would sneak in at night and ride into the pool on their bikes and skateboards. Then it was dirt bikes. He broke his arm twice. Anyway, then he went into the army and we worried, but it gave him direction and some control. He's still crazy, but racing on a track is better than on a street."

"Safer too. Have you seen him out there?" When Courtney shook her head, PJ continued. "They have an emergency team at the track for every race. A medical team, fire suppression crew. They wear some protective gear." Not as much as she'd hoped, but she knew who Asa and his friends were. They'd be safe—within limits—but still push it as far as they could. "He's really good at it. And when he comes off the track, he's totally full of joy. It's worth the nervousness when I see that expression."

"He's so fearless when he's on wheels of any kind. But... I like the tone in your voice when you talk about what makes him happy." Courtney paused and then went back to the subject. "Mainly I've accepted it. Drives my mom crazy, but he tries to shield her from most of what he gets up to."

Ha! PJ bet.

"Anyway, so Asa says you're amazing with custom paint. He showed us some pictures. He's proud of you."

PJ blushed. "He is? Well, wow, that's nice to hear." It was sweet that he showed her off like that. There was an Asa very few people got to know. One who was soft and tender all while being very protective. It was something she yearned for. Each thing he shared, every moment they reached a new level of trust and he let her in a little further made her greedy for more.

"It's pretty cool that I get to do what I love. It pays my bills and that's nice too. I get to be around cars, also a plus. Asa tells me you're a dental assistant."

"I am. I just work down in Burien. Did he try to get you to switch dentists? He does that a lot. I'm sorry."

PJ laughed because he *had*. "I've had the same dentist since I was a kid. But I think it's so adorable that he does it to everyone. If people only knew."

"At my graduation he brought the biggest freaking bouquet of roses I've ever seen. And then he had to hold it the whole time and never complained." Courtney smiled as she shook her head. "He was very proud of me, and my sister too. I'd say something like his bark is worse than his bite, but that's not true. It's just that he has a very small intimate circle. He hasn't added a woman to it before. Which is why they never really hold on when he walks away." She stood, moving to the windows. "You're in it, though."

"I think so. Yes." It was why she wasn't really that bothered by the fact that their larger circle included a few women he'd slept with. He never looked at anyone the way he looked at her. And that was more than enough to keep any worries away.

"I really have to ask you something. Is Asa as big a pain as he seems like he'd be to date? He's so bossy. That must drive you nuts."

"He's actually pretty sweet. I mean, he glowers at anyone who looks at me sideways, but he doesn't get too bossy about anything that's important to me. Your mom did a good job with him. He's a gentleman."

Courtney looked dubious. "He gets into fistfights with his friends for recreation. Has he told you about that?"

PJ laughed. "He has, and that remains my reaction too. I'd rather get a new pair of shoes or a book. But he's handsome and charming and he runs over to his mom's house to fix her leaky faucets. I can't complain."

Asa's baby sister smiled like PJ had just won a blue ribbon.

"Asa and our mom have a really deep connection. She fought for him. Years of her life she fought for him and never gave up until he was back home. He adores her."

PJ swallowed. He hadn't told her that story yet. And while she was hungry for details about him, she wanted Asa to tell her. To share himself by choice.

So she shifted the topic to something else, really liking Courtney Barrons.

CHAPTER

Eighteen

There were already about ten people at the restaurant when PJ and Asa arrived. They liked this place and their group often came in on a weeknight to hang out.

Duke stood at the bar with Duane, one of Twisted Steel's mechanics, and when he saw them both he raised a hand in greeting.

"Asa." Duke tipped his chin before turning to PJ with a big teasing smile. "Delightful, de-lovely Penelope. Nice to see you both. Though one of you is nicer to see than the other. Just sayin'." He winked and Asa groaned.

Then Duane made a comment about Mustangs that had Asa sputtering.

PJ joined in for a while, as she had her own very strong feelings on the subject, until the argument finally got down to some ridiculously esoteric level and she kissed Asa's cheek, patted Duke's forearm, and wandered off.

Mick arrived and joined them at the bar for a while as people came and went.

By the time Asa looked up, PJ was off with Duke and some of the others at a table halfway across the restaurant, already eating, smiling and apparently having a good time.

He wanted to be having a good time with her too. Asa began to extricate himself from the discussion so he could head over to her.

"Where'd your hot blond girlfriend get to anyway?" Mick looked around, and then once he caught sight of PJ he headed over like Asa wasn't even there.

Asa followed. "For a guy who started out pretty much hating her, you sure have changed your tune."

"I've had the time to get to know her and realize how wrong I was. I probably began to fall for her when she flipped me off. You don't deserve all that youth and beauty, so I'm just hanging around waiting for her to figure it out. Then I'll sweep her off her feet and you can eat shit."

Asa flipped Mick off. "It's nice for you to have dreams you'll never achieve. You need to set the bar way lower, though."

Mick flipped him off in return, but his attention had already shifted back to PJ. He bumped her fist as he slid into the booth across from her.

"You're eating already?" Asa noted the little plates from the conveyor belt on the table in front of her.

She laughed like he was crazy. "Yes, of course! You were all high on Mustang talk so I came over here to have a drink and eat and let Duke charm me. Plus I was able to watch you from my seat. You're very sexy when you get worked up about cars."

Duke snorted. "Gross."

Asa shot Duke a look. "Then get up so I can sit there."

Duke moved a space over and Asa slid into the empty spot at her side. He grabbed some tuna and eel. She gave him the eye and he grinned. "Don't tell me these are all California rolls."

PJ sniffed, such a perfect haughty sound that he got hard.

"You can always have my share of eel. Just saying. I'll also have you know California rolls are delicious."

He laughed, leaning over to kiss her quickly.

"Don't mind him. Asa is a sushi purist. Like an evangelist," a female voice said.

Duke's expression shuttered as Asa turned to catch sight of his ex-wife, Ellen, watching PJ like a bird watches a mouse.

PJ still smiled as she took in the newcomer, but Ellen was going to be surprised her supposed mouse wasn't so mousy after all.

"I'm Ellen. You're Duke's baby sister?"

PJ laughed, grabbing a plate of California rolls and winking at Asa. "No. He just teases me like I am. I'm PJ."

Ellen slid in across from them and Asa put an arm around the back of PJ's seat.

"Ah. So you're PJ. My family runs a rebuild shop in Olympia. I saw your work the other day. Metallic blue Impala. Blew me and my dad away."

That surprised Asa. He'd expected a dig, but there was real warmth in Ellen's praise.

PJ beamed. "Thanks. I have to tell you, I was a little nervous about the final blue. It was the first time I'd tried for that exact shade. The client, you know him, right?"

Ellen laughed. "Yes. So it's okay to tell me he was a picky asshole and you were worried no matter how perfect you got that blue he'd complain."

He hadn't expected this at all. But PJ and Ellen seemed to get along famously from the first word. Duke still watched her carefully, as did Asa. It was only wise.

Their group settled in, taking up multiple tables at the conveyor belt. People moved from table to table to visit with one another, pausing to eat and have a drink and then move on to a new group. It pleased Asa to see PJ at ease with his friends as well.

Most of them were protective of her, which he liked. The women seemed to like her, which was another plus. She loved cars. They loved cars. It was a great foundation.

She was good on her own. She didn't need him to constantly

be at her side, though he liked to be. He hadn't been entirely sure what to expect, as he'd never seriously seen women in their circle to avoid any problems. Even during the short period he and Ellen were married, they hadn't really hung out with a group.

But this was good. Better than he'd imagined.

Now though, he was going to have to tell her about Ellen, which he hoped would be no big deal.

PJ leaned over and kissed his cheek. "Be back in a few." She excused herself and he watched her disappear into the back where the ladies' room was.

"She doesn't know, does she?" Ellen asked Asa.

He sighed. "I haven't told her, no. I wasn't expecting to see you here, and now it's going to be weird no matter how I bring it up."

"It's going to be weird anyway. Wait, does she not know *I'm* your ex-wife, or does she not know you were married at all?"

Asa scrubbed his hands over his face and Duke and Mick both groaned.

"Don't judge! It didn't come up. Why would I tell her something unpleasant when it doesn't matter anyway?" He shrugged at Ellen. "No offense."

"None taken." Ellen rolled her eyes. "But not everyone is nice. Some people in this crowd like to play mind games. Also, she's hot, so you know some guys are going to see this as a way to get around you."

Duke burst out laughing. "Don't sweat it, Ellen." He looked at Asa. "You have to tell her, but mainly because it would be hurtful for her to hear it elsewhere. No one is going to try to snag PJ. Everyone knows she's with you."

"Including PJ. She'd ice any dude who tried." Mick shrugged.

PJ touched up her lipstick and headed over to order some more beers for their table.

For most of that night their group had been pretty much

the only people in the restaurant. But a group of dudebros had installed themselves at the long bar and the volume level had gone up considerably. She rolled her eyes inwardly as she made her way through them to get the attention of the bartender.

"Well, hello there. Buy you a drink, pretty lady?" This came from her left. One of the invading dudebros no doubt.

"No thanks." PJ continued to watch the bartender because she didn't want to look over and start anything.

"Aw, come on. Why you gotta be so mean? You think you're too good for me?"

Ugh. A drunk dudebro was dangerous. He had trouble hearing no. Liked using his size to intimidate women. No matter what she did, he'd be annoying, so she chose to ignore him. She'd said no and that was all he needed to know.

She pointed at a pitcher and held up two fingers when the bartender saw her. He nodded with a smile, indicating he'd bring the pitchers over shortly.

But when she turned to leave, the dudebro she'd been ignoring stepped into her path.

"I didn't say you could go."

PJ looked up into his sweaty face and then she looked around until she found the one dudebro who looked embarrassed. She motioned at the drunk one. "Are you fucking kidding me?" And then back to her problem dudebro, "Move out of the way and leave me alone." She'd just had an ugly scene two weeks ago with Gary Weston. She didn't want to do it again.

He stepped with her, keeping her from leaving. He grabbed her arm as she tried to pass. "The fuck you say? Big tits and blond in a bottle doesn't mean you can open your mouth to me like that, bitch."

Shocked, it took her a second to react. And then a wall of man showed up, breaking the hold dudebro had on PJ's arm before she could connect with his balls with her knee.

"You'd best tell the lady you're sorry and get yourself gone, son." It wasn't Asa, but Duane. Massive, but not Asa massive. Still, big enough to pick this jerk up and wipe the counter off with his body without breaking a sweat.

Dudebro doubled down, stepping a little closer. "Why, you her boyfriend?"

"No. He is." Duane tipped his chin in the other direction and they swung in unison...and froze at the sight of Asa stalking in their direction like a storm of fuck-your-face-up.

He headed straight to PJ and looked her over, his expression darkening at the red spot on her arm where the guy had grabbed her so hard.

"Outside." Asa said it to dudebro but continued to look at PJ. He traced across her cheekbone and kissed the same spot briefly. "Stay in here. I'll be right back."

The dudebro wasn't very bright.

"Look, man, she came on to me. You can't give me shit when your girl has a wandering eye. Am I right?"

Asa spun on his heel, took up two handfuls of dudebro, and carried him out the door, tossing him into the street.

Dudebro's friends rushed out. A few of them held their hands up, palm out, asking for Asa to let it go and they'd take their friend away.

But Asa wasn't done. He stalked out to the middle of the street, picked dudebro up one-handed, and dragged him back to where PJ now stood.

"This is my lady. You hurt her. That make you feel like a big man? Terrorizing someone half your size? A real man doesn't need to scare women. Or hurt them. You owe her an apology."

"Sorry. I'm sorry!"

Asa shoved him hard, sending him stumbling. "I see you anywhere near here and I will deliver the beating you deserve. Piece of shit."

The other dudebros scrambled to their friend and took off down the street without even looking over their shoulders.

Asa visibly got himself under control before he shifted his attention back to her. "You okay?"

She didn't even know what to say. The whole thing was so surreal. Nodding absently, she rubbed at the spot on her arm. She'd have a bruise there most likely. She bruised easily and he'd pressed his thumb in really hard.

Of course, Asa's attention went right to that and she cringed.

He touched her cheek again as he had inside. Like she was precious.

"Hey, baby girl." Duke approached with Mick and gave her a gentle hug. "I brought your stuff in case you guys wanted to duck out. The manager is glad you took it outside, but he's understandably anxious to have us all vacate the premises."

She wanted the ground to open up and swallow her. "This keeps getting better and better."

Duke thought that was hilarious. "Asa, your lovely lady seems to be under the impression this is the first time we've been asked to leave an establishment."

Asa grinned and she saw the light in his eyes. Noted the gleam. He was hot for her right then and there, and it was probably because he'd just tossed some dude out in the street like trash to protect PJ.

But it didn't offend her sensibilities. Whatever that meant about her, PJ just didn't care. It was hot seeing him be so badass to protect her. She wanted to lick him and thank him and go find that jerk and kick his face and also sleep and maybe have a doughnut.

"We get kicked out of a lot of places." Asa shrugged as he took PJ's things from Duke. "This isn't even the first time we've been asked to leave this particular restaurant. We'll stay away for a month or so and come back and things will be fine."

Duke and Asa seemed to find it hilarious, which made her feel a little better.

"You're an unruly lot."

Asa nodded solemnly and then winked.

Mick hugged her. "You okay, baby doll?" He looked her over carefully. Since that apology, he'd claimed her much the way Duke had. She was theirs because Asa was too.

"I just wanted to order some more pitchers. I didn't mean for it to turn into a fight."

"Aw, honey." Asa kissed the top of her head. "We've fought over far less."

Duke shook his head. "A person should be able to order a damned pitcher without being assaulted by a drunken frat boy. And the asshole who makes that impossible for women all the time needs to be thrown out into the street like garbage."

Mick and Duke did some sort of handshake/fist-bump thing and sauntered off.

Ellen waved as she came over. "It was nice meeting you. Do you have a card? I was about to ask you for it when all hell broke loose."

PJ pulled a card from her purse and handed it to the other woman, taking the one Ellen offered in return.

"I'll call you about doing some work down in the south Sound." Ellen waved and headed off with a knot of the people they'd come with. Many shouted their good-byes and locations for wherever they'd head next, but she could see in Asa's eyes that he and she weren't going anywhere but to his house.

He put her in the car and paused a moment before he got in on his side. He needed to pull it together because he didn't want to aim any of the violence he felt right then in her direction.

She'd had enough for one evening. And while he and his friends ate the adrenaline of fights in the street right up, he was sure it wasn't a regular part of her life. Nor would he want it to be. Especially when it was the result of some shitty treatment.

He slid into the seat and relaxed a little because it smelled like her in there.

"I've got another six weeks, maybe two months before I have to put her away for the winter," Asa said as he took them north, back to his place.

As much as he loved to drive his Caddy summer and early fall, once mid-October came it was time to bring her in for a while.

"What do you drive in the winter?"

He was glad that change of subject caught her interest.

"I have a few vehicles." She laughed at that response. "You laugh?"

"A *few*?" she managed to ask around her gales of laughter.

"You don't drive your Camaro all the time, so I don't see how you can judge."

She laughed some more, reaching out to pat his thigh. "Easily and often. Judging is one of my favorite things." Then she snorted, softening her tone. "Awww. I'm sorry. You're right, of course. I drive my Charger more than the Camaro. It has heated seats, which makes my ass very happy in the winter. How many is a few, though?"

He snorted. "Impudent."

"Does that mean you're going to discipline me? I thought we'd already established that. Will you discipline me extra hard?"

"You've had a rough night. Let's watch a movie and go to bed. I'll wake you up early in the morning."

"Asa, that guy was a dick. He touched me and I hate that. But that's not uncommon. That sort of reaction when you say no to a guy like him, I mean. You were there—and I'm going to hell for this—but you were so fucking hot when you picked him up like a pile of dirty rags and tossed him into the street."

Pleasure simmered low in his belly. "That so? I don't much like anyone touching you at all, much less trying to hurt you. The cops were called, which is why I didn't beat his ass. I hate that this is normal for women. Knowing this is the second time in a month you've been treated like this makes me crazy." He hadn't told her about his trip down to Centralia to *happen* by the bar Gary Weston had been hanging out in. But he wasn't worried about Weston saying anything. Once the swelling went down he wouldn't even look at PJ sideways.

"His face when he turned around after Duane said my boyfriend was coming. I bet he peed his pants a little."

"He accused you of coming on to him."

"Yes. Do you believe that?"

"*What?* Fuck no."

"Okay, don't get testy! I was just asking. Yes, that's another thing dudes like him do when you call them out."

If Asa ever saw that guy around again he'd finish what he started.

"Of course I'm testy. That guy better drink on the Eastside from now on."

"No. I drink on the Eastside too, with my sister. He needs to stay home until he learns manners."

The restaurant was close to his house, so it wasn't too much longer until they pulled into the garage and he closed the door, shutting the outside world away.

She got out and he followed her quickly, pulling her against him, her back to his front, before they reached the door to the house.

She arched back into his body on a moan. He caressed her belly and up over her breasts. He'd wanted her, had wanted to fill himself of her, wanted to share in that sweetness she gave him. That scene back there had gotten him amped up. It had been a long time since he'd reacted that fiercely to protect someone. Not since he'd left the army.

His system zinged with adrenaline. The need to mark and possess. To inspect and pet. To preen for. He'd held back on the way home because he hadn't wanted to scare her. He should have known she'd process the situation at the sushi place in her own way.

The light on the garage door opener clicked off, leaving them in the dark in his garage. All the smells he associated with things he loved best rose around him. His machines. Leather cleaner. And PJ. Sex and heat rose from her as he bent to breathe her in at the nape of her neck.

She let out a shuddering breath as he dragged his teeth against her skin. "Asa," she whispered, the sound tortured as she grabbed his hand, sliding it down her belly. He growled in her ear and burrowed into her pants and straight into her panties.

She was hot and slick and ready to go. He groaned, brushing his cock against her ass. With his free hand he trailed fingertips up under her shirt, pulling the cups of her bra down so he could play with her piercings.

He pressed a kiss to her shoulder as she writhed.

"Wet and hot. Ready for me."

"Yes," she gasped.

"Mine." Once the word left his mouth he knew it meant more than he'd even realized.

"Yes," she agreed again, riding his hand as he slid one finger against her clit and played against the inferno-hot entrance to her body.

His breath sped too as she pressed back against his body. She reached up and back, encircling his neck the best she could at her angle.

"Ride my fingers."

She made a sound, a plaintive growl. She wanted to come, his sweet Penelope Jean. Hated to wait. And it had seemed from pretty much the start that he'd been unable to resist her in the end. If she wanted it, he made sure it happened.

"It makes me crazy when you get so desperate and bratty for it that you tantrum just a little." He spoke, his lips against her skin.

She let go of his neck, slapping her palms on the door in front of where she stood.

She arched, pressing her nipple into his grasp, rolling her hips as she ground herself against his hand and came in a hot rush against his palm and fingers.

He spun her slowly to face him. "Feeling a little better?"

"Mmm." She smiled, eyes glassy.

He traced his fingertips, glossy with her, over her lips and groaned when she licked a trail behind his touch.

She grabbed his belt and in three movements his pants were open and his cock in her hands. He nearly blacked out when she went to her knees and took him into her mouth all the way, getting him nice and wet as she did.

He wanted to be gentle with her after that creep had man-handled her, but she had other plans. Inciting him on purpose, taking him as far back into her throat as she could.

There was something so scorching hot about it when she played with him like that. When she knew what he liked and made it so he could have it. She *knew* him in ways he had no idea it would be so special to be known.

The fist she had at the root of his cock slid up and down ever so slightly, but enough that he couldn't stop himself from thrusting, fucking her mouth in earnest.

He grabbed two handfuls of her hair and yanked her forward onto his cock, over and over. She moaned and made needy sounds as she sucked him.

"So fucking pretty. Your mouth on me all pink and glossy. Pretty and so, so dirty."

He brushed his fingertips over her cheek, aching at what he wanted. Turning away from it, not thinking she was ready.

Then she looked up at him as she swallowed him all the way down.

Challenge.

She needed it.

Wanted it.

As much as he did.

He pulled free of that luscious mouth, pumped his fist around himself twice more, and blew all over her mouth and down her neck and shirt.

A groan wrenched from his gut as he came, with each pulse as he watched his semen hit her skin, as her eyes widened but not with fear or disgust. No, PJ loved it. Loved that he'd done it, if for no other reason than that he loved it too.

He whipped his shirt off and helped her clean up the worst of it.

"Come on. There's a shower with our names on it. Then we should watch movies like we planned. I'll be up for another round shortly." He waggled his brows. Maybe he'd pull out the new toys, especially the cane. Maybe he'd save it for another time. They had plenty of it.

She tossed her sticky shirt in the laundry basket, along with her bra. He just followed behind her, watching her move through his house and feeling very satisfied with his life indeed.

CHAPTER
Nineteen

Asa's jeans were still open, so the V of tawny skin and that tantalizing trail of hair made her a little dizzy. That was why he'd gotten so close in the first place. He gave her such a smoldering look it made her wobbly. Despite the fact that they'd just had sex minutes before.

"We should go back to bed. You look stressed. Let me help you with that." His voice had gone low and coaxing. Teasing, laid-back Asa was one of her favorite flavors and as a result, even harder to resist.

"Stay back." PJ held out a hand to ward Asa off as he started to close the last three feet between them with that look on his face.

He pouted but then grinned as he ignored her and continued to stalk her way. "You can't honestly say that. Beautiful, you're so sexy right now. How can I be expected to get anything done the rest of the day if I can't have you before I go back to work?"

She burst out laughing. "Fuck off. I'm just putting my underpants back on because I let you get away with that the first time when you talked me over here for a lunchtime quickie! Was I so forgettable?"

"This is totally your fault, PJ." He gave her a very serious face and inched forward. She shook her head. "You're irresistible. I can't not want you. Even when I've just had you."

He was like a sex cobra. Swaying and dazzling her with his looks and all the stuff he said as he got closer and closer until he made a grab for her.

Yelping and then laughing, she hightailed it out of his bedroom and into the entryway, where she'd left her bag and shoes.

"I have things to do. I work with really demanding customers." PJ gave him a pointed look.

Which he ignored as he followed her out. "My hands still smell like you."

She shivered, loving it when he said stuff like that. "Good. I should rub all over you to scent you to mark my territory." It was a joke, but she meant it. She'd started to think of him in terms of *mine*. Since that day three weeks ago when they'd been out at sushi they'd drawn closer, and it had been so intense and wonderful and fantastic. She'd never been happier in the whole of her life.

She stopped in the entry and he was right there, his hands on her. Her resolve to go to work wobbled.

"You can rub on me any time you like."

"I plan to always take you up on that. Call me later."

He backed her against the front door and kissed her until she was goo all over again. He kissed her so long that she'd forgotten she was in the process of leaving until she opened her eyes to find him, gaze roving over her features.

He made her feel so fucking beautiful.

"Every time you touch me you do this." She looked up at him, reaching to brush his hair away from his eye. Unless he was working, he wore it down a lot more often around her because she'd mentioned how sexy she found it. And that was sweet and holy shit she was so fucking gone over this man.

"I always do what to you? Sex you up? It's because you're too delicious. I can't resist," he said.

"You make me forget everything else." She petted his beard because she could. He was hers.

He smiled, that softness he showed so few people, that tenderness he showed only her.

"I like it when you pay attention to me. What can I say?"

"That's good right there. You saying something, I mean." She kissed him and then managed to get out to the porch unmolested. "Bye. Don't forget to eat. I know you, you'll be at Twisted Steel until nine tonight and you'll get caught up and won't remember food until you have a headache."

His expression softened. "Okay."

"Not just ice cream and energy drinks either."

"Too far."

She laughed and he went out to the porch, watching her until she'd pulled away from his house and was heading down the street before he went back inside.

She had a job up north, so she called ahead to arrange lunch with Shawn. On the drive it hit her: the years she'd spent making this drive, the energy she'd put into building a place for herself at Colman—it was never going to happen.

It didn't matter how much she bled for her father, it wouldn't be enough. And maybe a life where she didn't worry every moment what her father might think, but instead thought about what *she* wanted, was better.

Fifteen minutes later Shawn and PJ sat at a rickety table in a hole-in-the-wall Mexican food place facing an overgrown parking lot in a strip mall many people had long forgotten.

But the tortillas were freshly made, the tamales were to die for, and for six bucks it was the best lunch within an hour of Colman's building.

"I'm glad you called," Shawn said as they cracked open their bottles of orange soda. "I've missed you."

"I know. You're coming to the dinner Mom is having, right?" PJ asked.

"The show trial for your boyfriend? You know Dad sees Asa as the source of your leaving Colman, right?"

"Um, no. Mainly because no one said, least of all him. He avoids me. I can't imagine why he'd care anyway. It's not like he makes an effort to have contact of any kind with me."

Shawn heaved a sigh. "He loves you, Penelope. But he's fucked up. He isn't a good dad. That's the truth. I don't know if he ever could be. He's telling everyone that you were finding a place at Colman just fine before Asa came into the picture. Whether he believes it and says it for that reason, or he's said it so many times he believes it by this point, I don't know."

Begging for scraps of her father's affection had left her disheartened and worn out. When she'd left Colman and had also been estranged from Asa, she'd been able to pour everything into her business, and it had been exactly the right thing.

"There are a lot of things I don't know. But I'm good at custom paint. It's not glamorous. It's hard work. It's expensive to do it right. I have to constantly innovate and update my skills. And I love it. I don't need to defend my life to anyone. And I'm not going to for Howard Colman Jr."

Shawn put his hands up. "Preaching to the choir. I just think Mom expects this dinner to be something it won't. As far as your work goes, I've always been proud of you. But I've seen enough to be thrilled by your success. You don't have to defend yourself to me. I love you. I just thought you should know."

"I appreciate it. I do need to know, even when it's tiresome and it makes me sad."

"I've only talked to you here and there for the last six weeks or so. I get updates through Julie but I don't know much about your private life. Tell me about him. All I know is that he's big, bad, and inked," Shawn said.

She nodded. "He is all those things. But he's kind. And gentle. He worries about how I'll feel about things. It's nice." She didn't need to tell Shawn about the bare-knuckles fighting or the kind of crazy stuff he and his buddies did on the regular. Shawn wouldn't understand, though he'd try because he loved her.

"He's smart and really talented. He and his partner, they're geniuses with machines. He..." PJ looked up at her brother. "He listens to me, Shawn. He listens to me and he takes me seriously."

"All right. Well, that's what I need, really. If you're happy, I'm good. You and I need to get together with Jay and Julie and work out when you're coming back to Colman."

She sat back and shrugged. "I don't know if I want to."

Shawn shook his head. "No way, PJ. You said resigning was your way of making your point but that you'd come back. That was the only reason I didn't make a bigger fuss at the time. You not being part of Colman *isn't* what I agreed to. Neither did Julie. Even Jay is unhappy. I'm holding you to the promise you made."

"As I was driving up here I realized how many times I'd made this trip just hoping I could get him to see how hard I was trying. And I realized it was never going to happen. Whatever his reasons, he's cool with not being close with me. Worse, he's cool forcing me into a place that would slowly destroy me over the years. Why should I do that? And make no mistake, if I returned I'd be saying that was what I was worth," PJ said.

Shawn didn't interrupt; he knew she wasn't done.

"Right now I don't have to share my profits, which are modest, but they pay my bills. I don't have to tiptoe around and pretend I'm not successful so as not to offend anyone that I might be doing better. My hours are my own. My choices are my own. Quitting was the best thing I ever did because when I had to put things together to make my business work, I realized I could do so much more than I thought possible. That encouragement is never going to come from my boss if I return to Colman."

Shawn sighed. "I'm sorry you felt that way. But we can change things. I miss you. I miss building a future with you and Julie and Jay. I used to see you at least five days a week. When was the last time I saw you in person, PJ? This is *our* company. Ours. Don't run off. Stand and fight."

"I do miss you and Julie, even Jay. But it takes a lot of energy to fight all the time, and I did a lot of it alone. I don't miss that. I don't miss feeling like no matter what I do they won't notice because I'm not a son."

"But we're all old enough to change that. I keep saying this to Jay and Julie. Why do we wait around for what Dad and Fee decide?"

"Because they're in charge."

"They're in charge because we allow it."

"Are you talking insurrection? I'm gone for not quite four months and you're already leading a revolution?"

He wasn't amused, though. "Is it such a bad idea, PJ? This is *my* company, but I'm stuck waiting for Fee to pull his thumb out so he can pretend it's his work and take credit. Julie is smarter than everyone above her but she waits. Jay, well, he's a dick, yes, but that's how he was raised. They made him this way. He's our brother and he's good at his job."

"I've been thinking about this a lot. At first I thought like you did. But now? Now I don't agree so much. Jay isn't good enough at his job that I'd believe he could lead Colman. Not right now. He's spineless."

Shawn's shocked expression made her sit forward and speak quietly. "It makes me so frustrated that you're surprised by that. I sat there after tossing him some of my biggest clients and he was still so worried about Fee and whatever he might say to Dad that he did nothing to help me. That's not leadership unless he planned to do that very thing. I get it; he was worried about his job, but come on. Until he grows a spine and stands up when he needs to, I don't think he's a better leader than Fee or Dad." She shrugged. "Leading is more than sitting at the head of that table. This is why I'm not convinced coming back is what I need. Or what Colman needs. I'd rather be successful on my own without tearing down Colman on my way out."

"Why do you see this in such either/or terms? Jay might just surprise you with how much skill he's got. Why assume he's taking this lying down?"

"What other assumptions can I make? I mean, really. I haven't heard a single word from him in months. I've left him messages. I've texted him a few times. Nothing. So okay. I hope his new income with my clients gets him some therapy and maybe some management classes. But he's doing nothing that I can see, so what other choices do I have?"

"Did you think we all should have quit in solidarity?"

She rolled her eyes. "Stop. I never asked for, nor do I expect, that. You're all happy in some way, so why would you leave? If I'd been listened to and valued, I'd have stayed too. I love my family, Shawn. I just don't think you all get to make me feel like shit for the rest of my life because I dropped out of college and have a ring in my eyebrow. Oh, and a uterus."

"I'm sitting here begging you to come back. So why would I want you to feel like shit? I want you back at Colman because it's yours. As much as it's mine and Julie's and Jay's. I think you judge him too harshly. Jay, I mean. He knows how to run a company. It's *all* he's known. It makes him slower to act, more conservative, because he's been educated that way," Shawn countered.

PJ shrugged. "We all have to live with the choices we make. Or don't make. He owes me a lot of words, and a lot of deeds. I haven't received any of them. So while I don't think he's Fee, I think he

needs to figure out who he is before I'd go tossing my power—
which is minor, really—behind him."

"If he comes to a meeting with you, me, and Julie to talk about
how we're going to take Colman into the future, would you consider that a meaningful step?"

"You've been planning, haven't you? Why not you then? Or
Julie?"

"Because Jay has been groomed for this his whole life. You have
no idea what it's like."

"I don't, no. But I'm making my way. Because no one at my
place of employment found it necessary to attempt to keep me on.
You need to remember that, because I sure as hell do."

"You said you wanted to make a point by leaving. We tried
to back you up. You can't have it both ways." Her favorite thing
about Shawn was that he never let her get past him with an argument he thought was fast and loose. It had always meant to her
that he believed her capable of backing up her choices.

"I'm not talking about you and Julie. I left. That's the way I'm
trying to have it. That way I can make my own mistakes and fix
them. That way I can look at myself in the mirror each morning
and know my boss thinks I'm worthy. I left. I thought it would
make a difference. I was wrong." She shrugged.

"You're just going to quit your plan? Along with quitting
your job."

She'd missed this sibling back-and-forth with Shawn. "Nope. I
quit my old job because Colman sells tires and that's all they want
to do. You're all great at it, but that's not what I want to do. My
job now is awesome. My plan was to be relevant to this industry.
It was to broaden our appeal and serve more customers than Colman did at that time. I'd hoped it would make a difference with
Dad, yes. I've sent him my receipts for the last three months. I've
forwarded him articles and pieces about what I'm doing. He hasn't
replied. My plan didn't work the way I hoped it would. I wanted

to come back. I wanted a place at Colman I'd helped build. But I can't do either of those things because I don't have the ear of anyone with a vote. So you can sit here and make it my fault that our brother won't stand up, or that our father is useless and would rather drink too much and play golf than let his children build for the future. But we both know the truth."

"I don't want you to give up because it's hard. It is hard. And I'm sorry you're the one who has to bear the weight of this. But if you walk off, it weakens us."

PJ threw her hands up, frustrated. "Then why wasn't this presented to me weeks ago? Why didn't anyone else bring it up? I've got to be the one to get punched in the face again because why? How does my leaving weaken you anyway? Shawn, has it not occurred to you that they don't want me back? That my leaving is exactly what they wanted?" She couldn't stop the crack in her voice and he softened his tone in response.

"What about our feelings? What about what Julie, Jay, and I think? We want you back."

"I'm still your sister. I love you and Julie and Jay. I just referred someone to you for tires this week, as it happens. But sometimes you need to let go so you can truly be better. I respect myself. The people I work with respect me. That means *everything*. I'll meet with you guys if you can actually make it happen, but it's going to take a lot more than I originally thought it would to get me back there. I'm not sure at this point if there is anything that could bring me to Colman again."

She couldn't make her father see her for the amazing person she was. She couldn't. But she could make every person who ever hired her know she was capable of really good work.

CHAPTER
Twenty

She came to the door looking so pretty he paused to just take a long look. This was his. It had long ceased to matter how she'd ended up in his life, only that she remained there.

He bent to kiss her.

"You look very handsome," she said, smoothing a palm down his shirtfront.

"Ha. I'm nothing compared to you. Do you want to stop for a drink before we go to the restaurant?" Asa asked.

Worry flashed across PJ's features. "Do you? I think it'll be fine. My mom is excited to meet you in person. Julie likes you. Shawn will because he's easy that way. Jay, well, who knows? But you've met him."

"Darlin', I'm fine. We'll be all right. I just hate seeing you stressed. Are you worried? Do you want me to take the piercing out?"

The outrage and surprise on her features made him feel a lot better. "You'd better not! You're who you are. A successful businessman. You own your own home. You take care of your mother and sisters. Plus that piercing is hot and as much a part of you as the color of your eyes."

He grinned, bending to kiss her. She defended him so ardently, even when he knew she was stressed out about dealing with her family.

"So beautiful. How'd I get so lucky?"

"I honestly don't know. You fought me so hard I was beginning to wonder if you'd ever come to your senses."

Laughing, he pulled her close. "I'm not always the smartest person. My mom says I need to live up to my potential. But you kept at it and thank god I finally listened."

"And now you get to eat dinner with my family. Lucky you. I'm going to warn you up front, my mother might use terms like 'in-laws' and 'marriage.' Just ignore her."

He remembered that he'd never told her about Ellen. *Shit shit shit*. It'd been weeks since that night PJ and Ellen had met. First he'd been waiting for the perfect moment to bring it up, and then he'd forgotten about it entirely.

He thought about it long enough that she noticed, giving him a look that said he needed to spill.

"I need to tell you something."

She crossed her arms over her chest and narrowed her gaze. "That's worrisome."

Even at a time like this she could make him laugh with her attitude. Still, he made sure to show none of that on his face.

"You know Ellen?" He could charm his way back into PJ's good graces. He just needed to get it out and tell her everything first.

"From the restaurant on fight night? Oh, are you going to tell me you and she had a thing sometime in the past? 'Cause duh."

If only he could hang it on that. "I was married. She was married. I mean, we were married to each other."

The amused smirk slid off her face. "You and Ellen were married and you're just telling me right now? Weeks after I met her? *Months* after we started seeing one another?"

"It was a long time ago. Seven years. It only lasted six months."

She shook her head, clearly upset. "That whole night! Everyone knew? Everyone but me."

This wasn't going the way he'd hoped. She wasn't mad, she was hurt.

"It wasn't like that. I was going to tell you that night but it was weird and then there was that whole thing with the douche-bag at the bar. We got back to my house and then we had sex. A lot of it, so it's not like I was going to bring it up. Then I forgot because it wasn't important. That's why we got divorced. Neither of us cared enough to stick it out."

"Asa, this is not okay."

"I didn't purposely hide it from you."

"Oh, but you did. You did, and you made that choice for me. Your sister, she started to talk about your father and I stopped her because I wanted you to share with me when you chose. I respected your right to do that. This, though?" PJ blew out a breath. "Why'd you get married to start with?"

"Stupidity. She thought she was pregnant, so I wanted to do the right thing. She didn't really want to get married, but she wanted to do the right thing too, and then she wasn't pregnant and it was awful. We were a bad fit from the start." It had been a tubal pregnancy, so by the time Ellen had gone through that they just didn't have any real foundation to build on and they'd broken it off.

"So bad she knows how you like your sushi and comes to dinner?"

"Are you jealous?" In hindsight, this line would have been better delivered with another tone. But he was so amused and flattered it showed right through, and she wasn't nearly as amused by the sentiment as he was.

"This is the part where I'm not laughing or making jokes. Do you see this part? Do you know how the chapter ends?" PJ asked.

This anger was different. He knew it to his toes. "I was lightening the mood. It was a failure. I apologize."

Her look told him how little she was moved by his declaration. "How would you feel if the tables were turned? If we were at dinner with my friends and then we chitchatted with some guy for hours and then weeks later I was all, 'Oh hey, that guy is my ex-husband. No big!'"

"I did not say it like that!"

"You didn't say it at all!" PJ said in a quiet voice so sharp it sliced to the bone.

He sucked in a breath. "Okay. I'm sorry. You're right. It was stupid not to tell you way before now. But it was something I did, something really dumb, and it happened a long time ago. What this is"—he waved a hand between them—"is not even in the same universe. I was married to her and she never knew me the way you know me. I didn't think about her the way I think about you. I won't say it meant nothing, because that would be shitty to her. And she's not a bad person. We didn't split because of anything horrible. Which makes me sad because it feels like a bigger failure that I never loved her and married her anyway."

She glared at him, stepping away to pace a bit.

Finally she turned back. "We need to leave for dinner. Being late will only mean lots of drama and upset."

"Are we okay?"

"Enough to go to dinner. Hopefully later we will be. Being lied to is a problem for me. I don't like it and I won't tolerate it. When people lie to me they're telling me I'm not worth the truth. If there's something else this big you need to disclose it right now. No kids, right? Other wives?"

He chanced getting close enough to hug her. "No kids. No other wives. She does really like you, though. Which weirds me out because she doesn't really like anyone. But you're irresistible, so I won't even say anything about you sleeping with Craig, and he's been at several events you and I have been to since we started dating."

Wow, that was a mistake to have said out loud.

She stepped back. "How is it you don't know when to stop speaking, Asa? That sentence should have ended with me being irresistible. So explain to me how you won't say anything about me sleeping with Craig? Craig *Salazar*?"

Uh-oh.

"Naturally I'm assuming that stopped when you and I started in seriously."

She blinked at him, so utterly incredulous he felt like kicking his toe in the dirt and hanging his head.

Finally she spoke. "I never slept with Craig. We've made out on several occasions. Usually when one or the other of us breaks up and the other is free. Kissing. That's it. No canes and floggers. No orgasms. His dick hasn't even been in my hand, much less in my mouth or body. He's my friend. He cares about me, but he is stone cold in love with someone else. Only she doesn't feel the same."

He started to speak and she put a hand up to stay him.

"Furthermore, if I *had* fucked him inside out in the middle of the street every third Tuesday, it still wouldn't matter. I don't care that you slept with other women. I knew you weren't a virgin when I came along. I don't want to hear about who you had sex with. It doesn't matter because you're with me now. This is about the fact that you had been married and you never shared that with me. Don't muddy the waters with this Craig stuff."

He paused, really thinking about what she'd said and realizing the huge missteps he'd taken. "I don't know how to do this right. I'm feeling my way along. I should have told you earlier on and most definitely that night you met her. I really am going to have to buy out the entire Godiva store to make up for my fuckups today, huh? Maybe some paint or a trip to Vancouver for the weekend where I'll keep you pleasured until you forgive me. Yes, the latter. I vote for that."

She sighed and tiptoed up to kiss him. "Caramels. Try Fran's. I like that better than Godiva, though if you go that way, nuts and chews, please." She opened her door and gave him a look over her shoulder. "And yes to Vancouver."

Hot damn. Weekend-in-a-luxury-hotel sex was something he'd been wanting with PJ for some time.

He put a hand at her elbow as they went down the steps. He hefted her overnight bag, not caring that it was heavy. Just pleased it meant she'd be in his bed that night.

After he finished an epic grovel. He knew that was necessary too. He'd hurt her trust in him. That was a problem he needed to fix.

He hit the remote and popped the trunk and PJ came to a stop. "One of those *few* other cars?"

He put her bag in the trunk of the BMW 7 Series crouched at the curb. "It is indeed." He loved the car. Smooth and powerful, he loved to road trip in it. He bet PJ was really fun on a road trip.

It also was safe, and if he couldn't surround her in all that steel of Motor City's glory days like the Caddy, he'd happily surround her in the finest German engineering.

Plus, it was an impressive fucking car. He knew enough about PJ to understand that the kind of guy she brought home to her family before didn't have a pierced cock. They'd be suspicious of him from go. So he'd keep in his piercing in his nose, but he wore nice clothes, drove an awesome car, and he cared about PJ.

If that didn't matter to them, *they* didn't care about PJ very much. So he hoped they'd all get along for her sake if for no other reason.

He followed her directions and then settled back into the seat and drove, just enjoying the time with her.

"This car is so quiet. It's like you can't tell an engine is running but for that purr beneath your feet."

"After driving the Caddy it's an adjustment, but she's so smooth, it's like really good scotch. And way easier to fit into a parking spot at a restaurant."

"Ha. And yet you do it. You parallel park in a car that's half a block long. It's your superpower. Well"—her voice changed, going low—"you have a few other superpowers, but that's one you can do in public."

He wanted to ask if she was all right, but it was clear she was a little tense and he figured asking would only make it worse. He let her lead with how much she wanted to talk.

She seemed in good enough humor and hopefully in a forgiving mood as they parked, and he sent out a prayer that her family wouldn't upset her. And that he'd be a good guy and not make anything worse.

It was a warm night with a light breeze; the sun wouldn't go down until after nine, but it was one of those Seattle summer nights when it was twilight for hours.

He put an arm around her, pulling her close as they walked across the street together and headed into the restaurant.

Once inside, they were led to a table where her entire family waited. She and Asa weren't late. She'd gotten them there fifteen minutes early, even with the thing she and Asa had had at her place.

She should have known they would have been there twenty minutes early just to make her feel bad even when she hadn't done anything wrong.

Julie grinned up at them, standing and heading over to hug her and smile at Asa. She held them in place, speaking quietly. "You're early. Shawn and I bet Jay fifty bucks. He said you'd be ten minutes early. I said fifteen, so I win. Shawn said twenty."

"How early were you?"

"I got here three minutes ago. Shawn and Jay only just put

napkins on their laps when you two walked in, so don't let them make you think they were here yesterday at dawn or something."

PJ cringed inwardly. This weird family stuff must seem so strange to Asa. It was pretty embarrassing when she thought about how it must look from the outside. Then again, he'd totally kept an entire marriage from her and she was still annoyed.

Just because she was mad didn't mean she wanted her family to make him feel bad. She hooked her hand at his arm and they went the rest of the way to the table, where her brothers stood and, after a poke from their mother, her father did as well.

Asa sent out so much charm PJ had to school her features. She gripped his arm a little tighter to keep from stroking his beard or kissing his neck. The man was lethal.

His hair had been drawn away from his face, exposing all that feral, masculine beauty. He wore a dark shirt with a tie that brought out the amber in his brown eyes. He was dressed appropriately for a meet-the-parents dinner. He cleaned up really well, while still being himself.

She introduced him to the siblings he hadn't met yet before they turned to her parents. "This is my mother, Lenore Colman, and my father, Howard Colman. Mom, Dad, this is Asa Barrons."

There was handshaking, though her father was cooler than usual; whether it was about Asa or the situation already existing with PJ leaving the company, she didn't know. And cared about less as each day passed.

"I think we should get a few bottles of wine for the table," Julie said as their server came over with bread once they'd all sat.

"I'll have a scotch and soda," her father said before Julie had finished her order.

PJ was sorry she hadn't taken Asa up on his offer to get a drink before they showed up because before they were finished with appetizers her father had consumed his fourth scotch.

As it was, she kept herself to one glass of wine because she didn't know what he might do. Which was disturbing as well as annoying and embarrassing.

Asa, though, kept it together. He asked Lenore about what she did, her hobbies and activities.

"We keep telling her she should run a party planning business." PJ smiled at her mother. "When you're invited over to Lenore's for a meal you always say yes, because it's going to be really good and she gives presents."

Julie laughed, putting her head on their mother's shoulder. "She does. When PJ and I had dinner with her recently she gave us each a silver frame with a picture of our grandmother in it."

"I was just asking PJ about that photograph a few days ago."

Of course, he'd been in her bed at the time and saw it on her dresser, but no one needed to hear *that* detail.

Her mother blushed as they kept talking about what everyone had been up to.

Finally, the most exasperated Lenore had ever been in public toward their father, she said, "Howard, you're awfully quiet tonight. I was just telling Penelope how much we've been admiring her work. From the pictures and articles Shawn sent over last week, remember?"

Her father grunted but said nothing. Asa's body language radiated anger though he kept a civil tongue and continued to talk with her siblings.

"Penelope tells me you're gifted with machines." Lenore shifted, her body language seemingly relaxed, though they all watched Howard somewhat warily as he ordered another drink.

"Excuse me a moment." Jay got up, dropping his napkin on his seat before walking off.

PJ never found it hard to talk about Asa's work. He never bragged on himself, so she had no problem doing it with her family. "He's pretty amazing. Sometimes these cars come in and they're a total mess. Half the original parts are totally destroyed because it was stored in a barn for sixty years or whatever. And then he shapes the metal and their shop machines new parts and when they're done it's totally art."

Asa squeezed her hand and she blushed. "Sorry, she asked *you*, I know. I got a little excited to brag on you."

He brought her hand to his mouth and kissed it. "It's nice to be bragged on." He turned to Lenore and they talked about restoration, and then transmissions when Shawn jumped in and Jay returned.

It wasn't too long after they'd finished eating when Asa excused himself along with Shawn and Jay.

"You know they're all going outside to look at Asa's BMW, right?" PJ said to Julie.

"Probably. Dad, you should go out there too," Julie said.

Howard curled his lip. "Why would I do that? I got enough of Penelope's *boyfriend* for one night."

"Howard!" Lenore sent him a stony glare, but he was too drunk to heed the warning on his wife's face.

"What? She quits her job and shacks up with this creature. She's an embarrassment to this family to come here with *that* at her side. This whole thing began when he came into the picture. Am I the only one who can see the connection?"

"Maybe it's hard to see clearly from the bottom of a tumbler of whiskey. I quit my job because I wanted to do something with my place at Colman and you didn't want to even listen to my ideas. Asa had nothing to do with that. Also, I live in my own apartment, so we're not shacking up. But even if I was living with him he still wouldn't have been connected to why I left Colman."

"You keep telling yourself that, Penelope. You don't seem to mind failing at things."

Everything just sort of froze for long moments as the pain of that sliced through her, tearing at her heart.

Her mother's face darkened with anger and Julie's eyes widened.

It was by will alone that she was able to stand without shaking on her wobbly knees. PJ grabbed her purse, pulling money from her wallet and tossing it at her father. "That covers our meal and the wine and tip. And on that loving, positive note, I'm going to leave."

"Penelope, wait." Her mother headed after her, along with Julie.

PJ paused at the front doors because she didn't want to carry all the drama out to Asa, but she did not want to have this scene in a restaurant waiting area either. She shook her head at her mother. "No. I've had enough for one night. I'm not going to stay to be insulted and listen to all that stuff about Asa."

"He's drunk. He doesn't know how to deal with you growing up and doing things on your own. You used to seek his approval; he misses that."

"And yet he continues to toss away any opportunity to give me even the smallest bit of his approval. This isn't about me growing up and him being a daddy who can't let go of his princess. Remember his comments about how I love failure? He ought to know. I've wasted years of my life begging for his approval. I've now accepted that will never happen. I'm done." It hurt for PJ to say those things, but she meant them, and once they'd been spoken, she had no choice but to hear.

"He doesn't know what he's saying."

"Mom, no. I love you, but please stop. I appreciate that you wanted to meet Asa, but please don't ask me to pretend I believe that." PJ hugged her mother. "He knows what he was saying. For a long time I thought it was my imagination that he felt that way. But he's been up-front about it all my life, so that's on me."

Her mother shook her head. "No. Penelope, he loves you."

"I don't need that kind of love." She hugged her mom once more and then her sister.

Julie kissed her cheek. "Call me tomorrow. I mean it."

"Okay. Drive safe. Love you both."

When she walked out, she nearly bumped into Asa, who was walking back across the street with Jay and Shawn.

He totally *had* been showing off his car. That made her feel a little better.

"What's going on?" Jay stopped her.

"I'm going now." She hugged Jay and thanked him quietly for being so welcoming to Asa and for the way he'd gone to ask the bartender to water down their father's drinks earlier.

"What happened in there?" Shawn asked.

"Too much scotch and ego." She hugged Shawn, relieved Asa hadn't asked anything yet. "I'm sure Julie can give you the rundown."

Asa said his good-byes to her brothers and put an arm around her shoulders as they went to the car.

CHAPTER
Twenty-one

Once he'd gotten back on the freeway she exhaled hard. "Oh my god. I'm so sorry. I can't believe that just happened in front of you."

"PJ, stop." Asa kept his gaze on the road, so she was free to stare her fill at his profile.

"That shitshow in there was so rude. Honestly, I'm horrified." That her father hadn't even made the smallest effort, that instead he'd gotten drunk and belligerent, had been a blow she still reeled from.

"Your dad was having a rough day by the looks of it. But that wasn't your fault, and the rest of your family was nice. Even Jay. He bragged about you, you know."

"Jay?"

He laughed. "Yes. He's proud of you. They all are, even your dad, I wager. You're different, but your siblings seem just fine with that."

"My whole life it's been 'Penelope Jean, don't be common. You're meant for better things, you won't achieve that if you color your hair wildly or pierce more than one hole in your ear.'"

"I'm glad you're not common, darlin'. I get what you mean, but you are singular. There's no one like you in all the world. I'm sorry your dad is having such a rough time with that."

"The summer I was fourteen I saw a sidewalk chalk artist at work and my mother got me these chalks to use so I could try it myself. I'd go out there at the top of our driveway every day and work, hosing if off and redoing it. One day I remember trying something to give it a three-dimensional quality. Have you seen what some of those street artists can do? Like huge chalk murals that look like people fishing in lakes or crevasses down to dark depths. That sort of thing. Anyway. My dad came out and made me hose it all off and throw the chalk into the trash. He said I could have fine art lessons if I wanted, but I couldn't deface the driveway with scribbles."

"Christ." He blew out a breath. "I'm sorry."

"When he gave me permission to paint the Colman logos on our cars it was one of the best days of my life. I felt like he finally understood that just because I was different it didn't mean I was worse. Or wrong. It was like he was all right with my being creative." It had felt like a respite from being a failure in his eyes all the time. "And we know how that ended up."

In the end he'd rather have her walk away because being different wasn't treasured in her life growing up, it was suspect. It made him wary of her because she didn't conform.

Even when she'd *tried* to conform she'd fucked it up.

And it didn't seem to matter either way, because her father still didn't want to talk to her, even at a dinner with her sitting right across from him.

"Are you ready to tell me what happened in there?" Asa asked quietly several minutes later.

Was she?

"Obviously whatever it was has something to do with me. At least partially. I want you to unburden yourself, and you can't if you worry how I'm going to feel. This isn't about how I feel, it's about how you feel."

Tenderness flooded her to near bursting. How did she get so

lucky that she found *this*? She never expected that love would be something so utterly certain. Asa had called to her from the start and now he fit in her life in a way that lightened her heart and made her feel grounded all at once.

"I'm in love with you, Asa. You know that, right?"

Wow, had she just said that out loud? After that freak show of an evening? After he'd lied to her and she'd caught him?

"Ack! Pretend I didn't say that."

He reached out to take her hand, squeezing it. "No way. I heard it and I'm holding you to it. You scare me. I'm scared I can't possibly measure up. You were meant for more than me."

"Shut up. This again?"

He barked a startled laugh. "And then you remind me you're perfectly capable of your own choices and decisions, so I'm not going to argue the point because as it happens I'm in love with you too. But I still want to hear about what happened in the restaurant."

Those words made it easier for her to tell Asa. "He thinks I'm a failure."

Asa's voice was quiet, but she heard the anger in it. "What? Honey, he's drunk and he clearly doesn't like me much. He's just being defensive. He doesn't mean it."

"No. No, I think he does. All these people who claim being drunk *made* them say offensive or hurtful things. Bull. Alcohol exposes your true feelings. The ones normal filters usually keep you from saying out loud. And it's not really about you, because he's made me feel like a failure my whole life."

Asa blew out a hard breath. "I don't get him at all. He's got four really great kids. You're all at the family business. *Were*, anyway. You all seem to understand and value what that means. What Colman Enterprises means. He's mad because you quit. But he pushed you there. Your quitting doesn't make you a failure. That's his failure—that he couldn't see such amazing talent. You chose an alternate path to succeed. It's petty and abusive to hang it on you like that."

It did feel abusive, but having him say it, having someone not in her family say it, meant a lot. It meant she hadn't been over-sensitive or imagining it outright. It was so damned nice that he saw it. To be believed.

"When I quit, it was liberating and nauseating all at the same time. I knew even as I was saying the words that it was the right thing to do. It was the right choice. I don't need him to ask me back, or even to admit he was wrong. For me, that's past, and if he'd just made the smallest effort I'd have been happy to move on. I would have forgiven just about anything. But there have to be some limits. You just don't say things like that. Even if you think them."

She blew out a breath, trying not to cry as the memory of that moment washed over her again. The shame. The sense of betrayal. He'd hurt her so carelessly but with so much vitriol she knew it was exactly how he felt.

PJ pressed the heel of her hand over her heart. It seemed odd that such a wonderful thing—the first time you tell someone you love them—could happen on a day when such a horrible thing had also happened.

"He said things to me. In public. In front of other people. Stuff that got to me because it's a lifetime worth of conditioning. Any-thing outside the plan as laid out by Howard Jr. is a *failure*. And then I'm horrified because I'm a twenty-five-year-old woman who wants her dad to be proud of her."

He growled and then sighed. "You're *supposed* to want your par-ents to be proud of you. I'm thirty-seven and I want my mother to be proud of me still. More than that, parents should be thrilled their kids still want it."

Asa hadn't been this angry at a person whose ass he couldn't beat in years. Rage simmered in his belly at how upset Howard Colman had made his daughter.

Failure? Was he kidding?

He'd enjoyed her sister and brother Shawn as well as her mother, and even Jay was all right. They all seemed to have a great deal of affection for PJ.

Her father had power over her, which normally, if your dad was cool, was a good thing. But the guy seemed to prefer to manipulate and shame his incredibly talented youngest child, and based on the few stories she'd told Asa, her father had been picking at her the whole of her life.

"You turned out pretty well. Thank goodness for it."

"I don't want to talk about it anymore. Not tonight. Thank you for coming with me," PJ said, her voice tired.

"Nope."

"What? Nope what?" At least now the sadness was tinged with annoyance and a little curiosity.

"I'm not having any attempts on your part to pretend this all away. Your father shredded your heart tonight, Penelope Jean. You told me you loved me, which means your heart is mine. I don't take kindly to things that are mine being misused. *You're mine.* I warned you I didn't play, and I don't. I'm deadly serious about loving you."

She tried to take her hand back but he wasn't having that either. Fuck Howard Jr. and his bullshit. He had no right to make any of his children feel this way.

"I need my hands!"

"Why?"

"Why?" An edge of irritation had pushed all the sorrow from her tone.

Asa smiled. "Yes. Why?"

"Because you're going to make me cry and I want to cover my face. But now I'm just annoyed, which is probably what you planned to start with."

He snorted. "You're super smart."

"Oh my god! You do a PJ impression?" She grinned and it was

like winning the lottery. That was far better than seeing her on the verge of tears because someone valued her enough to want to protect her. He didn't want her tears. He wanted her joy. That's what love was, and he wished her father understood that.

"Duke says he'd give it a seven and a half. We had a competition. I won fifty bucks." They'd both laughed their asses off. Duke had adopted PJ as the little sister he never had, and he seemed to have subtly campaigned on her behalf with their circle and in the industry enough to have really mattered. People respected Duke, so if he liked someone, it was taken as a good sign.

It also meant Duke teased her just like he did Asa. Well, not exactly the same, but the tone and affection were.

"Oh my god. I'm going to blush so hard the next time I see him," she said through laughter.

"I have others. Most of them I don't share because they're usually sounds you make when I do something you like," Asa said. "You know how much I love your noises."

"I can demonstrate for you and we can do a comparison."

"Yes."

"*Right on.*" She'd done a perfect impression of Duke's signature expression.

"Holy shit! How long have you been sandbagging that?"

"When I first met Duke it was at the track, like a year or so before I met you. I think you all had just decided to do some sponsorship of a local driver and he was up checking things out. Anyway, he just cracked me up with that beard of his. He had these purple boots," PJ said.

"Jesus, the Godzilla boots? He got those in Turkey off a street vendor. I've tried to kill them but they always make their way back to him, like Christine."

"Wow, so I already think you're the hottest man alive and you bust out a Stephen King reference. How can you continue to be so fucking sexy?"

No one gave compliments like PJ did. She had this way of seeing people always at an angle that surprised him and frequently touched him deeply. Each one was a little gift made just for him and no one else in the world.

It made him feel lucky.

At first it had been a struggle to allow himself to want her. But there had been no way around it because they had amazing chemistry. And then she'd been there in his life. Working at the shop, and then once he'd kissed her it had been a hard road to allow himself to need her. To accept that he needed her.

She was inside the walls he'd built as a kid to protect his heart, and she never did any damage. Even when he fucked up she let him work his way back to her. He did the work, even if he sometimes just didn't know what the hell he was doing.

Penelope Jean was worth the struggle. Worth the time to open up to. Because she understood him. She saw all of him and accepted it.

And because she had a magnificently sexy temper.

As he drove, Asa let it wash over him.

He knew what it was to be in love. Like full-tilt, *how the hell could I have thought anything else before this was love*–type stuff.

He'd never thought he'd have that tenderness as well as the heat and excitement. It was something he hadn't even imagined, much less known to want. But now that it was in his life he'd protect it.

"We should read *The Stand* and then watch all the versions of it on DVD. That would be awesome."

"We can do that in Vancouver. Read before we go up and then watch all the miniseries while we're there."

"All right. I'm totally up for that."

Asa spoke again. "You were talking about the Godzilla boots."

"Purple boots at a reception full of guys like Jay." She snorted. "Duke's at the bar, in line next to me. The dude in front of us turns around, sees me, and starts coming on to me. He's drunk and I'm ignoring him. And then. He gives me the finger guns. *Pew. Pew.* Finger. Guns. I die that he did this in a non-ironic fashion. He's clearly not going to go away so I say, 'Really, finger guns? Does that ever work for you?'"

Asa burst out laughing, so glad she was cheering up.

"This awesome dude who'd been next to me in purple boots with green lizards on them tips his chin my way, wearing a smart-ass grin. And he goes, 'Right on.'" Again, she said it exactly like his friend did. "It still makes me laugh, probably because he was already so tipsy and he's naturally surfer-dude laid-back, which I didn't know at the time. But I love it when he says that. If you can do me, I can do Duke. Wait. That sounded wrong."

He tried not to speed too much but it still felt like forever to get from the restaurant to his place.

Once he got off the freeway she made an exasperated sound and pulled her chirping phone from her bag. "It's Julie," PJ said to Asa before she answered. "Hey. Mom okay?"

Of course she worried about her mother when it should have been the other way around. He found it hard to imagine his mother ever tolerating someone saying such a thing to any of her kids without drawing blood. He didn't much like PJ's family right then. From where he stood, it sure seemed like most of them hadn't backed her up much in the past when it came to this shit from Howard. Aside from having an actual job and not being in prison, he parented a hell of a lot like Asa's father.

He was old enough to know that made him biased going in, so he tried to give them all the benefit of the doubt. How they reacted from this point on would cement his dislike or redeem them. All of them except Howard. That piece of shit was, as his sister Courtney liked to say, dead to him.

He tried to pretend he wasn't listening but gave up because she wasn't dumb. They pulled down his street and she turned to him as she hung up.

"Everything okay? Sounded like she was trying to reassure you."

"Jay and my dad had an argument. Jay had gone into the bar to ask them to water the drinks after the third one and somehow our dad figured it out, and you can only imagine what that looked like. Shawn called a cab and waited for it to take my dad home, and Julie dropped Mom off and settled her in with some tea."

He pulled into the driveway and they got out to head into the house. Not a word about what had happened to PJ, only this other shit?

Still, this was her family, so he attempted to keep his voice as neutral as possible. "Your mom okay? Do you want to go over there?"

"Julie said she set herself up in the guest room and was pretty ticked at my dad. He'll charm his way back, he always does. Whatever his flaws, she loves him. I'm done with it for tonight. Tomorrow I'll decide when I'll be ready to think about it again. For now, it's me and you."

He wanted to let her change the subject. Wanted to bury himself in her, anchor her so she knew no matter what he was always there.

But he needed to tell her a few things first. Not least of all because she'd been so brave and had told him all that stuff about her past. She'd given him trust even after he'd not told her about Ellen.

Asa needed to be a man worthy of her. So he pulled her into the living room instead of the bedroom.

"I do seem to recall you like the angle that couch gives you." PJ gave him a look over her shoulder that weakened his resolve.

"I do. But let's talk for a bit."

Her frown was calculated and he laughed, swatting her ass on his way past.

"Very nice try. I promise to show you just how nice in a bit." Asa pointed at the couch. "Sit."

"This sounds ominous."

He settled in next to her. "No reason for that." He took her hand. "Earlier tonight you told me Courtney had revealed some of the details from my childhood, but you wanted to hear them from me, so you waited." Asa swallowed hard. "That meant something to me. Well, more than one thing. But let's start with the trust you showed me, even when I didn't show you the same. I apologize for that. Honestly."

There was no reason not to accept a genuine apology. She wanted him to know why it was particularly upsetting to her. "I accept your apology. But, Asa? This is a problem for me. I need for you to understand that."

"I'm not going to promise to never be an idiot again. I will. I'm fucked up in a hundred ways. But I can promise to do my very best not to hurt you."

That was a good answer.

"Tell me one of those hundred ways then. Help me understand you."

"My mom was fifteen when she had me. She'd dropped out of school to follow this loser to Dallas. Estranged herself from her family. And then when my biological father got sent to prison for five years, his parents stole me from her. I lived with them until I was nearly seven. They punished her for her sins by keeping me away from her influence."

PJ shoved pity as far away as possible. If he saw any hint of it he'd close up. She didn't dare move and spoil the moment. So she waited and hoped he continued. After he was finished, later, when she wasn't in his presence, she'd have her full reaction to this story.

"We both had to be reminded of our nature, you see. That was Mr. Jeter's favorite. I needed to be beaten when I made the slightest infraction. It was the only way to cleanse me of the things my mother had done."

He shuddered, his gaze gone far away.

"Their mistake was to underestimate my mom. They thought continuing to dangle time with me was a way to keep her in line. Figured her obedience to those dictates meant she'd given up. She was a teenage girl with no education and no resources, while they were respected in their church and community. But she never gave up. She just did what she needed to do to keep her visitation rights, to see me. All the while she worked multiple jobs, got her GED, and saved to get an attorney to fight back."

PJ was really beginning to love Pat Barrons.

He licked his lips and she took a risk, linking her fingers with his. He let out a long, shuddering sigh and pulled her closer. She couldn't see his face.

Maybe that was easier for them both. She closed her eyes and leaned into the solid, comforting muscle of him.

"I was seven by the time I came to live with her permanently. She had Lettie about five months after that. Their dad, Lettie and Courtney's, stuck around awhile. He was okay at first. Or maybe he wasn't, but what I'd been used to was being forced to kneel for hours at a time in a closet while I prayed to be forgiven for my sins. I guess most people would have been okay in comparison."

She couldn't stop the snarl that ripped from her lips. There she was whining about her family and look at what he'd gone through.

"When she was pregnant with Courtney he walked out and never came back. Lettie was right around five. It took her a week to notice her dad wasn't around. That's how involved he'd been in her life. The state tried to find him to get him to pay support, but they never did. So my mom just stepped up and handled it. There was nothing else to be done. She worked her ass off, to the point that her health suffered, and she did it because that's what you do when you're a parent and she couldn't rely on anyone else to do it for her."

He buried his face at the nape of her neck, breathing her in and then biting hard enough to leave waves of goosepimples in his wake. "So when your father, who has every fucking privilege and opportunity handed to him, is a shitty, hateful creature to a child who only wants his affection, it really gets to me. And it gets to me because it's you."

She turned to face him, taking his hand again.

"There are a handful of people in the world I'm irrationally protective of. You're one of them. I can't shove it away when an asshole like Gary Weston humiliates you the way he did."

Uh-oh. "Tell me," she said on a sigh.

The war between sharing and keeping whatever he'd done quiet ran riot over his features.

"I'm going to tell you something. Not because I am sorry for it, but because I heard what you said tonight and I want to live up to my promise."

She narrowed her gaze at him.

"I punched him. Maybe twice. Not more than three times. But he said stuff, so there were mitigating circumstances."

"Elaborate."

He grinned and it lit his eyes. "I love it when you get mad. Goddamn."

"Don't try to eye fuck me. Just tell me what happened." But she couldn't hide the way a smile threatened at the corner of her mouth.

"I didn't go to his shop. I went to a bar I heard he drank at. I tried to speak with him. It got emphatic. He tossed some insults. I'm a gentleman. I handled that. He won't be speaking about you in public ever again. Trust that."

While she was horrified, at the same time it wasn't so very hard to admit part of her was comforted and, yes, titillated. He'd protected her. In a very elemental way. It was flattering and silly. And yet, once she'd experienced it she'd begun to crave it.

"You went there, he said I was a mouthy whore or whatever. No talent but a nice ass. You took exception and planted a fist in his face."

"The first was a kidney shot. Then he called you a whore and I popped him twice more, square in the face. He dropped like a stone. When he recovered, we discussed what his expected behavior was. He accepted how serious I was. I'm positive this won't be an issue. You don't need his shop anyway."

"No. I don't." PJ cupped his cheek and petted his beard. "But I do need you."

He stood, pulling her to her feet. "Thank god. Come upstairs with me."

CHAPTER
Twenty-Two

He pulled her upstairs to his bedroom as the energy between them tautened, heated, zinging along her nerves. PJ couldn't wait for whatever he had in store for her.

"Strip."

He sat, caressing her with his gaze.

Over the time they'd been together, she'd learned him. Taken cues from his reactions. Because she knew he liked to look at her, she took her time, meticulously stepping from her shoes and placing them in the corner.

Then she pulled the pins from her hair and it cascaded down around her face in waves. Each button down the front of the dress she wore opened with a twist of her fingers, exposing a little more of her skin until she shrugged from it, letting it slide off before stepping free.

"I'm really glad I had no idea what you were working with under that dress. More than your normal gorgeous body, that is."

She looked up at him through her lashes with a smile. "Do you like? I saw this and thought it might hold appeal for you."

Appeal.

"That's a tame word for what it holds for me," Asa said.

It wasn't just that she wore stockings. She'd already worn them when they started seeing each other, but once it was clear how much *he* liked them she wore them more often, making sure to buy the French heels he thought were so sexy.

That night she wore an all-new ensemble. She tended to wear blues and pinks, which worked on her skin so well. Right then she was wrapped in black silk. The front of the garter belt laced up like a corset with deep green ribbons, echoed in the matching push-up bra with green accents.

She took the bra off first and then moved to where he sat. She perched a foot at the edge of his seat and he watched, breath held, as she unhooked and then rolled down the right stocking, which she laid across his lap while she did the left.

She revealed herself to him slowly, finally removing the belt, leaving her in nothing more than a pretty pair of black panties.

"You usually like to do this part yourself."

He did indeed. Like unwrapping the best present he'd ever been given.

He stood, looking down into her face, struck with the weight of his blessings. A good weight.

He slid covetous hands all over her skin as he pulled the panties from her legs, loving the way she leaned on him as she stepped from them.

"*Now* this is perfect. You're perfect."

Her lips wobbled just a bit and he had to shove his anger at her father back yet again.

He kissed across her forehead, easing away the stress, delighting in the way she relaxed a little more with each touch.

"I'm going to have to insist all your attention be on me." He set her back from his body, taking long moments to circle her, to stare at and touch all the fierce beauty she possessed.

Of course she had all her attention on him. It humbled and incited him every time. But he wanted to underline that this was theirs. No bullshit from the outside would be acceptable in this space.

He took her hand and pulled her toward his bed. "Sit."

She did.

When he got this intense she didn't quite know what to do with herself. He was so hot and sexy and bossy and in charge that it blew her mind.

So she sat on the cool of his bed, on her side, and watched as he gathered things.

This too was part of the show.

He'd stay clothed until he was ready to be naked. Waiting for it only made her hotter. Having him touch her, his clothes against her naked skin, rendered her even more bare. Bare to everything he wanted.

He approached her, holding a blindfold.

"Been a very difficult day. I'm going to fuck all that away. But you need to let go totally."

He slid the blindfold on. Once the darkness took hold, she did indeed trust him and let go. Her skin came to life in ways it only did when her eyes were covered.

"Since our last experience with a cane didn't go so well, I got a new one."

She shivered. A crop was one thing, but a cane—well, a cane came close to her *no thank you* point. The last time they'd tried it he'd switched out to a flogger, which she preferred, loving the way the tails seemed to caress her even as they bit her skin.

He kissed her neck and she sighed, melting into him. Needing him to take over and make her forget everything but Asa and PJ.

It was one thing to make him hot, and most of the stuff he did made her hot too. But real pain wasn't where she liked her sex to be. She trusted him to try a new angle. Trusted him to make it really good for both of them.

She listened as he moved around. Things landed on the bed as he did. She wondered what each item was, which was probably why he did it.

"Your lips just curved up into a smug smile."

Of course she was smiling!

"So many other women could be right here, but they're not. I am. What's not to smile about?"

He hummed his pleasure at that. "No one could be here right now. Not this way. Only you."

His hands, warm and strong, caressed along her body until he stopped at her upper arms, lifting her gently, helping her to stand.

"Going to sit again, this time I want you over my lap."

He led her the few steps to where he'd been sitting before, where she'd come to him and removed her stockings and the rest of her lingerie.

The times they'd done this he'd had her standing, braced on the bed or a chair. This time, though, she let herself fall into the way he pushed her to her knees. Gently, of course. The strangeness of the fact that he was going to use a cane on her but always touched her with reverence was something she'd accepted.

But it still thrilled her.

More rustling as he sat. "Come here." He touched her again, helping her up, her belly across the steel of his thighs. "Palms flat on the floor."

She did as he said, arching as his fingertips traced down her spine, over the curve of her ass, tickling at the back of each thigh just below the swell of her butt cheeks.

Then the bulge in his forearm, the one resting across her back, flexed, and the sound of the cane split the air.

She jumped, but he didn't touch her. He was just making that sound. Ramping them both up.

Once she relaxed, he began again. Each new touch took a few

moments as she puzzled over what he was doing. He rolled the cane down her back and over her ass, which was nearly a massage.

Then nothing for long moments until a bright burst of sensation against her ass.

Whack.

She sucked in a breath and waited for the *nope too much* from the first time. He blew over the heat and it twisted through her. Not hurt, but delicious sensation.

He did it again and then once more before pausing.

"With me?"

She found her will to speak and managed to mumble a yes.

"Good. This cane is leather instead of rattan. Makes the prettiest welts on your skin, but it's less rigid and takes more of the impact."

His cock pressed against her hip as she writhed when he struck several more times. It hurt, but for just a breath, and then her body took over, rushing to fill her with feel-good chemicals.

Whatever it was, Asa was a master at it. He knew just where to hit and how hard. How often. He did it in a rhythm that seduced her nice and slow, the heat building but in a pleasant way. It seemed to flow straight through her right to her clit, and since that aligned with her interests, what did she have to do but enjoy it?

There were always plusses to giving over to him.

Asa liked this leather a lot. The creak as he held the cane was satisfying, and she seemed to like it far better than their last go.

The *thunk* of it each time he made contact echoed up his arm and made him harder and harder with every sound of pleasure he wrenched from her lips.

A pretty pink flush lived on her skin, and he put the cane aside to pet over her back and sides. She'd gone a little heavy and dreamy and he loved it.

He pulled the blindfold off and continued to stroke her skin until she was ready to be led to the bed.

"On your belly."

It'd be more comfortable for her that way, and it also gave him the chance to look at those welts as he pulled his clothes off.

Her head was turned in his direction and she watched him, a smile on her lips. He wanted to bottle that moment.

Instead he bent to blow over the heated skin on her ass and thighs, delighting in the way goosebumps rose. Her scent wafted to his nose and he licked a trail up the back of her thigh.

"I like that," she murmured.

"I aim to please."

"You do. It's a really lovely quality."

He slid her thighs apart, walking his fingers up to her pussy. He hissed as the heat of her greeted his touch. "So wet."

He wanted to shove his dick in her straight to his balls over and over, hard enough to knock pictures off the wall.

She needed to come first, though. He needed to hear it.

He moved up the bed, getting on his back. "PJ, come up here. I want you on my mouth."

He loved the way she roused, like a cat moving from a sunny spot. She stretched her back, arching with a knowing smile on her lips.

"You know exactly what you do to me," he murmured.

She straddled his waist and slid herself over his cock. That hot, wet pussy he'd just been talking about surrounded him. She groaned and did it again.

Magnificent.

He looked up at this magic he'd been unbelievably lucky to have found.

"Mmmm. I like this too."

He let her do it one last time and urged her up with a touch. "You have another task."

She hesitated just a moment in mid-grind, her gaze on his. The left corner of her mouth tipped up and she finished, making them both shiver a little.

"You know you're going to pay for that."

He scooted down and she moved up his body until she was where he'd told her to be.

"I really hope so. Or else why would I do those things?"

This part of what they had, it had been the best surprise of all. The humor and teasing back-and-forth had been unexpectedly hot. And totally unique to PJ. She wasn't afraid of him. She didn't do things because they were steps in a game. She wanted to please him. Wanted him to please her. But she genuinely gave herself over to their relationship on every level.

There was a joy in her that he'd never thought he'd crave the way he did. Being around her made him content. Being around her like this?

She knew what he wanted and bent forward to grip the headboard as he took the first lick.

And then he lost himself in her.

He left her shaking.

Asa Barrons more than anyone else she'd ever met knew how to push her every single button.

She hung her head, holding on to his headboard hard enough she might have heard the wood groan.

His beard abraded the inside of her thighs as he ate her pussy like he'd been starving for it. She'd be just a tiny bit sore. He'd told her he liked that, liked knowing he'd be on her mind.

That was hot too.

He sucked her clit between his lips and she nearly jumped off the bed. Here he dominated her like everything else. He wanted to touch and lick every part of her and took his time, setting a slow pace at first, building sensation and speed as he went until there was nothing left but a climax that hit her so hard and utterly that she could do nothing else but keep holding on to the headboard until he moved at last, helping her to her belly on the bed, a pillow under her hips.

Asa ignored the slight shake in his grip as he rolled the condom on and lined himself up before pushing all the way into her body.

"Earlier, as I looked at you, all I could imagine was fucking you so hard pictures came off the wall. But given the way the bed is situated, I think I can settle for making a lot of noise instead."

She grunted, pushing back at him, and he smiled. Okay then.

On his knees between her thighs, he looked down, hypnotized by the sight of his cock disappearing and pulling nearly all the way free from her before pushing in again. He held her hips up a little to adjust the angle.

Sweat beaded down his spine as orgasm settled in to his balls. So close.

She made these needy, breathy sounds into the pillow and they only drove him harder. He needed deeper and so he dug in, and whatever he stroked over inside her worked for her too because she was suddenly hotter and wetter as her body squeezed his cock.

And then there was nothing but pleasure as climax sucked him under. He continued to fuck into her deep and fast as wave after wave hit him until he finally flopped to the side to keep from crushing her and rolled from bed.

"Now then." He got back into bed and she sought his body immediately, resting her upper body on his as she looked at him.

"Being fucked is better than medication. I'm drowsy and feeling far better than I did before we got here."

It was his job to make her life as easy as he could, so if sexing her up was what he needed to do, it wasn't so big a chore, was it? He brushed the hair back from her face.

"Always available to play my part."

"I love you, Asa."

He cupped her cheek. "I love you too. So rest up, because you're going to need your energy for round two."

She started laughing and he joined her.

"Come on downstairs. We'll crack open a bottle of wine and drink it out on the deck. I got some of those anti-mosquito candles you love," he said.

"You did? You hate citronella."

"You love it. Now come on. There's something for you hanging on the back of the closet door."

She got up quickly and headed to look. He smiled at the happy sound she made and got up to receive her hug as she pulled on the deep purple robe he'd bought.

"I love it. So soft."

"I was walking by a shop and it was hanging just inside the door. I saw it and wanted it to be yours. Wanted to see it against your skin."

"It has a lotus on it. You didn't just find this at all. You went looking for it."

Busted.

He tried to stay gruff, but she saw right through him, so he shrugged. She petted his beard, which they both loved though he pretended to tolerate when he really wanted to preen around when she was done.

"You like me." She said this in a singsong voice, making him laugh.

He pulled on a pair of sleep pants. "I do. How can I not like a woman who can quote Arthur C. Clarke while having sex?"

They headed downstairs and she pulled down two glasses while he opened a bottle of wine.

"I'm what they call a Renaissance woman, Asa."

"So that's what it means? Saying no to anal with literary quotes?"

"Totally."

"I'm a lucky, lucky man."

She put the glasses down and lit the candles. "That so?"

He wanted to pat her ass, but he figured he'd give it a break after the caning. Instead he sat back, satisfied with his life, and poured two glasses of wine. "That's totally so."

CHAPTER
Twenty-Three

She opened her front door to find her sister standing on her porch.

"Hey, come in. I wasn't expecting to see you." PJ hugged Julie on her way past.

"I was in the neighborhood. I had to deal with the Department of Licensing and as it's just a few minutes away, I thought I'd take a chance and see if you were around."

"I just got home about ten minutes ago."

"I won't stay long. I know you have dinner at Asa's mom's tonight."

"Yes. She's making tamales. From scratch. I didn't eat any lunch today so I can have extra. Well, if I can manage it without looking like a hog."

"I have faith in you and your ability to eat a lot of what is going to be really good food."

"Apparently they're fantastic and legendary. Which are two things I love when it comes to food. She used to bring in extra money at the holidays making them by special order for people. Asa says she used to take orders for them months in advance for Christmas and New Year, so he's really leading me to expect some pretty awesome stuff."

"Try to put one in your purse for me. Or maybe not. Wouldn't that be a great way to introduce yourself to his mom? She finds a tamale in your purse, but you can say, 'Ma'am, this is so good I knew my sister had to taste it. I'm only human.'"

"Did you have drinks with lunch today?"

"I'm just naturally hilarious, Penelope."

Julie clearly had something to tell PJ. Her big sister wanted to share, so PJ needed to pay close attention.

"You actually are. What are you up to? Come through and help me look for something to wear. If you're thirsty there's juice and stuff in the fridge."

"I'm having dinner with Shawn in about an hour, so I'll last until then."

PJ pulled out two dresses. "So a dress is obviously in order. I need to look nice when I meet her. She's very important in Asa's life, so I really want to make a good impression."

"I like that. It says good things about him. I'm jealous, and happy for you too."

PJ smiled. "He has a marshmallow center. He thinks no one knows."

"Well, you look at him and before he says a word you're a little wary and then you see his eyes. He's intense, yes. But he's got kind eyes."

"He does, doesn't he?"

"You're in love."

PJ nodded. "Yes. Get this, I told him in the car on the way home from Salty's last week. But he loves me too, Julie. I know it's improbable, but he's someone special. He's everything I never knew I was missing until I had him."

"I like that. I like him, actually. He's insightful and deliciously alpha male. Mom has a crush too. And if he can love you after having looked that mess at the restaurant in the face for two hours, he's a keeper. So, I have to know. Does it get in the way? The piercing, I mean. When he's downstairs?"

"His nose piercing or the cock one?"

"These are words I just never expected to be saying in my day-to-day life, you know? My goodness. You're a thrill a minute, Penelope Jean."

"Neither piercing does a single *negative* thing when he gets up to any sort of sexing." PJ waggled her brows at her sister, who gave her a face. "Maybe Gavin can get something pierced when he gets back. Maybe he already did. Maybe *you* can get something pierced!"

"I've had all the piercing I plan to, but thanks. And stop with the Gavin talk. Maybe."

Ah! That was it. Something about Gavin. PJ grinned at her sister. "Have you heard from him?"

"No. I was thinking this last week that maybe I should just send him an e-mail. It's been a while. I send him birthday cards. Christmas cards. It's not like I just dropped off the planet, you know. Anyway, we're done with this topic now. We were just talking about your clothing options."

She let Julie off the hook and held the dresses up again. "Preferences?"

"The black-and-white one is super cute with the fit-and-flare thing. Plus you have those spectator pumps that'll match perfectly."

"Thanks!" PJ started changing. "You're coming to the show, right?"

"There's nothing that could make me miss it. I'm so excited to see your work on display."

A trade show had chosen cars with PJ's paint work to fill two of their slots on their custom floor. It was a huge deal with great exposure not just to the locals, but the trade show people, which got her work in front of even more potential clients.

"I'm proud of you." Julie handed her two Lucite bracelets, one black and one white. A smile bloomed over her face as Julie realized where they'd come from. "These were Gran Colman's."

"She used to let me play dress-up all the time. I had a little box at their house. We all did, remember? Anyway, after she died all that stuff went into storage. My box of dress-up stuff was in the trunk of the Z28 when it came to me. These were inside it. I love them. If you ever want to wear them just say so. They're meant to be shared."

Julie hugged her. "Come to think of it, after the will was read, a box of books came. All my mysteries were in it. I bet Grandpa stored each one of our boxes. I like that." She kissed PJ's cheek. "Anyway, I love the bracelets but they'd look wrong on me. On you they're perfect. Just like it's perfect that you're having so much success with work."

That meant a lot. "Thanks for being so supportive."

"Of course. I'm your sister. We need to meet, though. All of us. Shawn and I are having dinner tonight, like I said. He had a meeting with Fee today and wanted to talk about it. We'll loop Jay in once I hear what Shawn has to say. He's really upset right now. He and Dad are at odds."

"Fee must be in heaven."

"He *is* extra smug. But Dad has been keeping a low profile since the dinner. I think Mom is still punishing him. Which she should be. What he said was wrong. I told you this that night and I'll say it again. You *aren't* a failure. He was cruel to have said that."

It had hurt. And it had made her ashamed of having worked so hard for his approval all her life just to have him slap at her in such a petty way. Like he had no idea of her value.

"I don't know about meeting with you guys. I mean, I always want to meet for dinner or whatever, but I don't know if there's anything left for me at Colman. Especially now."

"Hear us out when the time comes. You're going to make your own choices and we all respect that too." Julie looked at her watch. "I should go."

PJ walked her sister out, hugging her and promising to call soon.

Asa watched her interact with his mother and knew he'd be getting two thumbs up from Pat later that night.

He'd told his mom and sister some of what had happened the week before, so it was extra nice that they'd been so welcoming and warm to PJ from the moment she'd walked through the door.

He'd brought women to his mom a few times over the years. Ellen, of course. His mom had been where Ellen was at the time, and a big part of why he'd married her was because he would have done anything to ensure his children didn't grow up without a dad. Now, years later, he knew he could have done that even if they hadn't married, but he didn't regret his choice at the time or right then, as he watched a woman who'd taught him what bone-deep, forever love was listening to his mom tell a story about Asa's childhood.

He hadn't known you could feel this way about another person, and everything he'd done until the point PJ walked into his life had brought him right where he needed to be to cross her path when he was ready for her. So he couldn't regret any of it.

"Help me bring in the good dishes." Courtney nudged him out of his thoughts.

He rose and headed to the sideboard, where his mother kept what she called the good dishes. The set of china Asa and his sisters had given her about ten years before wasn't actually that expensive or anything, but she loved it and brought it out on holidays, birthdays, and other special occasions.

PJ came in as he and Courtney were pulling out four place settings. "I'm supposed to tell you to remember the big platter."

"She trusts you with that? Good sign." Courtney gave PJ a thumbs-up and then thrust two stacks of plates her way. "Take those in; I'll grab the platter."

"Gotcha." PJ carried the dishes to the table and began to put them out.

"I figured you'd be prissy," his mother said to PJ as she worked.

Asa hurried up to see if he could prevent any more of those kinds of sentences.

Courtney snorted, grabbing his arm to slow him down. "She's going to say whatever she wants to say. You know how she is."

"If you had ever spent two minutes with PJ's father you'd understand why I want to protect her," he murmured to his sister.

"Mom isn't that guy. She's pushy and nosy and bossy, but she's not mean. But you know what? I like you this way."

Asa turned to face his sister. "What way?"

"Protective. That's what way. Oh sure, even if she was just a friend you'd look out for her because you're a good friend and it's in your nature. But...with her it's different. You're different. You're sweet. It's more than fast driving and motorcycles and all that crazy stuff you do. Please don't tattoo your face. That's an aside. Back to my subject. Mommy and Lettie and me, we know you're generous to a fault with people you love. I've seen you on dates. I've seen you with your *wife*. But you look at PJ like she's part of you. You look at her and your face brightens. You want to take care of her. You think about how she'll feel about this or that interaction. You're in love with her, aren't you?"

Asa nodded.

"Asa! I need that platter."

"Sorry, Mom. Coming right up." He turned, put the dishes he'd been holding on the table, and grabbed the platter, taking it to his mother.

"Thank you. I was just telling PJ I figured she'd be prissy. She laughed, though, so she knew what I meant. Don't frown, it makes your nose look worse." His mother looked back to PJ, who struggled against a smile. "Don't you think that thing in his nose makes him look like livestock?"

Courtney coughed over a laugh as she continued to set the table.

"I already got a request not to tattoo my face from Courtney, so we can skip this." Asa attempted to project some order, but as usual they all ignored him.

"No, ma'am. I think Asa is very handsome." PJ and his mother looked him over and he sighed. PJ smiled and was so pretty he couldn't help but smile back. "I saw the pictures of him with barely any hair at all when he was in the military. He was handsome then too. But I think the piercing and the tattoos and the hair give him a whole different type of good looks. He's very fierce. But he's that way in general, isn't he? He gets a look on his face when he's working on a car." She mimicked his expression and his mother burst out laughing.

"He got that look even when he was a baby." Her face went wistful for a moment. "When he's trying to exert control over something or someone, trying to learn something new or that sort of thing, he gets that face. He's a very serious boy."

"Definitely. Smart too. Creative. Handsome. He works hard. He didn't dump me after he met my family. You did an amazing job raising a good man."

Pat beamed at PJ and then over to Asa and finally to Courtney. "You were right. She gets him."

Asa winked at PJ, flattered, flustered, touched that she'd see him the way she did.

"Asa, put the tamales on the platter. PJ, put the rice in the bowl on the counter."

His mother headed to the table after she'd put out a pitcher of iced tea. Asa and PJ moved around each other in the kitchen in an easy rhythm after all the times they'd made dinner together.

He paused to kiss her. Just a quick peck and she smiled. Bending a little more, he took a deep breath and let her scent settle.

He was happy.

"Watch it, mister. I have food in my hands. You distract me too much," PJ teased.

"I'd apologize, but I'm not sorry for stealing a kiss." He indicated she head out to the table with the rice, and he followed with the tamales.

They settled, filling plates as they continued to talk. It was just like any other family dinner. Just like that, PJ had been welcomed at their table the same way Duke and Mick and Courtney's friends had. His mother had treated her like family.

And PJ had responded like family.

It didn't freak him out. He *liked* it. Liked how she fit into his life, liked how she made the effort to be with him the way she did, even with something as normal as hanging with his mom and sister.

He charged forward in his life. It's how he operated. He knew she was different, knew this thing between him and PJ was the real deal. The certainty of it was automatic, like breathing. He'd been missing this connection, though he hadn't had any real sense of just what it was before she'd come along.

His mom looked at him from her place at the head of the table and smiled. He'd presented PJ and she'd approved, and it didn't matter that he was thirty-seven years old and a grown-ass man. It meant something that his mother liked the woman he loved.

From then on, Asa knew his mother would include PJ when she thought of family. She'd be welcome—and expected—at family dinners and events. He probably should have told PJ that to start with. He grinned.

PJ eyed him warily and he found that pleased him. He liked to keep her on her toes.

After dinner, she helped clean up without having to be asked. She made his mom laugh. She and Courtney seemed to get on well too. The marked difference between this dinner and the one he'd had with her family was something he knew PJ hadn't missed.

He couldn't shield her heart from people she so desperately wanted to approve of her. But he was damned glad he could be part of the positive side of her life. Glad that he could love her and protect her as much as possible in the face of this bull with her father.

CHAPTER
Twenty-four

Asa came in just as she was unzipping the overalls she used while doing details work. She folded them, putting them in her duffel.

"I like this direction." He waggled his brows at her. "We should take this to your place. Or my place. Or any place."

"I'm having lunch with Julie and my brothers, remember?" PJ shook her hair out after she'd freed it from the bandana she'd had covering it.

He watched as she put on lipstick and changed from her work boots into flats.

"Since I can't take you anywhere and have my way with you, I'll let you know I'll be here until about four, then heading to the track for a while."

She tiptoed up to kiss him quickly. "Have fun."

"Come out when you finish."

"You need time with your friends without me."

"What do you think I do all goddamn day? I work with them. They're dirty and greasy and they smell bad. *You*, by comparison, are dirty but in the good way, not greasy, and you smell really good."

How it was that he managed to be so bossy and sexy at the

same time, she didn't know. It was a potent brew she could not resist. She shook her head as she grinned. "You're so grumpy when you don't get your way."

"It seems pretty obvious, then, that in order to keep me cheerful you just do as I ask." His frown was more of a glower, but when he sent it her way, it was toothless. When it came to PJ, Asa was a marshmallow and she knew it. He'd draw blood to protect her, but he put a hell of a lot of effort into making her happy.

"I know it does. It's one of the reasons I love you. I may come out but don't count on it. I haven't seen Audra in ages so I might see if she's free to do something," PJ said.

"All right. Text me to let me know. Can I come over after?" Asa sent puppy-dog eyes.

"You hate my apartment. Though to be fair, you hate every place that isn't your house."

"I have a big bed and my coffeemaker is nicer. My shower is bigger. So is my bed."

"And you're more in charge in your own house."

Busted. "So the solution is for you to come over to my house and spend the night."

"But you'll be out late racing and fighting and all that. I have work tomorrow."

It wasn't a complaint. There was no anger or resentment in her words at all. She totally accepted that part of his nature. That burning need to go hard and fast in so many parts of his life.

He reached into his back pocket and pulled out a ring with three keys on it. He dropped it in her palm. "Front door. Back door. Door from the garage into the house. I have lemon coffee cake. I'll make you come so fucking hard you see stars when I get home."

Really, how could she say no to that?

"This is an offer I can't possibly pass up. Say hey to everyone for me. I'll see you later," PJ said.

He hugged her, stealing a kiss. "Drive safely, okay?"

She nodded. "You too. Don't get arrested." She waved as she headed out, leaving him laughing in her wake.

In the old days, he'd have stayed out at the track and then drunk and fucked around for hours, crawling home after two.

But that was before PJ was waiting in his bed, in his home. He raced and talked cars and drank beer with his friends, and he was glad he had. PJ had been right about that. He'd needed the time with them without her too.

But by ten he was done and on his bike, headed home. To her.

His house was quiet, but her car was in his garage when he pulled his bike in. He'd insisted she start parking in his garage when she visited. When it got cold it'd keep her out of the elements.

Her scent was in the air as he came through the house, hanging up his things and taking his shoes off. He liked her red sweater draped over the back of a chair. Bits and pieces of his woman all through his space. Making it a little hers too.

He heard the music as he got to his bedroom. And there she was, on his bed, in a tiny tank top and an even tinier pair of panties, her glasses perched on her nose as she looked up at him from the book in her hands with a smile just for him.

"You're home. Did you have fun?"

"I'm home." He went to her then, pulling her up to her knees on the bed. She was home for him too.

He kissed her and she hummed in that way of hers, all pleased and feline.

"This is more fun than racing. But you weren't there for this, so I had to settle for racing. It was fun too."

She grinned, wrapping her arms around his neck. "Damn right. Glad you had fun otherwise."

"How was your lunch?"

"We plotted revolution."

"I can tell I need to be lying down for this." He pulled his clothes off and got in bed, shifting his arm so she could move into her place, snuggled at his side.

"Jay had some big ugly set-to with my father and Fee. My dad walked out after Fee said some nasty stuff about me to Jay. Wouldn't take a side. Fee threatened Jay, but for once, Jay stood up for himself and for all of us. Turns out Jay had done his home-work and found some leverage for us as siblings to make a power move to take over."

"I take it this is the revolution stuff you mean."

PJ nodded. "There's a poison pill provision in the contract my dad and Fee signed when my grandfather got ill and they took over. There's a way to combine to push them out. If we want."

"And do you? Want that?" Asa treaded carefully here.

"They said the new Colman would be one where I'd have con-trol of a paint and detail shop. My clients, Colman bays. It's what I hadn't dared to hope for. They said they appreciated my creativ-ity and my voice would be heard. This is our company. Grandpa would have wanted us to do this."

Asa didn't want her hurt. Jay hadn't done his job and it had harmed PJ. He hadn't protected her as a brother or as a co-worker, and though he knew she wouldn't want Asa to judge her brother too harshly, he did. Her father and uncle hurt her and Asa wanted to shield her from that too. He also wanted to punch Howard Col-man right in the mouth for telling PJ she was a failure, but that wasn't for thinking on because she needed him to support the choice she'd already made in her mind and heart.

When he first was getting to know her, she'd talked with a great deal of affection about Colman Enterprises and had always shown pride that it was a family business. If they succeeded, she'd be doing what she wanted and building for the next generation too. He knew she wanted that and so even though he worried about her getting hurt—again—he needed to help her get it.

"I want you to do what makes you happy. What makes you satisfied. I support that, no matter what it is that gets you there. But if any of them fucks up and you end up bearing all the heat for this, I will personally kick his or her ass."

"So romantic." But she laughed.

"You're going to do it."

She paused, choosing her words. "I've been thinking about it. Not just today, of course, but since I left. I had a plan when I resigned. I knew they'd realize how much I did and how integral I was to Colman and ask me back. Beg me maybe, but I wasn't going to make a big deal out of it. But they...didn't. I wasn't expecting that. So my dad and uncle, they don't care. They'd rather me be a silent cog in their machine than bring anything to the table on my own. I just couldn't choose that path. I made my own way. I'm not pretending I didn't have a leg up because of my name. But I built this business in large part because I'm good at it. And my brothers and sister, *they* see it and appreciate it. Not as well as they should, maybe. I guess I have to accept that it's never going to come from them in a way I need. But I get it elsewhere.

"The truth is, Colman means a lot to me. I can't just turn my back on it when it needs me. My father and uncle, they've stopped innovating. They're satisfied with tires and they don't think beyond that. Beyond when they both retire. That offends me. Maybe it won't when I'm their age. But yes, I'm going to do it because someone should fucking care about this business."

He kissed her forehead. "Yes, they should."

"What do you think? *And don't say* 'whatever makes you happy.' I don't need you to tell me what to do. I want your input."

"I think you should do it. It's going to be tough and there'll be a high chance of family drama, but you know that. You want to do this. If for no other reason than that, I'd support you. But you need to do this, and I understand that. I've got your back."

She went up to her elbow to look at him better. "You do. Thank you for that."

"My heart." He cupped her cheek. "Didn't see you coming at all. And once I did, you were faster and cornered me. Thank god you never fucking give up, huh?"

Laughing, she bent to kiss him. "You let me catch you. You wanted what I have going on."

He rolled, laying her flat on her back, looming over her. "Yes. I do, every moment of the day. Speaking of which, I promised you orgasms earlier."

"So hard I saw stars. If you wanted to be really accurate, I mean."

"Top drawer. Blue silk bag." He paused. "Yes, for now. Bring me the bag."

She licked her lips, her pupils big, a flush on her skin before she padded over to his dresser, where he kept most of their toys and gear. While her back was to him he took the opportunity to look at her ass in those little panties he'd be divesting her of shortly.

Then she turned and it was the way her nipples pressed against the front of her tank top that caught his attention.

She came to him, handing the bag over. He got to his feet, licking his way up her neck.

She took his hand and guided it to her pussy, pulling the fabric of her panties aside.

Ready? Hell yes. So hot and wet they both groaned.

"Of course I'm ready. I've been waiting for you," she murmured as he pulled his fingertips away.

When she said stuff like that it sort of unraveled him. That raw honesty regarding how much she desired him was the hottest thing.

One-handed, he pulled her tank top up and off. She smiled, one brow rising. "So." He opened the bag and slid the magnetic clamps into his palm. "We tried clamps before, but they weren't right for your piercings. Let's try these."

He kissed along her jaw and neck before playing with her nipples, making them harder.

He put each clamp on, letting the magnets and the bars through her piercings work together.

She sucked in a sharp breath as the sensation bolted through her. Still, more pain than she preferred was in her face.

"Give it a moment. I think it might help if you come."

He stroked over her arms and back as he kissed her, as she lost the tension of fighting the pain and gave over to it once it began to change into pleasure.

"Now you need the egg."

She swallowed hard but managed to grab the little case and bring it back to him.

"Put it in."

She rested a foot on his calf and slid the egg-shaped vibrator inside her pussy.

And hummed.

He played these games, but she always won because she was so sexy and gorgeous she got to him, challenged his control.

Asa took the remote from her and set it low, watching her nipples darken as she got hotter. And then that second flush of pleasure as the clamps worked against all that blood rushing to her nipples.

"Giving you pleasure is my addiction. Did you know that?"

She smiled.

"But my pleasure is to watch you give yourself pleasure."

He moved to sit back against the pillows and watch as she chose the wingback chair across from the bed.

And spread her thighs wide.

"I'll let you know what I want you to do with your hands," he admonished as she played her fingers against her clit. She did it again, her gaze locked on his.

"Someone needs it bad."

"It's your fault, Asa."

"How is it my fault, beautiful?"

"You're you. You're so sexy and hot and you're mine and I want to shout it out everywhere I go. *Yes, people, this is in my bed using all that on me.* I never imagined getting anything as amazing as you in my stocking on Christmas morning."

"That's good enough that I'll let you touch your clit. Slow. I don't want you to rush, even though I know how greedy you are. I'm going to use the flogger after this. Just thought you should know."

She gasped like she'd been underwater too long and he had to close his eyes just a moment to get himself back under control once more.

He got up to retrieve the longer-handled flogger. He squeezed it hard enough to make the leather creak, enough that she heard it too.

"I haven't used this one in a while. But after you come, I'm going to flog you until your skin is hot and pretty pink. Then I'll shove my cock in you and take those clamps off."

She shivered.

He moved to her, trailing the tails of the flogger over her shoulders. She turned her head and licked over his cock, eyes on him as she slid the flat of her tongue against the slit.

He flicked the next-highest setting on the egg, watching her eyelids go half-mast.

"Close?" He smeared the head of his cock and the bead of pre-come over her lips and she licked it off, making him grin.

"Yes." Her voice was a little shaky. She was trying to hold back, but he was making it harder and harder.

He wasn't into orgasm denial. It wasn't his kink. He wanted her coming often and hard.

He bent, pressing his lips to her ear. "Go on then."

She made a strangled sound and he straightened, taking in the sight of her, flushed and tousled, thighs spread, fingers stroking over her clit. So raw and carnal.

He caught that moment when she tipped into climax, when her gaze blurred and her lips parted.

He went to his knees then, moving her hand, licking hard and fast as he took her from one orgasm into the next.

It was too much. Every part of her was brilliantly, blindly soaring, her inner muscles clutching around that egg as he licked her hard and fast.

Her nipples throbbed as she came so thoroughly it seemed to seep from every pore.

She slumped when he finally backed off, kissing her thigh, slipping the egg free.

"Up."

He helped her to her feet, guiding her back to the bed.

Taking her hands, he guided them to the post. "Hold on here."

She'd never expected to like the flogger, but by that point he'd used them on her enough and with plenty of variety and she could proclaim it her favorite.

He started slow. A caress of the leather against her skin. Gentle. Rhythmic. Down her back, over her ass and thighs. Against her shoulders. He took care around her nipples, brushing the curves of her breasts instead of direct stimulation.

And then the first strike on the meat of her ass cheeks. He did it again and again. Moving subtly so the heat built carefully. He created pleasure like he worked on cars. Meticulously and with great creativity.

She closed her eyes, resting her forehead against the wood and letting herself fall away and become all sensation.

He'd be looking at her, watching the pink on her skin. Making sure he wasn't going too far, but getting harder and harder at the sight. Loving that precision.

He trailed the tails over her hip. "So beautiful. Jesus."

There was more heat and the soothing cool of his breath as he blew over her skin from time to time.

And then he tossed the flogger to the mattress. She roused at the sound of the condom wrapper tearing.

He kissed her neck. "Come on with me." He led her to the bench at the foot of his bed and sat. "On your knees, brace your hands on the footboard."

She obeyed; all the while his hands caressed.

"Close your eyes."

She did, and then there was an intense rush of sensation when he took the clamps off. There was no chance to gather her fraying wits because in one thrust he was inside her, fucking her hard and deep, and all she could do was gasp as she hovered on the edge of climax in one very long wave of pleasure.

He was so damned deep and she still pushed back, using her grip on his bed to leverage herself against him each time he thrust. The backs of her thighs stung as they brushed against the hairs on his thighs. It didn't matter.

She wanted him. All of him. Every intense thing he made her feel.

And he gave it.

This was making love. It didn't have to be sweet in a traditional sense. It was sweet for Asa and PJ. He loved her and cherished her, and the way he touched her, like he'd never get enough, humbled her to her toes.

Love did that. Laid you bare. Broke you open and opened you up. It made you want to be better.

He reached around her body, molding his body to her back, the heat of him against the skin he'd flogged, his fingers finding her wet and ready to come again.

And she did. Around him as he came too.

He pulled out and they both made their way to the mattress, her on her belly, him splayed out at her side, their fingers tangled as they got their breath again.

CHAPTER
Twenty-five

You've got like eleven billion roses out here," Julie called out.

PJ had been in her bedroom trying to figure out what to wear to the car show that night when the doorbell had rung and her sister went out to deal with it.

PJ pulled on her lotus robe and headed into the living room. "I think eleven billion might be an exaggeration."

She skidded to a halt as she took it all in.

Julie said, "Probably. But five dozen. That's close enough."

"Sixty and eleven billion? Not so close if you meant tacos or people, but roses? Yeah, that's close enough."

Her sister handed PJ two cards. "I think it's safe to say these are from Asa. But open the cards before I pass out from not knowing."

"I'm really glad you don't overstate things or exaggerate."

"Me too. God, what a drag that would be." Julie motioned to the cards. "Open."

They were in Asa's handwriting, which made her smile. He'd gone into the florist to do this himself that morning. "How lucky am I?"

She opened the card he'd marked with a *1* in the lower right corner.

My wild rose, you're going to wow everyone tonight. I love you, Asa.

She read it to herself before she tucked it back in the envelope. "They're from Asa."

"No lie."

The second card said, *There's some language of flowers stuff that says what color roses mean what things. So I got you all the colors of roses they had because you're everything.*

Julie poked her arm. "Oh my god, you're blushing and you look a little sniffly. What does it say?"

"I can't. He'd ... It's so sweet and lovely, but I don't want to expose him like that."

Julie hugged her. "Really? I love that. Yay to that."

Before she went back to get changed, PJ headed into the kitchen, pulling out smaller containers and spreading flowers all over her apartment, letting herself be happy about them and the lovely things he'd written.

"He frowns a lot. How does he make it hot? It's like a weird superpower," Julie said as PJ stepped into the red dress she'd decided to wear because she wanted to tuck red roses in her hair and the color was so similar.

PJ met her sister's gaze in the mirror. "I know. Zip me, please." Julie zipped and hooked the back of her dress.

"You're not going to protest that he's just misunderstood?"

PJ rolled her eyes and then trimmed some of the red roses to tuck into her hair. "He *totally* frowns a lot. He's grumpy. But it's adorable. Which must mean I love him. He ranges around being all *grrr* and *Hey you kids get off my lawn* all while he races cars and bikes he built or restored and has a piercing in his ween."

They both dissolved into giggles. "I'm never going to be able to look at him again without blushing."

"Whatever. Where is Asa?" PJ looked at her watch.

"Call him. I'm going to run over to Shawn's to pick him up. I'll see you soon. Love you."

PJ hugged her sister back. "Love you too. See you guys soon."

It wasn't more than five minutes later when Asa rolled up in a sleek black Jag. A paint job she'd finished not too very long ago.

He added to the wow factor when he stepped out wearing a suit and looking so ridiculously gorgeous she pressed her hand to her throat. At dinner with her parents he'd worn a tie and dress pants. But this. Shew. Gunmetal-gray suit with a dark blue shirt and a dark tie. Hair tied back. Intense gaze. Damn. He was *hers*.

She took in the long prowl of a walk as he headed up the steps and paused, looking her over slowly before he let himself reach her.

There she was, the lamp from her place backlighting her like an angel. If angels wore snug red dresses and roses in their hair.

He bent to brush his lips against her neck. "You look fucking delicious."

Just a few weeks before, he'd complimented her on a red blouse she'd been wearing. It had looked so pretty against the pale porcelain of her skin with those delightful freckles.

She'd been wearing red more often ever since. Including the auburn streaks throughout her golden-blond hair.

PJ did it because he liked it.

"Thank you." She smoothed down the front of his shirt and the tie. "I've never seen you in a suit before. I'm fully in support of you doing this again. I want to rumple you and muss you and lick you up and down like an ice cream cone."

Desire tugged him closer to her. Always. "My favorite."

"Going to keep me on my toes tonight, huh?"

He brought her to him, closing that small space left keeping them apart. After a breath, he led and they began to sway through the living room. She felt so good, the bounty of her body in his arms where she fit just right. "Only if that's where I need you so I can fuck you deeper."

She blinked up at him, her smile easy. Not at all weirded out by the stuff he said. "Romantical. Speaking of that, thank you for the roses and the cards. I love you."

"I love you too." He kissed her and stepped back before he got any harder.

"Are we waiting on Audra and Tom?"

As usual. Asa was used to what he called Duke-time. Which meant you had to add fifteen minutes to any time Duke said he'd be somewhere. But Audra was a thousand times worse. He had no idea how PJ could handle it on a regular basis.

"They're going to meet us there. As will Julie and Shawn. No reason to hang around here getting agitated as you wait for people who are perpetually late."

He snorted. "It's a little chilly out. Do you want a coat or something?"

She paused to grab a wrap and turn off all the lights.

"Where's your overnight bag?"

She pointed to the bag she used when she stayed over and he hefted it, holding the door for her and then waiting as she locked up.

"Why are you driving this? Did you get the client to loan it to you?" she asked as he tossed the duffel in the trunk and then opened her door.

"I'm the client."

He closed her door and went around to the driver's side.

PJ blinked, sure she'd heard him wrong. "What do you mean *you're* the client? I met the client. He looked at my tits for the entire exchange. I charged him extra for that!"

Asa burst out laughing. "I'm going to pop Henry the next time I see him. Asshole. I'm sorry he was a jerk, but it makes me laugh that you charged him extra for being a dick."

"I charged *you* extra. Why did you do that?"

"Because I wanted something that would be extra work and

thus would be expensive and I knew you'd try to do it for your materials or some shit, so I wanted you to do a job like you would for any other client. Henry—he's an army friend too—might have been an ass to you, but this paint job is fantastic and worth every penny."

"You didn't have to have some elaborate scheme. You could have just asked."

"You're mad that I wanted you to charge me a real rate instead of the guy-who-makes-me-come-hard rate?"

"I have the right to make that choice if I want to."

"But I don't want you to. I don't want price breaks. When we were first starting out, I remember how hard it was. How close to the margins we were. I didn't want to put you in a place where you felt you had to take a hit. I can afford it. And you just boosted the value. People will see it tonight too. I'll have it sold within the month, most likely."

He just—ugh! PJ worked to keep her voice level. "I counted to ten. Then I had to go to thirty. I appreciate that you thought of me and my business like that. And I know you can afford it. I would have charged you materials and time and that would have been *my choice*. You made that choice for me, and that's not cool. I'm usually fine with your need to control stuff. But this is not an area of my life I'll cede to anyone. Whether I give you a price break or not isn't about what *you want*. Don't you see? This is connected to that other stuff about control and trust. This is my stuff. My choice to make or not. My skills are mine, my time is mine, who I work with and for what rates is mine. You're not my keeper. I want to be with you, not live through you."

He blew out a breath. "I just didn't want you giving me a break you couldn't afford."

"I appreciate that you wanted to help me." She reached out to squeeze his hand. "I love that you want to protect me and keep me from harm. Talk to me, don't think for me, and we'll be good. It's not up to you to decide my pricing. That's my business. My choice. This going-around-me stuff, it is not cool."

"Okay. I see what you mean. I'm sorry. I'll do my best not to do it again."

"Your best is pretty awesome."

He used valet so they could get out close to the front doors, not wanting her to have to walk the mile through parking lots. He was a very nice man.

"I've been to what seems an incalculable number of trade shows in my life. My first was while I was still an infant. But this is better. This is totally cool."

Asa nodded, taking PJ's hand. "Absolutely. Better than cool. This is fantastic."

She walked along at his side, nerves jittering. He paused, pulling her out of the crowd and standing very close. "Penelope Jean, you are really good at what you do. That's why your stuff is here on someone else's dime, dig?"

She nodded. "I know. I do!"

Her mouth firmed and it took all his control not to kiss her as she got rid of the briefest frown.

"I know I do good work." This time he knew she believed it.

"There you are." His PJ was confident and strong. She knew she had talent. It was part of the reason people hired her. Her confidence was alluring.

"Next year I hope to have my own booth. With or without Colman."

"Do it," Asa challenged.

"I will. Speaking of that, where are you guys?"

"Restoration and custom work is across the hall from where your cars are. Let's go look at that first and then we can see what's going on over at the Twisted Steel booth."

"Debauchery, most likely."

He bent to kiss her, his mouth against the curve of her cheek. "You're perfect. I'm proud of you."

She clutched the front of his jacket, swaying a little. "Thank you. I love you." Her voice didn't get just a little thinner in the middle this time, her nervousness under control.

Right there in front of all those people in the exhibition hall, Asa blushed. "Fuck yeah." He turned her and they headed out into the main part of the large hall.

The cars with her paint were being featured by an auction house, so it wasn't too far away, just across a wide aisle where the edge of the Twisted Steel booth was. She could be over there to answer questions and network but also come his way to take a break.

He looked at the map in her hand. "Blue. So west. Go up here and hang a left."

"I'm relieved I don't have to set anything up this year. This time I can scope it out to see the lay of the land. Then when it comes time to set up next year I'll know what to expect."

PJ couldn't help the gigantic grin she got at the sight of her work. Most people wouldn't say, *Oh my god, that paint!* They'd think the entire car was fantastic and would hopefully think Cargrand Auctions was putting out only the very best.

It'd be the people who dealt with the auction house whose opinions would be so important. The shops like Twisted Steel were steady profit for her. But if she could do more with other types of businesses, with dealerships and the individual clients who wanted something extra special, she'd be growing *her* business just right.

And the truth was, if she went back to Colman and had the infrastructure of a billing department, the bays, and the industrial equipment for bigger jobs instead of having to rent that space herself, that would be a huge plus.

She already had offers to come on at other major paint shops. While flattering, she wanted to make it on her own.

"I have no idea how you managed to get this red so cherry." Asa looked closely.

She'd never reveal in public just how many tries it had taken to get that tone. "I'm just glad I liked chemistry. These lights really do make it pop."

"The metallic in that racing green, though. Yes, Penelope Jean, this is magic."

It'd been a risk. Racing green was a classic, traditional color and it appealed to a certain kind of customer. But the metallic was so subtle it managed to remain traditional while having just a smidge of rock star in it too.

She grinned. "I can't lie, I'm totally proud of that."

They looked around at the other cars. Asa shook hands with people because it seemed like he knew everyone.

PJ gave her card to a few people and they headed over to the Twisted Steel booth, where Duke was surrounded by several women, all gazing adoringly at him.

"I don't know how he does it," Asa said. "Everywhere you go it's this."

PJ looked up to Asa and then back to Duke. "Are you kidding me? How can you not know? He's gorgeous. Successful. Drives fast cars and motorcycles. He's got a slow, panty-dropping drawl. What's not to like?"

Asa frowned. "He's not me, that's what not to like."

PJ patted his arm. "I like you best. Your drawls are different. But it's impossible to ignore Duke's attributes. Even if yours totally overshadow his."

He appeared satisfied with that, and she wanted to kiss him for being so adorable but she resisted.

Once Duke saw Asa, he brought him over and they began talking about a rebuild of some sort. Duke's admirers moved on once actual business started being discussed and PJ smirked.

It was fine to see women gawk at Asa. He was gawkworthy.

But he was hers. So they could look their fill, but no touching. She remembered what he was like before they started seeing each other. He always had a passel of women rubbing up all over him, but as far as she could tell he never looked twice at anyone but her, so while sometimes she wanted to slap the mitts of the shop bunnies that came around, she'd had no reason to doubt his affections.

So she'd take the gawking because she had Asa, all of him, and they only got to look.

It was about an hour later when she finally caught sight of Shawn ambling her way.

He hugged her. "I just came from the other side of the hall, so I passed the cars on my way. You're kickass."

"Thank you."

"Julie is right behind me. She and Mom got caught by one of Dad's cronies."

True to his claim, her sister, her mother, and Jay came toward them. Lenore hugged her, kissing both cheeks.

"Well done, darling."

"She told everyone standing nearby that her daughter had painted the cars." Julie hugged her next, followed by Jay.

"Seriously quality stuff." Jay nodded, impressed. "I looked at their pricing sheets. You weren't kidding about profit potential for Colman."

"Not bad for a college dropout with a pierced face?"

He grinned, hugging her again. "I do miss arguing with you every day at work." He leaned close to whisper to her. "We heard from the attorney. I'll talk with you about it later, all right?"

She nodded and then looked back down the way they'd all come. "Did Dad get held up too?"

Her mother's mouth flattened into a line and Julie sighed.

That's when she knew he hadn't come. She'd waited over two hours and he wasn't going to show up.

She wanted it not to matter. Wished it didn't hurt as bad as it did. Even after he'd said all that stuff to her, she wanted him to come see her work. Because she was his child, if for nothing else.

"He's not here."

Asa came up, pausing to kiss her mother and sister before putting a hand at the small of PJ's back. "I see the Colmans are in the house. Nice to see you all. Did you get the chance to check out PJ's work?"

His body language changed once he truly took note of her expression. "What's going on?"

"Nothing. I'm done now. I'd like to go home." She wanted to pull the covers up over her head.

Her mom took PJ's hand. "He wasn't feeling well. He wanted to come."

PJ just looked at her mother. "Stop making excuses for him."

Jay shook his head. "PJ's right. But *we're* here. That's what matters."

"It does matter, yes. I'm happy you're all here. It means a lot to me. I'll talk to you all later. Call me about that thing, Jay."

Her mother hugged her. "He doesn't know how to be sorry. Don't give up on him."

They said their good-byes and Asa led her away.

CHAPTER
Twenty-six

Asa wasn't sure if he should keep to the plan, but then he decided, fuck Howard Colman. PJ deserved a special dinner in her honor for this, and he'd be damned if he let that asshole hurt her any more that night.

"I'm really hungry. You want to get some dinner? Celebrate you, my wild rose?"

She smiled, but it was sad at the edges. "Sure. I'm hungry."

He shoved all his annoyance down as far as he could. Her mother should have warned him about this so they could have prepared PJ for it rather than have her great night come crashing down around her ears because she got broadsided by it.

"You don't have to deal with all this Eastlake traffic. We can get something closer to your house, you know."

He rolled his eyes; even though she couldn't see, she'd know. "You said just a few days ago that you'd been craving Serafina, and that's where we're going."

"Okay then. Thank you," she said, her voice a little less flat.

He parked and took her inside and that's when she saw his mom and sister standing with her friends.

"Congratulations!"

PJ took in the scene with a smile on her face. "Aw, guys."

Asa just watched, approving of how her friends hugged her, excited for her success. His mom and sister hugged her and then Asa.

"You had this planned all along?" PJ asked him in a tone that made him so fucking glad he had.

"Your mother and sister did most of it. I just suggested the venue."

PJ didn't have to tiptoe up because she had on such high heels, but she kissed him, cupping his face. "I won't embarrass you too much when I tell you I know this was all your idea. I thought we established that I know that you're all soft and warm inside for me."

Asa ducked his head to brush his lips against hers, flattered but not wanting to belabor who did what. She needed to feel like everyone she loved was concerned about how she felt and what made her happy. He didn't need a blue ribbon to do it. PJ was pleased and felt cared for and that was the natural order of things.

Her family came in right as they were being seated. He tried not to be too hostile. Lenore had, as Asa had told PJ, taken care of preordering the food and had cocktails waiting for them, the flowers on the table and soft classical music playing in the background.

But she hadn't protected her daughter again, and he really didn't like that.

"What the hell is the deal?" he asked Jay later on. PJ was between Julie and Audra, listening to a story his mom was telling them at the other end of the table, so he could speak without worrying she'd overhear.

Jay shook his head. "I don't know. I thought he was coming. I talked to him at work yesterday and reminded him of it. He didn't say anything then."

"You people are really beginning to piss me off. She's important and she wants your goddamn love and you disappoint her over and over."

"I get that you've seen a lot of bullshit, but you don't know any-thing about us or our family. I love my sister; you don't have any right to claim otherwise."

"Yeah? I know your father called her a failure in a crowded restaurant. I know he didn't come to an event that was incredibly important to his child. I know he let her quit without even trying to stop her. I know all she wants is his approval, so much she bent herself into a pretzel for years and it still wasn't enough. And I know your mother could have given me a heads-up about this so I could have taken the time to prepare PJ for disappointment, and she didn't. I know what I need to know. Which is that your sister wants to do the right thing. She wants you all to be proud of her and support her and she's been let down right and left. You got some other way to spin any of that?"

Jay exhaled hard. "Chances are, my mom thought she could get him to come tonight and she worked up until the very last min-ute. She wasn't raised to contradict her husband. It's hard for her to stand up to him. She loves him and in a lot of ways is dependent on his affection and support. As for my father, you're right. PJ's wanted him to notice her since she was tiny and he just . . . I don't know. It's something about her in particular. We're trying, Asa. Trying to do what's right, not only for Colman and each of us, but for the four of us as the caretakers of something our grandfather built. None of us wants PJ hurt. None of us was happy our dad was a no-show. I like that you want to protect her, but cut us a break."

Asa snorted. "Not my job. You get yourself someone who loves you and she'll cut you a break when it comes to this sort of thing. But my job is PJ's well-being."

Jay nodded. "Fair enough. How about this? Give us a chance to do the right thing here."

"I've been doing that."

"We heard promising news from the attorney and we're going

to try to meet this coming week to talk about our options at Colman. We want to bring PJ back into the family and into the business."

Asa knew how much PJ wanted this, so he clenched back the words he preferred to say and instead shrugged. "All right, but my patience is thin when it comes to this."

"Mine too. It's time for us to step out of the box, and PJ's the best at that of all four of us."

At the end of the night, as everyone was out on the sidewalk saying their good-byes, Lenore waited with PJ, speaking to her quietly. Asa walked his mom and sister to their cars and headed over to see what was going on.

"I was just telling Penelope that I was sorry for her father not being here tonight and that I wanted to invite you over. We used to do a Friday-night dinner once a month, but over the last two years or so we've fallen away from it. We're in dire need of them again, I think. Would you come? This Friday?"

Asa looked to PJ. She needed to make this choice. He'd back whatever she said.

"We'll be there."

Her mother hugged her. "I love you, darling, and I'm so proud. I'll see you both Friday night at seven."

Shawn nodded his thanks to Asa, who shrugged. This was PJ's show. He'd had more than enough Colmans but for one.

"Thanks for being so nice to my mom. I know you're mad," PJ said as they started back to his house.

"I'm nice to you. Because I love you. And I'm not mad at you at all."

"I know." She rested her head in her hand. "Thanks for that dinner too. I know you put it together. Just because my mom set up a meal there doesn't mean I don't know you were the reason it all happened to start with."

"I love you. I want you to be happy. I'm proud of you, and

so is every person at that table tonight. Your family included. I don't know about your father, but you don't need to go over that right now."

She put a hand on his thigh and he let that touch settle his annoyance.

They'd get through. Her family needed to get on board. But one way or another, Asa would be sure PJ got her happy ending.

He'd planned on taking the Jag back to Twisted Steel, leaving it there, and switching to the BMW, but she looked tired and he didn't want her to have to wait around.

But when he parked at the curb she turned to face him. "You can't park this on the street."

"Of course I can. I park my extra cars in the driveway and at the curb all the time. Nothing has ever happened."

"What's in your garage?"

"What's the matter, baby?" She'd never cared where he parked what, and it was unusual for her to keep on at him.

She unbuckled his belt and then his suit pants. "Wait," he said around a tongue that felt too big. "A minute and we'll be inside."

"I don't want to wait."

She pumped her fist around him to the root and up again. It was late enough that the street outside the car was empty; most people were already at home and in bed.

She had that look she got when she wasn't going to be swayed. And with her hand on his dick, he wasn't too invested in trying to talk her out of whatever she wanted to do with it.

He leaned back, easing himself out of his pants a little better. Then she fucking leaned over, got his cock wet with her spit and he nearly came right then. His sweet Penelope Jean just spit on his cock as she gave him a hand job in public.

He got hot and shivery all at once at the carnal power of that.

"Jesus, that's dirty."

She cocked her head to look at him. "Yeah?"

He tipped his chin. "Yeah. Give me more."

She did it again, continuing to pump her fist around him, now wet with his precome and her saliva.

She leaned close, putting her head on his shoulder as she paused to give his piercing some love until he shuddered, right on the edge, before resuming her rhythm.

Her voice came, a sultry murmur in the dark. "I want you to come, Asa. I want you to feel good. We'll go inside and you'll be in me because I want that too and you always give me what I want. Do you realize how that makes me feel? Like a goddess. You're there for me. Not just tonight, but the entire time we've been together. Steady. Solid. Fierce. I love that you're like this now with me. So big and strong and yet you never scare me, not even a tiny bit."

He strained not to thrust up into her grip and sent the car rocking. He was so close and her voice was like a stroke of her fingertips up his spine.

She gave herself then, like the gift she was, and he couldn't do anything but come. And as he did, she shifted her skirt over his pants to protect his suit.

He cursed and then said her name as another wave of pleasure rocketed through him.

After what felt like twenty minutes he blew out one long breath and tipped his head back against the seat for a few moments.

When he could form words again, he sat straighter and tucked himself in. "I've never thought much of hand jobs one way or the other, to be honest with you. But that was one of the hottest fucking things I've experienced. You kill me in all the best ways." He kissed her hard and then looked down at where she'd folded her dress back. "Sorry about that."

She grinned up at him. "I'll throw it in the washing machine once we get inside. It's not the first time you've come on my clothes. At least this time I don't have to wash my hair."

Joy shot through him as he burst out laughing, hugging her to his side. "True, and I didn't even smear your lipstick."

"There's always next time."

"This is why you wanted me to park in the garage."

She shrugged. "It's all right. It was hotter out here. Though you have to unlock the door so I can go get this dress off."

"Yes. Do that. I'll bring in your stuff and meet you in the bedroom. I think you promised I could come inside you next."

He kissed her and went to go deal with the front door.

She headed inside, pausing to kiss him on the way past. The house felt like home to her as she headed to his laundry room and realized she couldn't unhook or unzip her dress.

She called his name when she heard him turn on his alarm.

"What is it?" He came in.

"I can't undo the back of my dress."

He was really good at getting her out of her clothes, so it wasn't long before she slipped free and tossed it in the washer.

"Mmm. I like that slip thing."

Suddenly it hit her. The utter fuckery of that night. The way he'd been at her side the whole time. The way it had felt with him out in his car. Dirty and taboo and yet it was Asa and PJ just the same. Hard, soft, romantic, in trouble, or in good times, it would always be PJ and Asa.

And here she stood in a laundry room in his house and he looked at her like she was magnificent when all she wore was a pretty but basic chemise.

What a thing it was to have this man see her as desirable. It made her weak in the knees.

She slid the straps from her shoulders and let it hit the ground, stepping free of the silk. She shimmied from her bra, letting it drop and smiling at the way his gaze followed it and then jerked back up to her breasts. She left the panties and heels on as she turned around, braced her hands on the dryer, and looked back over her shoulder at him.

"We've been tested twice now. I want to feel that piercing without a condom."

He groaned. "Goddamn. Look at you. My filthiest girl-next-door fantasy come to life, complete with a badass sense of humor and a lot of talent."

He'd already gotten rid of the jacket, shirt, tie, and shoes, but she was glad to be paying attention when he pulled his pants and boxers down and his cock sprang free. So hard it tapped his belly.

"I have excellent recovery time when my hot blonde thrusts her ass out at me and tells me to fuck her." He shoved her panties to the side and she closed her eyes a moment at the urgency in his touch.

He pushed in agonizingly slow. She squirmed and tried to move, but he held her in place with his forearm at the center of her back.

"Don't rush me. You feel so good I plan to enjoy every single second. You're so hot and wet. Fucking you this way tugs on my piercing." He shuddered and she swallowed hard.

He wasn't lying. Having him in her naked that way felt a million times better, and it had already been amazing.

Once he finally got all the way in he reached around her body, cupping her breasts as he pulled out slowly, only to reverse course just as he was nearly all the way out.

She'd expected hard and fast, the way he'd yanked her underpants aside. But instead he devastated her with hard and slow. He kept one hand on her nipple, playing with the bar, and the other slid down between her legs, where he made slow taps against her clit with the pad of his middle finger until she unraveled in the most delicious way.

He continued to fuck her at his own pace, touching her, kissing her wherever he could reach. Loving her and making everything all right again.

He came after making her come once more and grabbed some clean towels from the basket. "You don't have to wash your hair this time either, but no condoms is messier. Plus I want to rub soap on your tits."

She hugged him after he'd taken his pants off and they headed into the shower and then snuggled down into his bed.

"I'm sorry about your dad."

She sighed, snuggling closer. "No more tonight."

"All right. You've earned it. I love you."

"Love you too." She closed her eyes and only let herself think about the design she planned to do on a motorcycle that next day.

CHAPTER
Twenty-seven

P J took a deep breath as they walked up the front steps.

Asa put his arm around her. "Gonna be just fine. No matter what, I'm here."

She knocked and it was Shawn who opened up. He smiled at his sister, pulling her into a hug. "Come on in."

He shook Asa's hand and they walked through what Asa had imagined would be a cold, sterile mansion but was really a lovely but comfortable house. Clearly Lenore kept it up to entertain in frequently. Her touch was evident everywhere.

He definitely hadn't expected a fully set table on a wooden back deck with lit candles in hanging multicolored glass containers.

"Wow."

"I wasn't exaggerating when I said everyone accepts an invite to dinner at Lenore's."

He was impressed but also wondered why Lenore put more energy into candles and flowers and table settings than reining in her jerk of a husband.

"This is beautiful, Mrs. Colman."

She smiled at Asa, but hugged PJ first. "Thank you. I'm glad you're both here. Julie just ran to the store to get some Parmesan. I can't believe I forgot. Would either of you like a drink? We've got red and white wine, beer, soda, juice, those fizzy waters Jay likes so much..."

"I'll get us both a beer." PJ headed to one of the ice-filled buckets on a nearby table in the large open kitchen overlooking the deck and manicured back yard.

Jay came to join them, greeting PJ and Asa as he poured himself a glass of wine.

Lenore looked the deck over from her place near the stove. "It's chilly tonight, but I have the heaters out so that should keep everyone comfortable." Her mother moved around, adjusting, stirring, pouring. Occasionally she'd give an order for a child to do something, but mainly she knew what she wanted to do and everyone kept out of her way.

Julie returned with the cheese, which she then curled over the top of salads before taking them to the table.

But what Asa really wanted to know was where the hell Howard was. They'd been there about half an hour already and he hadn't shown himself.

Finally, he came out from what appeared to be a home office.

Lenore looked up, smiling. "Oh, there you are. I was beginning to think I was going to have to send an expedition into your office to find you. Dinner is ready."

The look on PJ's face broke Asa's heart. She wanted her dad to be proud of her. To see her as different, and wonderful for it.

Howard looked at Asa and for a moment, he attempted to pull some posturing, dick measuring bullshit. But the lion didn't give any thought to the concerns of the sheep, as his sister liked to say. Asa was an alpha dog, and soon enough Howard turned away.

"Penelope."

She nodded. "Dad. You remember Asa, don't you?"

Howard jerked his head and mumbled a yes. He didn't offer his hand to shake, which was fine with Asa, though he felt bad for everyone else who was clearly embarrassed.

"Let's all sit down." Lenore cut between Howard and PJ, taking her daughter's arm and heading outside. Julie hung back with Asa.

"Is she okay?" Julie asked him.

"She's been quiet. But she had a lot of work yesterday and today, so I'm hoping she hasn't had a lot of time to think about it."

"We're meeting tomorrow morning, so whatever he does tonight will have an impact on that. I wish it could play out otherwise, but I just don't see it at this point."

"Stop whispering and get out here," Lenore called to them.

Asa sat next to PJ, placing himself between her and her dad but far enough away that he was out of punching distance, which was probably for the best. PJ might not forgive him if he broke her dad's jaw.

Food was passed around as everyone attempted to make small talk.

Shawn refilled his wineglass. "Asa, I saw a motorcycle you built for my friend Ernie Patterson. Really excellent work."

"Ernie is a big guy; he needed that big fat back end."

"You have a Softail, don't you?" Jay asked, and they talked bikes and then shifted to cars and racing. Asa hoped Jay stepped up and took care of this thing with his dad like he'd promised, because he could see himself hanging out with Jay. He was a little stiff, but he wasn't a bad guy.

"Motorcycles are dangerous," Howard finally said.

No denying it. Asa nodded. "They are. I've known plenty of guys who've ended up in the hospital after getting into accidents."

"But you do it to look cool? Is that it?"

Asa wondered if Howard had always been like this, or if he'd started off all right and ended up an asshole.

"I do it because I like it. I try to make it safer, but I do it knowing and accepting it is an inherently dangerous activity. Some things you do despite the risks." He wanted to say more, but he kept his tongue. For PJ's sake.

"That makes you a bad bet for my daughter, doesn't it?"

"Dad. You're being rude," Shawn said.

"How am I being rude? It's a valid question."

Asa was pretty done with this piece of shit. "Mr. Colman, your daughter would be too good for *any* man. I'm a grease monkey. I bang out dents for a living. But I'm an honest man doing an honest day's work for what turns out to be a very comfortable living. For whatever reason, Penelope loves me, and of the two of us, I think I'm the one who understands how special that is. I have no plans to mess that up."

"How about you?" Shawn asked their dad. "Can you say the same? That you have no plans to mess up how much PJ loves you? Because I don't think you can right now."

Howard's face darkened. "You shut your mouth, Shawn. This is none of your concern. You think I haven't noticed how you've all started to challenge my authority? And how it all coincides with this *thing* insinuating himself into Penelope's life? And she's such a goddamn needy woman she's got to let him latch on."

Asa stood up and PJ did as well, holding her hand out. "Asa, please."

"Sir, I'm going to have to ask you to apologize to your daughter for that ugly accusation."

"Get the hell out of my house. He's common. Trash! Trying to get at our money through her thighs."

But it wasn't Asa who dealt with that insult, but Lenore, who slapped her husband's face.

"How dare you say such a vulgar, cruel thing to our daughter?"

Red faced, a hand on his cheek, Howard replied, "It's true. Look at her. She tarts up her natural good looks with crazy hair colors and all those tattoos. She consorts with these people." Howard indicated Asa. "She dropped out of college. She quit the job we gave her after that failure and this, the biggest failure of all, this creature who is clearly using her and she's too stupid to see it. Pretty fades, Penelope; what will you do then?"

PJ had gone totally pale. Asa helped her away from the table and back into the house. Shawn had intervened between his parents and Jay was telling everyone to stop talking and calm down.

Julie came in and pulled PJ into a hug. PJ tried not to cry, but Asa saw the strain and knew it was only a matter of time.

"I'm so sorry he said that," Julie said. "He's such an asshole. He's wrong, PJ. You are smart and strong and you are successful. Don't let him make you doubt that. You're coming tomorrow, right?"

PJ nodded and then everyone spilled inside as Lenore shut the sliding doors behind her.

"It's not enough that the whole neighborhood heard you? Calm yourself, Howard."

"Me? You slapped me in the face!"

"Take me home, please," PJ said to Asa. He didn't bother saying anything to anyone else, heading to the front door with PJ. But her father wasn't done.

"Yes, get her out of my house. You've been nothing but a disappointment to me since the day you were born."

Asa turned, heading back toward Howard, but Julie stepped in his way, her hand on his chest. "You'll only make things worse. He'll call the cops if you touch him. PJ is about to lose it; take her home. We'll deal with him. I promise you."

"You all keep saying that and I'm not seeing it." He turned, gathered PJ up, and took her away from that scene as fast as he could.

PJ was numb until about three blocks from Asa's house. Then it hit her that her father had just said all he had, and in front of Asa. Hell, *to* Asa.

Humiliation burned through her as tears sprang to her eyes. His mother had made tamales for their first meeting, and her family had done this to him. Twice.

Yes, she'd been growing away from her dad over the years, but this steady erosion of not just his paternal relationship with her but his basic civility had given way to something far worse.

He loathed her.

She heard it in his tone and she didn't know what to do with that. Distant was one thing. Disapproving was one thing. But loathing? He truly did think she was a failure. Worse, a whore who'd sell her pussy for love or attention.

Her mother had slapped him! And yelled at him. Jay had shouted at him too. Julie had been so upset when they'd hugged as they'd left.

She managed to get to the point where the garage door closed and then she couldn't hold the tears back anymore. Huge, hiccupping sobs hit as she put her head in her hands and gave over to them.

"Sit right there."

Asa got out and came to her side, unbuckled her seat belt, and lifted her into his arms. She tried to protest that she was fine, but she was incoherent from the crying and it felt really good to be held, so she snuggled into him as he kissed the top of her head.

How he managed to get the door open she didn't know, but he did and headed to his couch, where he sat, settling her in his lap.

"Get it all out." He rubbed circles over her back. "I've got you, Penelope. I'm not going to let go."

This made her cry even harder because it was so sweet. She cried as she gave up her hopes of ever truly connecting with her father. She cried as she realized things were about to change again after the breakfast meeting she had the following morning with her siblings too.

She cried for a long time until she just sort of dried up. Still, she was sore and her eyes hurt and her nose was runny and she'd gotten makeup on his shirt and he didn't even care.

"Now before you say a single word, I'm going to need you to listen to me first." Asa kissed her forehead. "Nothing he said tonight was true. You know that in your head, but when your dad says something so cruel, maybe it's harder to know in your heart. So let me tell you what my heart knows. You are smart and ambitious. You're capable and adaptable. He shamed himself tonight. Not you. Never you. Your hope that he would see you for all the wonderful things you truly are doesn't make you dumb, it makes you a woman with a big heart. It makes you my woman, and I love you and I hate that your father hurt you the way he did. I wish I could go back and undo it and make it never have happened. But I can't."

She nodded, so very numb. "I know. I've had to accept he's just not interested. He was never close with me. I was out with my grandpa a lot more than I ever was with him. But I had no idea he hated me."

She'd thought she was out of tears, but apparently not.

"I don't think he hates you. I think he resents you for some reason. He definitely doesn't like me, but he lashed out and has done several times. He wants to push you away. And right now I think that's the best place for you. Away from him. Do whatever you're going to do with your siblings at Colman, but you let your brothers and sister handle your father. He's hurt you enough."

PJ agreed.

PJ stirred her coffee slowly as her siblings settled in at the table.

Jay spoke first. "I'd ask how you are, but it's a stupid question after that scene last night. I'm so, so sorry that happened. He's wrong, PJ."

Shawn buttered some bread. "Mom came to my house after you guys left. She's beside herself with worry for you. I know you're angry and you have every right to be. But he broke something last night. Between them, I mean. I don't think she's going to forgive him."

PJ said, "I don't even know what I feel. Not all of it. I appreciate that you backed me up last night. I'm...still trying to get past the point where I start crying when I think about it too much, so let's talk Colman right now."

They put their heads together and began to plan exactly what they'd do that following Tuesday. It was a big meeting day, so Howard and Fee both would be around.

PJ formally accepted her siblings' offer of reemployment with her own division, and then they all drew up their new organizational chart for Colman Enterprises, with Howard Jr. and Fee Colman as consultants with offices on-site but a reduced workload.

"One last thing. Mom is giving us her vote. Grandma had a voting seat when Grandpa was alive. I guess Mom did too, back before Grandpa got sick. She never gave it up. She called me this morning to say that." Julie looked between them all.

Worry stabbed PJ. "If she does that, he'll leave her."

"She left her wedding rings in the safe at the house before she came home with me last night. PJ, she's done with him. He said some unforgivable things to you. To Jay. To all of us," Shawn said.

"What do you mean to Jay and the rest of you?"

Julie took one of PJ's hands. "After you left he started ranting about what a loser Jay was for being gay and how Shawn was spineless. I'm too masculine to ever get married. He told Mom he had no idea how we turned out to be so awful. He blamed it on her family. Finally Jay and Shawn took him into his room and made him stay there while I got Mom packed up. She called Aunt Jenny and they're going to go visit Aunt Mary in London in two weeks. Will you call Mom? She feels awful. I know she should have dealt with it earlier."

"How can I hold it against her? Yes, she made mistakes, but I'm not in her place. Her whole life is falling apart." Asa had been right. It was crappy parenting. But Lenore loved PJ, even if she wasn't always great at protecting her. PJ could keep her expectations low and still have her mom in her life.

"I think she needs that. All our lives are. That's the whole chrysalis thing right? We'll all be butterflies at the end," Julie said.

"Let's hope so. Do you think maybe Dad had a stroke or something? Maybe he's on pills or his drinking has finally taken a toll?" PJ wished there was something they could learn to make sense of this situation.

Jay shook his head. "He's been getting worse over the past five years. The last three especially. He and Fee have withdrawn from everyone else. Fee has fed him bullshit and he's eaten it up. He's turned into a bitter, entitled old man, and it's not a good look for him. I thought if I managed to get on Fee's good side I could finally get to Dad and make him hear me out. But he's closed himself down to us."

"I think he'll make a fuss just to hear himself shout," Julie said, "but in the end he'll get the hell out of the way. He'll see the writing on the wall. Fee? He's a wild card. He likes money but he hates work. If he can earn and not come to work, he'll probably let go. But he's a vindictive bastard, so you never know for sure."

CHAPTER
Twenty-eight

Wow. I'd let you fire me any day." Asa winked as she came out of the bedroom wearing a navy suit, her hair up in a French twist. She'd colored it the day before so the tips were as blue as the blouse she wore.

"You'll call me when it's over?" He hated that she had to go through the drama and upset of this business with her father and uncle. But he knew she'd do it because that's what needed to be done.

"Yes."

"I love you. Knock 'em dead."

"I love you too."

"Oh, wait a second." He held out a small box. Inside was a necklace with a charm. An *A* intertwined with a *P*. "Think of it as a talisman. I'll protect you even when I'm not in the same room."

She hugged him tight and then waited for him to put the necklace on her. "This is beautiful! How long have you been planning this?"

"Only a few weeks. One of Mick's buddies, a childhood friend of his, makes these. She just finished it yesterday and Mick brought it over himself. I just wanted you to have a piece of me with you wherever you were."

She took his hand and placed it on her chest, over her heart. "I do already. In here. But this necklace is perfect, and it'll totally make me feel better today as I pretty much put my dad on a raft and set him adrift."

"Hush, you. That's not what you're doing at all. You're being kinder than you have to be and you're doing it because you're you. Now go to work. Don't forget to call me."

"Okay, okay. See you later." She paused at the door. "I love you. Thank you." She touched the necklace. "For everything you are."

"Hey, Penelope?"

"Yes?"

"I think you should move in here."

She blinked, staring at him. "You just asked me to move in with you? Right now?"

"I did. I love you. I like being with you. I like waking up with you and having you here with me. You already have a set of keys." He figured this approach was best. She had enough stress. He'd take it as a given and not make any fuss. Hopefully she'd just give in and let him love her the way she had from pretty much the start.

"You're a trip, Asa Barrons. Yes, I'll move in, but I have three months left on my lease so it'll have to wait until then."

She blew him a kiss and was gone, leaving him smiling. She was moving in. That three months thing wasn't a big deal. Just because she paid rent didn't mean she couldn't move in with him. Mick needed a place; maybe he could take over the lease. He'd like it, even that fucked up hill.

Whatever the case, they'd work it out.

When Julie and PJ walked in the front doors of Colman Enterprises shortly before the meeting was to start, everything was already in place.

PJ had to give it to Jay, he really had stepped up and taken over.

She and Julie paused at the reception desk.

"Morning, Helen."

"PJ! It's good to see you. Are you back?"

Julie nodded. "She is. Today's her first day back so she probably won't be getting any calls, but if she does, we'll all be in the meeting until about noon. She'll be out in the workshop from now on, so there's a crew out there now getting her an office set up."

"I'm so glad to hear that. We missed you a lot around here."

"Are my father and uncle in yet?" Julie asked.

"Yes. I just took in food, they're in the conference room already. I think Jay just came through about five minutes ago too." Which they already knew.

They waited in Julie's office until Shawn and Jay joined them and then they went over the game plan one more time.

But when they opened the door to go to the meeting, their mother was on the other side.

"I'm here to cast my vote in person."

PJ shook her head. "Mom, you don't have to do this. We have your proxy."

Her mother shook her head. "No, PJ. I need to face him down. I loved him with all my heart for a long, long time. Loved him through his faults and his moods. Tried to give you more love when he gave you less. But he crossed a line. He crossed it more than once, and I was weak and let it continue. I wasn't a good mom then. I'm sorry."

PJ and her mother had gone out for a hike and spent hours talking about things. About Asa and her paint business, about her mother's growing realization that her father was turning into a bitter, hostile stranger who said and did the unforgivable. She'd told PJ it had been like a switch had been thrown and all that intensity of feeling she had for him had just gone dark.

"She deserves this chance," Shawn murmured.

She did. They just had to hope their mom wouldn't lose her nerve once she got face-to-face with their dad.

"Let's go."

To say Howard Colman Jr. was surprised by the sight of his youngest child and his estranged wife walking into his boardroom would have been an understatement.

But he took in the sight of all five of them and got it soon enough. His surprise went hard and so did PJ's resolve.

Jay folded his hands in front of him on the table and took their father and uncle in. "So as not to waste time, let's just get straight to the point. The five of us are claiming our rightful voting seats on the board of Colman Enterprises."

"Nice try. You're fired. Get out." Fee sneered.

Shawn waved a hand. "If you'd been paying attention instead of avoiding work all these years, you'd know there's a whole set of governing documents for Colman Enterprises. Grandpa had them in with all the legal stuff back when he first set up shop. In those documents, it designates full voting seats for each member of the immediate family running Colman. That's you, Dad, Mom, and all four of their children. Seven votes total."

"Six. One of my children quit her job," Howard interrupted.

Jay sighed. "Seven. We offered Penelope her job back and a division of her own. She started this morning. First order of business is to officially recognize and thank Howard Colman Jr. and his brother, Fee, for their years of service to Colman Enterprises. Yours will be tough shoes to fill, but we'll do our best."

"I'm not going anywhere, boy." Fee pointed a bony finger at Jay.

"Oh, but you are. And so is Dad. You'll each retain an office here and your salary until you begin to pull your retirement benefits. We will of course continue to provide your other benefits like health care and your gym membership, that sort of thing. But you're out."

Their father shook his head at Jay. "I don't know what the hell you're doing, Jay, but you don't have the stones to pull this off."

"You don't know a thing about me, old man. I'm done trying to make you see me. We've already voted to name Julie CFO. I'll be stepping in as CEO. Shawn will run the accounts, and PJ will have her custom design shop with a full roster of clients and a wait list."

"You have no right!" Their father stood up.

Shawn stepped in. "We have every right, because Grandpa knew what useless fools you both were and made sure there was a way to get around all this foot dragging. We are Colman Enterprises too. In fact, Julie and Jay know more about this company than either of you do. You crossed the line, Dad. You and Fee would happily just let this company dwindle and die off as long as it happened after you left. It's the CEO's job to be a steward for the business. You had your time, and your heart isn't in it. Go quietly and take your salary."

"It's more than you deserve." Lenore finally spoke. "You should be ashamed of yourself. I don't know who you are. Or what you think you're doing. But you broke your place in the family. Step aside and be quiet. Be happy your children are kinder than you are."

He pointed at PJ. "This is all your fault. You stirred everyone up."

"For my entire life I wanted your approval, and you thought I was a whore. Do you know what it felt like to learn that? I'll *never* forget that. I didn't stir anyone up. I wanted to do something I'm good at. And I wanted to do it here, where I could bring in customers and contribute my own thing to Colman. You stirred up your own problems. Whatever your deal is with me, I can't own it anymore. I can't make you love me. But I can make my mark in this company whether you like it or not."

Julie spoke up. "Just to let you both know, as of an hour ago, you've been removed from all accounts. You can keep your parking spots. Why don't you go on vacation? Golf. Relax and think about how it is you might manage to salvage your relationship with your family." She went to the door and opened it.

"He spent more time on you than he ever did his own children," Howard said suddenly into the silence.

PJ looked to her father. "What?"

"My father, your *precious* grandpa. He took *you* to the track instead of me or Fee. Took *you* to car shows. Left *you* the Z28."

"You're talking about stuff I did with Grandpa when I was a kid and you never could be bothered to spend time with me? Then? This is some sort of tantrum from a fifty-five-year-old man aimed at his daughter because he has daddy issues? You gave *me* daddy issues because you had them? Good lord. Go. Take your brother and go golfing for a few months. Maybe think about how if you showed even half the courage and compassion your father did, you could have been a decent parent."

He and Fee both tried more bluster. Jay showed them the paperwork and in the end, after a lot of arguing, they finally left.

"Okay, kids, get to work. I'm not paying you all to lollygag." Jay waved a hand at the door and PJ headed out to her shop, where they'd set up her office.

She put on her overalls and painted her own logo on the doors. Because it was hers now.

And then she worked for nine more hours, managing to text Asa here and there about what had happened. PJ was still stunned from watching her mother tell her father she was going on a trip for six weeks and that she planned to have her things moved into storage until her return, when she'd set up her own home.

But as she got into her car, she knew the other end of her journey was a place she could call home because of the man inside it. He made her safe.

Her brawling, ink-covered, motorcycle-riding, race-car-driving badass, who protected just as fiercely as he fought. Through all the turmoil and drama, he'd been there. Letting her work it all through. Helping when he could, listening. Always her number one fan.

That was something good to hold on to.

He heard the garage door open and went downstairs to meet her.

"I stopped by my apartment and brought some stuff. I mean, like I said, I can't move in for good until my lease is up. But it'll be nice to have more stuff here in the meantime."

"Come here." He took the suitcase, set it aside, and pulled her close. "Hi. Have a glass of wine while I get dinner made. Tell me about it at whatever pace you want to."

EPILOGUE

So really, I'm saying that when it comes to King, I like to see the movie adaptations as sort of a tribute to the work rather than an outright copy of the book. Scary stuff is internal. It's hard to make something so personal appeal universally, you know?"

He moved her leg to get at the bowl of chips. "I don't know. How can you read *The Shining* and then think Kubrick did it justice?"

"You're going to hell for that blasphemy, Asa."

She crawled from their very large hotel bed in their very swanky borrowed digs overlooking the beauty that was Vancouver's huge skyline. "I need more water. Want some?"

"I want more champagne."

She brought the bucket and glasses over and got back into bed. "Kubrick's version is fantastic. It's his take on King's material. An homage. Like I was just saying. Don't expect it to be what it can't be. You'll be happier."

"King wasn't happy."

"If you wrote the book, you get to be pissed it's not what you expected."

"You have a very detailed set of rules about life, Penelope Jean. I don't know how you remember them all."

"Basically, it's be nice to people, don't show your butt in public, and don't complain your sack of gold is too heavy. Everything in the rules is based on that."

He laughed, putting the chips aside again and getting her under him. "You should start your own calendar series. PJ's Rules for Life. I'd buy it."

He slid into her pussy easily, like he was meant to be there. Which he believed he was. And because they'd already had sex multiple times, so she was slick and hot.

A year ago he'd had no idea she existed; now he was sure he couldn't live without her. Funny how the world worked.

His PJ was unexpected. Loud. Funny. A pain in his ass. Uppity. Resourceful. Sexy. So much stronger than she gave herself credit for.

"There is nothing more beautiful than you," he said, kissing her as he began a slow thrust. He'd seen the youth and the beauty and had overlooked the person inside at first. It scared him sometimes, the idea that he could have missed her and made different choices and he'd be alone, or with some random person he didn't want to breathe in.

But she got in his face and made him see. Made him understand. Changed him to his very bones. He could race and fight and get grease under his nails and she didn't care. If he was happy, she was happy. Which seemed so deceptively simple, when really it was that she worked really hard to love him.

She wrapped her legs around him, arching up into each press he made into her body.

"Except being seen as beautiful by you."

"Damn, we're sickening."

She laughed. "So Duke says all the time. I think we're awesome."

"Okay then. We'll go with that."

He made her come again before he joined her and they napped, still wrapped around each other.

Two days and they'd go back to Seattle. They'd break ground on the new building that would house the Twisted Steel showroom and expand the shop space into the old showroom area. They'd signed the papers to buy the land the week before.

They'd go back and he'd open his eyes to see her next to him every morning. Come home to her every night. In just a year, everything had changed. She'd blown into his life and held on, and he'd been surprised and then oh-so-fucking-grateful for her.

Carmella Rossi has been secretly lusting after her hot, tattooed neighbor Duke Bradshaw for the last three years. His rumbly voice combined with the throaty purr of his custom bike never fail to send thrills down her spine. But when he comes to her with an amazing offer, will she be willing to put herself at risk for a guy who has heartbreaker written all over him?

Please see the next page
for a preview of

FALLING UNDER.

Carmella Rossi held the door open for Georgie, who hopped down with a happy look. Carmella understood; she wanted to dance around for joy too now that they weren't at her mother's house.

Medication delivered for the next three days—it wouldn't do to let her mom have any more than that; she'd just use it all and then not have enough and eventually end up in an ER somewhere trying to get pain scrips to get her through.

Carmella had learned the hard way that it was easier to simply dole out a few days' worth, which kept her mom from overdosing or getting herself arrested trying to hustle pills.

"Some people's mothers make pies," Carmella told the dog as they headed up the steps to the front porch.

Her key was in the lock when she and Georgie both paused at the throaty growl of a motorcycle approaching.

Duke Bradshaw. The hottest neighbor in the history of hot neighbors.

Considering the morning she'd just had with her mother, it was a nice treat to see all that long, hot, inked man get off a motorcycle and amble to his front door.

"Totally the best thing about this entire neighborhood," Carmella told the dog.

Georgie got in front of Carmella and sat. Ever protective and also sort of hot for Bradshaw, just like her human was.

Carmella looked to the front door. "We should go in. Come on. It's weird to wait out here like he's coming home for dinner at our house or something." Not like it wasn't weird to have a full conversation with a dog.

Georgie gave a doggie snort but shook, her tags jingling merrily as she followed Carmella up to the front door.

And that's when Duke Bradshaw pulled not into his driveway, but into Carmella's. That caught her attention as she unlocked the door to let Georgie inside. But the man brought Georgie bones from time to time, so the dog had no intention of leaving Carmella alone to greet the big, bad, tattooed biker who lived next door.

"Jeez, dog, he's on his motorcycle. He's not carrying bones in his pocket." Not that she was unaware that he quite frequently *appeared* to have something pretty hefty behind that zipper of his.

His bike was beyond gorgeous and the sight of it never failed to make her heart beat faster. Flat, matte black. No chrome at all. It was a custom rebuild of a 1963 BMW. It was understated and classic while still being really sexy and super masculine. It also sounded like sex—low and throaty, the bass of it settled into her belly in much the same way his voice did.

He keyed the bike off and pulled it back on the stand before sliding one long leg over. He wore a half helmet bearing the logo of his shop, the *T* and the *S* swirling together, looking sharp and badass.

His attention seemed to settle on her like a physical thing, freezing her to the spot.

And then he smiled and every erogenous zone—including a few she hadn't known existed until that moment—did the wave.

"Just the person I was looking for." Duke hung his helmet on a handlebar and headed up the steps toward her, still wearing black wraparound sunglasses and his jacket.

She wondered—not for the first time—if he ever wore the sunglasses while he had sex. Would you be able to see your own reflection as he fucked you?

Proud at the calm in her voice, Carmella smiled like she hadn't just been imagining riding his cock while he wore sunglasses so she could watch herself. "Me? Did Georgie get into something?" She gave a look toward the dog, whose normally erect ears were even perkier at the approach of the guy with the bones.

Duke bent to give Georgie a scratch behind the ears. "Nah. She's a sweetheart. It's her owner I'd like to talk about."

There was honey and lazy afternoons in his voice that day. Charming. He tucked his sunglasses into his shirt pocket and pale green eyes took her in. Laugh lines only made him more attractive.

He had a tiny smattering of salt-and-pepper at his temples, but it worked with the gold and caramel tones of hair that was long enough to touch his collar with just a little curl. Closely trimmed at the sides, long and thick at the top. He had some sort of nouveau rockabilly thing happening.

Her fingers itched to reach out and touch.

"Um." She shook her head, disgusted with how flustered he always seemed to make her. He'd been her neighbor for going on two years, so there was no reason to get fluttery, but every single time she spoke to him he seemed to turn her into a twit.

Georgie barked and Carmella pushed the storm door open. "Sorry, where are my manners? Come in."

She let the familiarity of her front entryway calm her a little as she bent to free Georgie from the harness and leash.

Duke's hand landed on her shoulder when she stood again. "Here, let me help you with your coat."

She shrugged free, suppressing a shiver as his fingers brushed the side of her neck. Carmella thanked him as he hung the coat on the peg next to his.

Removing herself from the temptation to touch him or his

leather jacket, Carmella stepped back with a smile. "You have excellent manners. Your parents did a good job."

"The army gets most of the credit for that." Again the grin.

"Want some tea? I was just going to make a pot." Of course, she'd been pondering whether or not to add a big dollop of whiskey to hers, but those were easily changed plans.

"Sure."

He placed his hand at the small of her back as he followed her through the house and into her kitchen. Which really threw a wrench into her plan of trying not to think about this big, tall, broad-shouldered man right behind her.

He took up a lot of space, his scent seemed to push itself ahead of everything else, and the electricity of his body seemed to hum from him at a frequency she wanted a lot more of.

Duke was a toucher. Not in a creepy way at all, but he frequently touched her when they spoke. In another man she'd have said something or made enough of a movement away that her *Don't touch me* would have been clear. But she *liked* it when he did it, so she allowed herself that sensual treat.

She pointed to a stool at the kitchen island. "Have a seat and tell me what brings you here at eleven in the morning."

Georgie kept staring at Duke lovingly until Carmella sighed. "George, leave the man alone." So easy. Give her a bone and she'd love you forever.

"Aw, she just wants some love. It's okay, I've got some." Duke leaned down and gave Georgie scratches and pets until she made a groaning sound of joy and fell over on her side.

Carmella wanted him to do something to *her* to make her create that sound too. And she bet he could. With any combination of his hands, his mouth, and that roll of quarters he carried around in his pocket that was probably a cock that got shit done.

And as if he'd heard her thoughts, he flicked his gaze up from the dog to her and smiled, bringing a blush to heat her cheeks and neck.

"I have a proposition for you."

She blinked, clearing her throat as she kept her hands busy putting tea bags in the mugs. "You do?" If it had anything to do with his penis, she was ready to accept.

He touched her hand briefly. "Our accounts payable person just quit. As in she's-moving-across-the-country-in-a-few-days-and-leaving-us-high-and-dry quit. I know you did books before for a few years and I hope you don't mind, but I called your old boss and he had nothing but great things to say about you. Asa and I would really love it if you took over as soon as possible. It could be a win-win for us both. You need a job. We need an employee. We pay well. We have good benefits. The hours are pretty flexible. The only time you have to be there is when we do inventory, but that's only once every six months and it's pretty easy."

Georgie growl-barked and Duke's attention shifted for a moment. "Oh, and we're dog friendly, so you could bring her with you if you wanted to."

"You called my old boss? He's my uncle. You know that, right?"

Duke laughed. "I did, yes. He told me several times, along with a few dire warnings that you were a good girl not to be messed with. He still had nothing but nice things to say about you. You have the experience we need. Our shop is bigger, but you under-stand the basics."

Her uncle's auto repair business had been a mainstay in North Seattle for thirty-five years. When the economy took a hit, he did too. And though things had begun to recover, he hadn't ever been the same. It'd been hard to compete with the quick-serve corpo-rate repair places and in the end, he'd taken it as a sign to close up and retire.

"He's family, so he has to say nice things about me." He was her mother's brother, and more of a parent to her than her mother had ever been.

A job would be really good. She'd been unemployed about

five months and it was wearing on her. Her unemployment was enough to keep the lights on, but not much more.

Duke's smile was one of the sexiest things about him, she realized as she nearly poured boiling water on her hand instead of in the mug.

"You know the industry. We're nice guys, I promise. We bring in food every Friday. Free soda in the fridge and ice cream bars in the freezer. I did mean it about the dog friendly thing. One of our guys has a Jack Russell terrier. Xena, as in the warrior princess? She hangs out a few days a week. She'll love Georgie. What do you say?"

Carmella should say that routinely being in close quarters with Duke Bradshaw was bad for all her promises to stay away from bikers and grease monkeys and the like.

It wasn't that she couldn't see his appeal. No, it was the opposite. He was pretty much a total package. He stood well over six feet. He was handsome. Like really handsome in that rugged, works-with-his-hands way, which in her opinion was the best kind of man. Duke wouldn't be thrown off by hard work. If something broke, he got it fixed. Broad shoulders, work-strong muscled arms and legs. She'd seen him in enough T-shirts to know he had detailed ink on his arms and belly. A really flat belly too. He moved with confidence, like he always knew exactly where he was going and how to get there.

Duke was at ease with himself. That sort of confidence was a sensual punch to the gut. She knew she wasn't alone in liking him. Friends were often at his house on the weekends and in the evenings. Never so rowdy that she considered calling the cops. Always cleaned up afterward.

He owned his business. Owned his home and a number of vehicles. At times he had a slow-as-molasses delivery with a hint of New England. And then he'd say *Right on* like some sort of Zen surfer.

No matter what he said, when he said it he made her hot and wet and tingly.

On top of all those things? He had an amazing ass.

She was beyond any ability to deny his appeal. If she could have ticked a bunch of her favorite man-type things and the result was rendered human, it would look a hell of a lot like the guy in her kitchen just then.

And none of that erased the fact that she couldn't afford a man like him. Her mother would love him, which was Carmella's general meter for unacceptability in a gentleman companion.

But he wasn't there asking her to nail him. He was offering her a job. And damn if she didn't need one of those. The number he rattled off as a starting salary was higher than her old one. She needed the benefits and the income and he was right, she was familiar with the industry, so it would probably be pretty easy to get started.

"Wow, you're doing a lot of thinking in there." He tapped her temple and she smiled.

"Not thinking gets a girl caught in too many dead ends." She paused. "You said you needed me right away?"

He nodded. "The sooner you can start, the better. Even if it's just a few hours here and there until you can start full-time."

"All right then. Sounds like you have a new office manager."